# My Lady
## of Plagues

# MY LADY

## OF PLAGUES

### AND OTHER GOTHIC FAIRY TALES

*Elana Gomel*

Trade Paperback Edition

Text © 2022 by Elana Gomel
Cover and interior art © 2022 by Nick Greenwood

*All persons, places and organizations in this book—save those clearly in the public domain—are fictitious, and any resemblance to actual persons, places or organizations living, dead or defunct, is purely coincidental.*

Editor & Publisher, Joe Morey

Copy editing and book design by F. J. Bergmann

ISBN: 978-1-957121-17-8

Weird House Press
Central Point, OR 97502
www.weirdhousepress.com
*Join the Weird House mailing list at our website!*

*There are so many people I want to thank for believing in me and supporting my work. My editor and publisher Joe Morey reached out to me with an idea for a collection of Gothic tales. My writer friends in Denver Horror Collective helped me to weather the long COVID-winter. My husband Jim Martin and my sons Ariel and Eliran Gomel are, as always, my emotional support team.*

    *But this book is dedicated to the woman who told me my first fairy tale and who has always been my role model and inspiration. To my mother, Maya Kaganskaya: lost too soon but never forgotten.*

# LIST OF ILLUSTRATIONS

# Table of Contents

# MY LADY OF PLAGUES

*A* grope around the house. Everywhere my questing fingers encounter the reminders of my lost world: the cool nobility of sateen (it feels like purple, but I know it is royal blue); the evasive, mocking swagger of silk; the knobby complication of lace. Occasionally I feel a prick of a rusted needle, or an old pair of scissors clutters to the floor. Blindness comes hard to the man who used to be the best tailor in town.

Parish people leave food on my doorstep; not much and only reluctantly. I have had broken glass in my milk pail and excrement smeared on my bread. Once or twice, I have felt the sting of a stone thrown with more malice than skill.

If it were not for the memory of her, they would have driven me away. But the magic of her lost presence still hovers over me, protecting me from the vengeance of her people. The very same people who snickered, and raised their brows, and shrugged with that inane air of knowing more than mere words can express, and spread ugly rumors, and pitied her husband.... Well, not many dared to pity the Lord. He was hated too much—hated and loved, with that craven devotion that distinguishes beaten dogs and oppressed commoners.

I have heard they are collecting gold, melting down wedding rings and worn-out bangles, to erect a statue of her in the town square.

They would have never dared to provoke him thus in the old days. But now he sits alone in the castle, drinking himself to death. His mercenaries are gone and that other, that invincible army that used to strut through our pestiferous streets is gone as well.

I still remember the first time I saw her. I was sitting cross-legged on the windowsill, plying my trade and enjoying the first pale sunshine, still fresh and unpolluted by the noisome vapors that would later rise from the crowded tenements.

I heard the hard clatter of horses' hooves and the occasional splash when they stepped into a puddle, and then laughter, and high arrogant voices. The cavalcade rounded the corner and stopped by my window.

I got up and bowed deeply, keeping my eyes down. But they did not move away, so I had to look up, and to meet her gaze.

She was sitting on a magnificent white mare, but my attention was naturally drawn to what she wore: a tawny kirtle of a lovely hue, not quite bronze but darker than gold. It was slashed at the sides to allow for riding and showed glimpses of dark-brown woven hose like a man's. The outer garment, a waisted *cote-hardie,* was the color of chestnut and embroidered with tiny golden stars. Her head was practically uncovered, just a stiffened band of maroon velvet, acting as a concession to her marriage and barely restraining the shining waterfall of her blond hair.

Was she beautiful? I don't think so. Her body was too hard; her bosom too small (I always had to enhance it with drapery or padding). Sometimes I mentally compared the Lady to my poor lost Mary, who would have been horrified rather than flattered by such a comparison. But Mary's plebeian body had been softer and rounder, her dark hair more manageable and her face more feminine. The Lady's skin had a marble-like pallor that, in combination with her straight nose, and small, tight-lipped mouth, made her look like a stone saint. Her probing eyes were large and almost transparent. They would have been more beautiful had her brows and lashes been a shade darker. Later I suggested dyeing them, to be rebuffed, of course, with that contemptuous absent-mindedness with which our Lady welcomed all advice.

"Are you the town's tailor?" she asked in a clear, ringing voice.

I bowed.

"We admired your work on the streets," said some toady behind her back. "What wonderful rags!"

Her retinue laughed.

I suspect it was the poor workmanship of their liveries that prompted me to lose my usual caution and respond to their half-bred insolence.

"I was taught by Eggbert of Tiw, the greatest tailor of our generation," I said, "and if my designs fall short of my training, perhaps the fault is our people's predicament as much as it is my own lack of skill."

They fell silent. I learned later that almost all of them were the Lady's own people, brought with her from that strange, cold country she called home. Now these white-skinned, broad-shouldered lads and lasses went desperate and wild in the verminous, humid warmth of our town.

The Lady looked at me searchingly and then smiled, revealing even, sugar-white teeth, the likes of which one sees only in small children among our folk.

"You'll come to the castle tomorrow," she said, "bringing samples of your work. My maids can only do rough sewing."

And so it began.

I knew I had to dress as humbly as possible, since I might encounter our Lord and tax-master. On the other hand, self-respect demanded a demonstration of my craft. At the end, I compromised by wearing a mourning suit of exquisite cut but dull fabric.

The weather had changed; it was muggy, the unclean air pressing on my face like a sodden cloth.

A woman stood at the street corner, the hem of her cloak heavy with mud. I gave her a wide berth. As I was passing by, her cowl slipped off to disclose a swollen, bald scalp with purple scabs like fish-scales.

I glimpsed the spire of the Cathedral, blurred by rain. After the deaths of my wife and daughter I never prayed. But I liked the solitude and the quiet of the deserted sanctuary. Sometimes I felt its beauty was not made by human hands but just quietly grew there, as pure as rock.

The castle, on the other hand, resembled a sprawling dead animal, the giant carcass of some grey-skinned, warty monster. A garlic-reeking guard escorted me to her Ladyship.

She was sitting in a small private chamber, wearing a loose robe of bleached linen. Because of her natural pallor, the robe made her look like a handsome ghost.

"Here you are!" she said by the way of greeting. "I have some nice fabrics but nobody to sew for me. I had a maid who designed wonderful dresses, but she died three weeks ago, from some horrible disease that swelled her to twice her size."

"Elephant fever" I said.

"What's *elephant?*"

"A kind of rat, as big as a kitten, with dirty white fur and a proboscis. They feed on sludge. Your Ladyship should not be troubled by them too much; they prefer the Lower Town."

A slovenly girl spread bolts of fabric before me. Her hands were covered with boils. I picked up a stretch of crudely dyed indigo poplin and found underneath some delicate ivory lace.

"Why are you keeping her?" I asked, nodding at the girl. "She's sick."

The almost-invisible eyebrows arched. "Her family is very poor. They need the money."

"They're no poorer than anybody else in our town," I said. "And she's disgusting. How can you let her touch you?"

I knew I was out of line, but somehow I cared not, even if she ordered me whipped or complained to her newlywed husband, who could, doubtlessly, invent a punishment more spectacular than old-fashioned flogging. I would like to believe that the deaths of my family made me indifferent to my own safety. But if I want to be honest with myself—and what is left to a blind man but self-insight?—I will have to admit that I was intoxicated by the image of her clean body under that flowing robe. After all, I was not just a stinking commoner, even if I did not boast a title. I belonged to the invisible aristocracy of beauty-makers.

"I don't let my maids touch me," she said. "I hate being touched, unless in love."

Afterward I flattered myself into believing that she had tried to seduce me. Of course, this was not so; why to waste womanly wiles where an order would suffice? She let slip this broad hint quite innocently, blinded by her own indifference to me. She seldom saw people, only humanity.

"I'm sure her disease is not contagious," she added, slightly flustered, as she realized, belatedly, what she had said. There was a lovely rose tinge on her throat. Emerald green, royal blue and salmon pink were the right colors for her.

There were heavy steps outside the chamber's door, and the bark of a dog, subsiding into low whimpering. I had been in the wake of his Lordship's passage before. But surprisingly, he did not enter his wife's room, did not even announce his presence by rapping on the door or yelling some obscenity.

Her color deepened.

"So, master tailor," she said harshly, "what do you suggest I do with my dowry?"

I picked some wine-colored silk.

"This," I said, "will do for a formal dress. I'll cut and sew it myself. You will need a necklace of rubies or garnets set in silver. As for the rest of the stuff—give it to your maids."

She looked at me in amazement. Then she laughed.

"I like insolence" she said, "because where I come from, we call it independence. But in this plague country everybody is crooked and blighted; there is no honest anger, only servile and silent rage. What is your name, tailor?"

"Tom."

"Well, Tom, I will do as you say. How long will it take you to make the dress?"

"A week," I said. "But I need to take your measurements, my Lady."

She stood up and shrugged her robe off. She wore nothing underneath.

I took out my tape and approached her.

"Wait," she said. "You remarked on my maid's illness; how do I know you're not plague-ridden like her?"

I showed her my hands, scrubbed with lye soap this morning.

"That's not enough," she said. "I have been told there are diseases here that strike only one part of the body which rots, invisible, under the clothes until the sufferer is obnoxious to his family but unnoticeable to strangers."

I took off my clothes. When I was naked, she knew I would not pollute her by anything but desire.

There was a new plague in town, and the taxes were raised.

The plague, called the Rose Fever, was spectacular. Death wears baroque fashions in our town, as if compensating the rabble for the ugliness of their lives.

The sufferers would show no symptoms for two days except heightened color and general vivacity. On the third day, scarlet rosettes would appear all over their bodies, and flowers of raw flesh would push out from under the skin. When death came, the corpse would resemble a bunch of bloody peonies.

I was not particularly concerned. I had little contact with my neighbors anyway. As for my taxes, the Lord's money simply went back to him, since I had been officially appointed dressmaker to her Ladyship.

Others were not so sanguine, but nobody dared to remonstrate. The Lord's black-clad mercenaries, with their faces masked by long scarves to prevent contagion, broke into homes, threw bedclothes, pots and pans out the window, searching for hidden gold. They were few in number, but our Lord had a more potent army at his beck and call: the plague demons, bound by the ancient compact between his family and the obscure powers of fetid air and swampy darkness.

For centuries, the Lords of our town had needed no army and no walls to defend their domain. The plagues that stalked our streets protected us from foreign invaders, repelling any would-be conqueror. The plagues took their own tithe, of course. We paid one tax in money and another tax in the sicknesses of our bodies and minds. But at least we lived our lives unmolested by war. And if we rotted, was not this the fate of all flesh? A tailor's craft is to make us forget that the body is only food for worms.

One day I was tempted outdoors by a gentle rain that had cleared the air and left rainbows in the sky. Coming into the empty marketplace, I saw a boy of about ten who was playing hide-and-seek with himself among the forlorn skeletons of locked stalls. The flush on his cheeks could not mask the deeper vermilion of death-rosettes. I hurriedly stepped back.

The Lady's cavalcade emerged from the opposite street. She was riding at the head, wearing an aquamarine surcote and a sleek grey gown of my making. I shouted a warning, but the child was already running toward her. And then her hand was on his curly head, and I stood petrified, a sick feeling in my stomach. Her attendants backed off.

"My Lady!" one of them screamed.

"What is it?" she asked.

"The child is sick!" shouted several voices in unison.

"So?" she said.

There was absolute silence, and now she and the boy were surrounded by the empty zone of a spontaneous quarantine. She dismounted.

"Pretty boy," she said. "Where is your mummy?"

"There," he made an uncertain gesture. "But she told me to go out into the fields and play until ..."

"Until what?"

He shrugged. I knew what had happened: the mother had sent the child away, hoping he would die somewhere and spare her the danger and the expenses of the burial. This is what the mothers in our town are like.

"Do you want to come with me to the castle?" she asked. A stir went over her huddled attendants. She faced them.

"Who will take the child?" she asked. When, naturally, there was no answer she smiled that forgiving and contemptuous smile we were to become so familiar with in the coming months. She lifted the boy. He rode pillion back to the castle with her.

In a couple of days, I heard he was returned to his mother, healthy and jubilant, his pockets filled with candy. His parents displayed him, a living miracle, to the crowds of hopeful neighbors, charging a penny for the privilege of touching his cool forehead.

I worked on a new seed-pearl embroidered stomacher for her as I had never worked on anything else. I felt the need to engage my fingers, to strain my eyes, and to empty my mind, as I sat for hours, picking the tiny pearls one by one and stitching each in its proper place among the interlocking whorls.

There had been no new cases of the Rose Fever.

The Lady's cavalcade swept through the town, her attendants laughing and exuberant. She rode on her white mare, the blond hair loose and sparkling with jewels. She distributed sugary delights to people starving for bread. Women raised their sickly infants, kneeling before her in the mud.

I was ordered to attend on her. The stomacher was finished, so stiff with embroidery and so elaborately wrought that the body underneath would have to mold itself to its perfect curves. I intended it as a sartorial allegory of her stubborn and perverse charity.

But she was oblivious to me and my craft, never more so than when she was in my arms. She was also oblivious to the danger to herself if the Lord found out about us. But he seemed to be growing even more wary of her and kept his distance.

We lay on her elaborately carved and canopied bed. The sweat on her body glistened in the uncertain candlelight for, contrary to her usual habits, the curtain was drawn.

"How did your family die?" she asked suddenly. I jerked. This was so like her, this straightforwardness that was indistinguishable from rudeness, honesty that verged on cruelty.

"A plague," I said curtly.

She waited. Her title and power were always there, an invisible garment on her nudity.

"One of those ephemeral curses that sweep the town only once, like a new and exotic fashion, and die out, our bodies too scanty for their appetite. This one prevented the victim from absorbing water. Whatever they drank, they vomited immediately. They could keep down hard food but no liquids. They died of thirst."

The gentle pattering of rain, the damp sheets, the moisture-sleeked furniture—and the dried-out bodies with the cracked lips and the furry tongues. My parents.

"One day we were sitting at dinner and my wife was holding a glass of milk to our baby daughter's lips. She had just been weaned. She drank the milk and it all poured back. She pointed at the puddle on the table and laughed."

She was such a sweet baby, pudgy and pink, with round dark eyes. I resented her crying and was repelled by her diapers. But sometimes I would play with her and tickle her tummy, marveling at the petal softness of her skin.

"Mary, my wife, started keening, and the baby bawled. I told Mary we should smother her rather than let her suffer, but she refused. She was a woman and weak."

"Perhaps she hoped to draw the plague demons to herself. Like all spirits, they seek to be willingly accepted and embraced. Then the child would recover." The Lady said.

"I told you, nobody recovered!" I snapped.

But when I stopped, she told me to go on, and words poured out of me like the water and milk that had poured out of the poor shriveling body of my daughter.

9

"I let her try until morning. By dawn the baby was so exhausted that she fell asleep and I hoped she would not wake. When I came out from the bedroom where I had locked myself in order not to witness this unnecessary torment, Mary was sitting in the kitchen, her head in her hands. When she heard my steps, she lifted her head and smiled. There was a half-filled glass of water on the table. She drank and the water ran down her chin and stained the front of her dress."

I fell silent. But the Lady's eyes were upon me, as if she waited for the ending and I hated her gaze, patient and remote like the gaze of God.

"I killed both of them!" I shouted. "Is that what you wanted to hear? I killed my wife and my daughter and that was the best thing I had ever done as husband and father! I let them go cleanly rather than in torment and in filth!"

"Had you waited, your daughter would have lived," she said.

I could have strangled her at that moment.

I jumped off the bed and groped for my clothes. She touched my shoulder. I pushed her away and saw, for the first time, what I had not seen in the darkness.

There was a tiny scarlet rosette under her right collarbone, as beautiful as a jewel.

My fat neighbor Sada knocked on my window. Her dewlaps wobbled excitedly as she poured out the latest news. The Lady was doing the rounds of the slums, clothed from head to toe in the black of a lay Sister of Charity. She went into the stinking holes, where abandoned pieces of humanity had been rotting for so long that nobody knew whether they were alive or dead. She opened the grime-locked casements; she bathed the pustule-covered bodies; she brought fresh fruit to people subsisting on garbage. And where she went, the plagues retreated.

"Perhaps they are afraid of her," I said.

"She is a saint!" Sada declared indignantly. "You are just jealous, Tom, because she does not want your trinkets anymore! Even His

Lordship dares not interfere with her good deeds. Some say he has had a change of heart. Worse men than he were saved by good women!"

"And better men were cuckolded too," I muttered under my breath but fortunately Sada, prattling on about the Lady's miracle of the day, did not hear. When she left, I finally ventured outside. It was unseasonably hot, the air was sulfur-yellow, and glistening puddles of steaming mud adorned the empty gardens.

My feet took me to the marketplace. Among the locked stalls, on the ground littered with festering potatoes and rotting apple peel, our Lady dispensed her charity. They had built a little canopy for her. There she was seated in a carved armchair, dressed in black flowing robes, both ridiculously unbecoming and too warm for the weather.

The square was crowded with rabble and the stench was unbearable. Having no desire to rub shoulders with my fellow townspeople, I jumped on one of the stalls.

Only two boys were left of her retinue; the rest, as I learned later, got infected as they followed her on her rounds. The two stood behind her with leaden expressions on their handsome north-bleached faces.

A woman was kneeling before her on the garbage-strewn ground. Her bald pate was shining like silver. Leprosy.

The Lady bent forward and took the woman's pitiful claws in her own hands. The crowd moaned; I felt my gorge rise as I remembered kissing those hands. For a second, they were frozen in this strange tableau and then the Lady let go and the woman rose unsteadily, turning around. I glimpsed a ravaged lion's face with fretted lips and sunken nose.

But even as I watched, silver flakes of dead skin showered upon the ground; the flesh twitched like putty; the sunken nose filling out, the split lips closing over the gaping cavern of the mouth, the skull darkening with the fuzz of furiously growing hair. And the woman threw up her arms, crying in a rusty, disused voice, "I'm cured! I'm cured!"

The crowd charged forward, like a dumb suffering animal, and rather than watch her trampled, I turned around and fled. I need not have feared; later I was told she had stood up and held them back with a gesture and a smile. At this point, she could have commanded them

11

to storm the castle and kill her Lord and they would have obeyed. Fortunately, she did not live to see their fickle adoration run its course.

There were signs and wonders; there was a dry rowan tree exploding into a fury of scarlet blossoms; a pavement weeping blood where her feet trod on it; a dead baby crying in a bird's reedy voice. I closed my eyes and stopped my ears.

People were cured and other people died; huge crowds milled in the town square and the cathedral was packed with wailing worshippers; in the marketplace fruit-mongers gave away apples to dirty beggar boys, and fishwives threw themselves on the ground in her path, and basket weavers publicly confessed their sins. The Lord brooded in the castle, and his guardsmen went to the mass. The two surviving Northerners wore white shirts decorated with crosses painted in their own blood. She wore black.

She came to my house late at night. Her attendants, their faces haggard with devotion, stood guard outside. She was draped in black fustian from head to toe, and her face was covered with a clumsy cheesecloth veil.

"I need new clothes," she said.

"I need to take your measurements, my Lady," I replied.

She nodded but hesitated. Her hand flew to her shadowed face. There were no competent glove makers in town to hide these swollen red joints under suede or leather. Then she lifted her veil, undid the clasps of her garment and took it off. The fabric came unstuck with a reluctant, ripping sound.

Her hair had thinned; and raw, weeping flesh glistened among its lanky strands. Her high brow was dotted with suppurating pimples. Thin strings of blood and pus oozed from her cracked nipples. Where her skin was still clear of boils and tumors, it was fever-flushed. Though she stood away from me, I could smell the sickroom stench.

"I have nothing that will fit your Ladyship," I said.

"Why?" she cried, and I could hear a slight lisp—some of her teeth must have fallen out. "I'm doing it for you, for all of you!"

"We are not worthy of your sacrifice," I replied.

She stood still and her eyes might have sought mine, but I turned away. She sighed, a rasping, laborious sound, and bent to retrieve her clothes. She paused at the door. "You will make me a black habit and bring it to the castle day after tomorrow," she said, her voice still striving to be imperious and failing, as her inflamed vocal cords unwillingly stirred to perform their duty. And then she was gone. I wanted to fumigate the place but gave it up. My vision was blurred but it was only tears.

There was no time for sewing a black habit. His Lordship had finally sobered up enough to discover that his sickly subjects were recovering apace, while his wife was gathering the demons of the plague to her breast, letting them feast on her once-beautiful body. I wonder what thoughts crawled through his alcohol-dulled brain. Was he amazed at her audacity or angered by her presumption?

If the town were cured completely, it would be attacked. A handful of his mercenaries would be no match for the armies of our greedy neighbors. At least, this is what he must have believed. Or was the reason more personal? Was it the disgust at her corrupted flesh that prompted the unexpectedly refined cruelty of his reaction? Was he suddenly sorry that her loveliness was now lost to him forever? Did he perhaps suspect that somebody else had enjoyed it?

The town criers went down the hushed streets, and notices were hung in the marketplace for the few capable of reading them.

The just angels that watched over our town were angered at the presumption of the people (the criers and notices said). They demanded their dues. New diseases, unheard-of in their puissance, would be unleashed, and each family would pay the plague tax, the tithe of mortality. This would happen—unless the Lady would take the sins of the community upon herself and set an example of proper humility. To do so, she should walk the Main Street naked, from the Castle to the Cathedral, on the first day of the glorious month of May. Everybody should look on and be humbled.

13

On the first day of the glorious month of May the cherry, apple, plum, pear and peach blossomed in great billows of white, pink, ivory, and mauve. Lilac and tulips and snapdragons and hollyhocks hid the festering pools and marshy ground.

But there was no one about to see nature's deceit. Petals and dust whirled in the wind, running unimpeded through the deserted streets. The doors were locked, the windows shuttered.

I would like to believe that by this final gesture the town redeemed itself. But this is just a weak fantasy. It was nothing but fear. It is not that we wanted to spare her but that we pitied ourselves; we could not face the suffering endured for our sake and preferred to turn away, so we could live on and enjoy the fruits of the redemption we neither deserved nor even understood. And then, of course, we were incapable of rebellion but quite capable of a little malice, a little nose-thumbing at our Lord.

I sat in my drawing room in darkness, listening to the soft susurrus of the empty air outside. I thought about all the people I cordially disliked or heartily despised, waiting behind the drawn blinds and closed shutters, calming restless children, impatient for it to be over, so they could go out and walk in the gardens, people healthy and alive because of her. I knew exactly when she would be passing by my house; I did not need to strain my ears, but I did anyway. And when I heard the shuffling sound, I threw the casement wide open and leaned forward into the sunlight to face her and look at her wounds and let her know that finally I accepted it all.

She walked in the middle of the unpaved track, treading on dandelions' silver heads. But they did not shine more brightly than her naked feet. The sun was like a dull coin above the glory of her hair. The wind lifted its glowing mass, and her body, freed of all disguise, blazed like a naked sword, without blemish or flaw; purity so awful it dimmed the daylight and clove the air. Its cruel perfection pierced my eyes and they flowed down my cheeks.

Later they found me whimpering on the floor in pain, my palms pressed so tightly to my empty sockets they had to wrench the fingers one by one. They were not gentle; they poured scorn at my lust that overruled decency and gratitude; they mocked me and might have killed me were they not subdued by her sacrifice. They refused to tell me anything, but I overheard their awed whispers and learned that her body was found at the door of the Cathedral, ravaged with all the plagues she had welcomed, a semi-liquid mass of rot, so foul the undertakers were loath to handle it. Her husband refused to bury her in the family vault, and her grave was in the common, marked with heaps of fresh flowers that are already beginning to dwindle.

I am going to die soon—a sightless tailor has no business in the world—and I know I am becoming a legend, a warning, a titillating label, a name to be spoken with a salacious grin. While her charity will be soon forgotten, my treachery will endure. And this is my sacrifice, which is greater than hers. I die as a master tailor should, for I have clothed her nakedness with my story.

# DEATH IN JERUSALEM

Mor is suspended in the heat like a fly in amber. The crowd is sprinkled with Arabs in galabiyeh, Orthodox Jews in dusty black coats, and young girls with navel rings. People jostle and push against each other. But Mor walks freely through the crush of bodies, buoyed by the roundness of her stomach, her gaily colored maternity dress glued to it by perspiration. People respect fertility in Jerusalem.

She is relieved when she reaches the old residential area of Rehavia, the ghostly echo of pre-war Europe lingering in the narrow alleyways lined with unkempt gardens. As she approaches her mother's house, she puts down her grocery bag to fish out the key that expertly eludes her sweaty fingers. She opens the gate into the small courtyard where a rusted bicycle rests in the meager shadow of an ancient wisteria. The heat is killing her. Leaning against the jamb to catch her breath, she closes her eyes and tries to cool off with a memory of blue steel and frozen candlelight.

The evening is almost bearable. This is the blessing of hilly Jerusalem as opposed to swampy, humid Tel-Aviv where in summer heat lies on the land like a rotting corpse. As the temperature drops and the light fades to lilac, Mor takes a shower and gingerly lowers herself into the beanbag in front of the TV. Channels flicker in a babel of voices and images as the carefully made-up anchors read out a litany of war, famine, disease, and death. Names and places change; the stories are the same.

Mor is listlessly chewing on a sandwich. She has no appetite; the heavy thing in her belly takes up too much space.

She goes to bed early. Stretching on her back, she automatically holds her breath, waiting for the baby's kick. Of course, nothing happens.

Sleepless in the dark, she touches her husband's pillow. Cold burns her fingertips.

The scrape of a chair and a man's voice saying: "May I?" She lifted her eyes and was instantly smitten.

It was summer, and the morning was hot, cloudless and blue, as all mornings would be for the next three months. But the man who sat by her in the campus cafeteria smelled of rain and fog, like the cool days Mor remembered from her two-year stay in New Jersey. He smiled, and his teeth were white and impossibly even. His eyes were the color of smoke.

They talked until she was close to being late for her class. The language of their conversation was English as it immediately transpired that "May I?" was the full extent of David's knowledge of Hebrew. He was from Toledo.

"I've been to Toledo," she said. "They make wonderful swords."

"Toledo, Ohio," he corrected. "I don't like cutting weapons."

Was he some sort of pacifist? A religious fanatic? A pilgrim? Just a tourist? Mor did not care. He was the most beautiful man she had ever seen.

Just a millisecond before she absolutely had to rush, he asked her whether she was free in the evening. She was so elated that her lecture went quite well, despite the fact that she had forgotten her notes in the cafeteria. Since her divorce, Mor's life consisted of a chain of relationships with wonderful beginnings and lousy endings. But as long as there was life, there was hope. She tried to be optimistic in order to distinguish herself from her mother. It made guilt bearable.

❀

They met at Dizengoff Square, which is not actually a square but a wide pedestrian overpass above a perpetual traffic jam. Its revolving fountain wobbled in the greyish twilight, occasionally coughing up an anemic jet of water. There were fat pigeons waddling and cooing around. They gave David a wide berth, and Mor was struck by a longing to be with him in the magic circle of protection that he seemed to draw around himself.

After a couple of drinks in a bar where flashing lights and deafening noise protected her from being recognized by a nosy friend or ex-lover, they walked along the beach promenade, the black oily sea lying heavy and silent beyond the fluorescent strip of sand. Moonlight dribbled from the tarry sky.

"I like your name," he said. "Mor. Does it mean something?"

"It's a kind of spice or incense mentioned in the Bible," she said, searching for the English word. "Oh, yeah. Myrrh."

"Really?" He sounded interested. "I thought it had something to do with death. You know, like *mortality*."

"Mortality, morbid, moribund." She shook her head. "You are right; it does sound like it belongs with these. Funny. I never thought about this. But it's a different root. *Mort*, death in French. Just a coincidence."

Her mother wanted to name her Hanna but Daddy had objected. She'd insisted, and so there were two names listed on Mor's birth certificate, even though she never used the other one. Another item to add to the list of grudges against her mother; another drop of sweetness to flavor her hazy recollections of the big burly man who had brought her to the kindergarten one fine morning and was dead of a heart attack in the afternoon.

The silence between them seemed restful and romantic, filled with unspoken promises. Mor tried to think what to ask him next and could not. Job, family, politics? What difference did it make? She would be happy to walk with him in this velvety dark for an eternity, just listening to the rhythmic hiss of the waves on the endless bone-white beach. But did he feel the same? He asked for her phone number, true, but made no definite promise to call. When she drove him back to his hotel (which turned out to be the Sea Crest, the most expensive one on the promenade), he politely thanked her for the perfect evening and left without as much as a peck on the cheek. She fought tears on the way back home and counted the crow's feet around her eyes as she brushed her teeth. Next day, just as she resigned herself to never seeing him again, he called.

When the phone vibrates on the kitchen counter, Mor stares at the flashing display and tries to remember who the caller is. Her memory is holed like cheese, some memories willfully expunged, some unaccountably gone. A school friend? A former colleague? Not a relative, certainly. She has none. An only daughter of an only daughter; and her mother's entire family buried in unmarked graves.

It does not matter. She needs nobody. She has her son.

Stroking her belly, she watches the phone quiver and jump like a living thing. When it finally calms down, she tosses it into the garbage bin.

They met every day for a week. Mor learned a little more about David: enough for her to decide he was the One. He was so reassuringly normal; so restful and commonsense; untainted by the feverish madness of the Middle East. He was an accountant, he said; and indeed, he was very good with numbers. His parents were dead; his numerous siblings scattered over an amazing geographical range; and there was no mention of an ex-wife or significant other. He read all the right books and had all the right opinions. He liked gadgets. Mor, being an adjunct professor in the department of Life Sciences, listened to his technobabble with an indulgent smile. The only negative she could find was that he was surprisingly indifferent to good food, despite the plethora of culinary temptations on every street corner. Rice-stuffed vine leaves; couscous; creamy hummus; freshly baked pitas; honey-almond cake—he consumed them as dutifully and apathetically as if they were medicine. Mor told herself that was a necessary counterweight to her own frequent indulgences that were beginning to show in her curves. Time to cut it; and indeed, David could be a walking advertisement for the virtues of abstemiousness, so trim and fit he was.

He told her his return ticket was for tomorrow. The despair she felt was strong enough to frighten her into a recoil from her infatuation. Did she really need him so much? She had her life, her friends, her job. She might meet somebody local, get married, have a family.

She was thirty-five. All of her school and army friends were married, most had children. The future stretched before her as blank and lifeless as the bony beach under the full moon where one walked alone.

For their last date, Mor put on a midnight-blue Bedouin-embroidered robe. She regretted not being the exotic, olive-skinned, Middle-Eastern type. Perhaps he would be more attracted to her if she were. But the generations of her ancestors dying under the washed-out skies of Poland had left their mark in her pale skin and green eyes.

They ate at the most expensive restaurant in Tel-Aviv. David had a lot of money and spent it freely, though never recklessly. He walked her to her apartment building and pecked her on the cheek, as he did every evening. Dully, she waited for him to turn around and walk away, as he did every evening.

"Can I come up for coffee?" he asked.

Inside the apartment, he turned off all the lights but because Tel-Aviv at night is bathed in the inflamed glow of its perpetually burning lights, they were left in the orange-tinted murk seeping through the slats of the Venetian blinds. Her neighbor's cat caterwauled in the yard and fell silent. She tangled with her robe, but his undressing was quick and tidy. Running her hand over his delightfully smooth chest she suddenly realized something she had only marginally noticed before on the rare occasions when they touched: how cool his flesh was, like a porcelain bowl filled with sherbet. Mor felt embarrassed by the drops of sweat gathering under her armpits and in the hollow of her neck. But David's body remained immaculate. His kisses were sterile; his mouth tasted of nothing.

His regular breathing did not speed up throughout their lovemaking. And then it stopped.

Mor lay in darkness, a cold heavy body on top of her. She could hear the squeak of tires outside, the laughter and chatter of pedestrians, barking of dogs—but nothing else. The innumerable small noises of the body's interior that had been the soundtrack of sex were gone. David's silken hair tickled her lips and pushed back her rising scream. And then he lifted his head and looked down at her.

"I'm sorry," he said, "but Death cannot die. Not even a little death. So that's all for me but don't worry, I'm satisfied."

She could see him clearly. His body was glowing in the dark, a bluish glow like candlelight seen through a thick slab of ice. His finely chiseled features were pierced by two black holes of eyes. The translucent flesh molded itself around the geometrical beauty of curving ribs and elegantly strung vertebrae, shining with hard steely light.

"Little death," she repeated blankly.

He sat up. Now on the left side of his chest, just above the nipple, she could see a wound-flower, a neat hole surrounded by petals of flesh that stirred restlessly, opening and closing like a sea anemone. The wound bled more metallic light.

"Orgasm," he said. "The French call it *la petite mort*."

"And you ..."

"I am Death."

In fact, he was only *a* death, one of many. Over the next couple of days, he explained it again and again: gently, patiently, and reassuringly.

There were, he said, a number of deaths (he talked of them in family terms, brothers, sisters, cousins). New ones appeared from time to time, and oldsters retired though, of course, none died. Each death was responsible for a specific mode of mortality, though in emergencies (he was vague as to what those might be) they could take over each other's domains. David's own responsibility was death by shooting.

How old was he? He did not know, could not remember. Had he ever been human? He did not know that either. Was there a God? This received a blank stare.

And in between these conversations, they went for ice cream, or swam in the sea, or toured the labyrinthine alleys of Old Jaffa, or made love. He brought her flowers every day. After a week he moved in, bringing his natty suitcase from the hotel. After two weeks he asked her to marry him.

This precipitated a crisis. She threw him out, yelling at him to go to hell. She cried for hours afterward, only stopping when she realized, with horror, that he might have done just that. Next morning, he was at her door with a fresh bunch of flowers.

She could not say "no." She was in love. "In love with death?" she asked herself with horrified incredulity. Of course, not; in love with a nice, gentle, even-tempered, caring man; a wonderful lover; a steadfast friend; a fun companion. So what if he was the rider on the pale horse—one of the whole cavalry, actually?

And yet she could not say "yes." She procrastinated, sobbed, made resolutions, and broke them on the spot. She pleaded with him to give her more time.

"Why can't we just live together?" she cried.

He explained that it would not be right. He wanted her to see how committed he was. And unless they were legally married, he could not give her his wedding gift. She tried to push the thought of the gift away from her deliberations—she was not to be bought, she told herself and believed it—but it sat at the back of her mind as a constant watchful presence.

One afternoon, as Mor was taking a long walk in Yarkon Park to try to unwind after another day of painful indecision, her cell phone rang. Her mother's officious neighbor Dvora called to tell her she was worried about Mrs. Shalev's state of mind. She managed to introduce a not-too-subtle remark about Mor's dereliction of her filial duties, with the unspoken "and the only child, too!" accompanying every word.

23

When her mother failed to pick up the phone, Mor drove up to Jerusalem. Just as she was rounding the last bend in the highway, the setting sun shone a peculiar golden-mauve light on the smooth bare hills with their clinging clusters of whitewashed dwellings. In such moments Jerusalem seemed not so much a city as a physical state: a lighting flicker of vertigo or a stab of pain.

Her mother was sitting in the darkened living room, softly crying. The usual half-an-hour of useless recriminations followed, with Mor getting so angry with her mother's drab misery that she felt like slapping her lined cheek. But eventually Mrs. Shalev rallied up sufficiently to make tea. Mother and daughter sat at the spotlessly clean kitchen table with a bowl of homemade cookies pushed closer to Mor's side. This was as near to reconciliation as they ever got.

"*Ima,*" said Mor suddenly. "*Ima,* did you ever see Death?"

Mrs. Shalev, who was mechanically stirring her tea, froze. Mor felt the embarrassment of a child breaking an unspoken family taboo. But she was doubly shocked when her mother glanced back at her with a sly, almost conspiratorial, smile, as if after all that time they finally got to share a grown-up secret.

"My mother did," she said. "Your grandmother, God rest her soul! She told me about it. When they were bringing them in, in the cattle-cars, she was squeezed close to a chink in the wall, and so she could breathe. There was snow outside. And there was a man standing on top of a snowdrift: an ordinary man, but wearing an office suit. In the depth of winter. And as the train was passing, and people cried and pleaded and screamed, he was writing something in his notebook. He never raised his eyes as the train passed. That was death, she said."

Mor felt a shiver pass down her spine.

"But she survived!" she remonstrated.

"Yes," her mother agreed. "For a while."

Two days later Dvora called again. When Mor came, she found her mother dead in bed. The family physician called it heart failure but privately admitted that an overdose of tranquilizers might have played a part.

They went to Cyprus to get married. Israel has no provisions for a civil ceremony. In the depth of her sleepless nights, Mor sometimes imagined a council or elderly rabbis solemnly deliberating whether a death may convert to Judaism.

After a brief honeymoon, they returned home as a married couple. Now, said David, they should have a reception for his family.

"At home?" Mor asked faintly.

"We will rent a banquet hall," David reassured her.

A catered dinner, of course, he said casually, a hundred and fifty people. No, not including your friends, we can have a separate reception for them; money's not a problem (of course, she thought, who ever heard of a pauper death?). No, love, not in Jaffa, that seaside is very pretty but it has to be in Jerusalem.

He explained that for his family a visit to the Holy City was a long-cherished dream that only the pressure of work had hitherto prevented them from realizing. Mor did not dare inquiring about the means of transportation, even though David's interest in airline schedules seemed to indicate that at least some of the deaths would be queuing for passport control at the Ben-Gurion Airport.

Standing at the entrance to the banquet hall, Mor welcomed the endless stream of visitors. The briskness of Jerusalem's mountain air was making her shiver in her turquoise dress (despite the sales assistant's insistence, she had rejected an elegant black-and-white outfit as being altogether too symbolic).

Candles burned on the tables. People with champagne flutes and plates of canapes in their hands laughed, chatted, embraced, wandered out onto the jasmine-scented patio.

"Wanda, Zoe, Jerome, Ervin," David introduced them one by one even when they arrived as couples. "Mark, Yolanda, Ahmed."

Only first names. Did it mean that they all had the same family name? The same name as was now her own?

"Maggie, Ruth, Xiaowei."

How many? God, how many of them?

"Guido, Carl, Donna."

Good-looking people, all of them: healthy, smiling, well dressed. Nobody looked to be below twenty or above fifty. No children.

"Liliana, Eric, George."

And properly diverse too: whites, Asians, blacks, and browns in roughly equal proportions. Mark was African American, and elegant Miranda looked like an Ethiopian model. Ahmed would blend into any Middle Eastern crowd. Susan, arriving on Roger's arm, belied her nondescript name by sloe eyes and *café-au-lait* skin.

"Kalia, Roman, Patricia."

"Nice to meet you!"

"Have a drink!"

"What a lovely place!"

They all spoke English but some with exotic accents: silky French, heavy Eastern European, or guttural Middle Eastern.

"Reginald, Oscar, Victoria."

Strangely old-fashioned names but nothing old-fashioned about their bearers. Women in Fendi and Prada dresses, men in Armani suits. Glitter of jewelry and expensive dental work.

"Mikhail, Gloria, Stefan."

She tried to guess their identities at first but then gave up, defeated by their impersonal gloss. But when she finally started to mingle, Mor found the answer.

At the entrance to the hall there was an old-fashioned mirror in a Venetian frame. And in the mirror, she could see her guests as they really were.

Liliana was the Plague Queen. Seen face-to-face, she was a slightly plump woman with crinkly brown hair and laughter lines. She was reflected in the mirror wearing a blood-red cloak that dragged on the floor, leaving a dark stain behind. Her features were the same but ravaged by open sores, the lips split and oozing pus, eyebrows missing. Holding a wineglass in a festering hand, this reflection pleasantly conversed with Mor's mirror double.

Mor blinked and swallowed, fighting nausea.

Stefan, a balding pompous guy, was reflected with ashy, hopeless eyes; his ingratiating smile—a rictus of pain; his neat tie—a twisted rope. Suicide.

Elegantly slim Ruth was transformed into a gaunt ravenous creature. Her diaphanous dress became in the mirror a transparent shroud that clung to her protruding ribs and swollen stomach. Famine.

George, the only man in the room wearing a tee with an Escher print instead of a formal shirt, incuriously glanced at his own image whose throat was slashed by a gaping wound. The Escher geometry was transformed into a chaos of bloody blobs. Murder.

Victoria's shiny blond hair was a couple of grey tufts on the mottled skull; her cream-and-peaches skin—a wrinkled parchment; her rose dress—a shapeless, stained shift. Old Age.

Mark was reflected as a walking mass of burns, bleeding tissue, and splintered bones. Accident, she thought. Zoe ... the others seem to defer to her and seeing her in the mirror, with the black leather harness molding her voluptuous body, her thrusting breasts like missiles, a bracelet of rusty iron splinters around her full arm, and her face covered by a helmet-like mask, Mor understood why. War was undoubtedly high on the deaths' social ladder.

There were, however, some visitors whose reflections left her puzzled. Maggie was one of them. When David introduced her, Mor saw a nice British woman, slightly older than the rest, looking like the aunt Mor would like to have but never did. She tried to maneuver her inside, but Maggie tantalizingly loitered on the patio. When she finally walked by the mirror, Mor glimpsed a strange scarecrow figure with stick-like arms and legs, her face painted with garish whorls.

She circulated among the guests, making polite remarks, feeling strangely detached (even curiosity was evaporating), when there was a commotion at the entrance. She saw David speaking to somebody whose only visible part was a pair of fluttering hands. She quickly went there when David stepped aside and brushed past her, muttering something about "bad taste." Mor found herself facing the late guest.

He was a short man with sandy hair and blue eyes magnified by rimless glasses. He looked pedantic and harmless.

"Your husband, I mean David ..." he began, seemingly flustered. His accent was a one Mor had heard before—it took her a moment to remember where.

"All my husband's friends are welcome," she said cautiously.

"Let me introduce ... Daniel."

David had come back. There was a tiny pause before he said the name. "Daniel is retired. He does not socialize much."

"I thought it was my duty to come," said the short man with dignity.

Mor offered him a drink and tried to steer him toward the mirror. But there was no need for subterfuge: he just walked there, planted his feet wide, and stared at his reflection.

The reflection was the same as the man.

And then she knew who her last visitor was.

"I'm sorry," said Daniel. "I know how you must feel. But I had to come. I'm glad David has found a Jewish wife. And I'm glad it's you."

"Do you know me?" she asked, swallowing, because her voice sounded as insignificant as the squeak of a mouse.

"I know all of you," he said.

She looked around. Should she appeal to Stefan, Death-Suicide, who had helped her mother escape? Or to Plague, Famine, Accident, Cancer, even War? Any other death to keep her company but this.

"You see, I'm retired now," continued Daniel, "and looking at the whole business from an historical perspective, I can't blame myself. I only followed orders."

"Whose orders?" Mor asked sarcastically. "God's? The Fuhrer's?"

"Your orders."

"Mine?!"

"Yours too, in a way. You're a human being, after all. You call the shots. We only do what we are told. A human hand pulls the trigger or signs an order, and we mop up the resulting mess."

"How convenient! However, I see the others shy away from you. Could it be even they don't approve of your methods?"

28

"Sheer prejudice," said Daniel. "Envy too. There is a great deal of jockeying for power going on among us. You'll find out. You are one of us now, after all. David's wedding gift is not to be sneered at!"

"Fuck you!" For one glorious moment Mor was so angry that she forgot her fear. "Do you think I'm doing this to be your sister-in-law? I love David. And anyway, what are you doing here, in this city, attending a Jewish wedding?"

Daniel only smiled, unperturbed:

"I have attended a lot of Jewish weddings," he said. "And of course, you love David. I have seen love sacrifices too. Eventually they tend to benefit somebody, though not always the party intended."

They moved into a bigger apartment in Tel-Aviv which David paid for out of pocket, despite the insane housing bubble going on in the city. Mor kept her mother's house in Jerusalem and rented it out. He suggested she stop teaching. There was no need, he said. She refused. She needed those hours on campus when she could pretend that life went on as usual—or better than usual. She was a married woman now. She had a diamond ring, a loving husband, and money in the bank. What else could she possibly want?

She did not want to know what David was doing when she was away. Every time she came home, she was afraid he would tell her. But he never did. They watched Netflix and ate dinners that he cooked. He went through the motions of eating conscientiously, even though it was a sheer charade. Mor soon realized that not only did he not need food but that he was incapable of tasting it. Despite that, his cooking was excellent.

When they made love, David's body glowed like ice, like frozen steel, the bluish petals of the wound-flower over his heart opening wide to disclose the dark seed of the bullet inside. On the hottest nights, when Mor's side of the bed was sticky with sweat, his body was cool and sleek. He was indefatigable; he was obliging; they would have sex for hours, until Mor, wearied and sore, would doze off and wake up screaming, to find her husband alert at her side.

Once she asked him whether deaths dreamed. He said no. Mor was sure he lied. But it was true he never slept, even though he sometimes pretended.

They were to have a party for her friends (all of whom loved David). She sent him out with a grocery list, having decided to cook herself. The idea of letting other people eat food prepared by Death made her queasy. She was chopping lettuce when the knife slipped and bit deeply into her thumb. Mor screamed and watched dark drops of blood pool in the shallow cups of lettuce leaves. And then the bleeding stopped, and the cut closed reluctantly like a disappointed mouth, the skin smoothing over, the pain receding—not into well-being but into a strange sort of numbness.

They had an Indian take-away for her party.

Once a week she goes shopping and she always ends up with another colorful package among her drab plastic bags. She comes back home and tears the bright paper to reveal a miniature garment. The clothes are all in delicate colors: cream, lilac, forest green. Pink and blue are vulgar. She intends to give the child a contemporary-Hebrew unisex name, like her own, fit for either gender—or none.

As she watches the TV on solitary evenings, she takes out an armful of baby clothes and keeps on folding and unfolding them, stroking them with her fingertips, checking the zippers and the buttons, her eyes on the screen. She seldom takes out the same piece on two consecutive nights. The amount of baby clothes one can accumulate in two years is considerable.

Her period was ten days late. She woke up every morning with a sense of tremulous well-being, which she was afraid to disrupt by certainty. But she could not procrastinate anymore, so she went to a pharmacy and bought a home pregnancy test. It showed negative. She called her gynecologist. He assured her that home tests were unreliable and directed her to the lab where they drew blood from her arm. She took a long walk and, for the first time in weeks, smiled at a dog-walker tangled among her charges and at old Mrs. Cohen with her Thai caretaker.

When she called the lab, they told her the result was negative. The nurse, sounding genuinely sorry, wished her better luck next time. Her gynecologist was puzzled and suggested a thorough check-up to determine the reason for amenorrhea in a young and healthy woman. Mor thanked him but did not bother. When she missed her next period, she was not even surprised.

The first time she saw her husband feed was on a bright and clear winter day. She had parked her car and was walking toward the campus gate, when she heard a sharp sound, which, from her military training, she recognized as a shot. Turning around, she saw people running, a small crowd milling at the sidewalk, a man down on his knees being sick, an elderly security guard ineffectually pushing through the packed bodies.

A boy in a soldier's uniform lay among the parked cars, his gun beside him, splattered red and yellow. The boy had no face.

The crowd buzzed like a swarm of bees, words "suicide," "accident," "terrorist attack" mingling into a senseless noise. Mor was resisting the realization that the blood and brain were not a special-effects simulation. Just as it finally sank in, she saw her husband standing by the body.

Mor did not call out to him; she knew immediately that he was invisible to everybody else. In the crystalline sunshine, his body glistened like dirty ice. Gunmetal-colored highlights slid along his limbs. By subtle distortions, his nakedness had shed all pretense of humanity. His arms and legs looked melted-down. But the wound-flower on his left side was alive, its fleshy petals moving hungrily; and when he knelt down and dipped his fingers in the boy's blood, it flashed a deep piercing crimson. The sun washed away the flimsy disguise of his face, revealing the starkness of old bone underneath.

Sometimes her in-laws would drop by. Coming back home, Mor would find Liliana chatting with her husband in the living room, or discover Mark and George sprawled in the armchairs, playing computer games. During the state visit by a U.S. dignitary, Zoe showed up.

The worst of it was that she did not need mirrors anymore. She could see their real shapes flickering through the misty outlines of their fake humanity. The mist kept getting thinner. When George visited, his necktie would flop wetly, soaked with the blood seeping from the slash on his throat. When they had Ruth over for dinner, the food blackened into ashes as she lifted it to her lips.

It finally occurred to Mor, eight months after the wedding, to ask David whether marriage to a mortal was an exception or a rule. She already knew that some deaths were married to each other. Stefan, Death-Suicide, and Gloria, Death-Drowning (a bloated pallid thing under her disguise of a petite waif with huge appealing eyes), were a devoted couple, always holding hands. But had some of them ever been mortal before joining the club?

David looked at her with expressionless eyes.

"We marry our own," he said. "Just as you people do."

She winced. She hated the way he had started talking about Jews. Was he a secret anti-Semite? No, ridiculous; he seemed to enjoy being in Israel and even suggested a couple of times they sell their new place in Tel-Aviv and move up to the Holy City. She resisted; the city was permeated by her mother's ghost like an old, curdled-up perfume lingering in an emptied closet. But she knew she would eventually give in.

Talma came for a visit. They had been best friends in high school and throughout the army service, but once Talma had married a nice boy from the Midwest and moved to Milwaukee, they mostly lost touch, sporadically "liking" each other on Facebook. Talma had a large family, yet she made time for Mor and swept aside her feeble excuses of being busy at work. Mor dreaded introducing David to her, even though she knew she was being paranoid. After all, they went out often enough and she had never seen a waiter faint or a diner blanch as brownish blood trickled off her husband's fingers onto his plate. Undoubtedly, everybody else saw David exactly as he wanted to be seen.

But what if he decided, prompted by his growing petty malice, to reveal himself to Talma? Or worse, to her three-year-old son Ron, whom she had brought with her?

Fortunately, it did not happen. David was all charm, and Talma liked him well enough—or seemed to, even though there was a faint puzzled frown on her forehead as he chatted to her about life in the Midwest. Mor knew he had never actually lived in Toledo, Ohio—it was as much of a lie as the statement that he lived at all. Mercifully, after an excruciating twenty minutes, he excused himself and left them alone in the kitchen to reminiscence, gossip, and covertly compare their fortunes. Mor, afraid of submerged things suddenly floating to the surface of the conversation, quickly offered her guest "mud" coffee, made by pouring boiling water over the coarsely ground Turkish blend. Talma had always liked this concoction and Mor had hated it; now, of course, it would not matter if it was real mud in her cup. Ron, Talma's son, was banging on the wall with a plastic rabbit.

"He is nice, your husband," Talma said, making it sound like a question. Mor nodded. Talma rescued the rabbit from Ron and told him to be quiet, which immediately elicited a wail of protest.

"I swear, this child will be the death of me!" Talma sighed. "When is your turn?"

"What turn?"

Talma nodded at Ron who was trying to stick a fork into a wall hanging.

"You're not getting any younger, you know."

The exile in Milwaukee had clearly done nothing to soften her friend's native bluntness.

"I have a medical problem," Mor admitted and was treated to a long recital of Talma's friends' struggles with infertility. She was relieved when Talma left, carrying the sleeping child in her arms.

Mor sat in the university cafeteria, poking at her lasagna and hoping that the cardboard taste was the fault of the new caterers. But she knew better.

Another slice of pizza, maybe? It did not matter. She was neither gaining nor losing any weight, no matter what she ate. At the beginning it felt liberating. But last night while she was mechanically putting potato chips in her mouth in front of the TV, one chip stuck to her palate. Taking it out, she discovered it was a piece of cellophane.

She took a sip of coffee and wondered why it was transparent. Then she realized it was actually water. In ages past, caffeine deprivation could drive her nuts. Now it made no difference. She might just as well drink water.... ... better for your skin... ... but then nothing was either better or worse for her skin nowadays. Her extensive collection of face creams and makeup had been tossed into garbage long time ago.

It was hot and muggy; the people in the courtyard were fanning themselves and wiping their foreheads. She used to wear tank tops all summer, and there would always be dark stains of sweat in her armpits. Now her long-sleeved white dress was spotless.

The scrape of a chair as somebody joined her at the table.

"May I?"

She lifted her eyes and met Daniel's.

She was speechless for a long time, observing him with the helpless attention of a mouse watching a cat. He was tucking into a pita sandwich and drinking Coke noisily. His appetite was very un-death-like.

"What are you doing here?" she finally asked.

"Traveling. I'm retired, you know."

"I should hope so!"

He lifted a conciliatory hand.

"I'm on your side!"

"It'll be a sad day when I need you on my side!"

"You already do." He examined the remnant of his sandwich and bit off a neat semi-circle of bread and hummus. His teeth, Mor noticed, with a shudder of revulsion, were big, square and yellow, as if he used to be a smoker. "Look, Hanna...."

"Don't you dare call me that!"

"I gave you this name," he said.

She stared at the table.

"You are like a child in a new school," said Daniel. "All those secrets whispered behind your back, old alliances, old loves, old hates, and here you are, a newcomer, and nobody to explain the ground rules to you."

"And you decided to be my guide out of the goodness of your heart, I suppose."

He shrugged:

"I do have a different perspective, you know. First, I'm very young. I still remember my mortal days."

"Were you human once?" she asked, horrified.

"All of us were."

Seeing her expression, he laughed.

"See? You didn't even know that. Your husband is not being very informative, is he? Well, David is singularly lacking in the two qualities indispensable to a death: wide education and a sense of humor."

"How do you become ... how do you become what you are?"

"The same way you become what you are. We are also chosen. Only we don't procreate, so the process is rather haphazard, nothing like your tidy matrilineal descent. Some of us just grow away from humankind until we discover our true vocation. It's a gradual process, you see. Kids who play with guns and explosives, that sort of thing. Some hear the call but cannot make the crossover and remain stranded on your side, pathetic failures in their own eyes, never mind how many body bags they send to the morgue. Ted Bundy and such ..."

"Ted Bundy," she repeated numbly.

He airily waved his hand.

"Quite a lot of those. They sense the vacancies."

"And the others?"

"Well, sometimes it is a sort of deathbed conversion, ecstatic experience, call it whatever you like. But it's going out of fashion.

35

Most people on deathbeds nowadays are drugged out of their senses. And then, of course, there are such as you."

"Such as me?"

"Yes. Marrying into the tribe."

"Are you suggesting I will become one of you?" Mor managed to keep her voice down only because she had subliminally recognized a couple of her students at the next table.

"Absolutely. Look, you'll never be a *Hausfrau*. Not that it's fashionable in our circles. No diapers to change and cooking gets on your nerves if you cannot taste the results. Plenty of your new relations are in-laws, so to speak. Stefan, for example, and Victoria. You should talk to her, by the way, she is a relatively new bride."

"Victoria? How can that be? Isn't she Old Age?'

Daniel nodded and finished his Coke in a single gulp.

"Then how ... I mean, people have died of old age since the beginning of time."

Daniel's face grew animated as he bent toward her.

"Precisely. That's the point. Deaths are not born but they die."

"How can a death die?"

"Never heard of John Donne?" asked Daniel smugly. "*'Death, thou shalt die.'* I thought you liked literature. Not *Christian* literature, perhaps. In any case, a death can only be killed by another death and that under very special conditions. That's why, as you may well imagine, we have rather mixed feelings about each other. We get together out of solidarity and even affection of sorts. There is a sense of family after centuries of gossiping. But we also need to keep an eye on each other. Not that it always helps. Victoria's predecessor was assassinated by Hunger and War, Ruth and Zoe, only they called themselves by different names then. We change names pretty often. I'm proud of my current choice. You're the only one to appreciate its meaning, really. *Daniel;* God judged me."

"Oh, cut it out!" said Mor impatiently. "Cheap theology! Why would Ruth and Zoe do such a thing? What's the gain?"

Daniel beamed at her.

"A very Jewish attitude, if I may say so. Practical, blunt and to

36

the point. Well, since there are so many of us, the only way to gain influence is to enlarge the sphere of one's activity. To some extent this does not depend on us at all. You humans are our real masters, even though most of us consider you mere cattle. But that's just the deplorable lack of education, as I said. Not many of us read Hegel or understand the master-slave dialectic. Anyway, once a new modality of death is discovered, a new ... executive comes into being by a process which, quite frankly, we don't quite understand ourselves. The twentieth century was a fertile one. Have you met John? In the sixties he was about to crown himself King of Death, but after the demolition of the Berlin Wall he has been semi-retired. Tending his garden, I assume, growing mushrooms."

"Mushrooms?" repeated Mor blankly. "Oh, I see. Mushroom clouds. And you?"

"I am a different matter," said Daniel evasively. "In any case we don't—quite—control the course of human history, but we can give a nudge now and then. Ruth and Zoe hoped that by eliminating Old Age they would enlarge their own respective domains. The political situation was favorable too. What they did not count on was that Mark's demure little bride, whom everybody considered half-witted, good perhaps for crib death but nothing more ambitious, would blossom overnight into the queen of geriatric wards."

"Why are you telling me this?" Mor's voice began rising again. "Are you grooming me to be your successor? If you think I'm about to take over the ovens ..."

"Please!" Daniel shook his head. "A little perspective! The ovens have been inactive for seventy years! No, Mor, I'm saying just the opposite. A death's existence is boring, devoid of pleasure, not fit for a woman like you. I don't need to tell you what our sex life is like. And no children, of course. I know what it means to your people. Your husband has trapped you on purpose, for his own amusement. He cannot love you, being what he is; but he cannot even appreciate you. You are a fighter; you are resisting being assimilated. But what if the force of your resistance is such that you'll be forever stuck in that twilight state, neither a death nor a living woman?"

Mor squeezed her eyes shut, staring into the warm blood-red murk under her eyelids. Then she opened them and looked at the creature in front of her.

"You have a proposition," she said. "What is it?"

The red-eye flight was short, four hours. Her night was ruined, first by waiting in the lounge among anxious first-time travelers burdened by duty-free purchases and squealing babies and then by the cramped aisle seat and talkative neighbor. But she emerged into the terminal at 5 a.m., feeling no worse—and no better—than after a good night's sleep. On the Gatwick express, she watched incuriously as the mellow foliage and the ugly rows of brick houses passed by.

She had expected London to be foggy and gloomy, but it was sunny and bright. Guided by her cellphone, she was in Holborn by eleven. She walked down Great Holborn Street until she came to an arched walkway leading into a cobbled courtyard. There she had to press the button several times before the grilled gate swung open.

The flat was tiny, filthy, and cluttered with dusty Victorian junk. The brownish liquid in her cup was either coffee or tea: even with her taste buds intact, she might not have known which. Maggie took out the ingredients for the beverage from an open fridge that was not plugged in, its interior choked with bundles of cobwebby herbs.

"Daniel thinks the world of you," Maggie declared. The contrast between her and her environment was brutal. She was carefully made up, smelled of lavender soap, and wore a neat mauve dress. As long as Mor did not look at her for longer than a few seconds, the illusion held.

"How nice," said Mor dryly. "The feeling is not mutual."

Maggie only smiled indulgently and sipped her indescribable beverage. Was she playing up her Britishness as a joke?

"Dear Daniel! He and I have a lot in common."

"How so?" Mor asked.

"We are both retired. Well, no. I'm semi-retired, I still do quite a bit of freelancing but it's nothing compared to what it was once. I pity

Daniel; so much work, and so spectacular, in such a short period, and then he is kicked out. There were certain affinities, you know, between what he did and my own skills."

Mor felt her gorge rise as the brownish liquid in her cup suddenly took on the tint of clotting blood. But the nausea passed quickly.

"It is ironic," continued Maggie affably, "I'm the oldest one and he is ... no, I take it back, he is not the youngest one, even though none of them, to my mind, is as talented as he is."

"Are you really the oldest?" Mor asked.

"Yes. I was the first-born. Even before your kind was quite sure of its direction. I was there when Neanderthals scattered ochre around the skeletons of the eaten ones. I was there when shamans danced, and withered babies in their mothers' wombs, and flayed men alive without even touching them. And I still enjoy the old art. There are people, right now, dear, who are sticking needles in voodoo dolls and call my name. Some things never change. When all the computer-guided missiles crumble to dust, I will still be there."

Maggie was smiling sweetly throughout the speech, but it was not her pink-glossed mouth that spoke the words. It was the other mouth, squirming beneath her disguise like a black worm: the slit in the whorl-painted visage of Death-Magic.

"But why here?" asked Mor. "Why London?"

Maggie shrugged:

"The Third World is too busy aping the First World. I need believers, not superstition-mongers. This land is soaked in history that it's beginning to rot like a bloated sponge. I was here before it began, and I will be here when it ends. But this is not about my plans, dear. Daniel has asked me for a favor, and I see no reason to refuse. David and I have never gotten along. His modus operandi is far too mechanical for me. No spirit. So ... shall we start?"

Mor nodded. Her throat went dry, and she gulped down the rest of the coffee-tea as she assumed some sort of ceremony was about to begin.

Instead, Maggie took a more comfortable position on her swaybacked couch.

"Once upon a time," she said to Maggie, "there was a boy who loved to play with guns. His family was dirt-poor and they could not afford to buy the weapons that he wanted. His father had the only gun in the family, an old Colt Browning. One day the boy came home and saw his father sitting at the kitchen table, the top of his head blown off. He looked at his old man for a while. And then he picked up the gun lying in the pool of blood, turned around and walked away."

Maggie reached under the torn cushion and pulled out a wreck of an antique gun, rusted and bent. Mor stared at it with revulsion.

"Old tales are right," Maggie went on. "The only power stronger than death is love. When we become deaths, old loves shrivel and fall away. But just as our bodies still bear the one mark of our lost mortality, the one spot reminding us of what we used to be, so do our souls. In a dusty corner of each death's still heart, the one true love of his or her life lies sleeping. If it's woken, the heart will beat once and stop forever. And the death shall die."

"David does not love anybody," said Mor.

"This gun is your husband's one true love."

Mor's fingers closed on the coarse metal. The rust stained them red.

They drove up to Jerusalem to check on her mother's house, which had stood empty since the last tenant had moved out two weeks before. The invisible Israeli fall was marked neither by the turning of the dusty leaves nor by the diminution of the oppressive heat of the day, but only by the melancholy lengthening of the night. It was dark when they got to Rehavia.

She had brought a bottle of red wine and a couple of fat aromatic candles that looked almost like memorial ones, only dyed deep scarlet. David turned off the TV and stretched on the sagging couch. In the candlelight, his real face poked through his unconvincing flesh. Its sharp angles aroused her now as she had once been aroused by his bland masculinity. She brushed the bone with her lips and thrust her tongue between the lipless teeth. The metallic fingers closed around her wrists like handcuffs, and with a shiver of remote pleasure she closed her eyes.

The charade was over; husband and wife were making love naked and sincere, all disguises discarded, all pretenses disavowed. The blind lead-colored balls in the sockets of his skull looked through her. And just for a moment she was tempted by the promise of immortality: freedom from desire, escape from pleasure and pain, time itself frozen in the clarity of her indifferent vision.

Her mock lovemaking died down as it always did nowadays. She sat astride the skeletal thing.

"Don't you ever miss it?" she asked. "The little death, *la petite mort?*"

"Why should I?" he said. "I have the real thing."

"But not with me," said Mor. "And I'm your wife."

He laughed. "I did not marry you for that!"

"Of course you did," said Mor.

Her hand snaked under the pile of her clothes and whipped out the gun. Quickly she pressed the muzzle to the wound-flower in her husband's chest and pulled the trigger.

For a second, poised over him, she thought it could not work. But then the body underneath her convulsed and dark heavy blood erupted from the wound, warm like vomit, splattering her belly and legs. At the same time, she felt a hot explosion inside herself. A single groan escaped her husband, the metallic bones of his face corroding and falling apart, the hard sleekness of his flesh growing soft and mushy, her fingers sinking into his arms and encountering only the pliancy of a child's bones that were snapping like twigs, while she was crying out, dying a thousand little deaths in one infinite moment of time.

When it was over, she found herself lying prone on the couch in darkness. The candles had gone out. Something scratchy was rubbing against her stomach and her thighs were glued together. She snapped on the light. The couch was littered with a pitifully small handful of bone fragments.

41

She took a shower and spent the rest of the night drinking tea, eating canned tuna, and watching movies in Arabic.

At dawn she showered again and went out, into the crystal-clear light of Jerusalem. So early, the city was empty and innocent, low buildings dissolving into the pink shadows on the bare stone hills. Mor drove to the pedestrian mall in Talpiot and stood by the parapet, looking at the glorious panorama of the Mount of Olives with the dim golden dome of the great mosque, and the dark lines of stunted trees winding down into the narrow valley of Gehenna.

She heard steps behind and turned. Daniel, looking fresh and dapper in a white shirt and jeans, smiled at her.

"Well done," he said.

She looked away. And then she looked back at him, incredulous. Over the left nipple, his shirt was stained by fresh blood.

"Thank you, Hanna. You have given me a new lease."

"You?" she gasped. "Coming back?"

"No, no. My old job is done. I have simply taken your late husband's vacant place. Nature—or whoever our manager is—abhors vacuum. I am too young to retire. I knew that when there was a job opening, I would be the first on the list. I'm sure I'll significantly improve on David's performance."

"I should have known," she said dully.

"Don't blame yourself. You did not imagine this morning would see all the guns beaten into ploughshares, did you?"

The city was waking up. A car honked, a child cried, a long strident call drifted up from a mosque in the valley.

"Just tell me one thing," she said. "What was your real name?"

He shook his head.

"I don't remember. Perhaps I did until last night but now, with my new position ... I remember some things. Piano playing, a woman with dark hair—my mother? Light on the linden leaves in spring. But it's fading, memory disappearing. Like that, see?"

He rolled up his shirtsleeve. On the white skin Mor could see disjointed blue strokes—the remnants of a tattoo—that were being absorbed into the body even as she watched.

42

"We all have our badges," he said. "I shan't be sorry to let this one go."

Mor looked into his eyes and smiled.

"You have miscalculated, Daniel," she said. "Or whoever you are. Killing is a spur to breeding. You should have been more careful about murdering your own. And now what will you do, you and your fellow maggots, when death becomes fruitful and multiplies? What will you feed on when life starts feeding on you?"

He stared at her uncomprehendingly.

"I am pregnant," she said.

"You can't be! You're still …"

"Death's wife. I know. But my husband died in my arms, and I am carrying his seed. I am not a pawn in your game, you smug bastard! I am the mother of the future King who will ride down this very mountain and call up the dead from their graves. He will mold ashes back into bodies and clothe burnt bones with flesh. And he will judge you as you deserve to be judged. My son is King of the living and the dead, and he will make each death beg for oblivion before he slays you all. And you, you will remember your name when you are called to his judgment!"

Daniel's right hand crept up, the fingers melting together, acquiring a metallic sheen, fusing into a small but deadly-looking gun. Mor laughed.

"I thought immunity from the family was part of the bargain! Fool that I was, to trust a death! But I have better protection. Go ahead, shoot me! Do it! Why can't you? Could it be you are sensing your King? Could it be my baby is already stronger than you?"

Daniel dropped his hand, which slowly resumed its normal appearance. There was fear in his eyes but also something else, something that looked like relief.

"Well," he said, "this was not planned. But this was bound to happen, sooner or later. And of course, this is the most appropriate place for it. The only place. I wonder what went through David's dull brain when he decided to take his Middle Eastern vacation. But even if he had a … guidance, this is irrelevant now. You are right, Mor. I

43

cannot touch you. And I can feel the thing in your womb even though it is tinier than a mustard seed. But I wonder what it'll be like when it's fully grown. It's conventional to wish a prospective mother joy but frankly, I wonder whether you'll have much joy in your baby. Think of your predecessors; they did not fare too well with their kingly sons, who broke their hearts before future generations bestowed upon the poor women heaps of silly titles. I wonder how you'll be known: Star of the Desert, perhaps? But in any case, Your Future Majesty, though I may be bound to obey your son, I am not going to welcome him with myrrh and frankincense. And though I may be the first one to be hauled before his judgment seat, I will maintain my innocence to the end. I only followed orders."

He turned and walked away, his back ramrod-straight, as he slowly dissolved into the sunlight. Mor shrugged.

"You will show him, won't you, love?" she said, cradling her flat stomach.

Every Friday Mor goes to the Wailing Wall, slowly wending her way through the narrow twisting lanes of the Arab Quarter's market, bright with tourist junk and fragrant with spices, coffee, and sweat. The business is not what it used to be and a couple of times she's been caught in disturbances, but she is not afraid. Nothing can happen to her.

Some of the shop owners recognize her and offer her bright blue beads against the evil eye, which she willingly buys. At the familiar corner stall, she rests her heavy belly, sitting on a scratched aluminum chair and sipping cardamom-flavored coffee from a tiny cup. She hears shots and glimpses a steely-blue apparition disappear among the fluttering rugs. She is unmoved, and so is Ali who continues his rapid monologue in garbled English and waves his hands when she offers to pay for the coffee. She is encountering more and more of the same attitude—reverence mixed with fear—among Jerusalem's numerous population of holy fools, beggars, preachers, certified nuts, and would-be messiahs.

The square in front of the Wailing Wall is beaten into dusty monochrome whiteness by the pitiless glare of the noon. A couple of soldiers lazing about in their glass booth throw her an indifferent glance. The women's section of the Wall is less crowded than usual, only some Orthodox heads hidden under untidy wigs are pressed to the eroded stones like a row of bushy little animals. Their men rock on the other side of the partition, their black hats and coats greedily soaking up the heat. Mor picks up a modesty shawl from the stand to cover up her bare shoulders, walks to the wall, kisses the warm powdery rock.

"Soon," she tells the unmoving weight in her womb. "Soon, honey."

At home she lights the Sabbath candles, fixes dinner, and sits in front of the TV, absorbing the latest litany of nuclear threats, military casualties, and political crises.

A Breaking News banner appears at the bottom of the screen, when Mor feels a sickening pang in her lower abdomen. She sits up, breathless, the dinner tray pushed aside. Yes, no doubt of it, the beginning of labor, just as she had been taught in those long-ago birth-preparation classes. A wave of exultation sweeps over her, overcoming another brutal spasm that feels as if somebody has grabbed a handful of her entrails and twisted them. The hem of her dress is soaked; her water has broken.

Mor reaches for the phone to call an ambulance. A hand closes on hers.

"No need," says a familiar voice.

Deftly, Maggie rearranges the cushions on the couch to prop up her back. Dazed, Mor looks around. Familiar faces look back at her. Ruth smiles shyly at her; Victoria pulls clean sheets out of a large tote bag; Zoe plugs in the kettle in the kitchen. Liliana shoos out the men who crowd at the door. George waves at her, somebody else—Mikhail?—flashes a V-sign.

Mor pushes Maggie aside and tries to stand up. But she can't; the pain is too strong.

"Why?" she cries. "What are you doing here?"

"We want to help you," says Ruth.

"We want to be here when the King is born," says Victoria.

"We want to welcome our leader," says Zoe.

She looks at them mutely and they look back: War, Famine, Plague. Old Age, Voodoo, all with shining hope in their eyes.

"Do you acknowledge my son, then?" asks Mor.

"He is our King," says Maggie. "We have been waiting for him since the beginning of time. And you are our Queen. You will intercede for us with your son."

The labor pains are almost continuous now; she can feel the baby impatiently pushing out of her womb. There are faint screams, booms of explosions, rattle of gunfire; it takes her a moment to realize they are coming from the TV.

"But aren't you afraid of him?" she cries. "Aren't you afraid, Death, that you shall die?"

She sees ambiguous smiles on their faces, but another twist of her guts makes her collapse on the couch, unable to push away Maggie's solicitous hand wiping sweat off her face. Zoe removes her helmet, and she sees the old brown bones of a skeleton rotting in some anonymous grave. The empty eyeholes are filled with light, and Mor still has the strength to wonder; is it the longing for oblivion, or the certainty of triumph?

# JACK THE GIANT-KILLER

*J*ack lived inside the giant.

And so did his Mam, his uncle and aunt, his five cousins, and his Goat. His father used to live inside the giant too but now he lived Outside, or so the pastor said. After his body was ceremoniously brought to the lip of the Colon and given a push that sent it spinning into darkness, Jack's father Robert was supposed to exit into the celestial radiance, reborn as a flier with iridescent wings, big and strong enough not to be afraid of predatory Parasites. He had left behind the dangerous labyrinth of the Guts, the treacherous bubbling of the Lungs, and the deadly seduction of the Heart. Even the ghosts of the Brain would be powerless to harm him.

This was what the pastor said, and Jack wanted to believe him. But by the time he grew up enough to hunt in the Guts on his own, he believed him no more.

Jack and his Mam lived in a hut perched at the entrance to the enormous cavern of the Stomach. This was far enough from the Guts with their deadly fauna but not inside the Stomach itself where the darkness was so thick that even the lumens harvested from the outer trunks of the Arteries did little to dispel it. True, they were close enough to the Heart to hear the Beat that lured men and women away from their families to be lost in the red Arterial Forest. But the Beat had not sounded in more than a generation.

Despite their domicile's good location, Jack and his Mam were poor. After Robert's death, their standard of living plummeted. Jack's Mam, whose name was Patricia, was of good solid Liver stock. But her family had renounced her after she married Robert, an adventurer with murky origins in the tribe of Venous travelers. Robert provided well for his wife and son. He was a great hunter, regularly bringing home plump Echidnas, many-legged Deer, and sweet Sugar-Sacks. Jack's Goat with his cute pink curtain of pseudopodia and five sparkling eyes was found by Robert in a dry streambed of the Stomach when he was just a tiny Larva, mewling piteously and thrashing around in pitch dark. Robert brought him home, and despite Patricia's misgivings, nursed it to adulthood. And that was a good idea because the Goat, whom Jack named Fred, turned out to be able to exude cheesy substance which was now Jack's and Patricia's chief staple. Occasionally Patricia would venture into the Arterial Forest to collect lumens and pick blood-fungi to sell at the market, but the proximity to the Heart made her nervous. She was a timid woman whose rapidly fading prettiness was her claim to self-worth.

Jack, on the other hand, loved traveling. He would often visit his five cousins who lived with their parents on the outskirts of the Arterial Forest in a spacious house with Capillary-woven walls. Unlike Jack's hut, the house had no roof. Jack's uncle Mervin always said that roofs were a waste of effort, even though his wife pointed to flying Lungworms and other Parasites that occasionally snatched babies and domestic pets. But Mervin, like his late brother, was cheery and optimistic, so he dismissed her misgivings—until it was too late.

One day Jack went deeper into the Guts that he had ever ventured before. He did not tell his Mam, knowing how apprehensive she was about her only child. But much as he loved Fred the five-eyed Goat, he was getting sick of cheesy milk for breakfast, lunch, and dinner, and hoped for some fresh game.

As he entered the gloom of the Stomach, the lumen he carried strapped to his chest flared up, and in its pink glow Jack could see the ribbed ceiling arching high above his head, viscous drips gathering in shadowy depressions and plinking upon the wet floor. Jack's boots, bequeathed to him by his father, were made of the finest Tardigrade leather, but they were getting worn as acid leached through their thinning soles. Jack knew how to mind his steps, avoiding particularly noxious pools that steamed orange vapors into the warm thick air. A translucent eyeless head poked out of one of the pools, its round mouth puckering as if kissing the air. Jack grasped his bone spear, but the Nematode disregarded him and withdrew back into the slime.

Jack went down. The gradient of the slope increased as he approached the maze of the Guts, and he had to use his spear to slow down his descent. The darkness coiled around Jack like an impatient lover, sidling up to him with odious intimacy. No matter how hard the lumen tried, its glow was swallowed up within a couple of inches from the course. Not for the first time, Jack wondered whether the darkness of the Stomach was of a different quality from the mere absence of light that was the norm in all the rest of the Body. The pastor preached that the reprobates—thieves, travelers, and wife-beaters—would find themselves in a limitless Stomach after death, fated to wander eternally through its thick gloom, preyed upon by Nematodes and Whipworms. Jack had his doubts about this story too.

The slickness under his feet was broken by flexible protrusions that grew into a thicket of pliant stems, reeking of spoiled milk. Jack lifted his lumen. In front of him, the slope evened out, becoming a field of wavering pink spikes. From between the spikes, worm-heads popped: transparent, blood-red, or purple; eyeless or adorned with multiple eyestalks; with tiny, pursed mouths or split into a toothy maw. These worms were mostly harmless, being tethered to the substratum of the Stomach and deriving their nourishment from it, but Jack knew most of them would not say no to live prey.

As he was approaching the Guts, the sweaty blanket of darkness lifted, and he was now in the ordinary gloom of the Body. He crossed the field of worms, taking care not to step onto the bodies writhing under the roots of the Capillaries, and stood at the entrance to the maze.

The entrance was an oval hole in the ribbed wall, just big enough for a grown man to walk through without bending. A pale illumination was leaking through; the Guts had their own lumens growing in clusters on the ceiling and the walls, whose light was supposed to be detrimental to health. Jack ducked through the hole.

He found himself in a meandering corridor with fleshy grey walls. The walls were riddled with tiny perforations that wheezed out puffs of steam. The corridor was oval in its section, the floor dipping into a shallow trough that was also peppered with vents. It was hard to walk on, but Jack had been here with his father, and knew that the real difficulty lay in the fact that the maze shifted unpredictably, the corridors winding around each other, joining or separating at will. And of course, there was the fauna of the Guts: the creatures whose only rule of behavior was eat or be eaten. Jack counted to be the one having a meal at the end of the hunt.

He hurried through the maze, increasingly concerned as to how empty it was. By now, Jack expected to encounter at least some life: a Hookworm, or a flock of Roly-Polies, or, if he were incredibly lucky, maybe a Deer. But the Guts seemed to have been swept clean.

Suddenly the corridor split into two passages in front of him, a thin membrane springing from the floor and dividing it in the middle. It was soft at first but quickly hardened into a crumbly wall. The passages were too narrow to squeeze through at first but then expanded. Jack saw a faint green glow coming from the right and went that way.

The passage led him to a grove of green Mushrooms. These were not the dormant fungi that his Mam picked in the Arterial Forest. They were alert and predatory creatures with stocky muscular bodies and swollen hatlike heads rimmed with gaping mouths. They were anchored in the layer of green muscle on the floor that rippled when it sensed Jack's proximity. This layer was the creature itself; the individual Mushrooms were its offspring that would eventually bud off and wander around, looking for prey to kill and anchor themselves in its body. But they were not mature enough yet to move on their own.

Jack stopped at a safe distance, pondering what to do. Mushrooms were venomous, spitting poison at any creature that came too close.

Its body would then be absorbed by the carpet-like muscle. Still, Jack knew how to protect himself. And Mushrooms were edible if one took the precaution of cutting off their poison glands. But their flesh stank of decay. If he managed to hack away one and scurry back home, it would fill their stomachs for a day or two but offer no pleasure. And they were about to visit his uncle Mervin, and Jack counted on bringing something special for the big family meal. He imagined the smile on his cousin Suzy's face when he swaggered into the family enclosure carrying in a Sugar-Sack or a Deer, just as his father had done.

Finally, he decided to chance it, to go deeper into the maze in search of a worthier game. Jack unrolled a Worm-hide cloak he carried on his back and wrapped himself from head to toe, carefully covering his face. He squeezed through the forest of spongy flesh, hearing the indignant hissing of immature Mushrooms and the smack of poison gobbets as they hit his cloak. His nostrils filled with a stench of rot. A couple of droplets found their way through, and landed on his flesh, raising blisters. Jack gritted his teeth. The thicket of Mushrooms was bigger than it had first appeared, and at some point, the muscular bodies blocked his way. He struck them with the butt of his spear, but he had to uncover his hand to do so, and it was immediately burning as the Mushrooms spat their poison. But finally, he was through, though his cloak and his hands were in a worse way than he had anticipated. These Mushrooms seemed more potent than the ones his father had told him about.

Beyond the grove, the corridor suddenly broadened out into a large cavity. Jack frowned. Was he somehow back at the Stomach? No, impossible. This cavity was well-lit; in fact, too well-lit. The dim greyish illumination reluctantly dribbled by the cancerous lumens of the rest of the Guts was here supplanted by a strong, even radiance.

Jack looked up and swallowed. There was no lumen on the concave ceiling. Instead, an enormous eye looked down at him, as big as his entire body. The eye was surrounded by a wreath of brightly glowing modules embedded in its puffy lids. But the eye was not like the primitive visual apparatuses of Mushrooms, Worms, and other

51

denizens of the Body. It was a human eye, albeit impossibly large, with a pale blue iris, a black pupil and bloodshot sclera. It even had sparse lashes the length of Jack's forearm. The eye blinked, and Jack backed off, deciding that the hunt would have to be postponed.

But there was nowhere to retreat. The Mushroom-infested passage he had come through had closed behind his back. Jack was locked in the cave with the enormous Eye in the ceiling observing his every move. And then he heard a wet slithering sound.

Another passage opened across the cave and emerging from it was a tangle of bright-red ribbons, weaving and unweaving, squirming, wriggling, sliding across each other. Jack's breath caught in his throat.

The Tape was the most feared of the Guts fauna: a creature of many shapes and many sizes, all of them deadly.

Jack hefted his spear in one hand and, clutching a sharp rib-bone knife in the other, rushed at the Tape as it was pouring out of the opening, piling up in slimy coils. Some Tapes were thousands of paces long, and Jack decided not to wait until more of the creature showed up.

He stabbed at the flat translucent body glowing with ruby light. The knife went deep, and Jack twisted it, cutting through the Tape that parted easily. He slashed again and again, cutting the Tape into bits of slimy ribbon. But each bit wriggled on its own, crawling over the rest. Two loopy headless worms reared up, their seeping ends sprouting a bunch of tendrils. In a welter of quick movements, the pieces of the Tape wove together, passing under and across each other, creating a loose basketwork that filled out into a rough approximation of a headless human body, with bulging belly and mismatched arms: two on one side, three on the other. One of them swiped at Jack. He ducked just in time as a misshapen hand with tentacled fingers tried to close around his neck. It slipped off, leaving behind a whiplash of burning pain. More Tape emerged from the opening and joined the growing body, knitting itself into a monstrous ragdoll, as tall as the ceiling of the cave, that advanced upon Jack, loose ends of its perpetually unraveling body trailing upon the ground and dripping foamy venom. It still had no head, and Jack hoped it could not see him, but any thought of escape was squashed when he realized that the only exit from the cave was the one through which more and more Tape was pouring out in an unending stream. Above him, the blue eye blinked leisurely.

Jack thought about his mother being left alone in the world. He thought of his cousin Suzy. He tried to convince himself he would see his father Outside, but he no longer believed Outside existed.

Jack lifted his spear with both hands as he pressed his back to the wall and took a defensive position. The Tape was now a swollen, big-bellied scarlet effigy that took up so much of the cave that more of the ribbonlike creature could not join in the construct but spread across the walls and the ceiling like ivy instead. Drops of its venom splattered around Jack but the cowl of his cloak provided some protection.

The Tape advanced, and Jack slashed and prodded and cut, but with every parting, the Tape sprouted miniature versions of itself, so eventually a whole crowd of red ragdolls, some as small as actual toys, advanced upon Jack. Whipping tendrils tried to wind around his arms and torso, disabling him. Every time he managed to cut them off; but with every stroke, he generated more of them.

Jack knew that was a battle he could not win, especially when he saw that the flat top of the woven Tape-creature bulged out, sprouting a rounded protrusion. The miniature versions of the main creature did the same, and the tendrils in these incipient heads spun around in frantic whirlwinds, generating solid lumps. They were growing eyes; and Jack knew that while he could fend off the blind and uncoordinated Tape attacks, he stood no chance when the creature finally saw him.

Jack looked up and saw the giant blue eye in the ceiling regarding him with wary amusement.

Discarding his spear and clutching his bone knife in his teeth, Jack jumped and caught a handful of Tape ribbons that now carpeted the walls of the cave, reaching up to the ceiling. The slimy living flesh quivered and tried to wriggle away from his grasping fingers; its venom burned like fire; but without eyes, the creature could not locate the intruder in its dispersed body. And before its eye spots could ripen and open, Jack scrambled up the wall and reached the ceiling. The blue eye blinked, as if in surprise. Jack reached out with his knife and drove it straight through the black pupil.

A rush of warm stinking liquid bathed his face as the glowing modules embedded in the eye's lids blinked out. He was clinging to the wall in absolute darkness. The cave shook; the walls palpitating, constricting, and expanding, spasming uncontrollably. Jack expected a shout—even some Worms cried out in death throes—but the silence of the Guts was filled only with the wet slithering of the coils of the Tape, as it withdrew in panic, trying to collect the scattered pieces of itself. The living ivy slipped out of Jack's hands, and he tumbled down, landing on the squirming pile of the Tape as pieces of it were beginning to develop into separate individuals and turning against each other. Its guiding intelligence gone, the Tape was only a mindless Parasite, breeding by simple fission.

Choking in its soupy stench, Jack groped his way along the margins of the cave, having recovered his spear. Suddenly his fingers encountered empty space. A new opening had appeared in the Guts, and Jack leaped through.

He made his way up to the Stomach with no further misadventure. Battered and shaken, Jack welcomed the blood-warm darkness inside the big cave; that at least was familiar. His lumen had been damaged in the Tape's attack and provided only a weak sputtering glow, but Jack knew his Mam would have collected more from the Arterial Forest where they grew among the delicate tracery of red branches and maroon twigs.

But when he finally reached their hut, it was empty.

Jack called for his mother but heard only the soft susurration of the Body that had accompanied him from the moment he was born. Their home had the air of abandonment, even though their meager possessions were all in place. The Capillary-woven rugs and blankets were undisturbed; his father's collection of grappling hooks was in place; and even the dried fungi and chunks of Nematode-flesh were in their jars in the kitchen. It took Jack no time at all to search their small domicile, but he persisted in looking everywhere for his Mam, his brain refusing to accept the possibility that both his parents were gone.

Suddenly he heard a piteous mewling from outside the hut. Fred, the five-eyed Goat, was hiding in the narrow crevice below the swaying tube of the Esophagus. It rose above the gloomy plain barely lit by the bluish glow from the bubbling ramparts of the Lungs in the distance. Jack embraced the animal, his pseudopodia gently stroking the boy's burned and scratched face. But when he finally let go, he saw that Fred was wounded: there were deep gouges in his back, and several of his eyes were plucked out.

"Who did it to you?" Jack asked but of course, the Goat did not reply.

Jack bathed his own wounds and tended to the Goat the best he could. Fortunately, the spring of pure water that bubbled from the base of the Esophagus was undefiled by the intruders, whoever they may have been. The Goat, in gratitude, exuded the cheesy substance that was its daily meal. Jack put it in his traveling satchel, together with his father's grappling hooks made of the finest bone harvested in far-away parts of the Skeleton. And so provisioned, he set off. Fred tried to follow but Jack told him to stay put, and the faithful Goat rolled up into a spore-ball, content to wait for his master in this inert form for as long as it took.

Normally he would have trudged up the Spleen Slope to get to his uncle, but it took a long time and Jack was impatient to see his relatives. So, he started to climb the undulating stalk of the Esophagus that disappeared into the upper reaches of the Body.

At first, Jack was dizzy, clinging fearfully to the pink-grey slick tube and driving the hooks deep into the pleated surface. His hands still throbbed from the Tape acid, and the higher he rose above the Slope, the more he felt like any moment he would tumble down. But the Esophagus responded to his jerkiness by swaying and contracting, trying to shake him off. Jack relaxed and forced himself to clamber up as lightly as he could. After that, his ascent became steady as he rose toward the distant scarlet glimmer of the Arterial Forest, reflected off the slick wall of the enclosed the Heart.

He searched in the gloom above for any sign of the Blue Eye but saw nothing. Jack had never heard of the Eye from his family and considered whether it could have been one of the phantoms of the Brain, even though they were not supposed to descend as low as the Stomach.

Suddenly he heard a whirring sound in the dark. Jack stopped climbing and listened. He turned down his lumen in order to be inconspicuous but then he could not see what was approaching.

The whirring sound grew stronger, and a narrow body, twice as long as Jack was tall, emerged from the gloom. Its head was a collection of serrated mandibles, fitted inside each other like a series of dolls, and from the innermost mouthpart a dripping stinger shot out and was reeled in with hypnotic regularity. The creature's segmented body was fringed with small transparent wings that beat the air, keeping it afloat. It was a Parasite of a kind Jack had never seen before.

The Parasite had no eyes, but Jack was in no doubt that it could sense him. The stinger reeled out, and its pointed end homed in on Jack, who pulled out his bone knife. But in order to do so, he had to release one of the grappling hooks that kept him tethered to the Esophagus, and the fleshy tube, as if reacting to his fright, suddenly contracted violently, all but throwing Jack off. He managed to cling on for dear life, but the Parasite did not relent. The stinger was thrown off its target by the Esophagus' contraction, but it stretched out even more, groping for Jack, as the creature hovered next to him, its spoiled-milk stink making Jack's eyes water. He tried to stab the stinger but was afraid to let go of the Esophagus. He was so high up that he could not see the floor of the Slope down below. He already imagined his body broken and bleeding, feasted upon by the smaller Nematodes and Worms.

The Parasite whirred closer, its many mouths stretching, opening up into a vortex of teeth. Jack grasped his lumen, squeezing it to its full power, and tossed it straight into the maw.

Lumens were living colonies, composed of many Animalcules,

so tiny they could barely be seen. They fed on even tinier Animalcules, and as long as they were treated right, they were harmless. But if startled or threatened, lumens could release their luminous energy in one burst of fire, scorching their enemies. And this was what happened. The lumen that Jack threw sailed into the Parasite's gut, illuminating its segmented body from within with a burst of white flame. The creature thrashed and flailed; the Esophagus shook; and Jack clung on with all his might. The whirring of the Parasite's wings ceased. Jack saw the burning body fall down to the plain, briefly illuminating Jack's empty hut before it collapsed in a sputtering heap.

Jack renewed his climb and was not molested any further. He reached the lip of the Arterial Forest and pulled himself off onto the soft mat of interwoven Capillaries which was the Forest's floor. The Esophagus snaked up above the Forest's canopy, leading to the legendary realms of the Throat and the Mouth, which no human being had ever seen in Jack's forefathers' lifetimes.

Jack had always liked the Arterial Forest, and after his father's death had tried to persuade his Mam to move up there in order to be closer to Uncle Mervin and Cousin Suzy, but Patricia objected. It was as if she secretly hoped for her husband's return from the dead, and so they stayed where they were. Now Jack regretted he was not more insistent. Perhaps whatever had happened to his Mam would not have happened if she were protected by the family. But very quickly he realized how misplaced his hopes for help were.

The Forest gleamed with its own inner light: scarlet, red, rosy, peach, and fuchsia; all the hues of life and warmth, as the sluggish currents of luminous substance circulated through its tangle of transparent trunks and interwoven branches. Jack had been told that this substance supported all life in the Body, but he did not believe it, as it seemed to be concentrated in one place only. But the radiance of the Forest always made him feel safe; and while there were predators hiding in its complicated arabesques of red limbs, such as shapeless Leucocytes that enveloped their prey with their sac-like bodies, they were not as dangerous as the denizens of the living dark.

He ran down the familiar path that his uncle Mervin had cleared through the Forest. But when he saw the woven walls of the enclosure ahead, Jack stopped in his tracks. There were huge holes torn in the walls. They listed and one of them had fallen and lay on the ground. Jack did not want to see what had happened here, but he knew he must.

At least, there was no sickening uncertainty as had been with the disappearance of his Mam. He found the bodies of his uncle Mervin, his Aunt Jemima, and four of his cousins under the collapsed walls of the enclosure. They had suffered no obvious wounds; nor were they bloated as with the aftereffects of the many venomous creatures of the Body. Nevertheless, they were dead; and rigor mortis had already set in.

Jack laid out their bodies in the clearing, crossing their arms on their chests. He half-wanted to say the same prayer the Pastor had said over his father as he had sent him on with the hope of the free life Outside. But he did not have time.

Because as much as he grieved their deaths, his sorrow was overshadowed by the impatience to go on. More important than what he had found was what he had not.

He had not found the bodies of his Mam Patricia or his cousin Suzy. And so, there was the hope they were still alive. It was not much to go on, but it was all he had.

As Jack was arranging the bodies, he felt a gaze on his back. Something was watching him from the luminous thicket of the Forest. Slowly, he turned around, grasping his knife.

The same Blue Eye that had watched his struggle with the Tape was now observing him from between the lattice of pink branches. Jack knew it was the same one, even though the Eye bore no sign of the wound Jack had inflicted with his spear. But the familiarity in its stare was unmistakable.

"What do you want from me?" Jack yelled angrily. "Who are you?"

The denizens of the Body, apart from the humans, were mindless; but people often talked to them out of loneliness. Jack talked to his

Goat, Fred, though he knew the creature could not understand him. But when he addressed the Eye, it was not simply to vent. Though the Eye belonged to no known creature, Jack felt that it was sentient.

The Eye popped out of its lair. It was tethered to a sinewy eyestalk that seemed to be part of the Forest, blending with its thicket.

"Can you talk?" Jack asked, but immediately realized it was a stupid question. It was an Eye, not a Mouth.

The Eye blinked again, and Jack had an inspiration.

"Blink one for yes, twice for no!" he commanded.

The Eye blinked once.

"Do you know what killed my family?" Jack asked.

The Eye blinked once.

"What was it?"

The Eye remained open.

"Was it a Parasite?"

Two blinks.

Jack was at a loss. There were too many dangerous creatures inside the Body for him to go through the entire list of them!

Suddenly the pliant surface under his feet shuddered, and he heard a distant rumble. The Eye's lid fluttered nervously.

The rumble grew, but it did not become a simple avalanche of noise; instead, it went up and down the musical scale, shaping itself into an almost-coherent utterance; an almost-comprehensible sentence, as if an impossibly loud voice was trying to articulate something through a handful of broken glass. Jack was battered and swept off his feet by the strength of its passion and yet at the same time, he did not feel endangered. To the contrary, he felt a peculiar tug toward the source of the noise as if something rooted itself in his chest and was gently reeling him in. He moved toward the thicket but then the noise died out and he stopped, disappointed and relieved in equal measure.

"What was that?" he asked, forgetting that the Eye could not answer, and it did not, only its lashes fluttered as if it was trying to signal something.

"Are my mother and Suzy still alive?" he asked.

The Eye blinked several times in rapid succession. Jack stared at it in bewilderment.

"Does it mean you don't know?"

One blink.

"Then who does?"

He did not expect the Eye to answer, but it did, in a way. The black pupil rolled sideways, and a path opened up before Jack, leading through the Arterial Forest whose lacy intertwined branches and contorted trunks shifted with a groan. Jack hesitated, remembering how the Eye had seemed to egg on the Tape when it had attacked Jack in the Guts.

But what else was he supposed to do? He had to find his mother and Suzy. So, he stepped onto the path.

Jack had been walking for a while without seeing anything new: the same glowing growths in the colors of red, scarlet, and pink; the same slowly circulating streams through the translucent flesh of the Forest. Once he stopped to drink from his water-bottle and to eat some of the Goat cheese. But he was driven on by the impatience and—he had to admit—curiosity.

Jack had always been different from his parents, his cousins, and the infrequent strangers who had visited his family from the other parts of the Body. All of them, even the Venous travelers on his father's side, were content with the basic framework of their lives. They may have been curious about specific subjects—where did Parasites come from or why was the Guts maze so unpredictable?—but they never questioned the foundations of their world, which was the Body. But Jack did. That was why he had listened to the pastor's words about the Outside first with incredulity and then with increasing anger. There had been a hollowness at the core of that sermon, which helped Jack crystallize his own attitude. It was not that he had any better idea of Outside, or even whether Outside actually existed. It was that he refused to accept what he was told.

Finally, the Forest thinned out and he saw a blue flicker in the sea of red. Jack peered through the interlacing branches.

There was a large clearing ahead, carpeted with a mat of swollen Capillaries. And beyond it was a curving wall, gleaming with blue, aqua and purple as lights played upon its wet membrane. It rose up far into the murk above, so Jack could not see where it ended, and its sides disappeared into the tangle of the Arterial Forest which seemed more active here, the red liquid rushing through the pulsing tubes with alacrity. But the strangest thing about the wall was that it pulsed, irregularly but with an increasing amplitude, contracting and expanding.

Jack was bewildered. He knew that the Lungs occasionally bubbled with activity, but he had left the Lungs below on the plain. And in any case, this thing seemed more intent somehow than the Lungs, swelling and pushing with visible effort as if trying to uproot itself from its substratum. Above it, Jack could discern sagging blue-red pipes, big enough to swallow him whole. And there was a low sound accompanying the thing's efforts: a hum that got under Jack's skin and into his head, teasing him with the promise of almost-words. Involuntarily, he stepped forward.

The Blue Eye popped out of the thicket, barring his way.

"What's up?" Jack snarled. "You wanted me to see this thing. What do you want now?"

The Eye fluttered its lashes but did not move away. Instead, it rolled back as if trying to see behind its back, and Jack followed the direction of its gaze.

The wet membrane that covered the pulsating thing was semi-translucent, and by peering from the side, Jack could get a glimpse of what lay beyond. And what lay beyond were people.

Caught in-between the skin and the muscular fibers that comprised the object were silhouettes of men, women, and children, frozen in contorted poses: some with their arms thrown up, some crouching low, some spread-eagled. There were quite a lot of them: Jack had never seen so many people at once in his entire life.

At first, he thought they were dead. But then he noticed a twitch here and there; a hand clenching into a fist; a head rotating. These were not corpses but living people caught under a sticky film and glued into their unnatural postures.

The hum Jack had been hearing intensified into a wave of sound that pulled him forward with irresistible strength as if the combined voices of all the people in the wall were calling out to him. And he almost heard the voices of his mother and Suzy in the chorus. He tried to force his way toward the wall, but the sound ebbed away, leaving him weak and disoriented.

The wall people twitched and shuddered. And Jack who, in his brief life, had learned the language of pain, knew what he was seeing. The people were being tortured.

"Is this the Heart?" he asked the Eye.

It blinked once.

"Can I release them?"

Another blink. Jack hefted his spear. The Eye blinked twice.

"What? Not this? Isn't it strong enough?"

Two blinks.

"Where can I find a better weapon?"

The black pupil rolled upward.

And Jack understood.

He had been climbing the Esophagus for what seemed like an eternity. Driving a bone hook into the peristaltic surface, hanging off it with one throbbing arm, pulling himself up. Repeating the process.

Jack was so tired he started hallucinating. He saw the face of his father floating just beyond his reach. Robert's lips were moving rapidly as if he were speaking, but Jack could not hear a word. Then Uncle Mervin showed up next to his brother, and the two of them seemed to engage in a spirited discussion. Finally, they floated away, leaving Jack grateful for their absence. He was too wrung out to pay attention to anything but his ascent. Fortunately, the surface of the Esophagus was not completely smooth but circled with concentric rings, which gave some purchase to his hands and feet.

Finally, after the interminable climb, the environment started changing. Dribbles of illumination from above diluted the uniform gloom. The Esophagus widened out into an umbrella shape, which made climbing even harder as Jack had to cling to the concave surface. But then he saw a ceiling above. There was a ragged hole torn in it, and a pale uniform light was streaming through it.

He grasped the lip of the hole and hoisted himself onto the flat surface. He lay face down, his arms trembling, his body so weak it did not feel possible to raise his head. If there were Parasites, Nematodes, or other predators around, they could make a free meal of him without him putting up any resistance.

Finally, Jack got his wind back and sat up. He was so shocked by what he was seeing that he forgot to be afraid.

The geography of the Body was not something he knew much about, though his parents had taught him as much as was necessary for survival. Jack had learned that the Body's main axis was vertical. People lived in the middle area, which was sometimes called the Trunk, though this term was not commonly used nowadays. Below the Guts was the precipitous plunge of the Colon where the dead were sent on their final journey. Nobody knew what—if anything—lay below. Above was the Arterial Forest, the Venous Rivers where Robert's kinsmen sailed on rafts, and the Heart, which was avoided as much as possible. The stony Ribs were quarried for bone but provided few places to inhabit. The sedate precinct of the Liver where the well-off folk tended their flocks of many-legged Worm-Sheep and fatty Piglets was the safest and the best place to live, though its inhabitants had to trade for lumens as there was no natural light source there. And above all of that lay the fabled realm of the Throat, the Mouth, and even higher up, the country of the Brain—where phantoms roamed. Many people, including Uncle Mervin, did not believe that the Brain even existed. But now Jack was about to prove them wrong.

Still, his environment did not quite correspond to the stories he had heard about the Brain, in which that fabled precinct was described as composed of arching passages and labyrinthine rooms flooded with mysterious light. There were no sweeping arches or towering spires here, though the empty space was larger than any Jack had ever seen.

Far above him stretched a dull red ceiling with elaborate moldings and decorative coffers. It seemed to be shaped like a dome, sloping down to the grey floor where Jack lay. In the distance, he could see a large maroon mass covered with white saucer-shaped suckers. At first, he thought it was alive, but it did not move. And closer to Jack was a fence composed of white boulders, each twice as large and broad as Jack himself. There were gaps between the boulders, and through them streamed the white light that was stronger than any lumen and more uniform than the wavering radiance of the Arterial Forest. Jack picked himself up and started walking toward the fence when somebody called his name.

Jack whirled around. A man stood nearby.

The stranger was tall and broad, bigger than the biggest man Jack had ever seen. He wore no clothes, which was unseemly as no civilized human would go around bare-assed. When the man came closer, Jack revised his estimation of the stranger's gender: his crotch was smooth, and there were no nipples on his broad chest. But even that was not as shocking as his face.

Wide, hairless, and flat, the face had a long toothy mouth, a tiny pug of a nose, and one single eye positioned straight in the center of the stranger's forehead. The eye was big and blue, fringed with sparce lashes. It winked at Jack.

"Who are you?" Jack demanded, squeezing his bone knife. "How do you know my name?"

"We have already met," the stranger replied. "In the Guts, and by the Heart. Unfortunately, I could not talk to you until you got closer to the Brain. Let me introduce myself. My name is Corb. And I am your Host."

"I've never visited with you," Jack responded belligerently.

The stranger laughed.

"You have been visiting with me since the day you were born, and so have your forefathers for many generations. I am the Body in which you live."

"How is it possible? We are inside the Body. How can a man be inside himself?"

"That's an excellent question, Jack. You are a smart boy, very smart. And you are also brave, as I saw in your fight with the Tape. This is why I have chosen you."

"Chosen me for what?"

"To kill me."

Corb the giant led Jack to the back of the domed room, close to the quiescent mass of suckers, which he told him was called the Tongue. There were plump little Animalcules nesting among the suckers, and Jack, who was very hungry, picked up a couple and sucked their jellylike juice. Corb did not touch them but encouraged Jack to eat his fill.

"It would be dangerous for you when it functioned properly," he explained. "The Tongue would have swept you down the Esophagus, and the Beasties who live there would have broken your body down, so it could nourish me. But it has been a long time since anything in the Body worked as it should."

"What happened?" Jack asked.

Corb shrugged.

"Senescence, decay. Who knows? I am the last of my race, Jack. Your kind have lived with us throughout our history. Pets, food, parasites. But now my body is breaking down, and your presence causes me daily pain and discomfort. You are breeding inside me, but other things are breeding too. They are fighting your kind, and you are fighting back. The more this warfare continues, the less I can be myself. My organs are rebelling too. The Heart has become a predator, scheming to take over and preying on your people, attracting them by its seductive call and imprisoning them to feed off their energies. It hates the Brain and wants it dead. And the Brain is the last hideaway where I still live. Me, Corb, my own self. A stranger in my own body."

Jack reached out and grasped Corb's thick arm. His fingers went through the skin and the muscles, sinking into the intangible fog.

"You are a Phantom!" Jack exclaimed.

"Yes. The Phantom of myself. A poor self, cowering in fear in a corner of the Brain, feeding on dusty memories. I don't want to live anymore, Jack. I want to be released. And only you can help me."

Jack was climbing down the Esophagus tube. It went much smoother than the upward climb: he was rested and well-fed. And more importantly, he had a better weapon than his father's dulled bone-knife and bent bone-spear.

"I have no control of my Organs," Corb had explained. "I cannot order the Heart to stop beating, or the Stomach to stop feeding. But there used to be a hierarchy inside the Body, Jack, and shreds of it still survive. The Brain has powers that others don't. It can forge a mental Sword that is deadly to any rebellious part of what used to be me."

"So why don't you wield it yourself?" Jack asked suspiciously.

Corb laughed: a grumbling belly-laugh.

"How can I, Jack? You see me: I have no material existence. I am a Phantom, a shard of memory, a dissolving bit of sadness. You, on the other hand, you are young and strong. You have fought off predatory Tapes and deadly Nematodes. You can kill the Heart. And if you do, the entire Body will die."

Now as Jack was nearing the Arterial Forest whose ruddy glow shone from below, he was ruminating over Corb's promises. The chief thing to do was that by killing the Heart, Jack would liberate his Mam and Suzy.

"I won't lie to you," Corb had said. "It's possible they are dead. The Heart lures people in with its seductive Beat and then imprisons them behind the wall of its Pericardium where it keeps them for a while, feeding off their life-force. Once it's exhausted, they die, and the Heart ingests their corpses. But your kin are strong and female, which helps, as females are more enduring than males. Perhaps they are still alive."

Corb had also explained why the other members of Jack's family, Uncle Mervin, his wife and four of their sons, had died when the Beat sounded. According to him, people varied in their susceptibility to the

Heart's blandishments: some found them irresistible; for some, it was so traumatic they died on hearing the Beat; and some, like Jack, were relatively immune to it. At the time, it had made sense. But now Jack was beginning to doubt Corb's story. What if the giant was actually intent to continue living and was sending Jack to the Heart as another sacrificial victim? Without the Heart, Corb had said, the entire Body would die, and so of course, would Corb, a Phantom of the Brain.

But he did give Jack a new weapon. Securely strapped to his back was what Corb called "a mental sword." It was made of a material Jack had never encountered: shiny and slick and unbelievably hard, harder than even the rare inner bone. Its edge was so sharp Jack had cut his finger simply by handling it.

"It is formed from the memory of what your kind used to have before you lived inside our Bodies," Corb had explained but Jack was impatient to get back to the familiar areas of the Trunk and try to rescue Patricia and Suzy. The sword gave him a sense of invincibility. No Parasite, not even a Tape or a dreaded Tardigrade, would stand a chance against its sharpness.

Jack was sorry he had not queried Corb more on what would happen if he managed to kill the Heart. Would the Body continue to provide shelter and sustenance to the humans inside it? Would the Arterial Forest still grow blood-fungi? Would the Venous Rivers still flow?

But there was nothing to do but go ahead, and Jack did. He jumped down onto the Forest's matted soil. The bodies of his family were left under the cover of their woven walls, but now Jack saw that these covers bunched up and moved. He approached cautiously.

The blind snout of a Nematode poked out, its concentric teeth rotating in its round mouth as it chewed on a piece of flesh. Outraged, Jack swiped with his new sword. And it did not disappoint: the blade went through the flailing body, neatly cutting it in two.

Having killed all the Parasites, he carefully covered the mangled bodies again. For a moment, he hesitated. Should he go to the Liver and call upon the pastor to perform funeral rites? No human corpse was left inside the Body for more than a couple of hours. All had to be given a decent burial by being thrown into the Colon, so their spirits may be reborn Outside.

But Jack knew he could not tarry. He remembered his father telling him that the duty to the living was greater than the duty to the dead. And so, Jack went forth through the ruby-colored Forest toward the Heart.

The pulsing trunks were not as compliant as the last time. They barred his way, crawling across the path, creating makeshift obstacles of interwoven twigs, their flexible branches winding around his neck trying to strangle him. The scarlet liquid boiled under their translucent tegument, agitated; and Jack heard a low hum, almost inaudible at first but then building up into a crescendo of rhythmic many-voiced sound. The Heart was gearing up for another Beat!

Jack sliced through the growth across his path. A fountain of warm red liquid erupted, bathing him from head to toe and leaving a salty residue on his lips. Jack knew the taste from the many times he had sucked a cut on his own fingers.

The hum grew until it reverberated in Jack's bones, rattling him from the inside. He ran, slashing at the quivering arteries.

And here was the Heart: swollen with life, slow and majestic as it inflated its blue-red walls as if taking a breath. It expanded, and the human bodies trapped under its tegument, writhed and flailed.

The Beat was now both inside and outside Jack, filling his entire world with the rhythmic irresistible call of life. He felt himself slumping down, succumbing to the mindless drowsy enchantment of his own flesh and blood.

Suddenly, he remembered his father's body spiraling into the darkness, the spark of life gone from the cocoon of flesh, flying free into the Outside.

Jack rushed at the towering Heart and struck with his sword.

The flood of blood swept him off his feet as he floundered in the salty red stream. His free hand closed around a quivering Artery, and he clung to it with all of his might. The Forest was in motion around him, branches whipping and trunks exploding. The Heart was erupting in powerful jets that leveled everything around it. Jack saw bodies swept by the flood, tossed, and turned in the red stream, but all he could do was hold on for dear life.

And finally, the strength of the flow abated, and he was able to open his eyes.

The Forest was leveled all around him; the trunks flattened and empty. Its scarlet luminescence was dimming. The deflated sack of the Heart lay in the enormous clearing like a pricked balloon. Surrounding it was a scatter of dark forms.

Jack waded through the pools of blood toward the bodies. Many of them were not only dead but half-ingested, missing faces and chunks of flesh, their limbs nothing but skeletal twigs. But a couple stirred, sitting up, trying to clear blood from their eyes.

"Mam!" Jack rushed toward a woman who was struggling unsteadily to stand up. Patricia threw her arms around her son.

"Suzy?" he asked but Patricia shook her head, and Jack realized Cousin Suzy was not among either the dead or the survivors.

"She was taken," Patricia muttered, trying to clear the thick plug of congealed blood from her throat. "A flying thing … came to your uncle's house…."

Jack swallowed remembering the flying creature that had attacked him on his way up. If it had taken Suzy, what chances did she have?

But there was no time to ponder it because something was happening. The ruby glow of the Forest was dimming into a scatter of embers, leaving Jack, his Mam, and the handful of survivors in the darkness as thick as the one that inhabited the cavern of the Stomach. Even the lumens that grew in the Forest were winking out. And the spongy surface under their feet shook and buckled. The tremors spread to the entire Body until the walls of flesh that had surrounded generations of humans were wobbling and shuddering, the air filled with creaks and groans.

Grasping his Mam's hand, Jack groped toward the edge of the dying Forest, urging the small group of people to follow them. The darkness was descending quickly, and the tremors intensified until the people had to crawl on their hands and knees, unable to stand upright.

Suddenly a gleam ahead drew Jack's attention. A fading glimmer of blue in the universe of black and red.

The Blue Eye stared at him from the pile of dead Arteries, its light almost gone, a film of white creeping over the dilated pupil.

"Corb!" Jack cried. "What's happening?"

He did not really expect the giant to be able to talk to him. But a voice sounded in his ears, remote and barely audible, as if coming from a long distance.

"Thank you, Jack!"

"Are you dying?"

"I am dead already, and the Body is in its death throes. It'll be gone soon."

"What will happen to us?"

"You may try to survive inside my corpse as scavengers. Many Parasites will. Or—you can cut your way to the Outside. Your sword will do it."

The group had finally made their way through the remnants of the Forest and approached the Outer Wall. It loomed above them, disappearing into the darkness. Even the white armature of the Ribs was barely seen in the encroaching gloom, and Jack heard the low buzzing of a Flying Worm. It was picked up by others of its kind, as the emboldened Parasites rampaged through the enfeebled and dying Body.

"Your choice, Jack," the echo of Corb's voice whispered inside his head. "Try to survive here or venture Outside. Only remember: there is a reason why your kind asked to be sheltered inside our Bodies. I am the last of my people, Jack. But sick and lonely as I am, I see both in and out. My Eye—my real Eye—has been watching Outside for generations of your kind. And you may not want to know what's there. You may want to stay here where it's safe!"

"What's Outside?" Jack cried so loudly that his Mam started, and other people turned to him. The voice in his mind laughed.

"You'll have to see for yourself. But something has killed all the giants, and it was not your kind, Jack. Except for the last one, me. So, thank you, Jack the Giant Killer, for setting me free from the horror Outside."

And the Blue Eye winked at him and dissolved in the dark.

Jack stood still for a moment. And then he strode to the Outer Wall and smote it with the shining blade of his sword.

With an enormous rumble, the Ribs cracked, the rubbery flesh gave way and parted. And Jack and his companions finally saw Outside.

And they wished they had not.

# TURANDOT

Turandot walked in her parched garden, her silks dragging on the ochre ground. She was reading a history of the Queendom but when she turned the page, the book dissolved into a shower of paper flakes, dust falling upon dust.

Turandot called her council.

"What can be done about the drought?" she asked, knowing the answer.

The Grand Vizier who had served her mother bowed deeply.

"The land is barren because so are you, Your Majesty," he said.

What maddened her most was the ease with which other women bore fruit. From time to time the belly of one of her handmaidens swelled and she would birth a bunch of grapes, a beautiful striped tiger cub, or even a human baby. But she, the ruler of the Queendom who incarnated the power of the land, was barren. And all the wisdom of the Lodges was impotent against such an unprecedented and shocking calamity.

She called upon her Grand Vizier again and demanded to know whether there was anything in the old writings of the lost Empire of the West that could shed light upon her predicament. The old man refused to answer at first, but then he reluctantly conceded that those benighted savages had some outlandish ideas on the subject of fertility, the ideas that challenged the ways of civilized society. They believed that offspring were produced by men acting upon women in some manner. But he insisted he did not know what the secret rite was supposed to be and strongly advised Turandot not to offend All-Mother by inquiring further into the matter. And yet she could not wait. If rains did not come within the next fortnight, the drought would bring about famine, unrest—and Turandot's own death. She had no choice.

Turandot's proclamation was read by criers in town squares and printed on sheets of yellow silk that were hung from the windows of and men's and women's Lodges. The Queen posed a riddle to her male subjects: how can a woman bear fruit through the intervention of a man? The man who could demonstrate the validity of his answer would share Turandot's throne as her consort. The punishment for failure was death.

The older generation was outraged, darkly hinting at the coming wrath of All-Mother. The younger people laughed and hoped for an exciting change. The courtiers shrugged and pitied the barren Queen whose life was measured in days until the inevitable coup that would put an end to this charade. But everybody loved to invent elaborately obscene jokes on the subject of men and women collaborating in the production of children. It was to Turandot's great mortification that the first seeker of the throne offered such a joke as an answer to her riddle.

The man was an inhabitant of the Marshes, the dreary backwater region where people were reputed to dissolve spontaneously into the mud, and he had the pale skin and colorless eyes of his birthplace. He knelt before the jasper throne where Turandot sat in her many-layered robes of black silk trimmed with purple and gold.

"Your Majesty," said he. "The wise men of the Empire of the West knew the answer to the riddle and I, alone of all Your subjects, have inherited their knowledge."

"And what is this fabled secret?" the Queen asked.

"The answer to Your riddle is," said the man, "that sexual intercourse between a man and a woman places the fruit in the woman's belly."

A wave of stifled giggles went around the Grand Hall and Turandot herself had to bite the inside of her cheek to keep a straight face.

"If it were so," she said, "surely no Lodge Virgin, barred from all contact with men, could bear fruit. And yet these women are often delivered of as many as ten babies a year."

"Then they are liars," said the pale-eyed man, "and secretly they entertain male visitors."

Many courtiers gasped at this audacity, and the fat Mistress of women's Lodges rose from her seat, red-faced with anger.

"Silence," ordered Turandot. "You are insulting the Lodge Mysteries, which are under Our protection. For this alone you deserve death. But we shall be lenient and shall grant you the opportunity to prove your assertion. Take a handmaiden of ours who has never borne fruit and lie with her. If by tomorrow she is proven fruitful, you will become my consort. If not, your head will be displayed on the palace wall tomorrow afternoon."

The Marsh man's head was brought to her on a platter before being put on a sturdy spike outside the Ceremonial Gate. Obeying some obscure impulse, Turandot closed his watery eyes.

"Surely," said the Grand Vizier, approaching her as she stood alone, among the dry flowerless stalks of her garden, watching the gaudy colors of the sunset enhanced by the ash from the burning forests. "Surely, if there is a male magic it cannot be anything as commonplace as the ordinary act performed by boys and girls for pleasure and by men and women for distraction."

Turandot glanced at his impassive face, his slight, straight-backed body. She suspected that he would be the one to deliver the blow to end her life, but until then he would treat her with all the deference due to a Queen.

"I have often thought…," began Turandot.

"Yes, Your Majesty?"

Turandot stretched her hand and her tame albino rat rose like a small pillar of salt in the yellow grass.

"Humanity is alone among living things. All animals breed true, only women can bear any fruit of the land. Is it the sign of our mastery? Or is it a curse of chaos? Could it be that men have a great, if unrevealed, part in the scheme of nature?"

"The wisest minds of the Queendom have asked these questions and have not found the answers," said the Vizier. "However, when I was young, I heard a legend that shows how the uneducated folk look at these matters. As Your Majesty knows, I come from the South. People there have much imagination but scant learning."

"Tell me," said Turandot.

"It is said we are not natives of the World. In fact—and this is a surprising flight of metaphysical fancy for such common people— the World itself is not real but rather a decaying labyrinth of dreams and desires of an age long gone by. The World is sly and mysterious, scribbled over with ancient ciphers. It seems we are lost in a dead men's riddle, perhaps the very riddle Your Majesty seeks to answer."

The second aspirant to the throne was a small plump man with bright shifty eyes. Turandot was wearing a red robe whose bodice was encrusted with rubies and garnets. Shewas sweating.

"The answer to the riddle, Your Majesty," said the man, "is that a woman's child is a man's dream. If a woman bears a fruit, then some man, somewhere, has dreamt of this creature, be it of human, animal or vegetable nature. The dream enters the woman's womb and becomes flesh."

"Is this also the secret wisdom of the Empire?" asked Turandot sarcastically. She disliked the man, all the more so because she was impressed by his answer.

The man squared his shoulders. "No. It is the result of my own research."

"Can you prove it?" asked Turandot.

The man became flustered. "It is difficult to prove, Your Majesty, since dreams fly far and wide. A man in the South can put a baby in the belly of a woman of the Marshes."

"But does this happen on the same night?" asked Turandot.

"Yes."

"In this case I shall send messengers to every corner of the land, ordering that on the night of the full moon, all the men from the age of ten and up are to hold a sleepless vigil. The Masters of the men's Lodges will make sure nobody slips away to bed. All the males of the Queendom will drink the juice of the bright-eye flower that dissipates dreams and promotes wakefulness. Next morning we shall see if any woman finds herself fruitful."

So it was done, and Turandot did not even have to wait for reports from far away, as no less than ten women on the palace grounds found themselves with swollen bellies, just as the men were going, grumbling and bleary-eyed, home to bed. The small sleek head appeared on the wall beside the large pale one, both intermittently pecked on by lethargic crows.

For three days nobody sought an audience. And then, in the early twilight when Turandot was dozing in the Great Hall under the monotonous swishing of the fans, a guard appeared to announce that another seeker had come with an answer to the riddle.

Turandot woke up with a start and stared at the man who walked in. He was young and slender, of medium height; his skin the color of cream but with a strange dusky undertone, as if his blood had clotted into tar. He was about to speak when Turandot raised her hand.

"What is your name?' she asked.

"Kaif, of the Mo-ruan family."

It was a minor but respected aristocratic family. Its members headed several men's Lodges.

"Kaif," repeated Turandot. "I am Queen, and I shall be merciful. If you are unsure of your answer, do not say anything. You may remain at the court and be rewarded."

Kaif bowed again. "I shall speak, Your Majesty."

Turandot sighed. "Speak!"

"The World was created by a male deity, whose name cannot be uttered. All-Mother usurped his power and treacherously killed him, scattering his body everywhere. The particles of his body alone possess creative power. They enter women's bellies and turn into babies, for women themselves are empty. These particles are everywhere: in water, air, and soil. But mostly they concentrate in men since men are made in the god's image. They are in men's semen, in men's brains, and in men's blood.

"However, having forgotten their god's name, men have become weak. Their semen is no more potent than water and their brains bleed power into dust. The last stronghold of the dead god's power is their blood. Your Majesty, a woman who cannot conceive by water, soil, semen or dream must have a man's blood. Only thus can she become fruitful."

At this terrible declaration Turandot saw her female courtiers grow red with indignation or pale with fear, while the males looked both sickened and bewildered. All-Mother's chief priestess started from her seat and a group of scholars traded furious whispers. But what shocked Turandot most was a sad smile on the face of the Grand Vizier.

"Very well," she said, struggling to preserve her composure, "we shall test your answer as we have tested the previous ones. You," she turned to her Master of Justice, "choose a convicted criminal, execute him, collect his blood, and bring it to us."

"No!" exclaimed Kaif.

It was an accurate measure of Turandot's diminished stature that her guards did not kill Kaif on the spot and let him continue.

"Your Majesty," he said, "order my execution without a test if it be Your will. But if it is Your pleasure to test my answer, know that a man's blood taken by force is as impotent as sewer water. The power of creation which is contained in male blood can only work upon a woman if it is freely given."

Confused and angry, Turandot leaned back, glancing in the direction of the Grand Vizier who instantly addressed Kaif.

"This is very clever, young man," he said sarcastically. "You have secured yourself against any testing, for where is a man foolish enough to give his blood for a child who is not his sister's?"

"I am willing to do it," said Kaif, "for Her Majesty's sake!"

She dismissed her servants and walked alone through the empty splendor of the Inner Apartments. Passing by a side door, she heard a creak and a rustle. She looked inside. One of her maids was squatting in the middle of the room, silken skirts hitched up to her waist. Something dark plopped onto the floor. The girl straightened, modestly tugged down her skirts and saw Turandot.

"Oh! Your Majesty!"

Turandot beckoned her to show the baby. It was a puppy with slick wet fur and disproportionately large head and paws, which it was restlessly moving as if trying to swim in the air.

"When did you first feel it growing?" she asked.

"Only a week ago. So, when I felt it coming out today, I knew it could not be human. Else I would have asked my friends to sit with me."

Turandot nodded. It generally took no less than six weeks of gestation to give birth to a human baby.

"Very well," said Turandot. "Bring her tomorrow to the Kennel Master. She will run with my hounds and wear a golden collar with your name on it."

The girl fell to her knees:

"Oh, thank You, Your Majesty!"

The small kindness rendered to the servant unexpectedly lightened Turandot's mood. She felt virtuous and deserving of fate's reciprocal kindness. But her gloom returned the moment she began to consider the actual mechanism of Kaif's proposition. Should she drink his blood? Bathe in it? Presuming she was capable of such a demeaning action, would not the people turn away from her in disgust? And what of the man himself, what of this inexplicable devotion that prompted him to offer his life for her? Turandot had long ago given up the illusion that behind obsequious smiles of the courtiers there was any shred of genuine feeling for her. Her younger sister, next in line for being Queen, would not be sorry to see her go. She could hardly remember the faces of her lovers. Perhaps only this maidservant and a couple of others whom Turandot treated with similar indulgence would shed a tear. But she had never seen Kaif until this day and had done nothing to earn his affection.

But if he was right, what difference did it make? Her first duty was to the Queendom. One man's life was a small price to pay for an end to the drought and the beginning of a glorious reign.

A servant approached her and told her the Grand Vizier was begging an audience. She was not surprised. She was shocked, though, at the old man's visible agitation.

"Your Majesty," he said, "send this madman away, into the custody of his family. If you desire to make him pay for his insulting words, this can be arranged later."

*How much 'later' do I have?* Turandot wanted to ask but instead she said, "His answer, though unusual, does not seem to me any madder than those of his predecessors."

The Vizier stared at her and she almost cringed under his hawk-like eyes. There was reproach in them and something else, which made her even more uncomfortable.

"Your Majesty," he said slowly, "do you remember the Southern legend I told you about the origin of the World? Well, there was one additional detail. The teller said that the reason we are imprisoned in the labyrinth of dreams is the terrible war that humanity had waged against itself, and that the cause for the war was that men resented women and that women were afraid of men. So, in that lost age, men found ways to enchant women so they would bring forth only sons; and women, rebelling, refused to bear children altogether, for then humanity was like all the other animals and bred true. And because the World was poisoned by their mutual hatred and by the spells they hurled against each other, it leached into nothingness, disintegrated, and our ancestors found refuge in the world of leftover dreams, which they could shape to their desire, though they have eventually lost this power. And their desire was that the sexes be forever at peace, and for that reason they made procreation simple and chancy, and as independent of human will as the movements of clouds. The Empire of the West tried to reverse the spell but broke the walls of the dream-labyrinth instead and found itself in the wasteland of dust and ashes. Now, would Your Majesty follow their example and doom the Queendom?"

Turandot winced as if struck and drew herself to her full height, a head taller than the frail old man.

"You forget yourself, Vizier!" She cried. "I'm Queen and I'll do what must be done! I will not be deterred by empty tales and metaphysical riddles!"

She swept out of the room in the rustle of her silks, her face burning with indignation.

She found herself at the black-lacquered door of the guest quarters. Nodding to the bored guards, she walked in.

Kaif was sleeping on the pallet. She stood looking down at him, in the grip of an emotional turmoil whose nature she did not want to understand. He opened his eyes and stared at her without moving a muscle, as perfectly poised as a snake. She was the Queen, and she could order the guards to kill him on the spot and yet she knew she had no power over him. Death was no threat to a man who wanted to die.

She saw that he had a locket around his neck. It had been hidden by his court clothes but now dangled freely over his smooth chest. She pulled it up until the chain snapped and opened it.

Inside was her own picture, one of the many distributed through the Queendom on her ascension to the Peacock Throne. Painted by a courtly flatterer, it was, nevertheless, accurate enough because her beauty needed no tricks of his art.

The eyes of the portrait were gouged with knife strokes.

She dropped the locket, turned to the door.

Still flat on his back, Kaif said, "If you order me killed now, my blood will make you fertile anyway. It is enough for a man to declare his willingness to die for the magic of his blood to start working his will on the woman of his choice."

"What is your will, then?" she asked.

"I want a son," he said. "My son will break the unnatural spell of female dominance and will make procreation as lawful as it must be. My god desires it, and so it will be done."

Next morning Turandot took her time being dressed. First, she was strapped into a whalebone corset padded with white silk. Over it her handmaidens put a bodice and trousers of emerald green, embroidered with golden flowers, and over them a sheer gown, so delicate it fluttered with her every breath. Her long black hair was braided and piled on top of her head with chrysalides, topazes and aquamarines cunningly inserted among the strands. Her face was dusted with pearl powder, her eyes encircled with kohl. No one could see her despair under this glittering armor.

She was borne into the Great Hall that was packed with courtiers in multicolored silks and peacock jewelry. But the gold and precious stones were dulled by their owners' anxiety; the bright fabrics were slowly darkening by sweat, and the faces beneath the layers of paint were pale and drawn. Outside, the sky was the color of a bruised skin.

On the dais in front of her throne Kaif waited, dressed in white. There was a long steel knife with a golden handle lying beside him and a bronze kitchen vessel.

She spoke, asking him to recant, promising royal riches to the men's Lodges and royal patronage to his family. His words were oily-smooth and meaningless. She realized, with a shudder of disgust, that he valued his faith more than his life.

He picked up the knife.

There was a commotion at the door.

A man dressed in the vermilion-and-black council robes made his way through the crowd and knelt before the throne.

"Your Majesty," said the Grand Vizier, "I have served Your foremothers for my entire life. I have given my strength, my courage, and my wisdom to the land. It is only fitting that now, when I have nothing more to give, I shall be privileged to offer my blood."

A small dagger hidden in his wide sleeve flashed in the dusty light and a jet of blood splattered Turandot, clinging to her robe in a scatter of scarlet beads. Kaif's howl of protest was lost in the multitude of screaming voices. But then the voices fell silent, awed by another sound, so long unheard that it was almost forgotten.

Beyond the dusty window, in the bruised sky, clouds were swiftly massing. Another roll of thunder shook them, and fat drops of water pattered on the thirsty soil.

Turandot was reclining on the couch, surrounded by the council. Her distended belly dragged her down like a prisoner's ball-and-chain.

The fat Mistress of the women's Lodges was speaking.

"By his sacrifice Ar-liran has prevented a greater mischief, but we are still left with a problem. The men liked Kaif from the beginning and now that his answer has been proven, they will admire him as a prophet. By executing him, Your Majesty, we shall make him a martyr. And then there will be no stopping his heresy."

Ar-liran, recalled Turandot, was the Vizier's name, but he seldom used it. It was embarrassingly common, country-sweet. His mother must have been a poor Southern girl who had doted upon her human child.

"It used to be you killed a man and there was an end of it," muttered the Master of the Guards, but he did not disagree with the Mistress's analysis.

"He could be imprisoned," suggested the Tea Master.

"If we want the rabble storming the palace gates, certainly," the Mistress said scornfully.

The baby gave another kick and Turandot bit her lip to stifle a groan. She lifted her hand, enforcing silence.

"Where is the Master of the men's Lodges?" she asked.

Embarrassed glances were exchanged and finally the Mistress of the women's Lodges spoke:

"He is with Kaif," she said, her unctuous voice oozing like over ripe honey. "He has declared him to be a mouthpiece of the Nameless God and ordered his hierophants to follow Kaif's teaching. Fortunately, many men are still loyal but there is a great deal of dissent in the men's Lodges."

Turandot closed her eyes; it was too hard to keep them open. If the Vizier was here, she thought dreamily, he would deal with this. And then she remembered he had dealt with this, and this is why he was not present at the council and never would be.

But she was here. She was still Queen.

She thought of what the Vizier had said about the labyrinth woven of human dreams and desires. One could try to escape the labyrinth and end up in the wilderness of ashes. Or one could try to redraw it.

Engaged in this silent internal battle, she missed what the Mistress of women's Lodges was saying. Apparently, it was something about declaring the unborn child to be the heir to the Peacock Throne.

"But what if it is a male? A male child cannot be the heir!" objected the Tea Master and was met with scornful silence. Everybody realized that from now on only a male child could be the heir.

"It will be a son!" the Mistress of Lodges said confidently. "And if Your Majesty wants to preserve Your position in the new court,"—there was no mistaking the venom in her voice—"I would advise taking Kaif as Your consort as soon as possible."

The baby kicked viciously, and Turandot shuddered. Not for the first time, she longed hopelessly for the easy, short pregnancy of every woman in the Queendom, for the colorful lottery of life that would reward her with a playful animal, or a lush vegetable, or a loving baby. She remembered the jokes and the camaraderie when a stout country woman birthed a pumpkin in the middle of a fair; the celebrations when a stoat or a bobcat born of a human mother was released into the wild; the feasts when a baby was presented to his sisters and brothers, aunts and uncles, to all relatives: vegetable, animal, and human.

And she knew it was ending. The World was changing because she had made it change.

"Make it so," she said.

There were ceremonies for taking a consort which had been done in old times. But Kaif rejected them, claiming they were an abomination in the Nameless God's eyes. He had conferred for hours with dark-veiled men who inundated the palace grounds, coming from small provincial Lodges where cultish unrest had been brewing for a long time. If anything could diminish Turandot's hatred for him it would be her conviction that he was the patsy of some vast conspiracy that would get rid of him when his part was done.

But most of the time she was too sick to do anything but focus on the growing fruit in her womb, trying to master the process that generations of women allowed to unfold on its own. She lay, heavy and swollen, on the pile of embroidered pillows, biting her fingers until they bled or staring at the endless rain beating on the panes.

The ceremony was done, at her insistence, at night and with a small number of attendants. So much power she still retained, even though she could feel it hammered into the soaked soil of her dissipating Queendom. The dark-veiled men chanted something unintelligible.

The women were pale and silent, except for the Lodge Mistress who sidled close to Kaif and congratulated him in her obsequious way. The baby kicked.

The pregnancy stretched on infinitely: two months, three, four.... By now her future son had become her only hold onto the Queendom. Kaif and his disciples, the worshippers of the Nameless God, reigned supreme in the men's Lodges and their veiled battalions marched through the streets every day, chanting, beating themselves with flails to atone for the god's murder, and harassing every passer-by who refused to join the procession.

Turandot woke up in the middle of the night. Her body was clammy and suddenly there was a sickening pain inside her as if somebody grabbed a handful of her innards and twisted them mercilessly.

Turandot cried for her maids. They did not come immediately because they had to report to the veiled men that Kaif had stationed outside the bedroom door. But come they did and were horrified by the unknown affliction that battered their ill-starred sovereign, squeezing blood out of her body with each new spasm. They sent for the Court Physician, and he came accompanied by the Lodge Mistress.

The Physician was baffled.

"It is the birth," Turandot gasped and saw the horror in his face.

She slowly re-emerged into consciousness. Her body felt battered beyond recovery. Somewhere far away a baby was crying: a thin, reedy sound.

The Mistress's face swam into her field of vision. The woman's expression was no longer insolent.

"Show me the baby!" Turandot said and spent a long time looking at the tiny, red, wrinkled creature. She had won the battle, but the victory tasted hollow. She thought of the labyrinth of dreams buckling and straining under the weight of human desire. Perhaps one day she would find the exit.

And perhaps the exit was already opened.

Kaif walked in with his usual serpentine smoothness, his face half-masked by his veil. But instead of hatred she felt pity for him: the man who had blundered into the future.

He stared at the baby, disbelieving his eyes.

"You have achieved your desire," Turandot said. "From now on, males will determine the nature of offspring. From now on, every child born of a man will be a woman."

# RATTLESNAKE

*I* smash mirrors everywhere. In my wake, shards of reflected sunlight litter ruined streets. Until they are splattered with red.

Mothers hide their baby boys from me, and when I root them out from cellars, attics or closets; they wail, squeezing the creature's rosy fingers. "He's just a little thing!" they cry. "How could he have offended you?" But I point to the snake between his thighs. It is tiny now when he is cuddled at his mother's breast. It will grow into a dragon that will hunt down and despoil women like his mother. Women like the one I used to be.

I don't know what I look like now, but my tail grows every time another man lies broken at my feet. It rustles and rattles as I drag it around piles of brick and stone. It should be hard for me. It is as long as a city block, composed of scaly segments that keep adding up like beads on a necklace. But I can barely feel it. My strength grows too, to keep up with my revenge.

Some women have taken to following me in worship: singing songs, beating drums, even trying to flush out men from their hiding places. It is satisfying, but not as satisfying as finding him will be.

Wild dogs roam the streets and run away when they hear my rattle. A salty wind blows from the sea. A restless sparkle of waves throws gold and silver my way.

It happened on the beach. I walked along the lacy fringe of the surf, my feet caressed by the water. The sun was setting. I was happy. I remember that. I don't remember what I was happy about. There are many things that have disappeared from my memory.

No, not disappeared. They have been stolen. By him.

He came from behind me. It was so sudden that when I found myself half-submerged in the chilly water, in the dark, my first thought was that the world had blinked somehow, and time lurched forward. But the pain told me otherwise. And though the sea had washed away most of the blood, enough remained to tell me I was no longer fit for the Temple. I was looking forward to my initiation into the vestal sisterhood. Now ... what was I? Worthless. Polluted. Discarded.

This was what I thought at the moment. Now I see how mistaken I was. He wanted to destroy me, but he has only made me stronger. He tried to lower me to the level of beasts; now I am above him, above all humanity.

The women behind me are chanting and shaking tambourines. But through the noise the dry clatter of my tail is still audible. It is flowing after me like a river of silver scales, sweeping aside the rubbish littering the street: bricks, broken glass, marble fragments.

Corpses.

When I glance down, I see a pair of legs, dark and sinewy like olive trunks, supporting the girth of my new body. And when I touch my forehead, something cold and oily slithers across my fingers.

I was beautiful. Now I am divine.

I stop before a small dwelling on a side street. It is still whole, one of the few. When I am done, nothing will be left of the city. The city that used to be mine but now is the hiding-hole of my rapist.

The familiar acrid smell assaults my nostrils, and my rattle is deafening. The women behind me fall silent. My hair—or whatever it is that crowns my head now—stands up in rage.

I did not see his face. But this stench—like burning dung, like carrion rotting under the midday sun—is how I will recognize him. He may have transformed himself into a mewling babe or an old man, but the stench of his violation will never go away until I find him. It is

90

now as horribly intimate as my own.

My tail flails and walls tremble and collapse in a cloud of dust. Two figures crawl out of the ruins. They stand up, holding hands.

The girl is irrelevant; I barely glance at her, just to ascertain her sex. But the male ...

My neck flushes with angry blood and something expands around my face like an unfolding flower. My hair rises with a hissing sound. My rattle beats summons to the execution.

He staggers toward me. He may be twelve or so.

He is male.

The girl steps forward.

"Medusa," she addresses me, and it takes me a moment to remember that is used to be my name. "My brother is innocent. He is my twin and I know his heart as I know my own. He would never assault a woman."

Her words wash over me. The hissing and the rattling drown them in irrelevance.

There is a snake between his thighs. He is a man. He is a rapist.

The swollen tension in my neck expands; my head is dragged up; my tail coils and lashes out.

The boy cries out—just a single strangled cry—and falls on his face. A bloody halo expands around his head that has hit the cobbles with a wet sound. A jerk on my tail as another segment is added to the rattle.

The girl drops onto her knees by her brother's body.

Is it him?

I look around at the field of rubble that the city has become. The sea flashes and dances beyond the embankment.

There must be more men left. Somewhere. The stench is still there; I can smell it, thick and nauseating.

I will find him.

I make to move forward but the girl jumps to her feet and bars my way.

"Great goddess of vengeance," she says, "Medusa the Gorgon who rights the wrongs of women. Let me show you my appreciation of your great work by washing the dust of our unworthy city off your feet."

I pause, uncertain how to react. This was how the vestals used to honor the immortals. Poseidon who I worshipped in those days—I used to bring clean sea water to pour over his statue in the Temple. But this girl … is it right that she should be *my* vestal?

And while I am hesitating, the girl lifts a bronze vessel filled with water. But instead of washing my feet with it, she brings it up to my face. And in the mirror of its calmness, I see myself.

I see the cobra-like cowl around my neck, swelling in rage, its fungal flesh flushed with venom. I see the armor of bony plates running down my breast and merging with the pewter scales of my tail. I see a tangle of oily verminous bodies whipping around my head.

And I see my own face.

It is him.

My rapist. The god whom I worshipped. Poseidon who took a mortal girl with no more thought than plucking a flower and left her, broken and defiled, on the beach. Poseidon who is forever beyond the reach of human revenge. Poseidon who is not a man.

Immortals do not care for our pain. They have no justice and no mercy. They do what they want.

She called me "goddess," that girl whose brother I just killed in retribution for a crime he has not committed. Yes, indeed, I am a goddess now. A rattlesnake of heaven. A creature who destroys because she can.

Looking into my own empty eyes, breathing in the burning smell of my own transformed flesh, I feel my hatred harden into the shell around my body, squeezing air out of my lungs. The worms on my head stiffen and tumble down in a shower of shards. The segments of my tail separate and fall like a line of dominoes. A stone cracks somewhere and I realize it is my breastbone.

*Vengeance is mine,* I think as I am turning to stone.

# DANCER FROM THE DANCE

*A* grey winter day, snowflakes descending on the whitish expanse of the wasteland like pieces of dandruff. A woman walking alone.

When she finally saw a glimmer of light, her rag-wrapped feet were so frozen she could hardly feel them. This would not do, would not do at all, because her feet were her most precious tools. Dedicated to her Art.

The city hunched in the snow like a beggar: dark jagged walls and the stink of smoke and filth. Martha waited until the midmorning when the gates were wide open, the guards ready for a break, and the stream of traders in full flood. Some places had laws against vagabonds, traveling musicians and fortune-tellers—all polite euphemisms for Artists. By such laws the sheep attempted to protect themselves against the sheepdogs, while the wolves—the mindless implacable gods of the Heavy Land—waited patiently at the door.

The bored guards did not even look at her as she went through the gateway that pierced the thick wall. She stopped to examine the old carvings of what appeared to be stylized arrowheads. At a second glance she realized those were lilac flower clusters. She knew that the name of the town, Sir-Annoir, meant the House of Lilac in the Old Speech: too pretty a name for this dispirited place.

She was looking for a cheap lodging when she spotted a tall building looming above the mean streets. It was a tower, its walls heavy with crumbling stonework, surrounded by a wilderness of skeletal shrubs and drifts of pus-yellow snow. The alley leading to the tower had a small, dilapidated guard house. Or rather, most people would consider it to be a guard house; but Martha knew better. The round-roofed brick structure was a shrine to the Arts.

She pushed the creaking door and entered. There were rotting fall leaves on the floor compacted into a frozen mass and the aisle was piled up with rubbish. The stained-glass windows were mostly broken but a surviving panel displayed the image of a flayed man writing on his own skin. And tucked into a corner she found a bronze figurine of a dancing woman, clothed with a greenish patina of age. Martha made a gesture of obeisance and silently promised to be back with proper offerings if ... no; *when* ... she Danced.

At the end Martha was unexpectedly lucky. She found a cheap inn of decaying wood and crumbling plaster. The proprietor, a wilted man with the dark splash of a birthmark on his cheek, looked her up and down and declared he needed a waitress. Before the night fell, she had learnt the circuitous routes among the scarred tables in the barroom and had gotten her meal of leftovers. And now she was safely ensconced in a little attic room above the stables. Nobody would bother her here. She had already dismissed her master, whose name was Burne, as only marginally more alive than the tables she had to scrub.

She looked out the window. The city was dark; people went early to sleep here. A new chapter was beginning in the story of her life which had only been a raw draft so far, a meaningless procession of hardships and humiliations, but leading to that one moment which she knew would redeem it all. The moment she would Dance. And as a confirmation of that pledge she repeated to herself every night, falling asleep in dingy hovels, or haystacks, or some anonymous man's sweaty arms, a rose flame suddenly shot up into the brittle air. It was burning on top of the tower she had seen earlier, and it was neither a bonfire nor a torch. It looked like an aurora borealis painted with the sugary colors of spring flowers. Her heart beating fast with this foretaste of the miraculous, Martha raised the sash and leaned forward into the biting cold. The flame grew brighter and changed color to mauve, pink and finally burgundy. It went out in a fountain of purple sparks.

She waited tables, washed and cleaned, helped Burne to cook the simple dishes their customers ate and to adulterate the cheap wine they drank. The curse of her secret life was the blessing of her everyday survival. Her big, strong, wide-shouldered body was not that of a Dancer, but it enabled her to perform twice the amount of manual labor an ordinary woman was capable of. At daytime she worked in the inn with her customary morose concentration and at night she practiced her Art.

Hidden under her bed in a silk-lined box were her mother's dainty shoes, too small for her own feet. Mother died young after a chaotic and misspent life. But she had Danced. So far, Martha had only danced.

The massacre happened at the beginning of spring, when the cherry trees lining the street were swathed in billows of white. After a blustery day the blossoms rained down and lay in fragrant heaps on the cobblestones. Martha was scrubbing the bar when she glanced out the window and froze in surprise. The heaps of blooms swirled and heaved, even though the tree boughs remained immobile. Masses of petals agglomerated into large solid lumps. And then the lumps began to evolve into unexpectedly familiar shapes. She blinked and realized what they were: body parts. Legs and arms, faintly pulsating hearts, horned uteri littered the street, all molded from white flowers. They crawled around, seeking each other and uniting into baroque combinations. A starfish of flailing arms groped its way along the dirty pavement, surrounded by lesser creatures: hands with a blinking eye stuck on the tip of the pinky; an

95

asthmatic, puffing lung; a leg butting a heart that tried to roll away; a nimble penis pursuing a floppy breast. It was a superior display of an Art that did not make Martha jealous because it was so different from her own.

A raggedy child was weaving among the white shapes. He fell, tripped by a leg adorned with a pair of floppy ears. A starfish of arms bore down heavily upon him, and other flower creatures piled on. A rosy tint spread through the heaving mass, deepening to splashes of red. Sated, the blossom creatures grew sluggish and dissolved back into piles of stained petals.

She heard a sniffing and turned around. Burne was looking over her shoulder. He refused to provide any information until he got drunk late in the evening.

"It is this damned sorcerer!" he announced. "Calls himself a flo— florist but he is just an evil magician, everybody knows that!"

"Flower Man?" Martha exclaimed. "Here?"

Floral magic was one of the rarest Arts, more esoteric than Sribing or Dancing. Martha had never met a practitioner.

"He's just a sorcerer!" Burne went on. "Killed his family too! I bet he boiled his parents' bones for his magic potions, for all they say it was black fever."

"So why do you suffer him here?" Martha asked. She expected a fellow Artist to have fallen a victim of the sheep long ago.

"Sir-Annoir. Some people still cleave to the old ways."

The House of Lilac. It explained his Art and the sheep's forbearance. His family must have ruled the town once. But not anymore: Martha knew that the town had an elected Mayor who lived in indecent splendor in the timbered Town Hall. So: the hall versus the tower; the pragmatic mayor versus the deposed prince; life versus Art. Martha, deep in thought, watched Burne collapse on the floor in drunken stupor.

His family had indeed ruled Sir-Annoir for a very long time, since the exodus from beyond the Heavy Land, or so it was said. Martha considered the exodus to be a myth, but she kept her unpopular opinion to herself. Most people fervently believed that there was a more capacious and freer world beyond the obsidian expanse that slowed time and warped space. She did not think so; the Heavy Land must stretch all the way into infinity, as boundless as people's stupidity. The world was a tiny circle of motion in the midst of stillness, kept alive and aflame by the Arts.

In any case, the sorcerer's family had been deposed some years ago when the current Mayor Roland Er-Ridan came to power on the wave of disgust with the old order's corruption. The sorcerer himself, or the Flower Man, as Martha secretly called him, was the last one left, his parents having died of the black fever and his siblings having mysteriously vanished. Served by a couple of decrepit retainers and his accursed minions, the Flower Man had kept largely to himself—until now.

One day a little girl, the daughter of one of the Mayor's sidekicks, was discovered dead in a bed of crocuses, yellow and purple flowers having grown through her eyeholes. After that the townspeople's patience gave out.

There was an unwonted crowd at the inn, ragged men, requiring a great deal of alcohol to keep their righteous anger boiling. There were confused shouts and a noise of pursuit. People in the barroom rushed to the door and Martha hurried after them, only to run smack into Burne who ordered her to stay indoors and "forget all this nonsense." She waited until Burne went into the kitchen and then slipped outside.

The darkness was luridly painted with torchlight and bonfires. Waves of humanity surged around and buffeted her. Doggedly pushing aside smelly bodies, she reached the Town Hall square.

The execution was almost over, the dark twitching mass feebly struggling among the scattering of stones. A tall, well-dressed man clove the crowd and walked to the body. In the smoky torchlight Martha could see his long face with an aquiline nose and dark smudges of shadow around the deep-seated eyes. Roland Er-Ridan, the town's Mayor. A hush fell, the mob breaking down into individuals who shamefacedly eyed their neighbors, now accomplices.

The Mayor looked down and fastidiously moved a stone with the tip of his suede boot.

"The sorcerer is dead," he declared. "The people's just anger has been assuaged. However, we are not savages to allow wanton desecration. The body will be left here, guarded, for the night. Tomorrow he will be burned without further abuse and the ashes scattered."

Martha knew that the Mayor's word was law. Roland, a canny politician, was both loved and feared. People started to drift away. She waited patiently until the square was empty and the two guards settled down by the fire. She walked over to the corpse, picking up a sputtering torch on the way.

"Hey!" shouted one of the guards.

"I only want to look," said Martha.

The second guard made a coarse joke, but she heard nothing. She just stood there, looking down at the white face. It was relatively undamaged, even though the limbs were crushed almost out of recognition and the chest caved in. A deep jagged fissure ran across the smooth forehead under the wave of dark curly hair. The expression was peaceful, long lashes resting on the exquisitely molded cheeks, deeply curved lips slightly parted. As she looked on, a bead of blood slid from the corner of the mouth. It rolled onto the filthy pavement but instead of dissolving into the mud, it became a hard glittering jewel.

Making sure the guards were not watching, Martha picked up the bloodstone and hurried back to the inn.

The cold spell was over; the air was like warm milk; and the raw dirt in the backyards was peppered with yellow and mauve stars. The gnarled pear tree near the inn exploded into a white cloud. Everything bloomed but the lilacs.

They were especially thick around the abandoned shrine to the Arts. There was one majestic bush, almost a tree. Every day Martha anxiously examined its smooth ashen bark, caressed the scratchy twigs, worried at the tight buds. Occasionally, she went down on her knees and peered at the tiny mount among the coiling roots. But nothing happened.

One evening, having scrubbed the last table and gotten rid of the last customer, she stepped outside to get some air. When she drew it in her lungs, the cloying sweetness was overpowering. All over the town, lilacs were in bloom.

The killings began the next night.

Because it was spring and every green thing that could put out flowers did so, the deaths were many and inventive. People were pierced through by the sword-shaped leaves of irises and suffocated by the sweetness of lilies. The bright blue carpet of forget-me-nots turned into a treacherous pool that drowned several kids. Snowdrops dripped milky poison on the treading feet of passers-by, who swelled until they burst. Lilies-of-the-valley rang their tiny bells, and listeners went deaf. Yellow crocuses brought yellow fever; purple crocuses brought palsy.

And then there were the lilacs.

Their branches whipped around and shed their fragrant loads. The heaps of blossoms frothed, heaved like the belly of a pregnant woman, and shaped themselves into caricatures of the human frame.

Rising from the tender ground, bright featureless figures stood upright, their smooth sexless bodies molded from interwoven florets. They glided through the frantically emptying streets and caught some stragglers: a child here, a dog there. The victims were enveloped in a sweet embrace that efficiently stifled their cries. And then a sack of skin and bones would be tossed aside, and the flower-creature would continue on its way, its color enhanced by blood: whiteness flushed with pink, mauve turned into purple, wine-red deepened into black.

The lilac creatures ruled the streets for several hours, while the hysterical townspeople cowered behind locked doors. Toward afternoon, they vacated the town center and migrated to the tower, circling it like sentinels. The tower itself bloomed like a giant obscene plant, wound around by sinewy vines with gross scarlet flowers.

Martha watched it all. And then she went to her room, fetched hot water from the kitchen and washed herself in a cracked tub. She stood naked in front of the dim yellowed mirror given to her by Burne. She knew well enough that her body, tall and big-boned, inherited from her unknown father, was unsuited to her Art. But by dint of endless harsh exercise, she had sheared away its fat. Now it was all taut muscles: hard thighs, bulging calves, small high breasts pulled up by the sinewy shoulders and forearms. It was beautiful, she thought, testament to her dedication. Her skin, normally sallow, was flushed, and her dark nipples sharp and hard.

She rubbed herself with musk oil from a bottle that had cost her a season's savings. And then she dressed in the clothes of her Art: a white linen blouse and a long tasseled skirt embroidered with secret charms and fringed with coins and glitter. The clothes were actually irrelevant: when an Artist Danced, his or her body flowed as freely as water, washing away and reshaping the obdurate thing that people called reality. But a bit of good luck would not hurt. So, while wearing her own large slippers, Martha put her mother's dainty pair into a cloth bag.

Burne was in the barroom drinking. He jumped up when he saw her. "Where are you going?"

She just shrugged.

"Stop it, Martha! You'll be killed! Don't go out, please!"

He tried to stop her. She pushed him away with all her considerable strength. He crashed into a table and was still.

It was late afternoon now, the air crisp and luminous. The tower bristled with blossoms like a florist's shop gone wild. She boldly

100

walked through the ranks of the lilac sentinels who drew aside and let her pass. They were beginning to wilt and smelled like stagnant water.

She lifted a curtain of briar roses and entered the tower. And stopped. It did not look like anything she had expected.

The space inside was large, much larger than the circumference of the tower. It was dank and dark. There were no flowers here. Veils of cold mist drifted in the air. The only source of light was a diffuse pale glow emanating from deep within the space. The rocky floor seemed to pull at her feet.

The veils of mist drew apart and she saw an armchair. A man was sitting in the armchair, his head bowed. Indistinct shapes loomed behind him, veiled by the curtain of curdled luminosity.

He lifted his head when she approached. The hammering of her heart threatened to incapacitate her as she confronted her dream lover. She had only seen these finely molded features broken and bloody. But now he was glowing with life, his skin fresh and rose-tinted, his dark ringlets almost cracking with energy, his sharply outlined lips parted in an ambiguous smile. Only his eyes were different from what she had expected. They were glassy, with no irises or whites, mere lumps of darkness.

Martha reminded herself that she, too, was an Artist. She tried to meet his gaze and failed.

"I was expecting you." His smile grew wider. "I guess I should thank you. It was a lucky choice, lilac."

"It was not by chance." Her voice sounded hoarse, and she had to clear her throat. "The name of the town has power. I understand such things."

"Do you?"

"I am a Dancer." She straightened up as she said these words, so new on her tongue, so old in her mind.

"Oh yeah? A minor Art, this, but it has its uses. Isn't it difficult for you to practice? Dancers need to be lighter, don't they? Anyway, you did well, all things considering."

He suddenly got up and came very close to her and she could see the sheen of saliva on his white teeth. He smelled of damp stone overlaid with flowery sweetness. No breath touched her cheek; his chest did not rise and fall.

Afterward she rested at his feet, giddy, aching, and joyful.

"Why did you do it?" he asked distractedly, drawing blood-red flowers in the mist with his finger.

"Because you are an Artist," she answered without hesitation.

"That's it? Not my winning personality?"

"This is what I realized when I first heard about you: that we are two of a kind," she persisted. "Most people are dead inside, just sheep who obey laws because they have neither the brains nor the guts to think and act for themselves. But people like us are different. We live for our Art. Of course," she added hastily, noting the flicker of his lashes, "your power is so much greater than mine, but we are of the same kind."

He smiled a strange secretive smile, and said, "It helps to pass the time. And I have a lot of time now. Being dead has its advantages." She turned away, feeling obscurely disappointed, and her eyes alighted on the floor, which she could see clearly now. It was not made of stone as she had previously thought. It was smooth, glassy, obsidian-like stone. The armchair rested in the center of a black disk about forty feet in diameter.

"This is ..." she said. Her voice caught and she started again. "This is the Heavy Land rock!"

He nodded.

"What is it doing here? How ..."

The Heavy Land surrounded the world on all sides and slowly advanced, year by year, in a creeping, glacially slow tide. It used to be believed that the tide could be stopped by exercise of the Arts. But the sheep-people had rebelled against the Artists in their midst and outlawed their practices. Now the Heavy Land was invincible. Still, its advance obeyed precise rules, one of which was that its outcroppings did not just spontaneously pop up in the midst of civilization!

He shrugged. "Well, that's the price."

"What do you mean?"

"Of that Art you value so highly. Where do you think mine comes from?"

"Training, talent..."

"Bullshit, girl. Training only produces those like you. And talent does not matter either. All power of the Arts comes from the Heavy Land."

"No!"

"Yes! I ran into the Heavy Land when I was fifteen. I spent a day lying on the rock, in that livid light that flickers like a man's death rattle but never dies. A month passed in the world. When I came back, I had my Art and a tiny spot of black appeared on the flags in the basement. This is how it's grown since then. When I am done with this town, it will have covered all of it."

Seemingly bored with explanations, he turned away and whistled. Something scuttled through the mist, a creature like a starved dog covered with curly roses. It shed petals and drops of blood.

The Flower Man patted its head, eliciting a whine of pain, got up and walked away into the mist.

"Stay here," he threw over his shoulder.

Martha pressed her hand hard over the slick rock. It was slippery, bland, and indifferent. Fire would not burn on it; water would slide off it; earth would not bury it; air itself would grow stale and unmoving above it. The Heavy Land. The weight of mediocrity.

The spring blossomed into a season of terror. Martha's lover had a quirky sense of humor which she was trying hard to appreciate. He also had power: more power than any Artist she had ever met or heard about. Having risen from the dead like a flower pushing up from the debris of winter, he was impervious to fatigue, remorse, and assassination. He slept on a whim, and his nightmares immediately became flesh and stalked the people of Sir-Annoir. He ate when he felt like eating, occasionally sharing a lavish dinner with Martha, occasionally tossing her inedible leftovers. He made love often, never hurting her so badly that the pain would outweigh the pleasure. And he never worked to improve his Art.

His latest project was giving parties for the pillars of the community, whose number diminished after every such entertainment. Nobody could leave Sir-Annoir, since the town walls were now wreathed and garlanded with enormous orchids whose toothy maws would crunch up any would-be escapees. The House of Lilac was threatened with famine, but the proportionate reduction of the population warded off outright starvation. The new ruler graciously offered fresh meat to his subjects but only the truly desperate ones took him up on his offer. The origin of the meat was too obscure—or perhaps, all too clear.

The next party was to be the largest one. Everybody who was somebody in town was invited. The rest—the poverty-stricken, the aged, the infirm, and the few surviving babies—would have houseguests to entertain them. The sorcerer's new minions were made of soil: hulking figures that rose from dug-up gardens and backyards. He did not bother with aesthetics anymore.

Martha stood at the entrance to the Flower Man's tower, looking up into the yellow sky. There was now a perpetual pall of dirty light hanging over the town. It was unseasonably warm and muggy.

She heard whimpering and turned wearily. Her clothes creaked: a smooth black corset, a skirt of gold chains, black-work-embroidered sleeves, and very high heels. She hated them; they cramped her leg muscles and she had to add more stretches to her daily exercises.

The creature sidling toward her was the rose-skinned dog. The creature suffered excruciating pain every minute of its existence because of the flowers, relentlessly pushing out through its flayed flesh. It constantly howled and wailed in harmonious cadences, so it was a pleasure to listen to its cries of anguish. For some reason it had developed a fondness for Martha, who would sneak it bits of food.

She sighed and went back into the tower. The billowing mist smelled of stale water and attar. And the circle of the Heavy Land rock had spread until its glistening surface could easily accommodate a large crowd.

Martha stood at its edge, her lips compressed into a pale line. Then she turned to the rose dog.

"Music!" she commanded.

It howled to the tune of a folk song. Martha stepped onto the rock. Her high-heeled shoes made a clacking sound as the rock tried to suck them in. She swayed, fighting against the gravity. She heard a snort and stopped.

She turned around and faced the Flower Man. He had changed as well. His clothes, once simple black, were now a riot of clashing color: the purple of irises encroaching on the yellow of daffodils and overrun with the corals of witch briar. His dark curls were braided with dahlias and amaranth. Fat pink worms coiled among the flowers.

"You are persistent," he said. "Quite putting me to shame with your industry. But why work so hard? I can create a whole ballet troupe for you."

Martha looked at him with her pale eyes:

"I want to Dance for your guests tonight," she said.

The guests were seated in concentric circles on the Heavy Land rock circle, the inexorable pull of it chaining them to their despair. The well-off burghers and merchants, the Town Hall hangers-on, and of course, the deposed Mayor himself.

The host sat on a high throne carved with a crest of his family. Martha perched on the footrest of the throne, staring defiantly at the crowd, meeting their hatred and tossing it back to them. She had refused to go along with the flower theme of the party and was wearing a simple black shift under a gauzy white over-garment. Her feet bled slowly. She had squeezed them into her mother's dancing shoes and had had to trim her toes down to the first knuckle. The Heavy Land pull prevented the wounds from festering but did not stop the pain.

The Flower Man's face was covered with a mask of tiny rosebuds. She knew what was under it.

"My people," said the Flower Man (the mask he wore making his voice somewhat indistinct). "I hope you are enjoying my hospitality.

In the old times our city, Sir-Annoir, was justly proud of its reputation as a cradle of the Arts. Together we shall return the House of Lilac to its ancient glory. We have a long and variegated program for tonight. Perhaps first ..."

Martha tugged at his hand.

"You promised," she said.

The opaque eyes looked at her indifferently through the petal-rimmed eyeholes.

"Well, why not?"

He clicked his fingers and music started out of nowhere: a variation on the old folk tune "Black-Eyed Susan." Its words were an obscene ditty that tipsy revelers bellowed out in pubs and country fairs.

"Now our Dancing friend will present us with a little show. Some of you, no doubt, have previously enjoyed Martha's talents as a scullion at Burne's Inn which, unfortunately, closed for lack of customers. Applause!"

A feeble clapping died out as Martha walked to the center of the Heavy Land rock circle. Tight-lipped, she surveyed the angry faces of the audience and blanked them out. She let the music, the crude catchy tune, enter her body as she had been trained to do, as she had trained herself to do, not resisting the primitive beat but allowing it to transform her as the black-eyed Susan was dancing in the circle of leering admirers with callused hands and beer-stained clothes, Susan, black-eyed because of the fight with her boyfriend last night but strong and sturdy and walking proud, the red-haired Susan with freckles on her large pink breasts that would feed large babies, Susan of the wide hips, the capable hands, the straight legs that bestrode the earth of which she was the queen, the queen of beer and babies and harvest moons, of food on the table and fire in the hearth. Martha Danced.

And as she heard the collective gasp of the audience, a sharp lance of pain shot up her legs, and she felt the black circle close around her just a little, its sharp edges puckering, as the outpost of the Heavy Land reluctantly shrank under her Dancing feet. Her eyes wide open, she saw everything, but at a remove; struggling to overcome the pain and not to falter; she saw her lover rise, the flower mask askew, and a pig snout poking from under it. And then the music died, and another melody was born: a slow melancholy dance that dimmed the misty light into a mournful dusk. She knew the tune, "Sea of Glass," and she immediately shifted into moving with it, letting the glassy quiet sea at sunset wash through her, the burnt orange and smoky silver of the flaming water, the clear sky, the woman crying at the brink of her lover's watery grave, and then the barely visible triangle of the sail at the horizon and the woman running, running toward her miraculously saved lover, running on water. Martha Danced.

And another jolt of pain, worse than the first one, her feet bleeding freely, and welts standing up on the exposed flesh as the tattered remnants of the shift, torn by her flowing body, fell onto the ground. The black circle shrank again, and the energy released from the Heavy Land lashed at Martha's body.

Again, the music disintegrated into a welter of sounds, but added to it was her lover's scream. His mask had fallen off, and they all saw the piggish visage that his face had become. But now even the face itself was slipping off, leaving behind a bloody featureless slick.

The music sputtered and died, but another tune was born. The rose dog howled, and its plaintive cry shaped itself into a version of the sentimental ballad "The Hawk in the Sky," and Martha Danced the sharp-eyed hawk circling over the battlefield, looking out for survivors, seeing crawling figures detach themselves from heaps of corpses and stand up shakily, looking up into the sky to the scythe-winged bird that had come to lead them back home.

The arena she Danced in was now barely large enough to let her move freely. Every time she brushed against its edge another welt appeared on her mutable flesh that blossomed in tune with the power of the music. The black rock flowed with her blood. But she felt as if she were suspended in a net woven of the gazes of her audience, a golden net that kept her up and would not let her fall.

Her lover waved the stumps of his disintegrating arms. He was now a skeleton messily clothed with flowers and raw flesh, his loose guts coiling around his hips and sliding down to pool at his feet. With the last feeble gust of power, he smashed the rose dog. A moment of silence, and then scattered voices rose in the audience, a medley of false starts that shaped itself into an impromptu choir singing off-key "The Victory of Love": the favorite song of young girls, wet nurses, fish wives, school boys, and undertakers; the song that everybody knew because it was sung, hummed, whistled, fiddled, and piped everywhere, at weddings, christenings and wakes; the song whose artless words promised that love would save the world. And Martha possessed for the one and only time in her life with the full power of Art, obediently Danced her love.

When she was done, the black circle of the Heavy Land had shrunk into nothingness and her lover was dead.

Somebody came up behind her and put an arm around her waist, steadying her. She felt a velvet cloak cover her nakedness. Blinking away tears, she looked into the Mayor's face.

"Let us thank our savior," he said and the audience, whipped into paroxysms of enthusiasm, clapped, and cheered.

Roland grasped Martha's hand.

"They will make you their queen," he whispered into her ear. "But they are fickle and difficult to rule. I know how to do it. Marry me and they will be yours forever."

Martha's eyes were watering with strain, her legs just about to collapse, and in the blur of pain all she could see were the rows of people's adoring faces, the faces of her fans who loved her and should never find out how much she despised them.

"Yes," she said.

Martha and Roland married and lived happily ever after. Sir-Annoir prospered under their benevolent guardianship that slowly extended over several nearby towns. The trade was brisk, the poor died in acceptable numbers, winters were not too cold, and summers scorched in moderation. The black wave of the Heavy Land would not lap at the city walls for many generations to come.

Martha bore six children: four sons and two daughters, all tall, strong and sturdy, having inherited their mother's large frame.

When she died in the fullness of age, having outlived her husband, she was given a magnificent funeral. The grateful citizens erected an ornate memorial on her tomb that occupied a privileged site where the tower had once stood. Some old lilac bushes had to be uprooted to make room for it.

The night after the funeral Martha's youngest son put an old, badly corroded bronze statuette of a dancing woman on his mother's grave. And then he ran away. Later people claimed they had seen him heading toward the Border, the edge of the Heavy Land.

# IN THE LAVA FIELDS

*here was a couple who lived on an old farm all alone. Their sheep kept disappearing, and their son went looking for them in the lava fields and disappeared too.*

All Icelandic stories seem to start with an old farm. The island is littered with them. Most of them are abandoned, rusted sheet metal and sparse grass tufting the caved-in roof. A few have been renovated into tourist rentals. Iceland has unaccountably become one of the prime tourist destinations in the world. Why would you flock to this land of bare rock bones sticking through the denuded soil; of empty lava fields where your vision dissolves in the black void; of Reykjavik, a small town pretending to be a big city?

After ten days in Reykjavik, I still did not know the answer to this question. Even as I was lying on the narrow bed in my Airbnb, listening to the sound of feet trampling on the slushy pavement above my head, I was trying to figure out whether I was doing something brave and edgy or something incredibly stupid. A time out of time; being a stranger in a strange land in order to find myself. It had seemed such a great idea at the time I booked a flight from Denver International. Now I was not sure.

My room was located in the subbasement of an old house with a peeling façade and small mean windows. When I first saw it, I almost ran away. In Denver, this would be a "bad part of town," not

111

suitable for a young woman on her own unless she was after drugs or bad boys. But here, it turns out, this was a very desirable part of town, just a ten-minute walk from the posh shopping street of Laugavegur. My room was perfectly fine; my hosts were polite and unobtrusive; and while there are drugs in Iceland like everywhere else, the crime that we take for granted in the US is pure fantasy here, on a par with elves or trolls. The homicide rate is minuscule. And yet Nordic noir mysteries and true-crime volumes in both Icelandic and English overflow the shelves in local bookstores. People in Iceland enjoy reading about dead bodies in the freezer for the same reason we enjoy reading about dragons. I wished my own true-crime obsession were equally detached from reality; and yet I succumbed on my first visit to the imposing Penninn Eymundsson bookstore, getting a volume entitled *Into Thin Air: Unexplained Disappearances and Murders in the Icelandic Countryside*. It seemed to mix freely tales of abduction by elves and cases of drunken tourists and sailors falling into lava crevices. You would think that after the Event that had cleaved my life into two, I would switch to a more cheerful genre but on the contrary, even here, on this dark island at the edge of the world, my mind demanded its daily dose of vicarious tragedy and violence. In some strange way, it offered me a relief from my own.

I did all the usual touristy things: walked around Tjornin, a large pond in the downtown area; shopped in what they call here "puffin stores," tourist traps selling lava necklaces and stuffed toy whales; visited Hallgrimskirka, a stark cathedral that seems to be dedicated to an angrier god than Christ. I even went to the Saga Museum filled with unnervingly realistic figures enacting horrors from Iceland's past: Black Death sufferers dying on the straw in cold stables; some Viking heroine threatening to slice off her own breast to intimidate the enemy (apparently it worked, as the enemy ran away); and bearded priests trying to convert beetle-browed Odin-worshippers. I was startled to find out Iceland became Christian only in the eleventh century, the last in Europe. I imagined all the pagan deities and demons of the Nordic countries crossing the cold sea to find refuge in the lava fields and smoking volcanoes. The sparsely populated country seems to have more elves and trolls than humans.

I stopped at one display in the Saga Museum. Garish against the dark background, it depicted a cloaked woman stealing away from a hollow surrounded by jagged rocks. Her face was hidden by a cowl, but she seemed to be glancing over her shoulder. In the hollow, in the bluish spotlight, lay a baby, its swaddling clothes in artful disarray around its splayed arms and legs.

I stared at it for such a long time that the man standing next to me said something. I shook my head. "English, please!"

"Oh, sorry! I was just saying, not a good way to advertise Iceland to tourists."

"Well, it seems to work. I'm here."

He smiled. "I am Aki."

He pronounced it in a strange way with a strong emphasis on the first syllable. Otherwise, his English was flawless.

"I'm Linda."

"Is it your first time in Iceland?"

"Yes. I love it here. Very different, like being in a fairy tale."

He laughed again. He seemed a bit older than me. Good looking, with dark smiling eyes and dark hair. Contrary to my stereotypical expectations, Icelanders on the average were no blonder than anybody else. He was wearing a beautiful hand-knitted Icelandic sheep wool sweater which I learned was called *lopapeysa*. Despite the fact that it looked like perfect winter clothing, it did not seem out of place on this cloudy, twilit Icelandic day.

"We are the land of magic. *Huldufólk,* the Hidden People. Not to mention waterfalls and geothermal energy. Where are you from, Linda?"

"Denver, Colorado."

"I've been to the States—California, NJ. But not Colorado. What are you doing in Iceland?"

I hesitated. Was he hitting on me? I was not ready for a relationship; Craig and I had split after the Event, and his emotional obtuseness still hurt.

*What's that to you? He has been out of your life for sixteen years. Why do you care?*

*How can you even say this?*

No, I needed solitude now. I needed to recover the Linda I had been before the Event. Having a fling with an Icelander was not on my itinerary.

But there was something about Aki that I found reassuring: the way he looked straight into my eyes; the laughter lines on his ruddy face; even that sweater that seemed, somehow, to embody the essence of this safest of all countries.

"I just needed a break," I said. "Being in a place where nobody knows me."

He nodded.

"I understand. Funny, this is why we Icelanders love to travel. Here, everybody knows you and your family going back generations. It's a small country. You know, most people here don't even have family names: just a first name and a patronymic."

"I heard about it."

"Anyway, Linda, if you have nothing better to do …"

I tensed. It was coming: an invitation to drinks in some downtown dive that "nobody knows about." Or would he come straight to the point?

He did. Aki took out a card from his jeans pocket and handed it to me.

"I am a tour guide," he said. "I organize small minibus tours into the countryside. Not your usual routes: the Golden Circle and the Blue Lagoon. No, I can show you places most tourists never see. The lava fields where dark elves live in caves. *Rangárþing eystra* where pre-Viking woodlands still survive with rare day trolls occasionally seen. Fjords where we can perhaps meet the Shore Laddie or *Matroll,* the Sea Troll. These," he pointed to the dramatic displays, "are like Hallmark. You need to see real Iceland."

I glanced at the business card. It said, in a nice script in English and German: "*Aki, your personal guide to Iceland. Discover the country of sagas and legends.*" There was also a website and a phone number.

I did not know whether to laugh at my own presumption or to feel disappointed. *Not every guy you meet abroad wants to get into your pants.* He was just a hustler.

On the other hand …

I planned to get out of Reykjavik at some point but did not feel up to boarding a giant bus with a raucous crowd of American retirees. Renting a car and just aimlessly driving around also felt stupid.

"I'll think about it," I said, pocketing the card.

"Sure. Give me a call any time."

He was about to leave when I pointed at the display with the woman and the baby.

"What is it about?"

Aki's face lit up, and that was when I decided to join his tour. His enthusiasm for Icelandic folklore was not fake.

"It's about *Útburðir.*"

"Ut…?"

"Sorry. This means the ghost of an abandoned child. In olden times, unwanted children were sometimes left in the lava fields to die of exposure. The ghost of such a baby becomes an *Útburður*—a horrible creature that looks like a disheveled raven with a human face. It crawls across the lava fields propelling itself on one arm and one knee. They howl at night and grab incautious passers-by. There is a legend of a woman who left her newborn to die. Later she wanted to go dancing but had no clothes. The *Útburður* visited her at night and offered its bloody swaddling-clothes for her to wear. She lost her mind."

I swallowed.

"It's pretty horrific," I said.

"I know. But other Icelandic ghosts and monsters are more picturesque. Look here."

He pointed to another display. A fissure opened in a craggy rock and peering from it was a nice-looking lad in an old-fashioned belted tunic with a silver buckle. He was beckoning to a young couple who stared at him with amazement. The couple were wearing modern clothes.

"He is one of the *Huldufólk,* the Hidden People," Aki explained. "They invite humans to stay with them in their underground country inside the lava rocks where they have farms and churches, just as we do. Sometimes they are reputed to kidnap strangers, but others say you only come if you want to, and you are free to leave."

"Are those Hidden People the same as trolls?" I asked.

"There are different kinds. These are often called dark elves. It's more respectable."

The elf-lad was smirking at the couple, and I decided that if I got such an invite, I would politely refuse. But Aki was trying to soften the stark horror of the *Útburður* tale, and I appreciated his effort, even though he could not know how close to the bone he had cut.

"Hope to see you again, Linda," he said before leaving the museum.

The minibus was small but very comfortable, with reclining seats and a drop screen behind the driver. It had the name of Aki's company in big letters on the side.

I hoped I would not be alone on the trip, even though when I made the call, Aki assured me that it would take place regardless of how many had joined. As much as I hated enormous tourist buses, I knew I would feel awkward being one-on-one with the guide. It would feel too much like a date.

To my relief, there were four more people waiting at the designated spot at Reykjavik's Bus Terminal. I strode toward them, pretending to be more confident than I felt. I realized that after two weeks talking to nobody but retail clerks and waiters, my people skills were a bit rusty.

Three women and a man. Even before introductions were made, I knew one couple were Americans. There is something about us that sets us apart from the rest of the world—and I do not mean it as a compliment.

I was right. The couple were Marsha and Bob Kane from Iowa. In their fifties, early retirees, their extra pounds and multiple layers of fleeces giving them the appearance of Mr. and Mrs. Michelin Man. They seemed to be genuinely happy to see a fellow American, which made me feel contrite about my uncharitable thoughts.

The two other women were more interesting. Sofia Valenti was an Italian from Como. She had that timeless elegance that many European women possess: striking without being beautiful. Sharp features, dark heavy brows, grey eyes, a slim lithe body like a ferret.

Gemma Waters was British. I had heard the expression "English rose" but had no particular image to connect it to until I saw Gemma. Her complexion had a peachy tint that a cosmetics company would pay to patent. Her age was hard to guess but I decided she was a bit older than me, maybe early forties. She volunteered that she worked for a pharmaceutical company, and it was her first time in Iceland, checking off an item on her bucket list. To confound my stereotypical expectations, she turned out to be single, while fierce-looking Sofia had a husband and two kids who wanted to take a day off sightseeing.

Aki was standing by the minibus, greeting each new arrival with a smile and handshake, and keeping up a stream of easy chatter, then instantly managed to cement all six of us into a group instead of being just an awkward collection of strangers. I envied this ability. After the Event, I had shut up, talking to Craig only when it was necessary. Sometimes, we would go for days without exchanging more than a couple of words. I could not really blame him for walking out.

I sat by the window, and Gemma asked whether she could sit beside me. She took off her puffer jacket and placed a bulging backpack by the seat. She was well provisioned: the pack held several bottles of water, a couple of containers of *skyr*, Icelandic yogurt, and a paperback. She noticed me looking at it and flashed a disarming smile.

"I always read on the Tube," she said, "so I thought, if the ride is too long, and we run out of tourist destinations …"

"Of course," I said. "I like to read myself. But I was looking at the book because I have the same one. I just bought it in that big bookstore on Laugavegur."

"The same. I love true crime. Is it popular in the US?"

117

"Very much so."

The book's jacket flashed its fake polar landscape at me: white on blue. *Into Thin Air: Unexplained Disappearances and Murders in the Icelandic Countryside.* I already knew that the real Icelandic countryside was black.

The back of the bus was piled with orange overalls and helmets. Aki winked at me. "A special treat," he said.

Was he singling me out? I told myself not to be an idiot. He just had the knack of making you feel special, which was surely a marketable skill in his profession.

We drove through the outskirts of Reykjavik, with Bob and Marsha taking pictures of random apartment buildings clad in corrugated iron, with blue and red sloping roofs. It was a typical Icelandic summer day with a dirty grey sky, the sun a white ghost rolling low above the horizon, and the temperature in the fifties. It would never get dark so close to the summer solstice. The city would be enveloped in the eerie twilight around the clock. It suited my mood: time out of time.

Aki kept up a stream of easy chatter, regaling us with random bits of Icelandic lore, from the fact that for a long time dog ownership was outlawed in the country due to fear of parasites (this elicited an outraged squeal from Marsha) to stories of the Cod War with Britain. I zoned out and was brought back to earth when Gemma offered me a container of *skyr*.

"It's like a different planet, isn't it?" she whispered conspiratorially.

"I know," I whispered back. "That's why I like it here."

"I wish ..."

"What?"

"I wish I did not have to land back on Planet Earth."

She and I were together in the sisterhood of women running away from themselves. I did not know what Gemma's trigger had been, but it did not matter. I gave her a conspiratorial smile and took the *skyr*, its acid tartness dissolving on my tongue like the essence of Iceland.

We suddenly stopped and I looked around.

Our minibus pulled in the lay-by of a narrow road. There were no trees around, of course; the Vikings had cut them all down, and only in very few areas you have thin strands of trembling birch and arctic willow. We were stuck in the middle of the corrugated black field like a tick on the back of a hippo, surrounded by folds and wrinkles of the island's bare skin. Black lava was weathered into scree and fissured by long gashes like unhealed scars. Low rugged hills with jagged crests stuck into the colorless sky. The black was splotched by the poisonous green of moss and lichen. This intensified the lava field's resemblance to an animal hide infested by parasites and slowly rotting.

"Come on, guys!" Aki jumped out. "I promised you real Iceland. Let me show you something few tourists ever see."

Bob and Marsha clambered down and looked around in bewilderment. Sofia's stony face bore an expression of disdain, as if she could not understand why this black emptiness was even considered a "landscape."

The sluggish air was cold and smelled of snow and gunpowder. The lava pebbles shifted under the soles of my hiking boots as if the field was trying to trip me. Aki pointed to the horizon where heavy clouds dragged their pregnant bellies over the land.

"See this?" he asked.

There was a row of razorback silhouettes against the dour sky. Animals? No, of course not. There are no large animals in Iceland. It was the land itself contorting itself into shapes of life as if trying to fool humans into forgetting its hostility to them.

"You have all heard about trolls and elves," Aki went on in his professionally melodious voice. "You must have seen *The Lord of the Rings* and movies like this. But what you may not know is that there are different kinds of elves in Iceland. There are dwarf elves, *Nissi*. There are light elves, *Ljosalfur*. And there are dark elves, *Dokkalfur*."

"Our grandson likes those video games with elves," Bob ventured. "What is it called, Marsha?"

Marsha shrugged.

"Elven Quest," Gemma said softly. I looked at her in surprise: she did not strike me as a gamer.

119

"Exactly," Aki nodded. "Magic swords and glowing armor. But Icelandic elves are much less friendly. Especially the dark elves who live in caves. They are second cousins to trolls but while trolls are big and stupid, dark elves are small and cunning. They are only seen by humans on special days like Christmas Eve when even rocks soften and open up to receive God's blessing. Then you may peek into the caverns where dark elves have their farms and churches, just like men do. But beware: dark elves can lure you in, and you will never see the light of day, enslaved in their underground farms and forced to labor to tend their flocks of ghoul cats and worm-dogs. The only way to escape is to fend them off until daylight; then they turn to stone. These rocks you see had not been there until twenty years ago. That was when a group of five teenagers went out to get drunk in the lava fields on Christmas eve. Only one came back and told the story. His companions were abducted by dark elves, but he ran away across the fields, cutting his feet so badly his boots were soaked in blood. But he managed to lead the elves on a chase until dawn when they all turned to rocks."

"And the police believed him?" Bob scoffed.

Aki smiled again. His sunny demeanor was jarring against this otherworldly terrain.

"They had no reason to disbelieve," he said. "Come on, let me show you what lies under the surface of the lava fields. I promise; it's an experience you won't forget."

"I'm ready," Sofia said. If voices had colors, hers would be deep purple, almost black.

Aki started pulling out orange suits and round helmets from the back of the minibus.

"We are going to explore a lava tube," he explained.

Bob and Marsha looked less than happy but apparently decided to get their money's worth and suited up. Sofia slipped into hers as elegantly as if it was a party dress. Gemma and I were the last ones to get ready because the idea of squeezing through a narrow tube like a baby being born did not appeal to me; Gemma because she was typing something into her phone. Aki cleared his throat.

"Are you ladies claustrophobic?" he asked. "You may stay outside, of course; but it's totally safe, approved by the Icelandic Tourist Board."

Gemma apologized, explaining that she had gotten a sudden text from home she needed to reply to, and promptly zipped into an orange suit over her tight-fitting lambswool sweater. I decided not to be the odd one out. I did not want to sit all alone in the midst of this black wasteland while the others were exploring. For some reason, I was reassured by the fact that the suit was relatively thin: more like a workman's overalls than an astronaut's hard-shell suit.

There was a pebbled path weaving among the petrified lava billows. As we walked, I noticed that the poisonous-green moss was getting lusher, covering the hard bones of the land with its meaty layers.

Gemma caught up with me.

"I found out something," she whispered. But then Aki stopped in front of an opening among rocks, and we all crowded around him.

I expected a cave, but this was just a yawning maw fringed with broken stone teeth. There was a little fence around it with some signs in Icelandic.

"We can't go in!" Bob objected. "It's too narrow!"

It was not, actually; even Bob and Marsha could easily slide in. But the sight of this raw wound in the lava was somehow too far removed from the polish of tourist sights to be welcoming. The band of bare rock around it was more weathered than the rest of the field and in the clotting twilight its color was closer to maroon than to black, as if the wound was bleeding out.

Aki was getting ready to launch into his litany of reassurance, but Sofia preempted him. She lowered her feet into the hole and slipped down the slope, her helmet light blinking on as she stood on the bottom of the tube.

Bob, apparently deciding that no Italian lady was going to beat him to it, huffed and puffed through, followed by Marsha. Gemma, casting an ambiguous glance at me, disappeared into the ground. Aki reached out to me.

"Come on, Linda," he said softly. "There is nothing to be afraid of. I'm here."

Echoes of the words I should have said but never did.

I took Aki's hand and slid feet first into the tube.

Inside it was not as dark as I expected. The multiple beams of light from my fellow tourists' headlamps pierced the greyish murk. Their reflections dappled the rough walls, black lava glistening like tar. All in all, it was underwhelming: a long tunnel with an uneven dipping ceiling and sloping floor. There were no fancy stalactites, or crystal outcroppings. It was a lava tube, plain and unadorned: the empty gullet of a slumbering volcanic beast.

Aki strode ahead, his head-beam reflected off the wall and populating my vision with floating blue circles. He kept talking but I zoned out.

*"You can't obsess over that, Linda! It's done. Over and finished. You need to look forward. To the future. Our future, if you still want it.*

*"Are you seriously saying that I should not think of ... that? Of my ..."*

The familiar replay was interrupted when one of the shapeless figures trudging through the light-splattered gloom squeezed over to my side. Gemma.

"Do you want to know what I found out?" she whispered conspiratorially.

I shook my head, as if I could physically shake out the sound of Craig's voice overlaid with another sound: a thin cry, a slam of the door.

"What?" I whispered back.

"Those lads he told us about, who disappeared in the lava fields? Twenty years ago? Well, it did happen. It's in the book. The one you also have."

I had not gotten far in the book. I had only looked at the Table of Contents, to make sure that no case had to do with murdered children.

The passage widened out into a small cave, its walls as smooth as polished jet. It must have been a gas bubble in the lava, I thought, though my knowledge of geology was rudimentary. No stalactites, no outcroppings, not even a graffiti, which I found somehow unsettling. The tube was easily accessible from the lava fields. If tourists came here often, as Aki claimed, why not locals?

"This is the entrance to the dark elves' farmstead," Aki said. "One night a year, on Christmas eve, it opens up and people can see what lives under the black rock."

"We are in June," Bob muttered.

"But Jesus was actually born in June," Aki smiled again, and this time, in a swirl of dancing shadows, it looked like a grimace. "Scientists calculated it. God was born on a Summer Solstice."

"What?" Bob bellowed indignantly. "No way!"

He and Aki seemed to be heading for a collision, testosterone thick in the air. I was getting increasingly uncomfortable with the situation. To defuse it, I pointed at the portion of the wall where it was flatter than the rest. It looked as if somebody had planed away a curve of the bubble, leaving behind a dull oval like a blacked-out mirror.

"What is it?" I asked.

"Oh, that!" Aki came over and touched the flat portion with his gloved hand. "It's the door."

"To the elves' kingdom?" Bob inquired acidly.

"Icelandic elves have no king," Aki responded. "They are free of allegiance to any royalty, just as we are since we won independence from the Danish Crown. Dark elves are independent farmers who live beneath the lava fields in the caves where they cultivate their livestock."

"Bats, I guess." Bob muttered, while Marsha tried to catch his eye to remind him of the meaning of "Iowa nice."

"No, actually." Aki responded. "Humans."

And before I could process this ghoulish comment, he tapped lightly on the wall.

The flat portion of the wall suddenly flapped open like one of those old-fashioned dumbwaiters, disclosing a deep cavity. And something crawled out—a hunched-up, horribly contorted figure, small like a child but sinewy and wrapped up with cords of naked

123

muscle glistening in the erratic beams of our headlights. It looked like a fire victim, with its spidery arms held up at its chest in the pugilistic stance of a burned corpse. The long fleshless fingers twitched and reached out, tipped with sharp talons. Quicker than the reaction time of my brain, the talons pierced Bob's neck, going through the layers of wool and polyester as if they were paper. It was so smooth and fast that it felt like a CGI animation until the horrible gurgling cry made it all real.

Bob was yanked back into the stone cavity, dragged with impossible speed; his suit ripped away as his body was swallowed up by the stone gullet. The hinged portion of the wall slammed shut, seamlessly blending with the dullness of lava.

I was left in the murk, blinking, trying to convince myself that it had actually happened. Superimposed upon the darkness was the impossible image of the creature's shallow muzzle, crisscrossed by twitching shadows. Had I seen what I thought I had seen? Did it really have eight eyes like a spider, unevenly scattered through its mangy fur?

Marsha threw herself at the wall, keening. Her screams woke me from my stupor, and I looked around, trying to locate Aki. Gemma knelt by the distraught Iowan while Sofia stood as if frozen, her headlamp shining straight into my face, blinding me. But Aki was nowhere to be found. Our guide had disappeared, together with Bob and whatever abomination had taken him.

Gemma finally managed to stop Marsha from smashing her fists on the lava wall. I helped her to bring the woman up as she sobbed and wailed.

"We must go!" I said. "Get out, call the police."

I had left my cellphone on the bus as Aki had told us to do. Not that I thought there would be any reception in this underground tunnel.

"Come on!" I urged Marsha. "We will be out in no time. The police will come, they'll find him."

She was beyond talking to, shocked into semi-unconsciousness. Gemma and I tried to guide her back the way we came but she was as unresponsive as a rag doll. And she was heavy. I turned to Sofia who seemed not to have moved an inch since the creature popped out of the lava.

"Come on!" I yelled. "Move! We need to get out of here!"

She did not budge. The beam of her headlamp painted a steady glowing circle on the wall that showed no sign of having opened up and swallowed a large man just minutes ago.

I came over and squinted through the blinding light.

Sofia's face was frozen, her mouth opened in a soundless cry. A glistening track of saliva wormed its way down her chin. Her eyes rolled up in her head, the whites like the carved marble of a statue.

I shook her shoulder. She collapsed in a heap.

There was no way Gemma and I could drag both her and Marsha out. But could we really leave her here?

While I hesitated, the wall behind Sofia bulged out as if the solid lava suddenly liquefied. Two sinewy arms, each as long as my entire body and tipped with skeletal claws popped out and grabbed Sofia, the claws hooking her like a fish. She was dragged backward through the curtain of flowing rock, her bootheels drumming on the rock. Again, it happened so quickly that my brain refused to parse it out. One moment Sofia was here; the next one she was gone. Shards of broken time; flashes of denied perception and unwanted memory.

I beat my fists on the wall. It was as solid as the entire weight of jagged dead rock that had swallowed us whole: the cold body of the witchy island crawling with hidden maggots.

"Come on, Linda," Gemma said with a composure that yanked me back from the spiraling maelstrom of shock. "We need to get out. Help me with Marsha."

The Iowan woman was all but comatose, but Gemma and I lifted her, draped her arms around our shoulders and half-carried, half-dragged her back the way we came. I remembered that the lava tube narrowed down toward the entrance, but we could get her through. Only the narrow part never came.

We were not in any kind of subterranean labyrinth. The tube was as straight as the ancient lava flow that had made it. There had not been any side tunnels or passages. We had walked no longer than ten minutes to get to the cave. But now we had been walking back for twice as long; and, even accounting for the slowness of our progress, we should have seen daylight already. But there was no daylight.

The darkness ahead and the darkness behind us were equally impenetrable, pressing in upon the pitiful puddle of light we carried with us. The smooth flowing walls offered no landmarks by which we could gauge our progress.

Gemma collapsed on the floor, letting go of Marsha who flopped down and lay still. I peered into her face, slapped her cheeks lightly.

"Come on, Marsha! Wake up!"

I recoiled. Her eyes were open and as white as a fish-belly, rolled up into her head.

Helplessly, I turned to Gemma, petrified of seeing the white of her eyes. But she was conscious, stirring and sitting up. She pulled a water bottle from her backpack and offered it to me.

"We need to rest," she whispered.

My legs were shaking: a delayed response to shock. I drank some water, passed the bottle back to Gemma.

"What the fuck is going on?" I asked the universe.

"I read the story in the book," Gemma said. "There were five teenagers who went out into the lava fields. But it was not on Christmas Eve. It was on Summer Solstice."

"Which, if you believe our guide, is the same thing," I muttered. "Where is he, Gemma? Did he sneak out when that ... that thing appeared? What the hell was that, anyway?"

"A dark elf, of course." Gemma replied.

"You don't really believe it...." My voice died down when I saw her face. She did.

"I am what you might call a sensitive," Gemma said. "I grew up in Suffolk. There was a barrow near our village. I would sneak out, go there at night when I was a child. I saw them. The Hidden People."

There was such a simplicity of utter conviction in her voice that I could say nothing in return. It frightened me. The shred of comfort I had had from not being alone underground suddenly evaporated.

126

"My parents did not approve," Gemma continued. "They took me to various doctors. I was sectioned for a while."

"Sectioned?"

"In a psychiatric hospital."

She must have seen my expression because she smiled crookedly.

"I've been officially cured. Declared sane. But that's why I came to Iceland. They know that the Hidden People exist. I would not be out of place here. I thought it would do me good to be in a country where I was not an oddball or a madwoman. But I did not expect the encounter to be so violent. The English Seelie did not harm me."

"What else did you find out from that book?" I asked.

"Well, four of the boys were never found and the assumption was that they had fallen into a ravine or perhaps somehow gotten to the fjord and drowned. But the fifth one was interrogated and denied any memory of what had happened. His name was Aki Sigurdsson."

"Aki ..." I whispered.

"Yes. He must have brought us here as an ... offering? Maybe he hopes we can be exchanged for his friends."

There had been four boys; five of us. When he had pressed his card upon me, had he been short of the quorum? Or had he actually liked me?

Yes, liked me enough to sacrifice me to the creatures living in the lava fields.

"We need to go," I said after a pause. "Get to the surface. These ... things cannot follow us there."

I did not know that, or course, but I needed something to encourage myself.

Gemma shrugged.

"Where is the surface?" she asked. "We should be there already. No, I think the elves don't want to let us go. We have seen their farmyard."

"Maybe Marsha and Sofia did but I didn't," I objected. "Did you?"

She shook her head and climbed to her feet. Together we lifted Marsha by her armpits. She was as inert as a corpse.

I shined my headlamp into the passage ahead, and that was when I noticed that the beam was no longer pure white. It was yellowing, growing feeble. The headlamp was running out of power.

Gemma saw the same thing because she bent down and turned off Marsha's headlamp.

"We need to conserve our batteries," she said tersely.

After another timeless interval of walking, dragging Marsha, a stitch in my side, the oppressive darkness closing around me like a fist, and my panicky breath burning in my throat. My headlamp was shedding pitiful glimmers of dying light, and Gemma's was hardly better.

I stopped again, letting Marsha's body drop. "We can't do it!" I gasped. "You ... you go. Get a signal. Call for help."

Gemma pivoted, looked at me with surprise and confusion that suddenly changed into something else as her eyes shifted to focus on what was behind my back.

"Too late," she breathed.

I turned around, my headlamp flaring up as if with one last gasp of defiance.

Aki was standing in the tube just a couple of yards behind us, his face smiling. That was how it looked: not Aki smiling but his face, a pale puffy mask stretching its lips in an unnaturally wide grimace, while the real Aki stared at us fixedly with his black insect eyes sunken into its eyeholes. His *lopapeysa* was streaked with red.

"Hello, ladies," he said.

Shouldn't there be loose rocks in a cave? He was only one man. Marsha was unconscious, but Gemma and I were young and strong, we could rush him, hit him on the head....

But there were no loose rocks in the gullet of the stone beast that was Iceland—the stone beast whose lightless innards bred the ecosystem of monsters. And even if there were, it would not help us. I saw a forest of shadows rising behind Aki's back, grasping many-fingered shadows as long arms were emerging out of solid rock. I did not have to look behind my back to know that there were more of them, blocking the way to the surface. A spidery touch slithered down my back.

"I counted on four tourists," Aki continued smugly. "One each for Tryggvi, Arngrimur, Erik, and Gylfi. I knew their … hosts would be very pleased with the lady elf-hunter from England. But I'm glad you joined us at the end, Linda. It's always good to have a spare. And who knows—I may even visit you some time in the future. When the *Dokkalfir* are done with you."

"You are crazy if you think you can get away with this!" Gemma yelled at him. "Five tourists disappearing—it will be a major international scandal! Iceland loves its tourists. The police will be at your doorstep by tomorrow!"

"Iceland loves its tourists because you are cash cows," Aki smirked. "Not that different from how the dark elves will love you. Humans are their livestock. Be assured that the Tourist Board doesn't want to endanger its supply of cattle. And of course, it doesn't want to quarrel with the Hidden People. You will have gone on a tour of the fjords in a kayak which overturned, and the five of your drowned. It might even increase tourism at the end. An exotic tragedy, you know. Good publicity. And now …"

The black rock behind his back shimmered and flowed. Something glimmered behind the stone waterfall: a glimpse of sullen red; a flicker of poisonous green. I squeezed my eyes shut, trying to gain another moment of consciousness before I was forced to see what Marsha and Sofia had seen; before my eyes rolled up into my head.

In the darkness, I heard Gemma cry out.

And then I heard the sound I had only heard once in my life and could never forget: a newborn baby's mewling cry.

My eyes flew open. I saw Gemma pressed to the wall, her hands over her face. I saw Marsha's body. I saw Aki looking back down the lava tube, behind the forest of waving fleshless arms emerging from the stone.

The arms were withdrawing, pulling back into the lava like the tentacles of sea anemones. And in the fading glow of my headlamps, I saw what was spooking them.

Crawling down the tube toward us was something floppy and ungainly; something like a giant raven, its disheveled feathers

129

glimmering with metallic reflections. But it was no bird; it supported itself on one hand and one knee, and the pimply grey flesh of its limbs was only sparsely tufted with plumage. Its head, poking out from the feathery cowl, was also bare: thick and lardy and pale, a microcephalic baby's swollen face under the broken skullcap. Its dripping lips puckered, and a piercing, unending cry emerged from its toothless mouth.

I heard Gemma cry; I saw Aki stumble back; but they had disappeared from my awareness that was focused like a laser beam on the thing before me.

I stepped forward, and falling down to my knees, embraced my baby.

It stopped crying and put its head on my shoulder. Its feathers tickled my cheek. It smelled of hot minerals, blood, and milk.

From the corner of my eye, I saw Aki spreadeagled against the lava as a fleshless hand grasped his neck and pulled him into the wall, his legs rattling in protest as he disappeared into the elves' hidden farmyard.

I held the *Útburður* until it eased itself from my embrace and crawled back into the darkness. Something light was left on the floor. I lifted it. It was a baby's blue onesie, splattered with blood.

Gemma and I huddled inside the ambulance under the thermal blanket as the rescue workers scurried around the lava tube's opening. Marsha had been already taken to the hospital in Reykjavik. The police wanted to talk to us, but judging by their lackadaisical attitude and superficial questions, we were in no danger of tough interrogation. Icelanders respected the Hidden People.

"What was it?" Gemma asked timidly. "It scared away the dark elves. I did not know there was anything that could do it. But it came to you and protected you. Why? Well," she added quickly, noting my reaction, "if you don't want to talk about it, I understand."

I sighed.

"No, I want to. I can, finally. Craig, my ex, he hated me talking about it. He thought I should forget. Let the dead past lie. It was not fault, he said, and there was nothing to talk about. But the silence drove a wedge between us. I thought he would never forgive me, you see? But now I know he has."

"He?"

"My son. I was sixteen, Gemma. A stupid little girl who got pregnant after a drunken fumble in the car. My family was religious. No abortion. But adoption, they said. Adoption was the answer. I signed the paperwork, and they took the baby away before I could even see his face. They assured me he was going to a good family. High earners. He will have a great life."

I swallowed. It physically hurt to talk—like tearing open a scar.

"I moved on. As long as I believed he was doing fine, growing up in a good family, I was fine too. I did not try to trace him. That was a closed adoption. My parents told me it was the best for all of us. But I told you, I was interested in true crime. Books, podcasts. It's a major industry in the States. So, I came across a podcast about a couple who killed their baby. The podcaster mentioned that the baby was adopted. After that I did some research...."

I stopped. Gemma squeezed my hand.

"It turned out my parents knew all along. It was a famous case. The couple are in jail, of course. Have been there for the last seventeen years, and hopefully will rot there forever."

"Why?" Gemma asked. "Why did they do it?"

"Who knows? He cried too much. They did not expect it would be so stressful, blah blah. Rich spoiled brats. Who took my child and killed him. And for seventeen years he has been looking for me. *Útburður* is the spirit of an abandoned baby. I thought they were angry, these spirits. But they are not. They are just looking for their mothers."

# THE TWO COURTS

She left the sun behind and walked into the steamy dusk. The air was warm and wet, shadows lay on the land and the sky was flesh-tinted. The rain threatened but did not fall; the darkness did not thicken, for it was the fifth time of the day, the interval between daylight and twilight when the doors of the Faerie stand open.

Squishy stems caught on her borrowed clothes. She was as tall as her brother, but his stiff leather outfit strained against her wider hips. The tower was nearing, its stocky outline thrust into the humid emptiness of the sky. As Anat came closer, a glistening segmented body, as thick as her forearm, slithered across the path and she caught a glimpse of a pale peaked face with two holes for eyes.

She shuddered but trudged on. The land was under a curse, and it was her fault. The rank weeds, the misshapen calves, the apple-tree blossoming in poisonous green—all these were clear signs of the displeasure of the Seelie Court on whose shifting borders her village was precariously perched. The Beautiful Ones would often enough be displeased for no reason at all, but Anat knew that this was not the case. Her brother's child was growing inside her.

She finally came to the tower standing alone in the meadow and touched the grey eroded stone. The tower was small and square with an arched doorway to the right. The doorway was bricked over and so was the only window. The brickwork appeared to be recent and shoddily done. Its cheap red stood out like a vulgar exclamation against the subdued lichen-covered stone. When she tapped on the bricks there was an answering tap from within.

She recoiled. There were no more taps, but she could hear a faint rustle as if something inside was rubbing against the wall. Anat pulled out her brother's dagger and started poking at the mortar.

As children, she and her brother had played on the boundaries of the Faerie. They had seen the tower from afar and had known its name, the Twins' Tower, and being twins themselves, they had felt an almost proprietary interest in it. Later they learned the obscure legend linked to it. According to the legend, the Immortal Queen had once given birth to twins. This was an omen of chaos, and so, to ensure balance, one of the twins was given to the Unseelie Court, the dark adversary of the Beautiful Ones. But the separated twins defied the prohibition. They met on the borders of twilight and kept on meeting secretly, thus breaking the rules of the Faerie, which, though incomprehensible by humans, were as immutable as the laws of nature. The twins were eventually caught and the one brought up at the Unseelie Court—the legend did not say whether it was the brother or the sister—was punished by imprisonment in the Twins' Tower. The legend was silent as to what happened to the other one. But somehow the balance had been restored.

Though Anat was not given to self-reflection, she realized that the legend had something to do with her incestuous relationship with her brother. They had, after all, grown up with the shadow of the Twins' Tower falling on their dreams. But now she had more pressing concerns than pondering the past.

Had their affair not led to a curse that threatened the village, it might have been swept under the carpet. But with the Beautiful Ones so visibly angry, the village would be sure to devise a fitting punishment to propitiate them. Running away was not an option. They had tried, and found themselves back at the gate of their own house. The Seelie Court knew of them and was unwilling to let go.

Desperation had made Anat audacious, though it had made her

brother merely sluggish. She did not share her idea with him. But if there was indeed a fairy prisoner in the Tower, why should she not release it? Humans, as everybody knew, had the one power denied to the Beautiful Ones, the power of unbinding. In the released prisoner they might gain an ally who would protect them.

The mortar fell out in large chunks. A brick was pushed out from within. A white hand appeared in the opening, fingers groping blindly. Anat caught the hand and squeezed it tight. The hand was silky and neither cold nor warm.

"I'm here to set you free!" Anat shouted into the dark hole. "What's your name?"

There was no reply. The hand lay limply in Anat's grasp and then withdrew. It must be the sister, Anat thought and was glad to have a woman on her side, for all that she was of the Unseelie Court.

She continued working, pausing only to wipe her face. The pearly sky was swollen with moisture, and she was afraid that the night would pour down like an inky waterfall and drown her.

The brickwork finally gave way, and she stepped into the darkness inside. It amazed her how dry the air was, dry and scratchy and full of prickly dust. She could dimly see the winding stairs. There was no sign of the prisoner.

She called again and then groped her way up. When she finally reached the top she could see nothing except a dim line of light around the bricked-up window. But she heard small furtive movements of something alive. Dry straw crunched under her feet.

She stepped toward the line of light and shoved until the rotten bricks tumbled outward. Twilight poured in through the jagged hole.

She was huddling on the clean stone floor, naked, hugging her knees with long sinuous arms, her face obscured by her long white hair. The hair was just a shade darker than her bleached skin and just as lusterless. In the land sweltering under the blanket of unshed rain her body seemed as devoid of moisture as old bone—not withered but angular and hard. She lifted her head and looked at Anat. Her face was indifferent and wrenchingly beautiful, a white oval starkly pierced with eyes and lips of the same dark wine color.

She uncoiled herself. And Anat saw that the prisoner was not a woman. A young boy stood before her, slender but wide-shouldered and tall, his nipples as dark as his lips, dry ringlets of white hair surrounding his delicate semi-erect penis.

"I have come to set you free," said Anat in a quivering voice. "I am ... I am a twin, like you."

The boy looked at her with dark stony eyes. Suddenly Anat doubted he understood human speech.

"Please help me," she blurted out. "I have slept with my brother and now I am pregnant with his child. Your ... the Seelie Court are punishing the village. They will kill us."

The boy approached her and stroked her hair. His body was as perfect and lifeless as marble.

And suddenly Anat understood what the Unseelie Court was.

The Seelie Court ruled the cycle of life, of copulation and spawning, of growth and decay. Their power was grimy, polluted, and corrupt. But denizens of the Unseelie Court were as clean and permanent as rock, sand and dust. They were not subject to the diseased flux of the flesh; they were not splattered by the filth of birth and the rot of death. She was filled with an unbearable longing to be like them, to be whole and pure.

The boy put his arms around her and pulled her close; not a violent act, but not a gentle one either. His lips tasted of sea pebbles, and she thought that there could be no blood in him. Another liquid, clean like salt water, flowed in his veins and engorged his penis. He pulled her down.

There was no pleasure or pain. She was looking into his long-lashed eyes and noticed, without surprise, that they were hard and polished like steel, and without pupils. The cleanliness of his magical body, so unlike her own swollen, polluted flesh, was what she came here to possess. By getting rid of the growing life inside her she would tame the tide of monstrous life that threatened her people. She relaxed in the stony embrace and wished with all her heart to be a rock or a scatter of sand, to live in the perpetual bliss of the inorganic.

❀

She woke up shivering and wet but not cold. Heavy warm moisture covered her thighs, and her back was glued to the floor. There was no sign of the Faerie boy. The fat buttery moon shone through the jagged opening of the window. The milk-warm air was pouring into the tower, saturating the last vestiges of dryness.

With a groan, Anat sat up and inspected herself. There was a puddle of dark liquid on the floor and two small runnels were feeding it. She traced them back with her fingers to her own swollen nipples. They dripped blood. Her thighs were painted with blood.

"So this is your gift?" she asked bitterly. "Making me into a sieve, a punctured sack?"

She felt soiled. She picked up her leather garment and tried to stanch the blood, but the leather was too hard to soak up anything. The worst thing was that she felt no pain or weakness, as if her body was eager for its new role. She had a vision of herself lying helpless in the tower while the streamlets of her blood fertilized the land, carving beds for themselves among the rank grasses and blowzy flowers; drawing clouds of beetles, mosquitoes, butterflies; rats and hares drinking and growing big and strong, litters of spotted wild kittens playing along the spongy shores; huge caterpillars and bloated golden spiders; new life breeding mindlessly and happily while she bled.

She crept down the stairs leaving a trail of blood like a snail. Outside she stood still for a long time, breathing the warm wet air perfumed with the piercing sweetness of the tiny star-shaped white blossoms that clustered around the base of the tower.

There was a scraggly wood ahead and as she walked toward it. Small animals followed her like ants drawn to a trail of honey: the bristling ball of a hedgehog; the fluid ribbon of a snake; the sail-like ear of a rabbit. She hated them and hated herself, but mostly she hated the creature that had perpetrated this cruel joke upon her. The Seelie Court often granted a boon in such a way that it became a curse. Apparently the Unseelie Court was no better than its adversary.

In the moonlight, she suddenly saw, on the margin of the woods, a creature like a large worm, burrowing into the mulch. In a curious inversion of perspective, it seemed to be getting smaller as she ran toward it.

It was a fat white worm with a segmented body and four soft flippers, its head hidden under the rotting leaves. With an effort, Anat picked up its squishy body, as large as a Scotch terrier. It was writhing frantically in her hands. But it was shrinking even as she was fighting to hold it, growing smaller every second.

There was a human face awkwardly perched on the conical worm-head like a slipping cap. She recognized the face, though it was covered with dirt and the large dark eyes with long curving lashes were blinking frantically, trying to clear it away. The white hair was matted; the perfect mouth trembling. The serenity was gone. The Faerie boy's face was now animated with a mixture of shame, hostility, and secret pride.

"You?" whispered Anat incredulously. "So, this is what you want? Being an animal, rooting in shit, living, dying?"

The boy's wormlike body kept shrinking but he still flapped his boneless arms, and curved his flexible spine, trying to break free; to burrow into the warm wet earth; to become a larva, perhaps; to spin a cocoon, to be reborn as—what? A buttercup, a beetle, a raccoon, or a baby?

"You let us live and die in pain, so you can play at being mortal?" screamed Anat. "I wanted you to make me pure and look what you've done! Used me as a brooding hen, stole my blood, plundered my womb!"

The boy, now the size of a carp, looked at her with mute glistening eyes that seemed ready to shed tears. It enraged her. Who would want to be a god if gods long to be insects?

"You want life?" cried Anat. "Get it!"

And she shoved the creature, now no thicker than her wrist, into her vagina headfirst. It hurt terribly for the worm thrashed and coiled. Anat pushed hard. Lubricated by dripping blood, her womb swallowed up the Faerie fetus.

And the bleeding stopped and so did the life of the land.

All the night noises, the chirping of crickets, the rustling of small animals in the grass, the soughing of branches in the wind, all ceased. A core of pain lodged in her belly. Anat looked around and saw the white night flowers closing one by one in the grass, and then the grass itself, lush and high, drying up, the field turning into an expanse of silver-grey like an old man's head, and then the ghostly stalks disintegrating into puffs of dust, and the small creatures thus exposed standing up on their hind feet and lifting suddenly human-like faces distorted with pain to the moon, their mouths stretched by mute screams, and then their bodies dissolving into the moonlight and tiny delicate skeletons tottering for a while and crashing down into separate piles of ivory bones. Snakes stood up on their tails like canes and their glistening skins unwound in long spirals; and then just the white bare stalk of a spine would be left; then it would be gone too. Butterflies rose into the night sky in swarms and their desiccated wings fell down like burnt petals. The trees in the forest ingested their own leaves and turned hard and heavy, like corals.

And after a while the field was a flat sheet of dust, faintly glimmering in the moonlight, the woods—a tangle of black wire. The only thing that broke the monotony of the landscape was the tower.

Anat walked back to it. When she approached, she saw that the doorway and the window were bricked over again. She laid her hand on the bricks and felt a flutter of movement within.

She left the tower and walked to the border of twilight, naked in the field of dust. She could not tell when she crossed the border, but she suddenly found herself in her family's backyard. Her horse whinnied softly from the stables, and her dog barked. The sky was turning pink.

Her brother was waiting for her at the door. He gasped when he saw her naked and quickly pulled her inside. He took her to her room, found some clothes and sat down in front of her. In the sickly light of the early morning, she saw his face, so like her own, high cheekbones and pale grey eyes.

"So?" he asked eagerly. "Will they forgive us?"

"No."

He buried his face in his hands, and she looked at him with a mixture of tenderness and contempt, for she could never understand how, being so like her, he could lack her strength.

"What shall we do?" he asked.

"We shall leave," she said. "The village is doomed. The Unseelie Court will take it over, and there will be no life here, just drought, stones, and dust. My children need a better place to be born."

"Children?"

"I'm going to have twins."

"Monsters like us!"

"So? We are holy monsters because we bring fertility to the land. And our children will be like us, life and death, embracing in the womb. We can make the land fruitful, even if the fruit is strange, and misshapen, and new. We can march into twilight, you and I, and take it away from the Beautiful Ones who are growing thin and dry, and set ourselves up as King and Queen."

He looked at her in fear.

"You are mad," he said. "The Unseelie Court has taken away your mind."

She shrugged and went to the window. A storm of petals blew in from the orchard. The petals were a beautiful lime-green in color.

"The Seelie and the Unseelie Courts are one," she said.

"No!"

"If you don't come with me, I'll go into twilight alone, bear my children and make them rulers of all, men and worms, foxes, maggots, fairies, eagles and cats. We shall make rivers flow with wine, and women bear quintuplets. No one will go hungry, and people will die laughing."

He did not answer. Anat walked out, into the new morning. Already the air was warm and moist like a lover's sweat. When she went into the stables to saddle her horse it shied away at first but then stood still and obedient, slightly trembling. She whistled to the dog and it growled, its tail between its legs; but when she galloped out of the yard, the dog ran after her.

Her babies moved in her womb, and she did not look back at the world of men, feeling its meaningless distinctions blur into each other like the purple and green of the blossoming land.

She was halfway to the borders of twilight when she heard the patter of hooves behind and turning, she saw her brother follow.

# ANGELO

When Angelo was a child, his mother told him that every flower had a fairy, and she described them. Inside the lilac lived a sullen, wizened creature, his face purplish with broken veins. The rose fairy had fanged mouths where her eyes should be. The peony's mistress bristled with tiny iridescent spikes. But when he insisted on seeing them, his mother shook her head. "You'll see the fairies when you're old enough, my boy," she said and laughed her sweet, mad laughter.

Angelo's mother died when he was fourteen. One day she left home and went into the fairy forest. She never came back. A week or so later, their yellow mutt slunk into the house with a rag of flesh dangling from his jaws. Angelo watched as the rest of his mother's body, crawling with black ants, was carried in by a couple of village lads, their faces pale with horror. His father hanged himself the next day.

Angelo grew up and became the supreme Judge of the small duchy perched on the borders of the fairy forest. The Duke respected his rectitude and let him do pretty much whatever he wanted. And what Angelo wanted was to enforce the law. In the country adjacent to the Seelie Court—to say nothing of an occasional raid by the Unseelie Court—the law was the only bulwark against the chaos that threatened to overwhelm man and his works.

The walled town that served as the capital of the duchy stood on the bank of a deep, winding river. Beyond the cleared fields, the mighty forest stretched toward the distant mountains; oaks and birches, and elms, and stands of dark pine shedding needles onto the dusty soil where nothing grew. And worse things—little hollows with miniature lakes, so small that dolls could have sailed them, and perhaps dolls did. Hills covered with feathery ferns whose stems were red as if dipped in blood; clearings thickly clustered with white and mauve orchids that blossomed all year-round, nourished by the decaying flesh of small animals that crawled into the thicket and never came out. It was not certain where the Seelie Court, presided over by Titania and Oberon, was located in this wilderness—provided, of course, that the Seelie Court had any precise location. As for the place of the Unseelie Court, nobody wanted even to speculate.

But wherever they were coming from, fairies never let men be at peace. Mostly, they restricted themselves to silly pranks, like stealing prayer-books or tangling threads on the loom. Sometimes, they would kill a dog or dry a cow's milk. Occasionally, a baby would disappear, and the distraught mother would discover a shriveled, mewling thing in the cradle instead. And very occasionally, a woman would be raped, or a man castrated.

Angelo succeeded in reviving some of the ancient protective laws that no longer made sense to the decadent inhabitants of the duchy. In particular, they objected to the regulations concerning marital fidelity and sexual purity which, they felt, were uncouth, embarrassing, and unfit for the modern age. But Angelo was relentless in meting out stiff punishments for adulterers and fornicators. He knew what unkind comments were made behind his back, the most printable of which was that he had ice in his veins instead of blood. But he did not care. The force behind his crusade was not prudishness but fear. He did not despise love and planned on getting married in due time. But he saw clearly what his fellow citizens preferred not to know: that desire was the gateway through which the inhabitants of the two Faerie Courts invaded the human world and played havoc with its laws and institutions.

In the course of his research, Angelo discovered an old ordinance that on pain of death prohibited all sexual intercourse for a fortnight before Midsummer Night's Eve. The Eve was the only truly dangerous time in the duchy. The fairy attacks at that time were as deadly as they were whimsical. In the dusk, a polite stranger, his face masked by a raised cloak, would ask a servant wench for a cup of water and let the cloak slip as he drank it. Next morning, the wench would be a babbling idiot. Or a pretty butterfly would alight on a child and leave him covered with running sores. Or flowers in the garden would pull out their roots and crawl away. Or ... There were many ways in which the Seelie Court celebrated Midsummer Night's Eve, on which date it temporarily reunited with its twin and enemy, the Unseelie Court, under the rule of Titania the Immortal Queen.

Angelo often considered how the dangers of the Eve might be minimized, if not avoided, and the old ordinance suggested a way. Its prescription was blunt: marital intercourse was as unlawful as fornication during these two perilous weeks.

Angelo prepared his campaign carefully. First, he talked to the Duke. The ruler of the principality was an indolent and cynical man, but he was not stupid. He was prepared to back any plan as long as its success would be attributed to him and its failure—to his underlings. He suddenly remembered an important state visit, appointed Angelo his plenipotentiary, and rode away.

Angelo instantly issued a proclamation that was greeted exactly as he expected it to be greeted. Not to be deterred by ribald laughter, he ordered all adults to attend daily lectures, prayer vigils and meditation workshops delivered by the armed constabulary. This kept them out of mischief at daytime. But even constables needed to sleep, and so policing every bedroom in the duchy, to say nothing of lofts, basements and haystacks, was out of the question. To enforce his law, Angelo needed to make an example of a transgressor. And a transgressor was conveniently found.

It was a foolish young man named Claudio, who seduced his cousin Juliet. The lovers were taken *in flagrante delicto* and the girl was found to be with child. This solved another problem: Angelo felt queasy

145

at the thought of executing a woman. He happily sent bawling Juliet home and jailed Claudio, ordering the gallows to be erected posthaste. However, he did not foresee the petitions, protests, delegations of dignitaries, attempted bribes, and death threats, all of which forced him to postpone the execution until the day of the summer solstice.

Finally, the delegations were turned away, the petitions denied, the death threats investigated and dealt with, and Angelo could relax. He decided to reward himself by spending the Midsummer Night in his study, poring over his precious volumes of Roman law. He knew he deserved a break. What he did not know was that the condemned man had a sister.

Isabella grew up playing with fairies in her father's garden. Tiny creatures with faces of wizened old men and gaudy wings had alighted on her shoulder and whispered strange stories in her ear. By now, she no longer remembered these stories, and her fairy companions had not visited her in a long time. But their dreamlike presence had stamped her with a kind of wholeness that only animals and very small children possess. She ate when she was hungry, and slept when she was tired, and obeyed no law but that of her own nature.

She bribed a couple of guards and positioned herself at the door of Angelo's study. When she heard him get up and walk around to stretch his legs, she pushed the door open and entered.

They had never seen each other before. Isabella was being educated in a convent and had only heard of her younger brother's impending execution ten hours earlier. She had spent eight of them riding back home. She had stolen the horse because Mother Superior would not let her go alone in the middle of the night. She was surprised and pleased that the Judge was not much older than herself and quite attractive. It made her task easier.

She dropped off her heavy cloak and stepped forth naked.

"If you release my brother," she said, "I'll sleep with you."

146

Angelo yelped and grabbed the dagger he always kept under his legal volumes. The duchy's outraged libertarians had made some half-hearted attempts on his life before. But he let the dagger drop when he saw what was in front of him. The hussy was as naked as the day she was born and as innocent of implements of murder.

"Cover yourself up!" he commanded. "Who let you in?"

She made no move to pick up her cloak and stared at him with a perplexed expression. Surprisingly, he liked her longish face with large brown eyes. He remembered the old superstition that one could recognize a fairy because the unusual color of its eyes would betray what material was used to fashion it. But her eyes were warm, common, and human.

"Cover yourself up!" he said again, a little more gently.

Still, she did not move. Angelo sighed. There was no need to prolong this awkward situation and test his own fortitude, which he knew to be considerable but not unlimited. He lifted her cloak and wrapped it around her.

"Who are you?" he asked. "And why do you think I want to sleep with you?"

Isabella was stunned. She did not really understand other people but had to adapt to their ways to get what she wanted. She had trained herself to read their intonations and facial expressions and had become quite adept at that. She could tell that the man was not faking. He really was not interested!

"Do you not find me desirable?" she asked in her dulcet voice.

The Judge frowned. "The whole situation is highly improper," he said. "You should not be here at all. Let me call the guards and they'll escort you safely home."

"But why?" Isabella asked innocently. "You make love to me. and let my brother go. This is simple and natural."

Angelo's rage at this insult to the law boiled over.

"You're a strumpet!" he snarled. "Your brother will hang tomorrow, and if you're not careful, you'll follow! Get out now!"

Isabella's hand flew to her mouth. The realization that her beauty was impotent to get her what she wanted shook her more than the Judge's threat and her brother's impending death. She backed off clumsily, tripped, and fell. The cloak slipped off again but now her nakedness had the additional—and unintended—appeal of helplessness.

Angelo sighed. "I cannot let your brother go! Don't you understand? He and this idiot paramour of his have opened the gates to the Two Courts. The Seelie and the Unseelie both are waiting on our borders! If they don't get their sacrifice, they'll destroy us! Are you willing to let it happen? Are you willing to unleash the Wild Hunt on our men, women, and children?"

Isabella lifted herself to her knees and smiled at him. Her self-confidence reasserted itself. She was not afraid of the Wild Hunt, and she lacked the imagination to be affected by others' fears.

"I'll go and bargain with the Two Courts myself," she announced. "The Queen, they say, values women more than men; she won't refuse. And then you can temper the harshness of the law with the sweetness of mercy and let my brother go."

Angelo was speechless. This was suicide. No one could go into the fairy forest on the Midsummer Night and come back alive. Such corpses as were recovered bore terrible mutilations. And this strumpet actually offered to suffer such a fate for her no-good brother!

Seeing confusion on his face, Isabella, still kneeling, reached out and put her narrow hand on his thigh—a move that brought the rest of her anatomy too close for comfort. Angelo shook her off and retreated behind his desk.

"I can't let you go!" he muttered. "Your blood will be on my head!"

"Is it better to have my brother's blood on your head?"

There were many answers he could make but suddenly the entire situation appeared to him embarrassing, compromising, and altogether intolerable. What if one of his scribes suddenly walked in and discovered a stark-naked woman in his study? He would never live it down!

"Go, then!" he declared irritably. "If you make a bargain with the Two Courts, I'll pardon your brother. More likely that your parents are going to mourn two children instead of one, but this is your own doing! Get up, make yourself decent, and leave. Go!"

Isabella went back home well pleased with herself. It was late afternoon, and it did not leave her much time to prepare, but she had boundless confidence in her own ability to face down the fairies, get her brother released, and achieve the life of ease, power, and plenty that was her due.

Juliet was sobbing in her room, and Isabella yelled at her to shut up as she went around ordering her maids to draw a bath and to prepare the clothes she needed. Her mother hovered at her door for a while but went away without asking any questions. Claudio was her second child, but sometimes when she looked at her daughter's bright impenetrable face, she felt he was the only one.

Isabella admired herself in the mirror. The memory of the Judge's rejection cast a fleeting shadow on the polished surface of her mind, but her beauty banished it. Her clothes were just right: a court dress of black velvet with ruffles of antique lace at the low-cut bodice; rubies around her throat and on her ears; and the white froth of fretted petticoats under the hooped overskirt. Most people would consider it a strange outfit for blundering around in the night forest, but she knew better. Titania was the Queen of air and darkness and had to be treated as royalty. She was convinced that the Seelie and Unseelie courts would appreciate the wisdom of her choosing the colors of their dominion: white, red, and black. Many years ago, the fairies in her father's garden had prophesized that she would grow up into these colors: her skin as white as snow, her lips as red as blood, her hair as black as a raven's wing. When she walked out into the warmth of the late afternoon, hobbling a little awkwardly on her high heels, it occurred to her that she was already grown up and her hair was blond, her lips pink, and her skin the color of skin. But she did not dwell on it.

Angelo's evening was irrevocably spoiled. He tried to concentrate on the law of primogeniture, but the outrageous image of the strumpet insinuated itself between him and the fine print. He sighed and closed the book. He was a man; he conceded as much. It was not his fault that he was subject to the same desires and temptations as any other man. He thought that perhaps he should visit Mariana. She was the woman he intended to marry someday.

But as he locked the door of his study (too late, he thought sourly), he realized that he did not want to see Mariana. And he also realized that his unease was not desire, which he had learnt from long experience to manage as necessary. It was guilt, and he did not know how to manage it.

The woman was going into the fairy forest on Midsummer Night. She was as good as dead. And he had allowed this; no, he had encouraged her.

He went back home and tried to drink but the rare Spanish wine tasted like vomit. Outside, the summer sky was growing deeper, the gold of the sun changing to copper, the shadows of the trees clawing the ground.

Abruptly, Angelo pushed open the casement and leaned out. There were no flowers in his gardens, just smooth turf and rocks.

Looking into the garden, Angelo thought that perhaps flowers were not the only things that housed fairies. Perhaps everything did. The scum on the pond might hide a creature with a smooth, featureless face the color of moldy bread. The decorative rocks might be alive with tiny, crawling bodies. The velvety lawn might hunch up into the shape of an emerald cat.

And why not human bodies? Perhaps there was a being in his stomach, a purple and yellow ball of slime. Perhaps his limbs were meat-puppets jerked for the amusement of an invisible puppeteer. Perhaps the thing between his legs was a blind leech with a mind of its own.

Angelo suddenly remembered Isabella's narrow, delicate hand. And then he imagined this hand lying in the grass and crawling with black ants.

He took off his court clothes, put on a nondescript dark doublet and a cloak, grabbed a dagger, and went out.

The forest was sleepy and purring like a ginger tomcat, golden-striped by the last rays of the setting sun. Isabella looked around for a fairy messenger that would take her to Titania's court, but the forest appeared to be empty. It was strange.

Isabella's eyes fell onto a thorny black bush that grew by the side of the path. It was leafless and bore shriveled black buds. She touched it, curious why it looked so winter-bare at the height of summer. A curved thorn bit into her palm. She cried out and sucked on the wound, but it was too late; drops of her blood rained upon the buds which instantly expanded and burst open, unfolding into giant white flowers with sword-like stamens. The flowers smelled of rot.

"Take me to the Queen!" Isabella cried, trying to still a quiver in her voice.

The dead-white fire of the blossoms consumed the bush, each flower exploding with new petals into a bristling ball. Adjacent blossoms attacked each other, their stamens swinging and clashing like swords at a tournament. With miraculous speed, the empty bark collapsed in upon itself, sucked dry by the voracious flowers that bit into each other with petal-rimmed maws. One of them, more predatory than the rest, consumed its brethren and swelled until it was almost the size of Isabella. As she backed off, the giant flower swiveled and pointed its sharp stamen at her.

"Take me to the Queen!" she repeated.

The thick petals flowed together, and the flower-ball became a mound of mock-flesh that quickly shaped itself into an eidolon. The creature tottered upright, opened its bulging eyes and looked at her. Its irises were the color of an abattoir.

Isabella gulped; the sending was animated by her own blood and would follow her, begging for more. This was bad enough, but the sending's shape was worse. Its pallid body was long and lean; its

151

head shiny and bald; its mouth—a gaping hole fringed with twitching petals. The sword-stamen stuck out obscenely at its crotch.

Isabella felt bile rise in her throat. She had seen enough animal couplings to develop a matter-of-fact attitude to the procedure. But this ... this *thing* was simultaneously threatening and vulgar, the stuff of shameful nightmares. And it had fed on her blood!

She retreated; the sending moved toward her. Desperately, she recalled the innocent companions of her childhood, but they seemed faded and far away.

She turned and ran, sobbing, through the thicket of chokeberry, velvet, lace, and taffeta being shredded by thorny branches. The creature glided after her at a leisurely pace. Its stamen-penis blossomed with curved bone hooks.

For the first time, Angelo entered the fairy forest. It was dipped in slimy light. Scant sunshine oozed down into the black earth that squelched under his feet. He gritted his teeth and persevered. His mind was filled with terrible images of Isabella raped, tortured, or dead. He strained his ears for screams of pain but heard only a remote murmur of trees.

Suddenly, something touched his leg. He jumped up and stifled a scream when he saw what it was. A little girl grasped the top of his boot with a tiny, dimpled hand.

Angelo backed off slowly, mindful of the Seelie (or was it the Unseelie?) penchant for cruel tricks. The toddler's face scrunched up, and she emitted a thin desperate wail. Then she plumped down among the tussocks of grass and started crying in earnest. She was wearing a dirty smock and one baby shoe.

Angelo hesitated. It was one of his best-kept secrets that he had a soft spot for cats and small children. And what if this was a real baby and not a fairy eidolon? Child-stealing was a specialty of the Unseelie Court, and it did happen that they lost interest and abandoned their prey in the woods.

Cautiously, he approached the wailing girl and picked her up.

She stopped crying and tearfully smiled at him. She was a pretty baby with curly hair and round face. There was a long, shallow scratch on her cheek, dry blood and dust matting her soft skin. Unthinkingly, Angelo moistened the edge of his cloak with his saliva and tried to rub it off.

Branches whipped Isabella's face as she tore through the brambles and undergrowth in blind panic. Her beautiful clothes hung in tatters; her hair was full of leaves and twigs; and her feet—she had lost her slippers—bled. But she hardly felt any pain. What she felt was the helplessness of a small, hunted animal.

Suddenly, the ground disappeared from under her feet. She stumbled, fell, and rolled down a grassy slope. She ended up flat on her back. Opening her eyes, she saw the pink sky with a single silvery star hanging low and the sunset clouds still smoldering above the treetops. Then she discovered she was lying in a small hollow cupped between gentle hills. It was fringed by a stand of aspens and thickly grown with tiny ferns.

Unsteadily, Isabella got to her feet. The panic had subsided, and its place was taken by burning shame at her failure. All she wanted now was to escape the forest, crawl back home, and hide under the blanket without seeing another human being—ever. But as she was untying the strings that attached the broken hoops of her overskirt to the bodice, she realized that among the people she was never going to see was Claudio. She had wanted to best Angelo more than she had wanted to save her brother. But now, tears came, and they were for him.

Suddenly, there was a rustle above her. The aspens parted and the white sending slipped through, shining with a pale glow. Its penis was now a spiny, writhing snake.

Isabella looked around but there was nowhere to run. The snake hissed and reared.

And suddenly, the voice of Mother Superior reading from a book on rhetoric rang in her ears. She had never taken her convent education seriously, but she knew it was the necessary stepping-stone toward her ultimate goal, and consequently, she was quite good at it. She faced the sending.

"I'm a pure virgin," she declared grandly. "Is this how you show your respect?"

The sending cocked its head. Isabella remembered the garden fairies' stories and songs, simple and straightforward like the prattle of children. Surely creatures like these had no defense against the wiles of legalism!

"You have tasted my blood, have you not?" she asked sternly.

The sending nodded a tiny, hesitant nod.

"This makes me your blood sister and thus prohibited to you under any condition. You may not even gaze at my nakedness under the penalty of ten strokes with a birch whip or temporary blindness. Both the Seelie and the Unseelie Courts recognize blood brotherhood and King Bronwen of the Unseelie and Queen Bramwen of the Seelie were blood brother and sister."

This much was true or at least a commonly told tale. The rest Isabella was making up as she went on. But would a sending made of bark, blossom and blood know any better?

"You have uncovered your sister's nakedness," Isabella continued, warming up to her theme. "If you are of the Seelie, of the Bright Court, you shall pay me restitution. If you are of the Unseelie, of the Dark Court, you shall be my slave for ten years. But since tonight, of all nights, the two courts unite, you shall do both."

The creature's snake-penis drooped and shrank. Isabella drew herself upright.

"Are you willing to do my bidding?" she asked severely. "Or shall I drag you before Queen Titania herself, the sovereign ruler of the Two Courts?"

The creature trembled and shed petals into the grass. Isabella reminded herself to go easy on it; she did not want to frighten it out of existence. She needed it for a job.

"If you do exactly as I say," she said, "I shall forgo the ten-year slavery."

The creature nodded energetically. Its crotch was now pristinely smooth.

"Well, come here," said Isabella, "and listen carefully...."

The moment Angelo's cloak moistened with his spittle and touched the girl's filthy cheek, he knew it was a terrible idea. He could not believe he had made this stupid mistake, when every child in the duchy knew that one should never let the Good Folk have anything that comes out of one's body, be it hair, nail parings, saliva, urine, semen, or blood. But the Judge often preferred to forget that he had a body which exuded various shameful substances, and being always clean himself, he could not abide dirt in others.

He jerked his hand away and dropped the girl. But it was too late. Her eyes blinked and milky whiteness flowed through them, filling them to the brim and spilling over onto her cheeks. Her smile did not waver, though. It just grew and grew as her lips stretched across her face, dividing her head into two. The upper part flipped off like the lid of a boiling pot and foamy white liquid poured out. Angelo gagged and turned around to flee.

But the girl was now in front of him, as if there were two of them, and perhaps there were but he did not dare look back. Only she was not a girl anymore. She had expanded into a woman-sized figure, exaggeratedly feminine, with high breasts and a tiny waist, molded of runny mucus. This nauseating parody of a female looked vaguely familiar, and to his horror, Angelo recognized her. The Unseelie creature had shaped itself into an obscene likeness of Isabella.

Now he did vomit, though having had little to eat the whole day, he mostly brought up bile. The creature dropped down on all fours, sniffing at the bile. Angelo was frantic with disgust.

The sun had set, but in the white light of the long summer dusk he could see it all with far more clarity than he wanted to. The Isabella thing sat down on its liquefying rump. It lifted its dripping arms to its chest, tugged at it, and twitched its shoulders like a woman getting out of a tight dress. The mucus flesh parted and something even more revolting popped out. A blunt, yellow muzzle pushed out from the slimy cocoon, its swollen tongue hanging like a dark banner. The creature that was being hatched had a dog's head and a woman's body. It was crawling with black ants that streamed out from its eyes like a child's clumsy drawing of tears. But the eyes themselves were glistening white, the color of saliva.

Angelo realized that he was tottering on the edge of insanity. Almost gleefully, he foresaw his own mad lurch through the forest, his clothes torn and filthy, mindless shriek bubbling up from his raw throat. And just as he visualized this picture in every excruciating detail, he realized how ridiculous it was.

The horror popped like a soap bubble. He wrinkled his nose at the creature's rotten smell. It stared at him expectantly.

"You poor thing!" said Angelo and patted the creature's wet, matted fur.

"There are," said Titania to Oberon, her lord, "three ways to please a mortal woman. Unfortunately, nobody knows what they are."

Her lord did not answer. He had been dead for a year. His body had become a hatchery for young fairies that swarmed in the rotting flesh, emerging from luminous larvae. One fairy fluttered upward and perched on Titania's outstretched, four-fingered hand. The second hand, made into a fist, hung down by the queen's scaly side.

The sprite had the muzzle of a weasel and the body of a boy. The queen of the Two Courts bent her head to look at the new creature. Her head was that of a giant crow, its faded black feathers scuffed on top where a golden crown had previously rested. Now the crown was placed on the mossy hillock and worked over by a crew of dung beetles. They were removing the rubies and emeralds from their settings and substituting dead men's eyes instead.

"Look at them," said Titania to the sprite. "Humans can be so funny!"

She opened her fist. The elongated palm was fringed with a strip of trembling grey-green filaments and in the middle of it moved two pale ticks.

"Poor clumsy creatures," said Titania, her beak opening wide in a yawn.

The dog-headed animal persisted in trotting after Angelo. It was rather clumsy, and its smell did not make it a pleasant companion either. But he did not have the heart to shoo it away. He remembered having read somewhere that sendings only survived for a short time. Perhaps being close to the source of its existence would give the creature a longer lease on life.

The sky was luminous, but the ground was mantled with shadows. Angelo ripped his cloak to shreds when it caught on a pine branch and skinned his knee on a boulder. But he persevered. He had to find Isabella. Clearly the dangers of the Two Courts were to the mind rather than to the body, but how would a weak woman withstand an assault of guilty nightmares?

There was a stand of aspens ahead of him, their delicate trembling canopies etched in black against the whiteness of the sky. Something dark and indistinct pushed between two trunks: another fairy or sending in the shape of a woman. Her semi-nude body shone in the twilight.

"Just leave off, will you?" he yelled at the fairy. "It doesn't work on me!"

The fairy started, and he realized he was being boorish.

"I'm sorry, Good Neighbor," he said, softening his tone. "I meant no disrespect. I'm looking for a woman who has been lost in your kingdom. Lead me to her and we'll both leave you to your … hmm, celebrations."

"Angelo?" said the fairy in amazement.

"How do they mate with all these skins on?" asked the weasel-headed sprite. "Do they shed them like snakes?"

Other fairies meanwhile had joined the audience. There was a double-bodied girl, with two pale trunks joined by a single head, a golden pince-nez perched askew on her nose. There was a colony of squirming pink worms interlaced together into a rough simulacrum of a human shape. There was a small, peaky child whose twin brother grew out of his chest.

"The males have these sharp implements," said the double-bodied girl authoritatively, "and they cut through their partners' shells."

"No, they tear them off," hissed the worms in unison, sounding like a man with a bad cold.

"The eggs hatch from within and break the shells," corrected Titania.

It was twilight now, the endless fairy dusk, the fifth time of day. The sky was grey and soft like a dove's breast. They were huddling together in the hollow. The grass was studded with the radiant cups of night-flowers. Shiny worms with human faces crawled on the ground and moths as big as sparrows flapped in the balmy air.

"I still can't believe you followed me here," Isabella said.

Angelo had spread the remnants of his cloak for her to sit on, but she insisted he should sit by her side, and he was painfully aware of her smooth shoulder touching his.

"I couldn't let you die in the Two Courts," he said.

She turned her head to look at him, her hair falling across his face. "I think we all die in the Two Courts," she said.

"What do you mean?"

"I was very frightened at first. But then I realized there is nothing to be afraid of because we carry our own Courts with us all the time. Day and night; birth and death; water and blood. This is all we are."

"I hope we're more than that," Angelo said, scandalized. "I have an immortal soul. I'm sure you do too."

Isabella laughed softly and stroked his cheek. Angelo opened his mouth to protest but Isabella's grubby fingers landed on his lips, so he kissed them instead.

"Now," Titania said with some satisfaction, "they are going to mate."

A gaggle of flower fairies surrounded her now, perched on her mighty shoulders, fluttering in the air around her head or clinging to the trees. They were delicate semi-transparent creatures, their bodies and gauzy wings colored according to their flower.

Titania held her hand rigidly outstretched, and in its hollow, the lovers were kissing.

"They're like doves," said the double-bodied girl. "So sweet!"

"Doves are good to eat," the worms hissed.

"It's so boring!" complained the child with a twin.

Titania grabbed the weasel-fairy with her free hand, bit off his head and slurped the stream of blood that jetted from the neck. The smell of blood drove several flower fairies into a feeding frenzy, and they buzzed around her until she swatted them.

Dropping the headless body, Titania focused her cartwheel eyes on the lovers.

"It's taking them too long," she grumbled.

"When will she whelp?" the turquoise bluebell fairy hummed.

"She has to lay eggs first," the double-bodied girl explained.

"You're so smart!" exclaimed the bluebell fairy in admiration.

"Will she eat him afterward?" the pink dog-rose fairy asked.

"No chance," the yellow daisy fairy grumbled.

The peaky child grabbed the bluebell fairy and fed her to his twin.

"Be done, be done!" Titania cried impatiently. "What's so special about you? Dog and cats do it; and flies and beetles too! Hurry!"

"It's making me nervous," the daisy fairy complained.

She reached inside herself and pulled out a skein of tangled intestines. Spreading them into a dripping web, she flew toward a large beech tree that hummed softly to itself. A flock of tiny cherubic babies with greenish lanterns fluttered in and out of the tree's canopy.

Several of them blundered into the daisy fairy's web and got stuck. She hauled the web with its catch back into her belly, and it snapped shut with a wet sound.

"Are they still looking for the right appendages?" the worms hissed.

The double-bodied girl shivered. "There is something in the air...." she whispered. Her two bodies threw their arms around each other as if looking for shelter.

A shudder passed through Titania's giant bulk, and the whole forest trembled, leaves raining down on the grass. Oberon's decaying corpse split in the middle, and a great mass of fairy larvae plopped out.

"I wish they'd stop!" cried Titania in distress.

The peaky child with a twin caught another flower fairy.

"It'll be over soon," he said, baring his small, pointed teeth. "They mated. She will bear young. He will kill them, so he can mate again. Death and life, life and death, the Two Courts together. There is nothing else."

"Who are you to teach us?" the double-bodied girl screamed at him in sudden fury. "Rot-eater! All of you, Unseelie buggers, you're mulch!"

She snatched her pince-nez and pitched it at the boy. But her aim went awry because the second body tried to stop the attack. Instead of hitting him, the pince-nez smacked into the dog-rose fairy and brought her down. The fairy, helplessly twitching on the grass, was immediately attacked by the dung beetles who had run out of the eyes for Titania's crown. The dog-rose fairy was quickly dismembered and carried away. The worms tittered.

"Oh, shut up, all of you!" cried the fairy queen. "I should not have allowed this to happen! And now I can't make it stop!"

There was an acrid smell of burning in the air. The lush grass of the fairy clearing was turning brown as if singed by invisible flame. The flowers dotting the ground writhed in distress. A large poppy swayed wildly as its scarlet cup filled with smoke. One by one, the flowers caught fire.

"Stop it!" Titania wailed. "What do you want from us? Why do you have to come to the Two Courts and burn them to the ground?"

The double-bodied girl, trying to comfort the frightened worms, hugged them so tightly with her four arms that the colony disintegrated, and its components wriggled away in panic. The peaky child's twin broke away and crawled after them, snapping at the stragglers.

With a moan of pain, Titania grasped her beak and tore off her bird face. Underneath there was the muzzle of a grey fox, its teeth bared in a grimace of defiance. The fairy larvae milled about her feet and cried out in plaintive voices.

Titania was clawing at her faces, peeling them off and tossing them onto the heaving ground. A she-wolf, a sheep, a writhing sea anemone, an earwig, a chimp, a clump of rose petals, a snake with human eyes, a woman with a forget-me-not growing out of each eye socket … She was screaming, a high-pitched, monotonous sound. The towering mass of her body shook uncontrollably, but the hand in which she held the lovers was rigid, defying the chaos that now spread to all the inhabitants of the Two Courts.

The last face was blank. Swaying over the devastation of her kingdom, Titania put all her remaining strength into bending her fingers. Slowly, she closed her fist.

"Yes!" Titania cried in triumph.

But even as the word left her lips, a quick tongue of fire leapt out, licked her scaly forearm, ran up to the shoulder, smoldered in the dark feathers of her head. Wreathed in flame, Titania became a giant torch illuminating the ruins of the fairyland. She burnt over the debris of magic as the sky darkened into the night and the moon rose peacefully into the dark sky.

Some tenacious root was digging into Isabella's back. The air was getting colder, the ground lumpier, and then a gust of wind brought the pungent smell of smoke.

They jumped up and saw that among the trees a small fire was burning. Angelo beat it down with Isabella's petticoat. Peering at

161

the dying embers, he saw a scatter of tiny bodies among the jerking shadows. He thought they were insects and mites until he made out the contorted shapes of their multiform agony.

"Did you see it?" he asked Isabella. "I mean, when we were ..."

"Yes," she said. "I saw."

She had seen indeed, in snatches of vision, in the periphery of her pleasure: the luminescent sky swarming with angelic insects, and the animal paw, larger than the hand of God, holding them under the scrutiny of an animal eye. She had felt the air ignite and the earth tremble. And now there were scorch marks on her petticoat.

"We destroyed the Two Courts," he said, puzzled. "How? Why?"

"We broke the law," said Isabella, "and the poor creatures were shocked to death."

"Law? The fairies are denizens of chaos. They have no law."

"Wrong. Nothing is as law-abiding as the wild things. They have to eat, to breed, and to die. We are free to make the law or to break it."

"This is sophistry," he muttered.

She shrugged. "Suit yourself."

He offered her his arm, and they walked out of the forest in silence. When they were nearing the outskirts of the town, Angelo spoke.

"I'll release your brother, of course," he said, clearing his throat. "I cannot execute a man for a crime I'm guilty of myself. Anyway, the danger to the duchy seems to have been averted."

"Oh no!" Isabella exclaimed.

"What?"

"I sent a ... well, a messenger to the jail. Claudio must be home already."

"The guards won't release anybody without my personal order."

"It was your personal order," Isabella confessed. "I made it ... the sending ... in your image."

"How could you do it?"

"It's not hard if you can visualize the person clearly. And I ... I remembered your face well."

Angelo opened his mouth to deliver a stinging rebuke and closed it again.

They came to the gate of Isabella's family mansion. The gate was open, the windows lit, and the sounds of cheering spilled out into the street. The sending had apparently done its job.

"Well," Angelo muttered, avoiding her eyes, "it's a little too late now, and your family must be celebrating Claudio's return, so I'll postpone my conversation with your father till tomorrow morning. It's more seemly this way."

"Conversation?"

"I mean my suit. Asking for your hand in marriage."

"What?" Isabella stared at him in consternation. "I can't marry you! I have other plans!"

And indeed, when the Duke came back from his state visit, Isabella married him. Angelo married Mariana, who had been patiently waiting for him in her moated grange. The Duchess had been known to refer to the Judge's wife rather unkindly as "that whey-faced bitch." But despite this tension among the mighty, the town prospered, untroubled by incursions from the Two Courts. Everybody agreed that this was due to the secret ritual of powerful magic performed annually by the Duchess and the Supreme Judge as they solemnly walked into the fairy forest every Midsummer Night's Eve and returned at dawn.

# GREEN BIRD

*L*ast night, a flock of ghost starlings landed on my porch. I knew they were ghosts because of the noise they made—a soft but discordant susurrus, like multiple envelopes being torn open at the same time but not quite in sync. Natural starlings don't make this kind of noise. And do natural starlings even fly at night?

I lay in bed, staring at the ashen rectangle of the window, the full moon peeking from between the cypresses in the garden. I saw a swift, winged silhouette streak by, leaving behind a shadowy tracing of silver on the night sky, as if the bird was plucking invisible cords in its flight.

"Bernadette?" I mouthed.

That was stupid, I knew. Ghost birds don't talk to the living. And starlings are supposed to be ghosts of stillborn babies.

After a while the flitting ceased, and I drifted back into sleep.

Next morning, as I made my way to the police station, I saw a man sweeping the pavement at the intersection of Annunciation Avenue and the Place of Sorrows. Shards of glass glittered in the sunlight.

"What happened?" I asked the man. I had seen him before—a grizzled street sweeper—but his name escaped me. Strangely for a policeman, I am not good at remembering names, only faces. But he did recognize me.

"Inspector Rocco?" he smiled, showing an uneven row of yellowing teeth listing like old gravestones. "A drunken brawl. One of them pulled a knife. The second one is in the morgue. They'll tell you all about it in the station, I'm sure."

I was not. But I thanked him as he resumed the rhythmic movement of his broom on the ancient cobblestones. I saw poorly washed-away pinkish stains on the worn pavement, adding to the accumulation of blood and grime that had been building up since the Land sprang into being and the City Below was built millennia ago.

Sitting on the architrave above the entrance to the station was a ghost raven. In daylight, ghost birds are easy to distinguish from their natural counterparts: there is a glimmering halo around them, as unstable as the film of oil on water. They seem both more solid and more elusive, somehow: they stand out from their surroundings like a pebble dropped onto a flat drawing, and yet it hurts your eyes to look at them directly.

This raven was bigger than its natural kind, and it stared at me with a bird eye that had a human iris, blue and muddy. It flew away silently into the brightness of the sky, which, for a moment, seemed to be crisscrossed with a transparent webbing. I blinked, and it dissolved away.

When I walked into the station, few of my colleagues were in, and those who were suddenly found something urgent to do with the piles of paperwork on their desks. They all seemed to avoid my gaze, and nothing much was said beyond the muttered "Good morning." I was neither surprised nor angry. Demotion and misfortune always mark their victims with an invisible "Keep Away" sign. And I had had both. After Bernadette's death, I was told, in no uncertain terms, that I could not continue as a lead detective in active cases. My actions were still under investigation, but I had no illusion about what the end result would be. Desk duty at best; discharge at worst. For now, I was told to go over cold cases before filing them away. I did not object; nor would I object to being kicked out of service at the age of thirty-five and having to earn my living as a security guard for the Five Hundred Families in their gated compounds on the Forum Hill. I had done what I had to do. And if I could not save Bernadette, what business did I have saving others?

I went down to the archive where old Gianna presided over her kingdom of yellowed paper stacks and mouse droppings. At least her attitude was no different from her usual: a grunt in lieu of a greeting. She was an equal-opportunity people hater.

My new office was a rickety desk in the corner of the archive that held several files marked with the yellow "Suspended" stamp. My task was to stamp them with the red "Closed" label, after which they would be permanently buried. I could finish it all in half an hour, go home, and brood.

I quickly went through the files, dreading to see the familiar name. But of course, even Superintendent Flavio would not be so tactless as to give me Bernadette's file to retire. Or would he? Well, it was not a cold case. Not anymore. I took care of that.

I struggled with the temptation to stamp all the files without opening them, and to skulk back home where a half-full bottle of red wine waited on the kitchen table. Instead, I sat at the desk, balancing it with my knee, and started reading the first file. After five minutes, I realized I was not going anywhere.

I had never heard of this case, which was not surprising because it was fifteen years old. At the time I had been struggling to find a way to convince my father I was not made to be a vintner. Newspapers arrived once a month to our village and were mostly filled with gossip about the Five Hundred Families. On the other hand, they probably had covered it up because it took place on the Forum Hill.

Marco de Luca's wife was stabbed to death in the garden of their villa, her body sprawled across the sundial. Her jewels were missing, so it was assumed to be a robbery. But what set the murder apart was that her three-month-old twins were missing too.

I studied the yellowed daguerreotype attached to the murdered woman's description. Since then, new photography techniques, from collotype to plates, had emerged that provided much better-quality

167

portraits of the living and the dead. The daguerreotype only made it possible to surmise that Anna Livia had a great chignon of dark hair attached to what seemed to be an undifferentiated blob of a face. But I had no doubt that she had been beautiful. A de Luca would not have married a plain woman.

I tried to remember what I knew about him. It was not much: my job normally took me to the gang-infested areas of the Cloaca, well below the Forum Hill. I had heard of the de Luca family, and while it was not the richest or the largest among the Five Hundred, it was not on the bottom of the pole either. Had not a de Luca run recently for the Senate? The run was unsuccessful, and now I wondered whether that old scandal might have had something to do with it. The "husband did it" always applied, even when the husband, by virtue of his position, would not be prosecuted unless an unquestionable proof of his guilt was found. And even then, a conviction was not guaranteed, which was the reason I was sitting in this dank basement.

But reading through the Anna Livia file, I realized that the investigating officer had not been intimidated by the Forum domicile and the array of influential relatives. Marco had been called in for interrogation more than once. However, he had an ironclad alibi, attested to by several members in his exclusive gentlemen's club, called the Peacock. According to his statement, which never varied, he came home to find his wife dead and the cribs of the twins in the nursery empty. The nursemaid had been given a day off, and the only other person in the villa, a cook, claimed to have heard and seen nothing.

I checked the name of the investigating officer. Gianfranco Balboa. It did not ring any bells.

I went back to Gianna's desk. She was cataloguing some old evidence boxes, writing down numbers in the ledger in her old-fashioned feminine script that was as precise as copperplate. I put the Anna Livia file before her.

"Where is the evidence box for this case?" I asked. She glared at me over her glasses but checked the ledger and waddled deep into the labyrinth of the stacks where even the new-fangled electricity lamps failed to dispel the accumulated gloom of decades of murders, rapes, burglaries, and frauds. She lingered there for a long time and when she came back, empty-handed, she had the grace to look crestfallen.

I did not need her self-serving explanations. The Anna Livia evidence box had been removed.

The Flower Precinct was not the worst area of the Cloaca. Many high-end brothels were located there, and as I passed along the Via Rossa, I occasionally met the eyes of girls behind their beaded curtains sparkling like jewels in the soft candlelight. The brothels apparently did not like electricity, keeping to the old-fashioned candles and gaslight that did a better job of erasing signs of drunkenness, fatigue, or despair.

I was not a saint but since Bernadette's death, a woman's face had lost its magic for me. Everywhere I looked, I saw a bird's curving beak and a bird's unblinking eye hiding under the thin layer of human flesh. As if in response to my gloomy thoughts, I heard a whirring of wings above my head. I looked up into the roof of the sky and saw an owl momentarily obscure the pinprick stars. It was a natural bird, but ghost birds often followed their living counterparts. And indeed, a winged silhouette standing out against the flat indigo background streaked across. I sent a wordless plea to deliver a message to Bernadette, as I always did nowadays. And as always, there was no response.

The augurs who claim to be able to speak to ghost birds are all fakes; that was what my father used to say. And yet after the death of my baby brother Roberto, I saw him leaving the house of our village augur. He dropped his eyes in embarrassment and pretended not to see me; and with the arrogance of youth, I condemned him for his inconsistency. Now I knew better.

Gianfranco Balboa lived in a run-down apartment building near the market. The building was very old, but its stone shell had been hollowed out and filled with a maze of shoddily constructed rooms and mean corridors. There was no electricity, of course, and the smoky gas fixture on the landing threatened to set the entire building on fire. I knocked on the scuffed door, and after a long interval, the shambling steps announced that the lodger was at home.

The man who peered at me suspiciously through the crack had the jaundiced complexion of somebody who likes his raki undiluted. He looked as old as my father, though he probably was not.

"Inspector Gianfranco Balboa?" I asked.

"Inspector? Not anymore. And who are you?"

I introduced myself. He tried to slam the door on me, but I pushed my foot in.

"The de Luca case," I said.

We sat at the bare table stained with wineglass-rings and candle drippings. There was little else in the one-room apartment besides the messy bed that tried unsuccessfully to disguise itself as a sofa and a large collection of bottles. I saw my own future in twenty years—a disgraced police officer, drinking his loneliness away in an anonymous rooming house.

"Why are you interested in this case all of a sudden?" Balboa asked. He did not offer me a drink, even though he was nursing a large glass of suspiciously colored liquid. I explained that I was put in charge of the cold cases unit, omitting to mention that the entire unit was myself. He cackled; his face was so complexly pleated and wrinkled that it looked like a paper mask.

"You mean you've gotten on the nerves of Il Commissario? Or pissed off one of the Five Hundred Families? No ... wait. Did you say your name was Rocco?"

I winced; the old fart was not as totally clueless as I expected.

"The wife's murder, wasn't it? You went after a guy who decided to join the birds before his time. Jumped out the window, didn't he?"

I nodded.

"He was exonerated later, right? So, police brutality, the whole shebang."

"He was guilty," I said.

"But you did not have the proof. And now it's too late; he is on the wing. Speaking of which, too bad Anna Livia was offed by her husband. She could have helped you."

170

I stared at him. Balboa drained his glass and cast a longing glance at another bottle.

"What do you mean?" I said.

"You know about augurs, don't you?"

"Of course. There was a push to force the department to use them, but the Commissario put his foot down. They are all frauds."

"You are pretty sure of yourself, aren't you? Anyway, there are two kinds of augurs: public and private. The public ones are the ones charging big bucks for luring in the ghost bird of your dear dead uncle and making sure it pecks on the ghost-corn to spell out whatever message you want to hear."

"In other words, frauds."

"That is as it may be. But there is another kind: private augurs. Ladies—mostly ladies but some gentlemen too—who have the gift, as they call it. They are often shy about advertising it. Most don't need money, or if they accept donations, it's all hush-hush. But they are good, many of them are. And Anna Livia was."

I blinked. That was unexpected.

"So why is it important?"

Balboa apparently decided not to pretend to be sober anymore, pulling the bottle from under the table, and refilled this glass. The sharp smell of anise assaulted my nostrils. I may not have the nose for wine bouquet my father had wanted me to develop but I knew fortified raki when I smelled it. It's not called "Lion's Milk" for nothing.

"It's important because her husband didn't like her mucking around with ghost fliers. And the rumor is, one of them told her something she was not supposed to know. Something he did not want her to know."

I walked back home through the Flower Quarter immersed in thought. It felt good. For a moment, I was the old Rocco again, the hot upcoming detective out of the Training College, ready to take on the world and its malefactors. It helped that there were no ghost birds around. They don't follow the sun in the same way natural

171

birds do but there is a correspondence between the manner of death and the preferred time of manifestation. Ghost owls whose hooting at night makes children shiver and crawl under the blanket are supposed to be the spirits of murder victims, while ghost starlings, the spirits of stillborn and exposed infants, fly just before dawn. That was why in the first months after Bernadette's murder I had haunted the woods around my house, listening for owls or nighthawks. Useless, of course; even if they were around, I had no way to recognize the bird-spirit of my wife or to communicate with it. You need an augur for that.

But what could a ghost bird have told Anna Livia that put her life in danger?

Balboa had told me that Anna Livia used to give sittings for her friends and relatives, all belonging to the Five Hundred families. Apparently, she also charged a hefty payment for that, which was surprising considering her husband's position and reputed wealth. And in one of the sittings, she said something that eventually led to her death.

It was incredibly vague. Balboa was convinced that Marco de Luca was responsible for his wife's death despite his ironclad alibi. He had been seen by a number of people at the Peacock during the time of the murder. He could have hired somebody, of course, but why?

And then there was the disappearance of the twins. Everybody believed they were dead, thrown into the Styx through one of the many manholes in the Cloaca, so no search was ever done for their bodies. But why would a father order the assassination of his own children? The Five Hundred were very conscious of family lines, and the pressure to get married and produce heirs started early.

Speaking of which, I did not know if Marco de Luca had remarried. I normally skipped gossip columns, so my awareness of the goings-on among the rich and powerful was pretty sketchy. I decided to check this out.

The Via Rossa was crowded this late at night; johns perambulating up and down the gaslit street, peering at the girls behind their glittering curtains. Suddenly I heard a commotion ahead.

At one of the smaller windows, a man was struggling with security guards, yelling out a stream of obscenities. A scatter of broken glass lay on the pavement. I pushed through, pulling out my badge.

"Police! What's going on?"

One of the security gorillas reluctantly let go of the man. He was very young, a teenager. Good-looking, with jet-black eyes, white skin, and lips so red I suspected they were painted. In fact, I thought he was a working boy rather than a client. But what was he doing here? Boys like him had their own quarter.

"They are keeping my sister prisoner!" the boy shouted. "Tell them to let her go!"

"Whoa, whoa," a gorilla interjected. "We are a licensed establishment, no illegal trade here!"

"Where is your sister?" I asked the boy.

He pointed to the broken window. Crouching in the corner was a young girl in a skimpy sequined outfit, her long black hair falling over her face.

"My sister is not a whore!" the boy yelled. "She is an augur! We were trying to set up our own bird-speaking stall when these goons broke in and took Barbarina away."

I saw the goons exchange dubious glances. Something was wrong here: the Flower Quarter seldom had any difficulty in legally drafting young and stupid girls, so why would they kidnap one?

"Come here!" I commanded the girl. She uncoiled from her position and came over to the window. My jaw dropped. I had never seen a male and a female looking so alike. She and the boy could easily take each other's places with a simple swap of clothing.

"Are you Barbarina?" I asked.

"Yes, sir."

Her voice was higher pitched than the boy's, but she had exactly the same slummy accent.

"And is this man your brother?"

"Yes sir. He is my brother Renzo."

"He claims you are being held in this brothel against your will. Is this true?"

Tears flowed down her cheeks.

"They told me they would kill Renzo if I did not … if I did not do what they told me …"

I had heard enough.

"You two are coming with me," I commanded.

One of the goons stepped forward.

"You have no right …"

He shut up when he saw the police-issued pistol in my hand. I felt a rare flash of satisfaction; it was good to be a representative of the law, for a change.

I took the two of them to the station, where Gianna made tea and brought in some bread and olives. They told me their story, each picking up when the other fell silent. With my eyes closed, I could imagine it was one person speaking, using slightly different voices.

They grew up on a baby farm in the Cloaca, one of those places where whores, too kind-hearted to throw their newborns into the underground river, dump them to be slowly starved. But Renzo and Barbarina not only survived but flourished, relatively speaking, in no small measure due to the fact that somebody regularly paid a gold florin to the baby farm's owner to take care of them. They had no idea who it was and did not seem to be very interested. In general, they were so wrapped up in each other that I felt as if my words filtered to them through a layer of cotton wool.

Having outgrown the farm, they left it with the intention of making their own way in the world, using what they assured me was Barbarina's talent in speaking to ghost-birds.

"Can you do it too?" I asked Renzo.

"No," he said curtly.

So here was the first wedge between them that could eventually push them apart enough for each to develop their own personality.

According to them, while they were busy trying to set up a market stall, the goons appeared … and I had heard the rest of it before.

Now there was the question of what to do with them. I could not let them go; my detective's sense was telling me this may be the biggest case of my dwindling career. If I had to go out, I would rather go out with a bang. I needed to keep them where I could find them anytime. I could arrest Renzo for disorderly conduct, but it would mean separating him from his sister.

Eventually I did something entirely unprofessional but that was par for the course by now. My house in the woods was outside the boundaries of the City Below, on the border of the countryside where fields and vineyards interspersed with small villages stretched all the way to the limits of the world, abutting upon the Dome of Heaven. Bought with Bernadette's family money, it was as isolated and spacious as you could possibly have without living on the Forum Hill. Now its large rooms mocked me with their emptiness.

As we left the station, I asked them how old they were. They did not know.

Renzo and Barbarina ensconced in a spare bedroom, I no longer bothered to come to the station. Il Commissario sent me a letter requesting me to apply for an indefinite leave of absence without pay. Otherwise, the letter threatened "disciplinary measures." I tore it up.

I went to see Marco de Luca. The attempt was short-lived. His sumptuous marble villa surrounded by thickets of myrtle and rose gardens was patrolled by private guards. After asking them to bring my note to the Senator, I found myself out on the dusty road with my coat torn. To my satisfaction, one of the guards would probably sport a cast on his arm for some time. I did, however, show up at de Luca's election speech, mingling with the crowd of hangers-on and hoi polloi, and elbowing my way through to get a good look. The results were disappointing. He was just an inconspicuous-looking older man with a dusty receding hair line and gold epaulettes on his bowed shoulders. He was running for the Speaker of the lower chamber, and his oratory would put a nervy rabbit to sleep. I elbowed my way out.

I decided to talk to Balboa again. However, when I came to the rooming house, I found a group of black-clad women who were ceremoniously affixing an open birdcage above the front door. I addressed the oldest of them whose balding head seemed to suggest that her ghost-bird would be a vulture.

"Who died, mother?"

The crone hissed at me but relented when I shoved a couple of liras into her palsied hand. Being a professional mourner, she was not interested in the lives of those on the wing, only their proper burial rituals, but she was naturally curious, and what she told me was enough.

Balboa had been found dead on the floor of his shabby sitting room; rags stuffed into his mouth to suffocate him. That was a cruel way to die, but I had no illusions about the kind of people I was dealing with.

On my way back home, I stopped at the Church of the Holy Ghost. I had not been to a church since Bernadette's death and even before that, I had counted myself among agnostics: those who claimed that ghost-birds were just mindless reflections of the dead, fading away with time like a silver collotype. After all, wouldn't the Land be overrun by ghosts if all the dead remained around forever, circling between the ground and firmament?

But even so, when I stepped into the cool dusk of the nave with fluted columns marching away like slender tree trunks and the sweet scent of incense in the air, I felt a childhood awe wash over me. There was a giant painting of the Holy Ghost above the altar, cleverly lit up by the hidden electric lamps, and depicting a white dove whose outstretched wings covered the flat disc of the Land with the City Below in the middle, its white towers reflected upside down in the blue dome of the sky. The statue of the Holy Mother stood by the side, her head bowed, the swaddled form of the Redeemer in her arms. A bank of lit candles cast dancing reflection upon her porcelain face. I lit a candle for my parents whose ghost-birds never came back to visit me. I wanted to put up one for Bernadette but could not bring myself to do it. It would mean acknowledging that she was irrevocably gone.

At home, I found Renzo and Barbarina busy in the kitchen. They were whispering together but fell silent when they saw me. Using my meager larder supplies, Barbarina had made pasta e fagioli. I had to acknowledge that it was nice to have real food for dinner and to be able to share it with others.

This said, the twins were not great company. They were as jumpy as a pair of wild rabbits and shied away from any in-depth discussion of their past. However, after we shared a bottle of red wine, their tongues loosened a bit.

"Didn't the nurses at the baby farm ever tell you who your parents were?" I asked.

Renzo shook his head. He had seemingly appointed himself the twins' spokesman, while Barbarina was shy and withdrawn, fiddling with her long jet-black hair. Renzo's was shorter, which, along with the pitch of their voices and the slight roundness of Barbarina's chest, distinguished between them.

"No," he said. "They never talked about it. Most kids there didn't want to know anyway."

"Did you?"

He shrugged.

"We assumed our mother was a pricey whore. Paying for her brats with her clients' money."

"Is that what you think?" I addressed Barbarina.

"Our mother is dead," she said, for the first time lifting her eyes and meeting mine. I blinked. There was something smoldering there, wilder and stranger than Renzo's adolescent cynicism.

"How do you know?"

"I'm an augur."

She must have caught an expression on my face because she frowned.

"You are an unbeliever, aren't you? Well, how can you mistrust your own eyes. Look!"

She pointed to the window which I had unlatched and left open because the evening was sultry. There, among the bats noiselessly darting through the heavy air, was a ghost magpie. It landed on the stunted cypress in my backyard, observing us with its amber-colored eyes. One was noticeably brighter than the other.

I shrugged.

"I don't deny that these are shadows of the ones we lost. But they come with no message. They show up, sometimes for years, sometimes for days, and then disappear. Most people don't even know for sure whether a ghost-bird haunting their yard is the ghost of their dead parent or sibling, or of some stranger. I know some say they recognize their loved ones but ..."

"But you haven't," Barbarina finished for me. "She has never come back, right?"

I fidgeted. The conversation was getting uncomfortable. I was here to interrogate the twins, not the other way round.

"My sister can do it for you," Renzo said suddenly.

"Do what?"

"She can call the ghost-bird of the person you lost. And it will come. I know you think we are frauds. Slum-brats, trying to claw their way up from the gutter. But we have as much integrity as the fat cats on the Forum. My sister's gift is real. And she will do it for free. You helped us in the Flower Quarter, and we don't forget those who help us."

I had never seen a full séance. Before Bernadette's death, I had scoffed at the credulity of the easily fleeced fools. Afterward, it was just too painful. So, I did not know whether Barbarina's preparations were par for the course or something the twins had cooked up to impress their audience of one.

I cleared out my living room, taking out all the old junk that I had not had the heart to touch for months. There were no pictures of Bernadette, though. I had taken them away after her death. It was too much, meeting my dead wife's glassy collotype gaze. So how had Barbarina initially known that the person I lost was a woman? Well, that was not a hard guess.

Only a large oval table in the middle of the room remained, covered with a black cloth. I lit all the candles I could find. Even though the house had electricity, Barbarina insisted ghost-birds were averse to this new-fangled invention. It was her show.

And indeed, it was, as she came into the room wearing a long black robe that emphasized the startling pallor of her face. It would have been even more impressive had I not recognized the robe as a dustcover from my storeroom.

Renzo followed in his street clothes, carrying a large ceramic dish which I used to hold dry pasta. I felt like an idiot, hovering by the table, and trying not to laugh.

Renzo placed the dish in the middle of the table, and then the twins held hands and murmured something inaudible, their eyes closed. It went on for some time, and I was just about to call it quits when Barbarina opened her eyes and reached for the dish. Only now did I see that its rim was plastered with bits of paper, each inscribed with a letter of the alphabet. Two bigger pieces had the words "Yes" and "No" in sloppy handwriting.

Barbarina's hand hovered above the middle of the dish, and she made a gesture as if she was scattering something. I blinked, trying to convince myself it was an optical illusion. Dropping from her empty palm, seeds of corn drummed into the dish.

A trick. She must have hidden them in her sleeve; I've seen mountebanks at the fair doing the same thing....

A small pile accumulated in the center of the dish and with the tip of her index finger, she pushed the seeds around, so each letter had two or three in front of it. The "Yes" and "No" pieces had more.

And then the seeds started to glow.

It was faint but unmistakable. A pale glow that gradually grew warmer, becoming golden-yellow like the sunshine on a ripening cornfield. Each tiny pile coruscated with a jewel-like glitter.

My mouth fell open, and I saw a smirk of satisfaction on Renzo's face. It brought me back to reality. The twins were trying to pull something over me; and I had to be on my guard.

Barbarina spread her arms, the sleeves of her makeshift robes fluttering like a raven's wings. She threw her head back, her mouth gaping open. Her eyes rolled back inside her head.

And then a beat of intangible wings, and a bird flew into the room through the open window, alighting in the center of the table, its more-real-than-real presence transforming the rest of the room into a domain of faded shadows and random objects. We were accidental. The bird was the only one who had to be there, its presence definite and absolute.

It was a beautiful bird of a kind I had never seen before. The size of a crow, it had a bright-green plumage, shading off into lighter jade on its belly and deepening into emerald on the head and the tips of the wings. Its head was sleek and cocked inquisitively as it stared at us with its sloe-black eyes. Its tail feathers were long and slender, fanning out in the shape of a lute.

Barbarina's knees buckled, and she would have fallen had Renzo not caught her. Brother and sister clung together, and then Barbarina straightened up, shedding her trance in an instant. Suddenly she was quite businesslike as she addressed the bird.

"Dear Green Bird, thank you for coming again."

Again?

"This man wants to hear from his wife. Her name is Bernadette. Can you guide her to him?"

The bird hopped, its talons bunching up the tablecloth. Were all ghost-birds that tangible?

It dipped its beak in one fluid movement and speared the glowing seed in front of the piece of paper with "No" on it. It threw back its head displaying the prismatic feathers on its throat and gulped it down. A kernel of light traveled down its gullet. I just stared. I had never seen, or heard of, anything like this.

"Why not, dear Green Bird?" Barbarina insisted. "Has the ghost-bird of Rocco's wife been released from the cage?"

The bird performed the same pantomime, this time in front of the piece of paper with the word "Yes." Barbarina turned to me.

"Sorry," she started, "but you have to rejoice that ..."

She fell silent because the Green Bird was not finished. Hopping around the table, it pecked on glowing seeds, each corresponding to a letter, spelling out a name. The name I knew all too well.

*Stefano Costa.*

Bernadette's killer. The man I had pushed off the balcony of his fancy Forum villa when I crept in and saw the smirk on his face as he went through his collection of trophies: women's shoes, scarves, and undies. One of them was Bernadette's.

The situation was hushed up only because Costa's own family had gotten wind of his proclivities and contemplated putting him away somewhere in the countryside where he would not embarrass his Senator brother. But it did not mean that they had forgiven his killer.

I rounded on the twins.

"What the hell is going on?" I shouted. "Who put you up to this?"

"We do not ..." Renzo began but I had had enough. I lurched forward and grabbed the dragging tail plumage of the Green Bird, intending to wring the neck of this fraudulent overgrown chicken.

My hand closed on thin air.

The Green Bird turned its head to look at me and I swear, I saw a glint of amusement and something almost like flirting. And then it rose unhurriedly into the air, its wings making a tangible whirring sound, and disappeared into the night.

Stefano Costa had been a serial killer. It was Bernadette's bad luck that she crossed paths with him one bright morning when she sipped hot chocolate in her favorite café. Bernadette was open-minded; she would not shrink away from chatting with a male stranger if he was presentable and clever. And Costa was. That was how he had lured in his victims, whose exact number had never been established. I imagine he offered Bernadette a walk on the Via Libertad. Perhaps he offered her a ride home in his new car. There were very few cars in the city, all belonging to members of the Five Hundred. Bernadette would have been curious. She was a thoroughly modern woman, bright and inquisitive, laughing at the ancient superstitions and outdated rules of propriety. She would have accepted.

Bernadette never came home.

And now I was sitting in the waiting room of Senator Amato Costa, Stefano's elder brother.

He came out of the office deep in an animated conversation with a man I assumed was his secretary. He gave a start when he saw me, even though it was the first time we met face-to-face. It confirmed my suspicion that the Costa family had been keeping tabs on me.

He dismissed his secretary and stood before me. He was a big man, with what is known as the "classic" profile, similar to the carved statues of our illustrious ancestors. He cultivated this image by wearing an old-fashioned surcoat rather than a modern suit. From close-up, I could see a resemblance to his younger brother.

"Detective Rocco, I presume?" he asked.

I nodded. He ushered me into his office and closed the door.

"First," he said, "let me offer my sincere condolences at the loss of your wife."

I expected to hear mockery in his voice, but he sounded sincere.

"Your brother was responsible for my loss," I said.

"My brother was a piece of dung," the Senator said, "and I pray that his ghost-bird is being perpetually torn to pieces by celestial falcons to feed their hungry hatchlings. But this is over and done with. My brother is dead, for which the family thanks you. So, what can I do for you today?"

There was a reason Amato Costa was universally believed to be the next Speaker of the Senate. I could not but admire his sangfroid. So I cut to the chase.

"Marco de Luca," I said.

Costa raised an eyebrow.

"What about him?"

"You were one of the five club members who vouched for his presence at the Peacock on the day his wife was killed."

"Was I? I don't remember. It was a long time ago. But yes, I must have."

"Was it true?"

Senator Costa's classically carved nostrils quivered.

"I just confessed to you, Detective, that my brother was a killer. Why would I shield somebody who is neither a family member nor a friend?"

He had a point. I had done some research on the inner politics of the Five Hundred and I knew that the Costa and de Luca families did not get along.

"So who killed Anna Livia and abducted her children?" I asked.

"I don't know. And before you suggest that my brother might have been responsible, let me remind you that he was twelve at the time. Stefano was precocious but not that precocious. Also, as far as I remember, Anna Livia was not ... molested."

I winced. Reminding me what Bernadette had gone through before her death was meant to throw me off. But I had spent too many sleepless nights imagining her last moments to be easily distracted.

"I am not suggesting that your brother was responsible. I am suggesting you were."

When I arrived home late that night, the house stood dark and silent. The twins had flown the coop.

I opened a new bottle of Chianti and sat by the window, smoking and drinking. The sweet smell of star jasmine Bernadette had planted just weeks before her murder mingled with the smoke of my cigar.

I was convinced that by accessing my contacts in the underworld of the Cloaca I could easily pick up the twins' trail. They were too distinctive, too unusual. And despite their tough exterior, not street-smart enough.

But should I? I had no illusions that Amato Costa would not have me followed. Whatever I found out, he would eventually know too.

Our conversation kept replaying in my mind. When I accused him, he did not seem outraged or frightened. He was palpably amused.

"Really? You think I killed Anna Livia? You forget that if I and four other men provided an alibi for her husband, the very same men provided an alibi for me."

"I am not saying you killed Anna Livia yourself. You may have paid someone to kill her, but I doubt it. What I know for sure is that you arranged for her children to be kidnapped and raised at the baby farm. You paid good money to the nurses, so the twins would be treated well. One of the nurses remembers you."

The amusement on his face mutated into something I could not quite put a name on. Respect? Suspicion? Hesitation?

Finally, I realized what it was. Uncertainty.

Senator Costa poked his head out and told his secretary that under no condition should he be disturbed. Then he closed the door and turned back to me.

"You are good, Inspector. I used to feel sorry for you because of what a member of my family has done to yours, but now I am beginning to suspect I underestimated you. But you are wrong. I did not arrange for Anna Livia's children to be abducted. I saved them from abduction and certain death."

The story he told me made sense—almost. According to him, after leaving the club on that fateful evening, he went strolling on the Forum among the myrtle gardens and vanity vineyards. He saw a man hurrying away, carrying what he thought were two packages. And then he heard a baby cry.

"I ordered him to stop," Amato had said. "He was a ruffian, one of the Cloaca's professional banditti. I held a blade to his throat as he told me what he had been hired to do. He said he received a large sum of golden florins to kill a woman and throw her babies into the Styx. He had no compunction about the first part of his assignment; that was what he did for a living. But throwing babies into the underground river ... he was a superstitious sort and seeing a ghost-bird following him after he took the children away, he got spooked. He was still hesitating when I came across him, but the babies' crying and the weight of money in his purse was tilting the balance of his conscience. He was looking for the nearest pit when our paths crossed."

"Did you know who the babies were?" I asked.

Amato nodded. "Marco was the only one among the Families with recently born twins of opposite sexes. But I could not figure out why he would order such an atrocious thing. He seemed to be overjoyed when they were born. His family is dwindling; it's not like they had an overabundance of offspring."

"I see that you were not surprised that he ordered his wife's murder," I said.

Amato smiled. "Divorce is rare among the Families because it is both dishonorable and expensive. But in this case, it would have been all but impossible because Anna Livia was neither unfaithful nor barren. She was …" he hesitated.

"She was?" I prompted.

"She was an augur. And the things she prophesied put people on edge. Including her own husband."

They came for me at night.

I woke up even before I heard the smash of broken glass. Later I realized that there had been another sound preceding it: a stealthy, whirring, flapping sound in the dark.

I had my service pistol on my nightstand, but as I fumbled for it, they were in the bedroom, and I knew I was outnumbered. They had one of those new electric torches and shined it in my face, effectively blinding me. Still, I could see there were at least three of them.

I rolled off the bed, grabbing my pistol and trying to take aim. One of them fired first. The bullet grazed my cheek.

I fired back but I knew I missed. I was cornered between the edge of the bed and the wall. In a shootout, I was badly outnumbered. My only advantage was that I did not think they would want to leave a bullet-riddled bedroom behind. Their orders must have been to use discretion.

I took aim again into the blinding circle of light. And then it was not blinding anymore.

A flock of ghost-ravens materialized between me and my assailants, their oily black feathers sucking the light out of the air and rendering it dusty and dim. They cawed as they launched themselves upon the goons.

185

Ghost-birds cannot inflict material damage, but they never attack people anyway, and the fact that these did must have spooked those hired guns. Everything was lost in the melee of black bodies, milling shadows, curses, and an occasional thunderous shot. But I did not pause to see how it would end. I jumped out the window and rolled on my unkempt lawn, cursing my own negligence as nettles and thorny weeds whipped my naked arms and legs. When I reached the shelter of the hedge, I suddenly realized I could see pretty well, even though it was a night of the new moon.

Sitting on the hedge and shedding a pleasant emerald glow was the Green Bird. It—or should I say, she—cocked her head, and winked at me. And then she rose into the air, flying low to the ground and disregarding such material obstacles as lilac bushes and picket fences. Occasionally she would pause, hanging in the air like a hummingbird, her wings vibrating, and glance back at me to make sure I followed. I did my best to keep up, disregarding my rapidly growing collection of scratches and bruises. My cheek was bleeding from the bullet graze, but all in all, I counted myself incredibly lucky.

The Green Bird led me to an abandoned house on an empty lot where a solid middle-class neighborhood abutted the slums. There she rapidly rose, dwindling in size but getting brighter until she looked like a falling star reversing its descent. I tried to follow her with my eyes, but she was so bright that a network of ghostly shimmering lines imprinted itself on my field of vision. I blinked and it was gone, just as the Green Bird winked out of existence. I was back in the dark. Semi-naked and shivering.

But not alone. Two shadows separated from the house and came toward me.

"What took you so long?" Renzo asked.

The abandoned house was actually an opium den, but Renzo and Barbarina had gotten rid of the human flotsam that collected in the place.

"We asked them to leave," Renzo explained, "and they did."

Apparently, the twins' ghostly fame preceded them.

We huddled in the kitchen, drinking cheap wine and eating bread with olive oil. I had noticed before how escape from certain death improves your appetite.

"It was Amato Costa," I told them. "The man who saved you from the Styx and paid for your upbringing. He sent the killers after me."

"Why would he do such a thing?" Barbarina asked. She was still under the impression that people were neatly divided into good and bad.

"Because he told me too much."

"She was a powerful augur," Amato had said. "Once in a generation, or more. Nobody liked her, though; she was morose and blank-eyed, though presentable enough. As long as she did private seances for the bored wives of the Families, to convey simpering messages from the dearly departed, she was tolerated. But then she started telling all and sundry of the incredible revelation she received from the birds, it became too much. She wanted to come before the Council of the Families or if they refused to listen, to preach in churches. People should know the truth, she said. And this could not be tolerated."

"What was the truth she wanted to tell?" I asked.

"That the birds are not the dead. We are."

Did Amato believe it himself? I suspected he did not. But Anna Livia's supposed revelation was a useful weapon to hold against the Council if they ever interfered with his ambitions. It must have been the major reason he had saved Anna Livia's children, hoping one or both of them inherited her gift. At the very least, he could always pull them out of his sleeve in order to blackmail their father.

"The Green Bird has been coming to us since we were toddlers," Renzo explained. "She took care of us."

"She is our mother," Barbarina said placidly.

187

I nodded. I had already figured out that the Green Bird was the ghost of Anna Livia.

"How long have you known it?" I asked.

The twins shrugged. I already realized that their perception of time was blurred, imprecise; much like their perception of the boundaries of their identities.

"She told us she would take us to the City Above," Renzo said.

The City Above ... When Amato told me what Anna Livia had preached to her followers on the Forum, I laughed. This was as insane as any of the rantings of ragged haruspices on street corners, trying to pass off their wing-clipped magpies as avian angels.

"Didn't anybody ask her why we bother to eat and wash and use bathrooms if we are already dead?" I inquired. But Amato frowned, and I realized he was taking it far more seriously than I expected.

"Did you see those open cages the devout place above the entrance to the house where somebody died?" he asked.

"Sure."

"Well, what Anna Livia claimed the birds told her was that the City Below is our cage. We lived in some other place in previous lives, some other city, perhaps? But we are expiating our sins here. And when we die, we are actually released from the cage, and can fly away to our real city. She even claimed you can see that celestial abode, which she called the Eternal City, of the City Above, if you look hard enough at the firmament."

I frowned, thinking of the transparent bars and struts I sometimes thought I saw in the blueness of the sky. An optical illusion, of course.

"So why are the ghost-birds hanging around?"

"Because they have some unfinished business here."

And now talking to the twins, I mulled it over. Dead or living; perhaps it was a matter of perspective. Perhaps all that counted was that the ghost-birds flapped around the living, trying to attract our attention, to make us do ... what? Climb into the sky? Knock on the firmament?

Listen to them?

I looked at the twins, their identical faces splotched by the play of shadows. Now I knew why their mother had died. I had solved my last case.

But one question still remained, and it niggled at me like a piece of lettuce stuck between your teeth after a sumptuous dinner.

Why did Marco order his kids to be thrown into the Styx?

Even if he got spooked by Anna Livia; even if the heads of the more powerful families told him in no uncertain terms to silence his augur wife or else; why did he want his newborns to be murdered? The Five Hundred Families competed with each other in the number and health of their offspring. Barren wives were unceremoniously discarded. Renzo and Barbarina were rare: healthy, thriving, opposite-sex twins. Marco could have married somebody else and kept on producing more babies. Why hadn't he?

"Did the Green Bird always watch over you?" I asked.

The twins nodded vigorously.

"Always," Renzo said. "She can only speak through Barbarina, but she watched over us equally."

"She is our mother," Barbarina repeated, smiling.

"And who is your father?" I asked.

Their faces went blank; and again, I was struck by how coordinated they were, how eerily similar. Normal siblings, even twins, are not like that. Normal siblings ... human siblings.

"I don't know," Renzo finally said, but I saw ... something in his eyes. Suspicion?

I got up. "We need to find a better place to hide," I said. "The killers will search the neighborhood."

The sky was getting lighter. I squinted into the pinks and blues of the dawn. And again, I saw—or thought I saw—the transparent grid of struts and bars against the light. But now there was something else as well: a hint of glassy towers, a sketch of radiant walls. I blinked and it was gone.

"We will go to the Cloaca," Renzo declared. "I know a guy. He will let us stay for a while."

*And then what?* I wanted to ask. Amato and his goons would eventually flush us out. There was no place to hide permanently in the

City. The Forum had spies everywhere, from the mean alleys to the prosperous suburbia.

But there were still villages, like the one where I was born. I still had cousins there. They could hide us.

But Amato's killers would not let us be. They would hunt us down to the ends of the earth—literally. Would we have to take our last stand with our backs pressed against the dome of heaven where it touched the flatness of the earth?

I decided not to be morbid. We were alive for now; that was all that counted. Amato may have believed that we were dead, locked up in some purgatory cage for our forgotten sins. As long as my heart kept on pumping blood through my veins, I refused to entertain this idea.

As we left the house, I sidled up to Barbarina.

"You know, don't you?" I whispered. "You know who your father is."

She nodded. "The Green Bird told me," she whispered back. "She did not want Renzo to know."

*Children of the dead.*

I thought of the frescos I had seen in the Cathedral of the Holy Ghost. A woman in white, her face frozen in ecstasy, her eyes closed, and the outstretched wings of the white dove hovering above her. It was a tenet of our religion that the Redeemer of the City had been born of the Ghost Dove and had flown away to his abode in the sky when his mission was accomplished. Most people nowadays considered the story a metaphor. Only true devotees believed it to be factually true.

Was Marco among those? Or perhaps he simply discovered that the twins were not his and did not care about their provenance. He just wanted to get rid of the bastards.

For all I knew, the Green Bird may have lied. Who said that the dead were more honest than the living?

Renzo was walking ahead of the two of us when he stopped suddenly. I almost ran into him.

Among the trees of the neighboring overgrown garden, I saw a stealthy movement.

190

Amato's goons had not given up, after all.

"Down!" I whispered and flopped down on my belly into the dewy grass. The twins followed suit. If we could hide until the dawn, they would give up. People were beginning to come out, and hired guns were not popular in the mean streets of the Cloaca.

They seemed to be heading away from the hedge between the two gardens, toward the gate.

A dark shadow dropped out of the sky, fringed wings outstretched, yellow talons curving toward me. The bald vulture head flushed with dark blood. The muddy eyes framed by folds of inflamed skin.

I had seen those eyes before. I had met them when I had sent Stefano Costa, a serial rapist and killer, to fly over the railings of the balcony and into the void beyond.

The ghost-vulture inflated the scaly pouch of skin at the base of his neck. A croak was all he could produce, but in the morning hush, it sounded as loud as a shout.

The men beyond the hedge stopped. One of them turned around, his pistol aiming in our direction.

My own pistol was empty. Useless. The twins were behind me, hiding in the grass.

I got up and walked toward the killers, my hands up in the air.

"I surrender," I said.

The next words were drowned in the bubbling of blood as a bullet went through my trachea.

The air around me was as sharp and crystal-clear as ice. It was blue but with the kind of uncompromising blueness I had never experienced.

I stretched my wings. They were dappled in brown and grey, with smooth, silky plumage. A falcon? A kite? I never knew the difference.

I rose toward the crisscrossing grid of transparent struts above me. Now that my eyesight was attuned to a different wavelength, I could see clearly the flat disk of the Land below and the curving cage around it, imprisoning our small holding of the City. I tried to look up to see its counterpart: the Eternal City Above, but all I could see was the sky and the bars of the cage lining its painted dome.

What was the unfinished task that still kept me imprisoned? Or was the story a lie? Was there nothing else but the cage?

Below me, I heard hoarse croaking as a murder of ravens pursued a wounded vulture. Its feathers floated in the hard air, as the ravens mercilessly pecked and tore at Stefano Costa's battered wings. I hoped they would kill him, but can you really kill the dead?

I glanced back, noticing a flash of green among the oily raven plumage.

The ceiling of the sky was close above me, and I decided I would dash myself against it if no opening was in sight. Man or bird, I was not going to live in jail. I was a policeman. I put others behind bars.

A patch of blue detached itself from the underside of the sky, and as it did, I glimpsed, for the first time, something faintly outlined beyond it. A hint of towers; a glimpse of crenellated walls.

A bluebird dropped toward me; her wings outstretched.

"Bernadette!" I cried.

Bernadette banked as she approached, her wings touching mine.

# THE BONE FOREST

laia never came back.

Her stepmother sent her into the woods to bring back her little half-brother Alessandro. The boy came running in, rosy-cheeked and happy, holding a basket filled with goldenberries. He said his sister was just behind him; she had stopped to tie her shoes while he scampered ahead. But their parents waited until nightfall, and she did not come back.

Then her father Fede went into the woods to retrieve his eldest daughter. His wife Urrea begged him to wait until sunrise, pointing out that the woods were haunted by shapeshifting spider-owls, two-legged foxes, wolves with human tongues and other monstrosities. She also pointed out that she, her son, and her youngest daughter Nekane, who was just a baby at the time, would be left unprotected. She strongly indicated that Alaia was old enough to know what was good for her, and perhaps she had decided to run away. She even accused Fede of being more faithful to the memory of his dead first wife, Alaia's mother, than he was to his living family. He did not listen.

He went into the woods and never came back.

Nekane grew up and went looking for her half-sister whose face she did not remember. She went into the dark woods and met a spider-owl who tried to trap her in its sticky net; and an unctuous fox who tried to deceive her with its honeyed words; and a wolf who talked incessantly, but only nonsense. She found her sister and brought her back.

That was the story. But it was not true.

Nekane was a quiet girl who spent her days working at the spinning wheel, transforming fluffy batches of discarded sheep wool into the yarn that she then wove into sturdy cloth and cut and sewed into kyrtles and tunics. Her family spent the money she brought in but was embarrassed by her industriousness. She did not have to work. Her father Bittor was a village elder, and he expected his daughter to dress well, go to dances and parties, and eventually make a good match. But Nekane only wore the simple clothes she made herself, which she refused to adorn with ribbons and flowers like the other village girls did. She was so shy she hid in the attic when the family had guests. She had no friends or suitors.

Finally, the family gave in and allowed her to live in the attic room where she had her spinning wheel, her loom, and her sewing workshop. The room was small and cramped, barely large enough to accommodate the pallet where Nekane slept. But it had a window. And it opened out onto the Bone Forest.

Spinning her wheel or plying her shuttle, Nekane would gaze out into the green distance. Closer to the boundaries of the village, the woods were permitted and tame. They consisted of broadleaf tress—larch, ash, wild chestnut—and their sun-saturated glades and shadowy recesses offered goldenberries and mushrooms in summer, firewood in winter. But some distance away, the forest changed. The bright green of broadleaf gave way to the somber murkiness of firs and pines. Their dark-green pall covered the land that fell away in ridges and hollows like gargantuan pleats on a piece of fabric, all the way to the ghostly mountains in the west. The scar of a single road leading out of the village toward the King's Keep puckered the garment of the forest. Nekane never looked in that direction.

Stories of what lived inside the Bone Forest varied depending on the teller. Lads and lasses of Nekane's generation giggled about foxes who took human form and flashed their voluptuous naked bodies through the screen of ivy. Oldsters dispensed stern warnings against wolves who, in ages past, would venture into the village and carry away lambs and babies. Barn owls were pointed to as proofs of a much larger and more dangerous variety that lived in the depth of heartwoods. But for Nekane, the most fascinating of the tales was the one about the Bone Lady.

The tale which she had patiently pieced together from snippets of conversations at spinning parties for unmarried girl,s to which she would be reluctantly invited, was both simple and odd. It stated that somewhere in the middle of the Bone Forest stood a hut made of bones. It was not built on a foundation like human houses but was supported by two clawed bony legs that could carry it away wherever its owner wanted. The hut had no doors or windows, and inside it lived the Bone Lady. If she liked you, she would gift you gold and jewels. And if she did not, she would extract all the bones from your body and add them to her ever-growing abode.

For Nekane, the fascination of this tale lay not in the promise of riches but in the description of the Lady. She was said to have no face.

Nekane felt the same way about herself. She was nobody. People who talked to her, including her own parents, did not look her straight in the eyes, as if she had no eyes to return their gaze. When she was a child, she thought it was because she was ugly. But when her father brought a silver mirror from the market for her mother, Nekane slipped into the bedroom and studied her own reflection. Her mother had been a famous beauty in her time, and Nekane was sure her ugliness was fate's payback to the family. But she was surprised that the reflection displayed no obvious deformity. It showed a slight girl with freckle-dusted skin, sleek black hair, and hazel eyes. She was neither ugly nor beautiful; neither short nor tall; neither smart nor stupid. She was invisible. A quiet mouse, hiding in the attic, spinning her wheel. She embraced her invisibility. In her dreams, she saw the Bone Lady gliding among the towering trees, her face as blank as a polished slice of marble.

Occasionally she would imagine her brother coming back from the King's Keep and taking her away. Nekane was only eight years old when Alessandro had run away, but she remembered him making a ragdoll especially for her. It was more attention than anybody else had shown her in her entire life. Her parents had their youngest son, five-year-old Edur, to dote on, which was understandable: a son was a gain to his parents; a daughter, with her need for a dowry, a loss. Something had happened between her father and Alessandro that had led to the latter's name never being mentioned in the house. Nekane did not know what it had been and felt no pressing need to find out. She was indifferent to people, finding their interactions incomprehensible and tiresome. There was always something else underneath their spoken words, as if there was some other language she did not know. Alessandro was only a name, a vague idle daydream. She did not even remember his face.

Once Urrea, her mother, followed her to her attic room. Nekane was outraged; her room was her own, the only place where she could hide from the world's onslaught of loud noises and obscure emotions. Urrea started haranguing her about her "weirdness" and the need to be out and about in order to attract a suitor.

"Your father and I are working hard for you!" she yelled. "You are almost fifteen, and you have a dowry laid away in trunks, but nobody has knocked on our door asking for your hand! When I was your age, I was already married!"

Urrea's loud voice grated on Nekane's nerves like a screech of a rusty door hinge. She knew her mother was right, but this knowledge only made her angrier. Turning to Urrea, she yelled back, "You are not my mother! I have another mother who lives in the woods, and you stole me from her!"

Urrea's large face paled until it looked as white as a fish belly. She opened her mouth, then closed it. And then she turned around and marched out of the attic, slamming the door behind her.

Nekane was shocked. She did not mean it seriously: it was a spontaneous tale, born out of her frustration and embarrassment at her own lack of marriageability. Nekane sometimes had difficulties in distinguishing between truth and storytelling, but she had never actually thought she was a foundling. The resemblance between her mother and herself was unmistakable, though Urrea's bold handsomeness had somehow become Nekane's shy plainness.

But after this conversation, Nekane began venturing into the woods: first, early in the morning when the household was asleep, penetrating no deeper than a couple of paces into the damp green murk, her feet sinking into the mulch and releasing a pungent mushroom smell. Gradually she was emboldened. Eventually, she would go so far that the sounds of village life, the mooing of cattle and the shouts of farmhands, would dissolve in the whisper of the trees. But she never crossed the barrier created by faded yellow ribbons and streamers tied to a stand of gloomy firs that interrupted the light-saturated growth of ash, birch, and chestnut. The ribbons marked the beginning of the Bone Forest. That was where all the trails petered out.

One day she sneaked into the woods and walked so close to the boundary that she actually touched a faded yellow ribbon fluttering at the bony finger of a dark fir. The ribbon was discolored and frail, washed by rain and snow. It was late in the spring, and the woods were alive with white cow parsley, azure bluebells, and sunny buttercups. But beyond the line of firs, the ground was bare and covered with grey bark scales like ashes. The tip of Nekane's foot, shod in homemade woven slippers, nosed across the line, as delicately as a curious kitten. Nothing happened. She pushed her entire foot across the boundary, scattering rusty desiccated needles.

In the depth of the Bone Forest, an owl hooted.

Nothing surprising about it, perhaps, except that it was mid-morning. Nekane, spooked, ran back to the village. A couple of lads raking hay straightened up when they saw a girl's silhouette flit out of the woods. But they went back to their work when they saw who it was: plain Nekane in her plain brown kyrtle, which, as opposed to other village girls, she did not bother to decorate with ribbons, embroidery, or fresh flowers.

When Nekane reached home, she saw her mother trying to entice Edur into having his oatmeal. Mother and daughter did not acknowledge each other. Since Nekane's outburst, Urrea seemed to avoid her. Nekane went to her usual perch in the attic room, but she was distracted. The single hoot by an impossible daytime owl stirred something deep inside her. Her normally sluggish blood seemed to bubble with excitement.

Standing by the window, she stared into the woods, trying to see through the familiar play of light and shadow to what lay beneath. But there was only green and more green; a deceptively lush cover of the hidden bones of the land.

Restless, Nekane shifted her gaze to the dusty road winding through the woods toward the faraway King's Keep. Normally, the road was empty; only on market days would there be an occasional itinerant peddler's wagon making its creaky way to the village.

But now there was movement on the road. Nekane squinted into the green light.

A lone rider was entering the village, his glossy roan stallion and gleaming breastplate standing out from the familiarity of the farmhouses and barns like a shout.

The rider stopped by Nekane's house.

The commotion in the living room was so loud that Nekane lay on her bed in the attic, fingers in her ears, trying and failing to screen it out. The raised voices reverberated in her head like flashes of pain.

"You never wanted to have anything to do with us anyway!" Urrea said.

"Tired of collecting scraps from the King's table?" Her father Bittor.

"I want to see my sister!" A deep masculine voice, hoarse and unfamiliar, and yet making her shiver under her blanket.

Finally, it all died down, and she heard the clop of the stallion's hooves as it departed from the house. Her mother called her down to dinner, her throat clogged with tears.

Nekane went down and slipped to the outhouse, and then across the hedge in the back yard, and made her way to the inn called The

Bone Lady. The faded tin sign depicting a veiled woman in a white dress with an owl on her shoulder creaked in the rising wind. The roan stallion was being led into the stables by a serving boy. Nekane went into the bar, where early drinkers fell silent over their ale when they saw her. Eyes downcast, she made her way to the table in the corner.

The man stood up. "Nekane?" he asked uncertainly.

They stared at each other; the man's strangeness almost painful to her. He had a thin sunburnt face with an ugly scar on his left cheek. His clothes were expensively dyed but torn and poorly mended.

Nekane sat down, and the man ordered ale for her, to the consternation of the host. She could not drink it anyway; her throat was locked.

"You have grown up," the man said finally.

She nodded. It did not escape her that he did not add, "into a beauty."

"Why are Mum and Dad so angry at you?" she forced out.

Alessandro laughed.

"You mean that cow who gave birth to us, and that unctuous slimeball who married her? Bittor is not our father, Nekane. Now he has his own spoiled brat to dote on, so why would he need another man's spawn? I ran away the moment I could because I knew what they had done. And I came back to see what they were doing to you."

Nekane waited till nightfall to pack. She put on her plainest kyrtle, which she had woven and sewn herself out of pure lambswool. She tied her spindle, her needle, and her scissors in a carrier knot with a bit of bread. It did occur to her to take a kitchen knife for protection, but she decided against it.

She left when the night fell, and the full moon floated above the ragged line of the Bone Forest. Urrea's and Bittor's snores were coming from the bedroom.

Alessandro would be waiting for her at the inn, his roan stallion saddled and ready to go, to carry brother and sister back to the fabled King's Keep.

Nekane spared one glance at the pitched roof of the inn with its Bone Lady sign. And then she slipped into the woods, making her way to the fir barrier.

Moonlight turned the woods into an alien terrain of silver lace stretched between black columns. Something quick darted across Nekane's path. When she reached the ribbons marking the barrier, they seemed to writhe in the still air. She stepped across.

The fir grove drank away the moonlight, turning the woods into an impenetrable space of furry shadows. But Nekane went ahead, more by touch than by sight.

Suddenly something glimmered ahead: a faint greenish smear of luminescence that was not moonlight. To Nekane's light-starved sight, this was irresistible. She angled her path toward the glimmer. Fortunately, the denseness of firs meant there was little undergrowth to snare her. As long as she did not stumble over a fallen tree or fell into an invisible hollow, she was fine.

The glimmer grew brighter, even though it was still strangely self-contained, illuminating nothing but itself. It resolved into a web of glowing filaments, a delicate network of otherworldly radiance. It spread across the rough background of darkness like a giant spiderweb, studded with indistinct clods.

As Nekane came closer, she realized it *was* a spiderweb. A shaggy body hung suspended in the middle of the web, a lump of uncouth darkness. Then the body twitched and unfolded. Two long protrusions shot out from its sides, a rounded horned dome lifted up from its shoulders, bony legs fell down to the ground, grappling it with clawed feet. The owl stepped forward, still attached to its web by a bluish umbilical cord.

It was as tall as Nekane, and much more massive, though it was hard to tell just how much of this mass was fluffed hairlike feathers. The feathers had the same consistency as the web; or rather, the web was woven from the excretions of the owl's body, though they only began to glow at some distance from the trunk. The only spots of light in the owl's flat face were its saucer-shaped amber eyes with spindly pupils. Between them, a bony beak gaped open, exhibiting needlelike teeth. As the owl came closer, Nekane realized that it was unraveling as it walked, more and more of its soft body spinning out into its web. The web flared out, and Nekane saw what the shapeless clods were: the remnants of forest animals, badgers and hares and lynxes, drained and shriveled into desiccated hunks. Among them, the ivory skull of a child hung like a Christmas decoration.

Nekane backed off, but the owl flapped its vestigial wings, and suddenly, the web billowed forth, snapping around Nekane like a shroud. A wave of rotten stench mixed with a musty bird-smell made Nekane's eyes water. The web was torn in several places, hanging in tatters, but as Nekane tried to push her arm through, it contracted. The owl's amber eyes stared into Nekane's with the self-assurance of a predator.

Nekane suddenly felt as if a layer of grime that had muffled her experience for as long as she remembered herself was washed away. Every beat of her heart was clear and strong; every breath she took went deep into her lungs; every second was precious and irreplaceable. Even the stench, as sharp as a naked blade, was a call to awakening.

"Mr. Owl," she said, "my sister Alaia walked this way, and I follow in her footsteps. Please let me pass."

The web drew close, its sticky strands, beaded with glowing acid, brushing against Nekane's sleeves. The owl hooted as more of its body unraveled, spinning itself out.

'Mr. Owl," Nekane cried, "I will spin you a new web if you let me pass. You shed your feathers and pull your muscles, but I can deliver you from pain. Look!"

She untied the knot she carried her things in and took out her wooden spindle.

"I am the best spinner in the village," she said. "I can spin a web that will be the marvel of the Bone Forest. Let me help you."

The owl hooted uncertainly. And then it flapped its wings that were worn down to mere nubs by the unraveling of its fluffy body, and the web withdrew slightly. But it still curved around, imprisoning Nekane in its sticky barrier.

201

Spindle in hand, Nekane approached the owl. From close up, she saw that she was right in her assessment of the creature. It was a ball of living yarn, tangled filaments of feather and muscle through and through. Even its long, clawed legs turned out to be composed of braided fibers, the claws—hardened bunches of feathers.

Nekane took out her spindle and started spinning. Pulling at the living tendrils, she dropped the spindle and lifted it in the same smooth familiar movement that had soothed her since babyhood. Her entire life had been a lie. But this, the muscle memory of her fingers, the pleasure in seeing a mess of fibers resolve itself into an orderly thread; that was the truth.

The sticky liquid on the web burned her fingers; the stench of the owl's feathers burned her throat; but Nekane persevered. And when she was done, the web was no longer torn or tattered. Healthy and sturdy, it surrounded the owl like a halo. And the owl's feathery body fluffed out, retaining its glossy volume.

The owl stepped away, the web contracting, withdrawing into its body. Its light dimmed but the forest was no longer completely dark. The predawn sky pearled above the firs.

"Thank you, Mr. Owl," Nekane said.

Suddenly the creature stretched its vestigial wing toward Nekane. "Take a feather," it clicked. "If you need me, blow on it and I will come."

She pulled out a soft dappled plume and put it in her pocket.

For a while she stumbled through the tangled scaly firs, growing so close together that hardly an inch of free space was to be seen. The hem of her kyrtle caught upon a branch and ripped; her pinned up sleeves snagged on twigs. Nekane knew she could always repair to make new clothes, but it hurt to have her handiwork destroyed by the indifference of the woods.

And suddenly, between the trunks, she saw a space free of gnarly roots, and deadwood. Nekane found a trail. Winding between mounds of rotting needles and moss-covered boulders, the trail seemed too wide and well-marked to be made by animals. Surely, people had walked here!

The sky lightened to washed-out pinks and blues, and the moon paled into a watermelon seed, white and moist. The firs were coming to an end. Daylight was filtering through the widely spaced trees ahead. Was it the end of the Bone Forest? She felt the bile of disappointment rising in her throat.

But when she came to the edge, she saw that the Bone Forest went on, though its character changed dramatically.

The land fell away here, in a slope covered with brambles and thorny bushes. At the bottom of the ravine, a sluggish creek wound its way through the woods, overhung with slender willows. Beyond the creek, the land rose again in a shallow sweep, and the ridge bristled with broadleaf: ash, and larch, and hornbeam. The trail she had been following led down to the creek and miraculously, to a little stone bridge arching over the green water. It continued on the opposite bank, rising through the trees.

Nekane hurried down to the creek. A shape rose from the bushes, barring her way.

It was a girl, the same age as Nekane, and dressed in the same plain way. Like Nekane, she carried a bundle tied to the end of a small pole over her shoulder.

Nekane drew away, shocked. She had no friends her own age, and though she could not help but know every villager by sight, she did not understand why this girl looked so familiar. It took her a couple of heartbeats to realize what she was seeing.

The girl wore Nekane's face.

The same hazel eyes; the same black hair; the same faint dusting of freckles on the paper-white skin. Not only that: the girl's homespun kyrtle was the same brown grey as Nekane's, cut in the same way, and had rips and tears that corresponded to the damage done to Nekane's outfit by scrambling through the trees.

But as the first shock subsided, Nekane realized that the girl's supercilious expression looked alien to her. Surely, she never smirked like this!

And then a faint but unmistakable hint of red in the girl's sleek black hair told Nekane what she was.

"Lady Fox," Nekane said, "please let me pass. I am searching for my sister Alaia."

The fox-girl laughed. "Your sister?" she said. "You have no sister. You have two brothers: one you hate, and one who hates you. You hate little Edur because he took away your mother's scant affection. And Alessandro hates you because you are not beautiful enough to sell in the King's Keep and thus to restore his failing fortunes. Do you really believe he came to fetch you because he suddenly felt remorse for abandoning you after all those years? No, he came because you were of a marriageable age, and he hoped you would be pretty enough to bargain away. He was disappointed."

The fox-girl's voice was unlike Nekane's: shrill and high-pitched. Nekane rejoiced in that sign of their dissimilarity until she remembered reading that people did not hear their own voices in the same way others heard them. This memory distracted her from fully taking in the content of the fox-girl's words. Still, it was close enough to the truth to hurt.

"If this is so, Lady Fox," she said, "why is Alessandro waiting for me at the inn to take me to the King's Keep if he has no use for me there?"

"Are you sure he is?" the fox-girl countered. "You didn't see him there, did you, because you foolishly ran away to the Bone Forest. In fact, he is halfway back to the Keep."

Nekane bit her lip. She had no way of knowing whether the fox-girl was speaking the truth short of going back.

But wasn't it exactly what the fox wanted?

"But why would Alessandro lie to me about Bittor not being our father?" she asked. "There is no profit to him in such a lie."

"To tie you closely to himself," the fox-girl retorted. "An unmarried maiden has to obey her eldest male relative. If Bittor is not your father, this role falls to Alessandro who could force you into an advantageous marriage—or worse."

Again, the fox-girl's words were plausible enough for Nekane to experience them like whiplashes—sly, honey insinuations that stung like nettles.

*It does not matter,* Nekane reminded herself. *I know what I am doing. This is just the Bone Forest throwing its wiles at me*

She dropped her eyes, pretending to be upset and confused. It did not take much play-acting; just a tiny exaggeration of her actual feelings.

"Thank you for telling me the truth, Lady Fox," she whispered. "I see it now. My parents are disappointed in me, and I let myself believe Alessandro's deceitful words because they made me feel better. But now I realize it was all a lie, and he was trying to take advantage of me. He is no better than the rest of them!"

"You should go back," the fox-girl said. "Try to make peace with your parents, as they are the only ones who may take you back. Accept the truth, Nekane: nobody will ever marry you, and nobody will ever care for you. Your fate is to be a spinster; your abode will always be the small attic room until God finally calls you to His kingdom."

"It may be too long for me to wait," Nekane whispered. "What good is my life going to be? Friendless, loveless, forlorn."

"It's true," the fox-girl agreed eagerly. "Perhaps hastening to God's kingdom will be better for you, and for your family. A spinster is a burden on her parents. Look: this creek is cool and inviting; its water deep and dark. All it takes is a step off the bridge."

Nekane wiped almost-real tears.

"You are right, Lady Fox," she whispered. "I am no good to anybody. My life is meaningless."

She moved toward the bridge and the fox-girl stepped aside to let her climb onto the railing. Nekane paused as if struck by a thought.

"I may still do one last good thing in my useless life," she said. "I want to thank you, Lady Fox, for opening my eyes to the futility of my existence. The one useful skill I have managed to acquire is that of a seamstress. I see your kyrtle is as torn as mine. My attire does not matter anymore, but yours does. Let me repair the damage, and I promise your kyrtle will look as good as new."

The fox-girl hesitated, but one glance at the ugly rip in her long sleeve changed her mind. Foxes are fastidious animals; and in whatever shape they appear, they want to look their best.

205

"Do it," the fox-girl agreed.

Nekane took out her needle and thread and came close to the fox-girl to stitch the rips in her kyrtle that mirrored the ones in her own: right to left. From close up, she smelled the sharp hot vulpine smell emanating from the creature.

The needle flew in Nekane's fingers, obedient to her will. And before the fox realized what was happening, the kyrtle's sleeves were sewn to the bodice, and the hem was stitched tight around the ankles, incapacitating the creature. It gave an outraged hiss, as Nekane pushed it, and it toppled into the creek. The water licked away its false semblance of humanity, revealing the animal underneath: the long narrow snout with discolored needle teeth; the lice-infested red fur; the bald ears standing above the flat forehead. The fox struggled and mewled, but the sewn dress held it as securely as a sack. A mangy tail frothed the water as Nekane ran across the bridge.

The creature made a coughing sound as the soaked fabric dragged it down. A wave washed its mutating face, and for a moment Nekane saw her own features dissolving, desperate, and pleading.

She hesitated. Then she bent over the side of the bridge and lowered her pole. The fox grasped it with its teeth, and Nekane dragged the pitiful, dripping bundle onto the bank.

"If you do anything to harm me again, I will kill you," she said and meant it.

"I pay my debts." the fox rasped. "You saved me from death. Take a hair from my head. If you blow on it, I will come."

Nekane did as she was told and ran up the steep bank.

Breathless, she scrambled up the slope and, tearing through a stand of wild raspberries, found the trail again. It led her to an oak grove. It was not as dark here as among the firs, but the gnarly trees crowded her, their massive trunks and leathery leaves plunging her into an unsettling greyish twilight. Acorns peppered the trail, shooting from under her feet, as she tried to slow down her panicky flight. Eventually, Nekane needed to catch her breath. She sat down leaning against the fissured bole of an old oak and took out her bread.

Something dripped onto her shoulder. Nekane jumped up.

A long clownish face peered at her from above; a slinky grey body draped along the thick horizontal branch. The body was sparsely furred with discolored hair that made it blend with the chiaroscuro of leafy light and shadow. A long warty tongue lolled out, foamy saliva dribbling down.

Nekane, disgusted, rubbed at her shoulder and scowled at the wolf. "Come down, you lazy good-for-nothing!" she scolded the creature.

The wormy body uncoiled and slid down from the branch. The wolf stood before Nekane on his hind legs, his muzzle towering above her head. His front legs hung down awkwardly, ending in semi-human paws with long clawed fingers. His belly was pink and bald, his tiny penis flopping along his thigh, much to Nekane's chagrin. His face was an incongruous mix of human and canine: a muzzle protruding from beneath the large porous nose; the sad brown eyes with no white peering from beneath the bushy eyebrows.

"I am looking for my sister," Nekane said. "Will you show me the way to the Bone Lady's abode?"

The wolf bayed. His tongue snaked out and flopped on the ground, spraying foamy saliva. Nekane wrinkled her nose in disgust and stepped away. Surely, this ungainly creature was no danger—and no help—to her! The spider-owl tried to trap her body; the fox-girl tried to trap her mind; what could the wolfman do? Nekane could easily outrun him if he came after her.

The tongue curled on the ground like a pink snake, and Nekane stared at it, fascinated and disgusted in equal measure. It writhed and flopped; it unspooled from the wolfman's mouth like an endless run of ribbon; it fouled the ground with foamy saliva. And as it crept toward her, she heard voices.

Multiple and indistinct like the lapping of waves on the shore, the voices hissed and chatted. They mocked her. They told her she was not one of them. They spat and insulted and degraded. And they did all of this without any words. Their malicious inanity did not require any meaning. Just the rising wave of rejecting voices was enough to drown her.

Nekane pressed her hands to her ears, but it did not help. The voices were inside her brain, silencing any thought and any emotion, feeling her mind with the clatter of pebbles that was simultaneously unbearable and inescapable.

Nekane staggered and fell. For a moment, she tried to push against the noise and almost succeeded. She tried to get up, to scramble away from this dreadful onslaught of meaninglessness that was worse than any wounding words and any physical assault. But she could not. She was immobilized. The wet blanket of the tongue wound and tightened around her legs.

She tried to crawl away, but the tongue snapped like that of a lizard and dragged her back. And all the while, the mob shouted in her brain, casting her out and yet not letting her go. They needed an outcast, a perpetual victim, somebody to mock and revile. And she would be their target, simmering in the filthy saliva of their gossip for the rest of her miserable life.

Nekane fumbled in her bundle and pulled out her scissors. Biting her lips until they bled, she grasped the revoltingly warm tongue and snipped through.

The voices rose to a crescendo of hate that drowned Nekane in unconsciousness. When she came to, she was lying on the ground, the length of the pink tongue lying beside her like a leech, still feebly spasming as it bled. Nekane scrambled away, clasping her scissors and looking around fearfully. Surely the mutilated wolfman would come after her! Or was he dead?

At first, the oak grove appeared to be empty, but then she saw a slinky grey body trot from between the knobby boles and approach her.

He was no wolfman anymore. A spare canine shape nosed at the dying tongue on the ground and pushed it away with its clawed paw. He looked no different from the big dogs that the village shepherds trained to guard their flocks: a natural animal, cunning but not malicious. And blessedly silent.

The wolf yawned, exposing yellow fangs and the stub of a tongue.

"I am sorry I had to do it," Nekane said.

The wolf shook his head and wrote in the dust of the path with his paw.

"Men lived like parasites inside of me," he wrote. "You banished them. Take some fur from my tail, blow on it when you need me, and I will come."

Nekane did as she was told and went on.

And now the character of the Bone Forest changed again. The oaks did not disappear; on the contrary, they grew ever bigger and craggier, some as squat as they were tall. Their denuded branches clawed at the pale sky. Their sparse leaves lay on the ground, slate-colored and thick. When Nekane kicked one off the path, it clattered away like a piece of bone.

There were no more flowers, or clumps of grass, or moss. The forest had lost its green; it was now grey and brown and white. Even the light that dribbled through the lattice of boughs was the color of dust.

Nekane stopped by one of the trees that bent over the trail, almost barring it. Its swollen trunk was hung with fissured protrusions. She thought it was a burl until she saw the screaming mouth and the bulging eyes.

The deeper into the Bone Grove she went, the more faces she saw. They protruded out of the trunks as if trying to pull themselves out of the wood. Their mouths gaped; their eyes were screwed shut or bulged in fear; their necks were knotted with the effort to escape. But there was no escape from the trees whose contorted branches opened up in skeletal hands and whose gnarly roots ended in fleshless feet. Bones were everywhere, lying on the dead ground like fallen leaves.

Nekane was examining every tree-face, but she knew it was useless. She did not know her father's or her sister's face. Until yesterday, she had not known they existed.

"Our father Fede was a widower," Alessandro had told her. "He had an almost-grown daughter, Alaia, by his dead wife. I remember her making porridge for me. I liked her better than my own mother because she was kind and pretty and used to play hide-and-seek with me in the woods."

"Was Mother jealous of her?" Nekane had asked.

"Very. They fought all the time, Father and Mother. I hated it."

"I remember none of it."

"You were a babe in arms. Of course, you would not."

"What happened to Alaia?"

"She disappeared in the Bone Forest. Mother later told me I was with her, but I don't believe it. I have no recollection of going out on that day. I believe she had sent Alaia away and lied to Father. He went to retrieve his daughter and never came back. Bittor was already waiting in the wings; I swear they must have had something going on while Father was alive. They got married a month after he disappeared; Bittor had to bribe the pastor to get a special dispensation. After that, Mother insisted that Bittor was our father and that we had to address him as Papa. You did because you knew no better. I did because I had to. But I have always known it was a lie."

"So, I am the daughter of ... Fede?"

"Yes. And I am his son. We owe nothing to that slimeball Bittor. I left as soon as I was able to, but I came back for you, Nekane. You are my sister. We are both children of Fede, whose name has been erased by his faithless wife."

Nekane sped along the trail. The sky was different here too: the color of lead and with no sun to be seen. The light that filtered through the tracery of brittle branches was dirty and dim. The Bone Forest was plunged in a permanent dusk.

Finally, the trees fell away and Nekane stepped into a clearing. In front of her was the House of Bones.

Built of ivory humeri and yellowing tibias, the house stood on two skeletal legs that scrabbled in the dust as it shuffled around. It had no windows and no doors. Its roof, made of interlacing ribcages, was decorated by grinning skulls along the rim.

Nekane straightened up and addressed the House of Bones.

"Dear Lady," she said. "I have come to bring my sister Alaia home. Please let her go."

The house turned around. The front wall was as blank as the back but as Nekane watched, the two clasped skeletal hands in the middle unclasped and pulled the vertical rails of tibias aside, creating an opening into the darkness. A ladder made of ribs clattered down and a small figure stepped out and onto the first rung. As she reached the ground, she seemed to have grown bigger.

The Lady faced Nekane—or at least, Nekane thought she was looking at her through her impenetrable veil, though it was as blank as the bone walls of the house. The woman, no taller than Nekane herself, was dressed in a torn and smudged frock that used to be white but was now yellowed and specked with bone dust. Her hair was hidden under a linen headdress with a heavy curtainlike flap of fabric in front.

Nekane bowed and repeated her request.

The Bone Lady was silent for a long time until Nekane thought she had no power of speech. But then a voice, rusty from disuse, issued from behind the veil.

"I am Alaia."

Alessandro knocked on the table with his empty tankard, asking for more ale. The host's lips thinned but so far, Alessandro had paid his tab, so there was no reason for the innkeeper to feel antsy. Except, of course, that the innkeeper, like everybody else in this shitty little village, was apprehensive of strangers. He did not recognize Alessandro. Not many did. Taking the King's coin for the last six years had changed him considerably.

He drained his ale and stared morosely out the window. She had not come. And now Alessandro was confronted with a choice: go back to the Keep with his tail between his legs or wait some more. The third option—going back to his mother's house and confronting the family again—was too unpalatable to consider.

Somebody plunked themselves down on the bench in front of Alessandro. He lifted his eyes and coughed furiously as the dregs of the ale went down the wrong way.

"We need to talk, son," Bittor said.

Alessandro regained his wits.

"I am not your son!" he hissed. "Don't call me that!"

"You called me Papa for a while, if I remember correctly."

"I did not know any better. You and my bitch of a mother killed my real father!"

Bittor sighed.

"I know you believe this nonsense but it's not true. I confess that I was not heartbroken when Fede disappeared. Your mother and I ... well, we had a thing going on. It's true. But I am no killer, though I would be justified in giving him a good beating. You may not remember it, but Fede was a brute and a drunkard who mistreated his eldest daughter and his wife. He was partial to you, his son, but it was only a matter of time before he started on his youngest children."

"You are lying," Alessandro said but he did not sound at all confident. Fleeting images like dissolving dregs of a nightmare floated through his head: a man's face purple with rage as he yells something incomprehensible; a girl cowering in the corner, her hands over her head; his own tiny body squeezed under the table as he hides from the tempest of filthy words and broken crockery raging through the house....

"I am not," Bittor said. "Alaia left because she could no longer stand her father's abuse. He went looking for her because he felt guilty. I hope he was taken in by the Bone Lady, who yanked out his skeleton and used it as scaffolding. After I married Urrea, I swore to myself that I would treat my family right. I tried to be a proper father to you. I never laid a finger on you, did I?"

Alessandro stared into his empty tankard. He said nothing; but his silence was all the answer Bittor needed.

"You are a man now," Bittor continued. "If you have decided to make your own way in the world, it is your right. No matter how your mother and I want you back, we cannot keep you by force. But please, leave Nekane alone. Don't try to tempt her away with your tales. Let her stay with her family where she belongs."

"Nekane is my sister!" Alessandro responded. "She is Fede's daughter, as I am his son!"

Bittor shook his head.

"You are Fede's son, true," he said, "and I am afraid you have inherited your father's temper. But Nekane is not his daughter. She is mine."

Nekane gaped at the Bone Lady. She had believed the Lady was keeping her unknown sister hostage. It had never occurred to her that Alaia could be staying in the Bone Forest of her own free will.

"Can I see your face, then?" she asked dubiously.

"Don't you believe me?" the veiled woman asked. Nekane could hear anger, and something else as well: strange overlapping echoes, as if more than one voice spoke from behind the veil. "I am Alaia."

"You are my sister?" Nekane repeated incredulously.

"Don't you believe me?" the Lady repeated, and the echoes multiplied, tripping over each other. Nekane thought quickly.

"Of course, I believe you, Lady," she said, bowing. "But I have not seen my sister's face since I was a babe. I braved the dangers of the Bone Forest to gaze at it again. May I be vouchsafed this privilege?"

The Bone Lady hesitated, and then with a jerk, she lifted her veil.

A rounded blank surface like the eroded brow of a boulder stared at Nekane with no eyes. The pale mushroom-like flesh rippled slightly, and faint outlines of features seemed to surface and then be absorbed again into the undifferentiated softness. The voices issued from behind this wavering curtain of blank skin.

"Do you recognize me now?" the voices sung spitefully. "Little Nekane, little bastard! Don't you recognize your big sister?"

"I came here to release you from captivity," Nekane whispered.

"Captivity? I was never captive, little Nekane. Your whore of a mother and my drunken fool of a father, they were the ones who held me prisoner. I escaped. My father went after me when he realized he had lost his punching-bag of a daughter. Of course, when I caught him, he swore he was remorseful over his outbursts. He begged forgiveness for slapping my face. He wanted me to come back. He was still pleading with me when I pulled out his bones and planted his face on one of my oaks."

"You killed our father?" Nekane whispered. "Why?"

The faceless woman laughed.

"Our father? He is not your father, little Nekane. You are a bastard. Your whore of a mother, whom my father married after my mother, his true wife, died of swamp fever, played around with a smarmy shopkeeper. I saw them in the barn and told Fede. And what do you know? Instead of thanking me, he slapped me. He yelled at me. What should I have done, what do you think?"

Nekane bowed her head. Everything she knew, or thought she knew, about herself was changing, bits and pieces rearranging themselves like the broken ice on a frozen lake.

"Was he a violent man, then?" she asked.

The faceless figure shrugged.

"No worse than other men. No worse than other people. You haven't learned your lesson, little Nekane, whose name means 'sorrow'. Sorrow is what other people bring. Families are monsters that swallow you alive, and grind you down, and spit you out. You came to the Bone Forest looking for solitude because only in solitude can we be ourselves. And this is what I will give you. Your bones in my house; your face on my trees; your voice in my mouth."

"I don't want it!" Nekane cried. "I thought I would find a sister! I thought I would find a friend!"

"You are no sister of mine," the Bone Lady responded, "and as for friends, who needs them?"

And coming closer, the skin curtain on the faceless visage twitched and drew apart, and Nekane saw a raw weeping surface with clusters of mouths, all moving their lips in unison, spitting out hatred. The voices of men and women absorbed into the self-consuming vortex of resentment that was the Bone Lady. Her wasted hand reached out to Nekane, and she felt the bones in her body creak and strain as they tried to wriggle out of the covering of the flesh.

"You see what I have overcome," the voices whispered, and trilled, and hissed. "Nobody will ever look at me again with anger, or lust, or contempt. The faces of my enemies decorate my trees; their bones build my home; their names are forgotten; their lives are erased."

Nekane backed off, but she was struggling against herself, her muscles pulling against her bones, her body wracked by an internal strife. She fell to her knees. The Bone Lady approached.

Nekane reached into her pocket and drew out the feather that the spider-owl gave to her.

"Mr. Owl," she cried. "I spun your web; please help me!"

A thunderous flapping of wings above her head; a momentary darkening of the glade as fleeting shadows swept over it. The spider-owl came, and he did not come alone. A flock of greyish-brown fluffy bodies descended upon the Bone Lady, spinning their sticky webs and throwing them like lassoes, trying to ensnare her.

The many mouths of the Bone Lady screamed, and the piercing sound went through Nekane's head like a javelin. Pressing her hands to her ears, she staggered out of the glade and onto the trail. Casting one last glance over her shoulder, she saw that the scream had felled some of the spider-owls, who flapped desperately on the ground, tangled in their own webs. But one was still aloft, still trying to stop the Lady. Muttering thanks, Nekane ran.

She slowed down when she reached the oak grove. Somewhere here was the tree with her father's face on it. Her father? Alaia had said she was Bittor's daughter. Could she believe her?

Even if she could, what difference did it make? Her past life flashed before Nekane's eyes, rearranging itself like pieces of colored glass in a kaleidoscope. Bittor had been good to her. He was not the perfect father of her dreams, but he was who he was, and he tried his best by providing for her. She should be grateful for this.

Still, the man who had presided over her birth was here somewhere. Should she try to find his face?

A noise like the lapping of waves upon the shore came from behind, and Nekane felt the sickening tag of bones trying to burrow their way out of her skin. She looked back.

The Bone Lady sped down the trail, her filthy white gown hung with spider silk.

Nekane pulled out the fox-girl's clump of fur. "Sister Fox," she cried, "I would not let you drown; please help me!"

Another wrench that almost tore her joints apart. The skin on the Bone Lady's featureless visage twitched, and grinning mouths surfaced and went back under like darting fish in a shallow pond.

A bundle of orange energy bounded down the trail.

The fox was in her natural state, not wearing a borrowed human form. A fluffy red vixen, she leaped at the Bone Lady, her needlelike teeth bared, going for the jugular. The tug on Nekane's bones slackened. She staggered to her feet and ran, pausing only to catch a glimpse of the writhing white-and-red pile as the Bone Lady tried to fend off the attacking animal.

And now she was at the creek, its stone bridge within reach. Nekane realized that beyond it, she would be in the familiar terrain, close enough to the boundary of the Bone Forest to reach the village before sunset. Even though the inflamed ball of the sun was touching the spindly fir tops, there was still time for her to reach safety.

She stepped onto the bridge, and it shuddered and lurched under her. A sickening crack made her gasp and hold onto the railing for dear life. The bridge, so well-made that it had stood for hundreds of years, was tilting and falling apart; the stone, which is the bone of the earth, was splintering under the alien drag.

Nekane looked back. The Bone Lady stood on top of the bank; her dress no longer white but stained with blood. A red fluffy tail was bound around her shoulders like a trophy. Her mouths screamed in rage.

The bridge creaked and listed, flakes of stone peppering the placid surface of the water. Nekane clung to the railing but felt it wriggle out of her slippery hands like a snake. At least her bones seemed to work in tandem with her muscles, not rebelling against the body that housed them. Either the Bone Lady did not care to absorb her false sister anymore, or she could not exert her magic upon stone and bone at the same time.

Nekane realized she was going to drown. With trembling hand, she reached into her pocket. The disintegrating bridge buckled like a maddened horse trying to shake off its rider.

216

"Brother Wolf," Nekane cried. "I delivered you of the screaming voices in your head; please help me!"

"Bastard!" the many mouths of Alaia cried. "A cuckoo! A whore's get! Die!"

A grey slinking shape trotted from behind the Bone Lady.

Like the fox, the wolf had reverted to its natural shape: a mangy thin animal with shifty eyes and lice-ridden fur. But as an animal, it knew cunning and stealth. It knew how to feed by lying in wait and attacking its prey from behind. It was no longer distracted by the fug of alien words and alien thoughts. Its life was simple: track, hunt, kill.

And it did.

Leaping upon Alaia from behind, it sank its teeth into her throat. A fountain of blood sprayed the animal as it worried and shook its prey.

The white-clad form collapsed upon the ground. The mouths stopped their screaming. The residual tug upon Nekane's bones snapped.

The featureless head turned toward her, and human features rose from beneath the white moist skin like an archipelago after an earthquake: a sharp nose, a thin mouth, large brown eyes. For the first and last time, Nekane looked at the face of her stepsister.

The wolf dipped its muzzle and began to feed. Turning away, Nekane scrambled over the ruins of the bridge, and plunged through the firs, tears drying on her face.

Alessandro saddled his roan stallion and put water and food into the saddlebags. Everything was ready. Still, he lingered by the inn, staring in the direction of his childhood home that, he knew, was no longer his and perhaps had never been.

He wanted to see Nekane one last time. Bittor's revelation that they were only half-siblings should have changed his feelings, but it did not. He had come back to the village hoping to find in Nekane an ally in his quest to avenge their father. Now it no longer mattered. Bittor was not an ogre but a pathetic little man, trying to do his best for his strangely blended family. His mother was not a whore and a traitress but a silly woman mourning her lost beauty. And Nekane was his sister, no matter who her father was. When they had met after all this time, the little girl had become a fearless and curious woman, an ally he could use in the cutthroat world of the King's Keep. And when he saw her needlework, he realized she could make both of them rich. Here in the village, she was derided as a spinster. At the court, she would be famous, and the fine ladies would be vying for her dresses. That was why he had wanted her to come with him. And she had seemed eager. But he had been waiting for twenty-four hours and she had not come.

Alessandro put his foot in the stirrup when he heard a voice calling his name.

Nekane ran toward him. She looked like she had been dragged through the hedge backward: her kyrtle in tatters, her hair undone, her headdress missing. There were bloody scratches on her face. But she promptly leapt into the saddle behind him.

"Let's go!" she breathed.

She was breathing heavily, and Alessandro forbore asking questions until they were on the road, and the buttery moon floated above the treetops of the Bone Forest.

"Did you say goodbye to Mother and … and Bittor?" he asked.

Nekane laughed; and her voice was as hollow as a rattle of bones.

"I have not said my goodbyes to the people who were responsible for my conception," she said. "But I did see our sister Alaia and bid her farewell. Pray that you and I shall never have to part like that, brother."

# WINGS

She walked the empty streets of yet another town, walked slowly, because her glass shoes—the last, the very last pair, she hoped—were clouding with blood that seeped from her raw feet. At first she thought it was early in the morning because there was no sun in the milky-white sky. But then she realized the transit had deposited her in a fifth-time zone. She spotted a small café and went in. A slovenly waitress, her coarse black hair falling in a solid mass onto her stooped shoulders, brought her a cup of spicy coffee and a stale puff pastry.

Pounding music filled the cavernous room, coming from some clunky mechanical contraption she instantly despised. She was idly looking out the window, sipping her coffee (not bad, after all) when a group of laughing schoolgirls passed by. One of them looked back, her eyes the color of the sky over Thebes. Was it her daughter? She swallowed the familiar grief. No use wondering. Her daughter might pass her now and then in one of her myriad disguises: a laughing urchin, or a majestic swan; a swirl of fresh snow or a piano tune; a slim borzoi or a lady in a dress worth a kingdom's ransom. And she would never know, never recognize her own flesh and blood or be recognized by her.

She got up and went into the bathroom at the back of the café. Standing in front of the cracked mirror, she dragged a plastic comb through the tangle of her yellow curls. In proper sunlight they still shone like gold—the coin with which she had bought her immortality. Her beauty had not withered in her endless peregrinations but grown refined, her slender body pared down to the pure architecture of her bones. Her eyes were of an even purer blue than the eyes of the schoolgirl but her skin had been burnished by the sun so that she looked almost like one of those barbarian slaves who used to serve in the Temple of her mother-in-law.

Never mind. When she found her husband, it would all be restored. Her love, her daughter, her complexion. Her world.

She washed her face, adjusted her tatty jeans and, hoisting up her backpack, went out. In some fifth-time zones periods of light and darkness chased each other around like fighting cats, but here the white dusk just went on and on.

She considered her options. The latest instructions, coming from her mother-in-law in a dream, as maddeningly vivid as it was obscure, seemed to suggest she had to cross a desert. Was it in this zone or the next one? Was it really a desert or some oblique symbol based on one of those childish word games the immortals were so fond of? This was so much more difficult than the first time because there was no set task to fulfill, no definite obstacle to overcome, nothing except those horrible glass shoes, two pairs of which had already shattered on her travel-worn feet. There should be three pairs to wear out but what if the bitch, in a senile fit of pique, had decided to multiply the sacred number or had forgotten about it altogether? There was nobody to restrain her now, no higher authority to appeal to. The others were … She closed her eyes and saw giant lumps of mossy rock vaguely resembling human shapes hunched over their petrified banquet table.

The street was deserted. She suspected that were she to go back to the café she would find it deserted as well. She plodded on.

The sullen quiet was broken by a flapping sound. Startled, she looked up. A flock of birds wheeled over her head, their plump bodies and pointed wings black against the colorless sky. Her heart gave a leap. Doves, her mother-in-law's flunkeys!

The doves alighted on the sidewalk in a perfect circle with her at the center. She was surrounded by pearly-grey bosoms and unblinking eyes the color of blood. Their cooing drummed in the dead air.

"What do you want?" She shouted, enraged. "Spying on me? Go tell that bitch I won't give up!"

No response but something did happen: a sudden shift like an intangible gust of wind. The doves stepped forward, hemming her in. No, they did not. The circle was shrinking because they were growing.

Was there no end to her tricks? Wearily amused, she watched the doves balloon out. They became the size of chickens, eagles, ostriches. And still they kept on growing. Suddenly she was not amused any more. The acrid smell of bird-shit clogged her nose. The doves loomed over her, their stubby beaks drooling. She drove her fist into the nearest bird-breast but it drowned in the flea-infested down. The cooing rose to an unendurable pitch. She felt a sharp pain in her left shoulder and then a hot trickle of blood down her back.

"You can't do it!" She yelled. "It's not part of the bargain!" But even as another peck penetrated her sleeve, she remembered that there had been no bargain.

She managed to push through what felt like a barricade of frowzy pillows and was running down the street when a thunderous whirring above made her realize the giant doves had taken to the air. Splats of guano fell around her like acid rain. She covered her head and angled toward the nearest house. But then the swirling of agitated air buffeted her, lifted her off her feet and slammed her against the hard pavement. From the corner of her eye she saw a larger shape swooping down among the cloud of panicky giant birds. And a dark curtain fell over her, cutting off the anemic light.

She came to lying on something warm and gritty. Sand. Sand and the sea; the deep aquamarine glow; the familiar tang of salt like a message from home. She sat up and saw an empty beach fringed by the dazzle of placid wavelets.

Turning around, she discovered a man meticulously going through the things in her backpack. She opened her mouth to protest when he looked up and shook the pack open. It had been reduced to a torn rag.

The memory of the confrontation with the doves made her wince. So undignified!

"Are you OK?" the man asked.

She looked at him closely. Medium height; dressed in faded army fatigues. Black hair, dark eyes, eagle-face: all strong angles and hard restless lines. Some of them were due to age; older than he seemed at first glance.

"Have we transited?" she asked.

He shrugged.

"If this is what you call it. We're in a different place."

"Different zone," she said.

She looked around. The beach continued inland, dotted here and there with clumps of succulent plants and then rising into the folds of sand dunes. The air was balmy and crystal clear.

"Are you hungry?" he asked.

She nodded. He spread a tablecloth on the sand and placed on it two apples, a flat loaf of white bread, a water flask, and some stewed vegetables in a tin can. She would not eat apples because they were her mother-in-law's fruit. The tinned stuff was repulsive for a different reason but she was ravenous.

She caught him staring at her and smiled inwardly. The magic was there; it was just the matter of using it properly. When the quest was over; when she sat on the golden throne and held the water-mirror; when the scattered pages of *Theogony* were put in the right order ... everything would be as it should be. Again.

"What's your name?" she asked.

He shrugged. "I don't know. Since I found myself in this ... this," he made an expansive gesture, "I don't know who I am. Sometimes I suspect I must be dead or dreaming. It's not my world, that's for sure."

"It's nobody's world," she said.

"What do you mean?"

She brushed the crumbs off her shirt and stretched, aware that the movement set off the swell of her breasts.

"The gods have died. Most of them, anyway. When I was a child, I was taught the universe is a book written by the gods and each has a chapter to him- or herself. Well, the writers are dead, and the book has been torn apart. You have zones now, pages randomly glued together. And we are moved across them by chance or malice."

"Malice?"

"As I said, not all of them died. Too bad."

He looked sharply at her. (*He really has interesting eyes,* she thought, *but the wrong color. He cannot be a Hellene.*) He shook his head.

"So somebody must set it right!"

"Yes," she said. "Somebody must set it right."

For the rest of the afternoon, they explored the beach. They climbed to the top of the dune and discovered a semi-desert scrubland. There was a tiny spring surrounded by low bushes with leathery leaves. So they had fresh water, and the soldier's pack contained more tins. She made a face.

"It's very ingenious," he said in an aggrieved voice. "They keep forever."

"It's a barbarians' invention," she said. "They work in metal and smoke and create things that cough, and spatter, and stink. We make things of beauty."

They bathed in the sea. As she swam, she felt the gentle nudging of rainbow fish whose school followed her around. A dolphin came and smiled at her with his clownish mouth. And when she came out, water streaming down her perfect body like liquid draperies, she felt the warmth of the soldier's gaze on her skin.

He told her about his wanderings. Some zones he mentioned seemed familiar but most were totally strange. A white city with straight boulevards shaded by broad-leafed trees—but the leaves bled, the sidewalks twitched, and the buildings were subdivided into tiny chambers like nautilus shells. A world of purple dusk populated by midgets with scarlet mouths and dead eyes. Dragons with blunt scaly faces, their heavy dewlaps sprinkled by fresh blood as they fought over the carcass of an emaciated woman.

"The Chaos is rising again," she said.

It turned out he kept a diary. After some prodding, he took it out, a large notebook in a scuffed leather cover, and opened it with a bashfulness she found endearing. Uncomprehendingly, she looked at the twisted characters running across the page.

"I can't read this," she said.

"Aren't we speaking the same language?"

"Probably not."

"How come we understand each other?"

"Maybe it only seems to us we do. Or maybe with all the world-pages mixed together we all have the gift of tongues now. Anyway, what's that?"

"A poem," he said. "I found it in the ruins."

"What does it say?"

"The love that moves the sun and other stars."

"Yes!" she exclaimed. "Yes, this is exactly right!"

The sun was dropping toward the clear slash of the horizon separating the silver sea from the rose-tinted gentle sky. He put his hands on her shoulders, pulled her close and kissed her. She was gratified by this acknowledgment of her magic but that was enough for now, and with a tiny twitch of her finger she made him release her and shrink away. Seeing a mortified expression on his face—he, of course, felt that it was some failure of his manhood—she relented.

"I'm a virgin," she said.

He blushed and stammered an apology.

She laughed.

"I have a husband and a daughter. But this is one of her cruel jokes. When you have Hymenaeus for a brother-in-law, it does not take much to restore your maidenhead."

"Hymenaeus?"

"God of marriage, he calls himself. Prurient pasty-faced little bastard."

"And you are…?"

"I'm Psyche."

The sun hung just above the horizon, a soft orange ball amidst the glory of gold, velvety grey and royal blue.

"I've heard your story, a long time ago."

"All the stories are mixed together now that *Theogony*, the Book of Gods, has been torn. Time is broken. Chronos' body had been dismembered, the pieces scattered."

"What I know … you were the beauty of the family and your father sold you.…"

"I met her, that Beauty who married the Beast. She's not as pretty as she thinks. No, my father loved me and even my sisters.… They envied me, true, but I don't think they ever really wanted to hurt me."

*The smell of olive oil, and the blue shine of the cloudless sky, and her bare feet pattering on the marble, and her sister's scornful voice "You think you're so pretty!" and her own triumphant laughter. "I am!"*

"Our family was rich, and our city was old and prosperous, and beginning to get paunchy round the middle. Like a middle-aged man, abandoning his wife and falling in love with a teenager. They looked for a new goddess and found me."

"They worshipped you?" He sounded scandalized by the idea, and she thought: *he's a barbarian, after all.*

"Yes. It's not unusual. It wasn't the first time a girl was chosen to be crowned and anointed in the Temple. But nobody expected her wrath."

"Her?"

"The goddess of love. The ruler of nesting doves, spawning salmon, rutting deer and nursing babies. The Queen of the world. Aphrodite. My mother-in-law."

"Why does she hate you so much?"

"Because I'm more beautiful than she is."

He looked at her with those strange deep-seated eyes and she felt a shiver of disquiet run down her spine. What was it? She did not know; she was not good at categorizing ambiguous emotions because for so long she had lived within the simple clear-cut lines of love and hate.

"You are the most beautiful woman I have ever seen," he said quietly.

She turned away, staring into the molten gold of the horizon.

"I'm sorry," he said. "I shouldn't have…. You are married."

"Marriage is a human thing. Gods don't care. Nature does not care. As long as babies keep coming … this is all that matters. Love keeps the world on track. 'The love that moves the sun and other stars.'"

"It is not right," he said.

"Yes, it is. My brother-in-law Hymenaeus, he puts shackles on desire. My daughter sets it free."

"Your daughter?"

"Her name is Pleasure. Born of the union of Eros and Psyche, Love and Soul."

"I remember, as a child, going into the Temple, genuflecting before the pink-marble statue, of the goddess, touching her draperies, trying to sneak a peek into the water-mirror she held in her hand. The water that fertilizes the thirsty soil so that the crops may grow, and women conceive … it is under her command. Still."

They were lying on the blanket near the small fire that the soldier had built with pieces of driftwood. The indigo sky was sown with stars and the sea glowed with a faint greenish sheen.

"But when you saw her, was she like that? Like her Temple statue?"

"No, not at all. She was surrounded by stinking pigeons. She was stark naked, no draperies, and her body was running to fat. And her face was hungry—not the hunger of passion but of a perpetual petty dissatisfaction. She was getting old, like all of them, like all the gods, and she hated that. The gods have no memory; they are creatures of desire. But with their end approaching they suddenly desired the one thing that was denied them: the past."

The whispery silence was shattered by mighty splashes. Broken water cascaded off a giant body in a waterfall of stars. The beach was suddenly alive with thrashing orange tentacles, coiling and whipping through the air. The soldier jumped up but Psyche stopped him.

"It is the Kraken," she said. "He no longer obeys her."

The soldier tried to push her behind his broad back, but Psyche stepped forward. A tentacle as thick as her waist wound itself around her. She patted the rough, pitted skin. The tentacle withdrew and the Kraken submerged again, leaving behind luminescent streaks of disturbed plankton.

"You see?" she said. "Her allies are abandoning her. She is old and spent. She can no longer make the ocean brim with fish and the air thrum with birds. She has lost her own desire and cannot kindle the desire that keeps the world alive. I can!"

The soldier turned away from her.

"Yes, they left me on the mountainside, tied to a post. It was after the drought, the fire, and the famine; after the oracle made it clear the goddess of love was outraged at the upstart girl taking her place and demanded a sacrifice."

"A human sacrifice?"

"It's done in Hellas."

He snorted disapprovingly.

They had slept briefly. Now there was a little greying in the east and she could see his face better: a hard face, lines like scars, the face of a man on speaking terms with death. But now Death was dead as well, Hades slumped on his black throne.

"After the first hour of weeping and cursing I decided I was not going to let her see my tears anymore."

"To fight well you need to hate your enemy," he said.

"I was bored. Seems strange being bored while you're dying, but so it was. I amused myself by watching the birds. Swallows, finches, robins. Only doves did not come. Well, they would have come later, together with vultures."

The soldier nodded.

"I imagined myself growing wings and flying away. Then I must have fainted. But I saw the darkness in the sky, the winged shape coming toward me...."

She fell silent. The sky blossomed in sullen reds and pearly pinks.

"Why did he lock you up with nobody for company?"

"It's not true!" Psyche cried. "He built a palace for me! It was a wonderful place, filled with pearls, sapphires, rubies, and emeralds! I had Smyrna figs to eat and Thessalian wines to drink! True, I had nobody to talk to because the slaves had their tongues cut out. But who needs talk when you have love?"

"You must have," the soldier said dryly, "because according to the tale I know, you asked him to bring your sisters over."

"I did not ask for them! He must have arranged their visit to please me."

"Didn't quite work out," the soldier pointed out.

"It was my fault! I should not have listened to them! A fool's words are poison."

"What did they say?"

"They wanted to know who I was married to."

"Rather natural, don't you think so?"

Psyche turned away, pouting.

"Sorry," the soldier apologized. "My manners are not great, I know, but when you spend most of your time with molten metal and burning fire, you lose the knack of talking to ladies."

She went on with her tale, even though something in what he had said nagged at her. "They tried to convince me I was making love to a monster. I knew it was nonsense. The bedchamber was always pitch-dark, true, but I knew every inch of my lover's skin. I could have picked him out by touch in a crowd of thousands."

"It could have been an illusion," he said.

"Of course. But my pleasure was not an illusion, and neither was the baby in my womb."

"Then why…?"

"Because I wanted to *know*. Oh, he talked to me. He refused to give me his name or tell me who he was, but we talked. I did not have much to say then, a naive girl just out of my father's house with vague dreams and unfocused ambitions. But he told me wonderful tales: about speaking flowers and singing bees; about strange slimy creatures at the bottom of the sea that carry imperishable flame in their flesh; about birds crossing oceans to find a home that no longer exists; about lovers separated and reunited. He was sweet and wistful. He was not like *them*, the other gods; he was born in their twilight and inherited none of their swagger and brutality."

"So what did you do?"

"I hid an oil lamp in the bedchamber. And when he fell asleep, I lit it."

*A feeble flame flaring in darkness and his face and body swimming up from the shadows. This redeemed it all: anger, frustration, fatigue, dingy inns, monsters and sunless days; they were all redeemed by that one moment of vision. If only she could make it the end of her story rather than the beginning.…*

"Did you scratch yourself on one of his arrows?"

"There are no arrows, it's a superstition. My husband does not spill blood. A touch of his wings is all it takes."

"Does he have wings? How could you possibly not know it while sleeping with him?"

"He was my first man," Psyche pouted, "how was I to know how it's supposed to be? But they were so lovely, his wings: huge, soft and rosy-white, spread on the bed like a pile of Persian silks. I wanted to stroke them, to find out how they moved, to feel the muscles that roped them to his body."

"But then …"

"But then a drop of oil fell upon his bare arm," said Psyche, getting up and turning away to stare into the sea that was growing dim as clouds veiled the sky. "You know the rest of the story. How he was burnt and had to fly away, under his mother's curse; how I followed him, swollen with my baby, to the abode of the immortals; how I faced my mother-in-law and forced her to set three tasks at the completion of which I would be reunited with my husband; how I fulfilled the tasks with the help of kind creatures, large and small— and trust me, it was not easy to haul the water of life in a bucket when my own water was about to break—and how the goddess had to wake her son from the enchanted sleep and allow him to embrace his wife; and how my divine daughter was born. I'm tired of talking. Do we have anything to eat?"

"So what are you doing here?" the soldier asked.

Psyche did not answer, squinting into the pearly space where the cirrus-shrouded sky and the grey sea melted into each other. It was marred by moving dots.

"Doves!" she cried. "We have to move!"

The soldier shook his head.

"These are gulls," he said.

"Still," she insisted, "we're going to transit soon. We'd better be prepared. I don't want to be stuck in a fifth-time zone again."

"What's that?"

"There are four times of day, but there are zones in which a fifth is added. It is the worst: muddled and ambiguous, neither light nor darkness."

The soldier started packing. She saw he was putting her spare clothing into his backpack.

"Hey!" she protested.

"You did not answer my question," the soldier said. "In the tale I know you were reunited with Eros and accepted into the company of the immortals. The story was over. Finished. So how is it that you're here and alone?"

Psyche bit her lips, tasting the ocean tang of blood. *What does it matter?* she told herself.

"It's the second time," she said.

"The second quest?"

"Yes. I told you, she hates me. And when the other gods died—
the Sky-Father and his wife Hera—there was nobody to restrain her.
She is the Queen now. You see the results."

"She did it again?"

"Yes. Took my daughter, separated me from my husband, and
sent me on a new search for him."

The soldier straightened up.

"So," he said, "you're tramping from zone to zone, attacked by
monsters, fighting giant birds, wearing those things—are they really
glass? And all for this Eros, this boy wonder. And where is he? Hiding
behind Mummy's skirts on Olympus?"

"Shut up!" Psyche flushed with anger. "You have no right to
speak of him this way. What do you know? You're just a barbarian!"

"I may be," said the soldier levelly, "but I know what I see."

She turned her back on him. He came over and put his arms
around her. Psyche buried her head in his shoulder, angry with herself
for the tears that had always flown too freely, the heritage of the fierce
temper tantrums of her childhood.

"Don't cry," the soldier whispered. "I love you."

Psyche started.

"Don't say that!" she cried. "How long have you known me?"

"How long did it take you to fall in love with Eros? Do you even
remember his face?"

She disengaged herself. "We'd better go up the dunes," she said
without looking at him. "Transits are easier when you are on a higher
ground."

They trudged up the slippery sand slope and Psyche tried to
explain.

"Eros and Hymenaeus have no father. She needed no male
because she was a force unto herself, equal sister to Sky-Father. But
now she has become a malicious tub of lard. The world has fallen
apart because the force that binds it is no more."

"'The love that moves the sun and other stars.' But Eros is Love.
So where is he?"

Psyche grabbed his hand, pointing upward. A jagged black line appeared in the sky. The line widened and the dune they stood on shuddered, sloughing rivulets of sand.

"Transit is coming!"

He hugged her hard, squeezing the breath out of her.

"We'll go together!" he shouted.

And they did.

So this was the desert.

They stood in the wilderness of red stone under the lowering sky of purple and orange. The terrain was folded and wrinkled like the skin of an old animal and colored in the shades of drying blood. There was no sun; the light was heavy as if ready at any moment to congeal into darkness. Twisted spires of rock thrust from piles of rubble.

Somehow, they had lost their clothes and all their belongings during the transit. They faced each other naked, a man and a woman. The syrupy light painted the soldier's chest hair black and tinged Psyche's body with rose. The glittering fragments of the glass shoes shone on the ground.

"My things!" she cried.

"You don't need them now," he said, "You're coming with me."

"I need to find my husband!"

"Your husband is dead."

"Yes," Psyche said. "He is dead because I killed him."

*Scarlet drops of blood like scattered jewels on the rosy wings ...*

She turned away, staring into the furnace of the sky.

"He would not protect me. He would always take her side. He spent more time with her than he did with me and our daughter. I did not know you could kill a god. I wanted to teach him a lesson. But the gods were dying anyway...."

She felt the soldier's hand on her shoulder.

"I'll protect you," he said gently. "You see, it's all done now. Your quest is done. You are coming with me."

"You're not a god," she said.

"I will *make* myself a god. Look!"

234

He spread his arms wide, and a glow of liquid silver flowed over his body from his toes up, subtly changing his proportions, streamlining him, smoothing out the bumps and valleys of old scars, melting his arms and solidifying them into the elegant scythe-shapes of narrow wings fringed with metallic feathers, and then flowing over his face like a veil and covering it with the shining bird-mask, its sharp alien features washed with blood as it reflected the red light.

"Icarus!" she cried in recognition.

He inclined his head—the liquid metal of his body as pliant as flesh.

"My love," he said.

She stepped back.

"No!" she said.

"But ..."

"I am Psyche. The Book of Gods has been scattered, but one story still endures: the tale of Soul's search for Love. As long as the story continues, there is hope. If I give up, the sun will go out and the stars will fall from the sky. But if I find him, if I take his mother's place on the golden throne, the world may still be restored."

"He's dead!" Icarus cried.

"When Death is dead, who is to keep him in the eternal darkness?"

"I can give you wings," he said.

"I have wings of my own," she said. "Yours will burn but mine will endure because they are the wings of desire. And desire is immortal."

A distant rumble started in the hills, coming closer, gathering momentum, and the earth shook, as if an enormous animal on whose hide they perched were waking up. Shards of rock flew; the sky darkened.

Psyche opened up her arms and sprang into the air, borne on the iridescent butterfly wings that sprouted from her shoulders, frail as soap bubbles, shivering in the violent wind. But they bore her up as the terrain underneath convulsed and shattered, gaping fissures crisscrossing the hills, converging upon the silver figure that stood still, his face lifted up to her.

235

"How do you know I am not him?" he cried.

Startled, she tried to bank, to turn back. But the wind picked her up and hurled her into the star-studded void over the clashing pieces of the world; of light and dark; of seas, cities, and deserts; of birds and fish; and dying gods and spawning monsters. Caught in the maelstrom, Psyche flew on, tears drying on her face.

# MELISSA AND THE STONE TROLL

nce there was a little girl who loved to eat. She ate bread and butter, ham and eggs, cherries and apricots. She particularly liked honey-cake, and so her parents named her Melissa, which means "honey."

Famine came to her village, and her parents died. Melissa survived, but she became gaunt and pinched. She wandered into the dark forest, where she met a stone troll.

"Little girl, why are you sad?" he asked.

"I am hungry!"

"Don't your parents feed you well?"

Only then did Melissa remember that her parents were dead.

"Look at me," said the troll. "I never want for sustenance; and I never grow wrinkled and sad. We are what we eat. I eat rock, and rock is eternal."

Indeed, the troll's face was as white as alabaster and his eyes as blue as sapphires. Poor Melissa thought she had never seen anyone so beautiful.

"Tell you what," said the troll. "I'll trade with you. I'll take your hunger and I'll give you my satiety. You'll never lack food again."

"But I don't want to eat rocks!" said Melissa. "They'll break my teeth!"

"You can eat ashes and coals," the troll said. "They'll make you as bright and lively as fire."

Melissa, who was too hungry to remember that one should not trade with trolls, agreed.

The troll took her human appetite and immediately metamorphosed into a handsome young man. He walked happily away, only pausing to throw over his shoulder:

"Oh, I forgot to tell you. There is one catch. You can eat coal and ashes, you can even swallow flame, and it'll keep you alive. But human food will be poison to you."

Melissa wandered in the forest for many days until she came to the king's palace. There she was hired as a kitchen wench. This suited her just fine because she could rake ashes, clean fireplaces, and collect coals. She swallowed fire and it made her eyes bright, her hair red, and her temper volatile. But she still missed human food. She confronted the chef and made him teach her everything he knew about cooking. In a short while, she forced him to resign—like everybody else, the chef was afraid of this fiery girl with her unpredictable flares of anger.

So, Melissa, who now called herself Cinderella because she ate cinders, became the cook. She cooked wonderful dishes, far more elaborate than the old chef's best creations. But she could never taste her own food; she could only remember the country fare lovingly prepared for her by her parents. And often her tears fell into the pot she was stirring, adding an additional flavor to it.

The king, pleased with the improvement of his table, wished to meet the new cook. And when Melissa appeared, he was instantly smitten with her sparkling beauty and proposed marriage to her. Melissa looked at the young king and for the first time since her parents' death felt a hunger for another person's company. For fire only consumes itself, while food is made to be shared with others.

But the king's evil counselor remonstrated and told the king those wonderful dishes were surely a slow poison. For how else to explain that the girl never tasted her own creations?

Melissa saw the doubt in the king's eyes. She took a slice of her marvelous honey cake and put it into her mouth.

And the trade with the troll was undone. She became, once again, a country girl, sweet as honey and soft as butter. But the king, who wanted a spirited, impetuous wife, decided not to marry her after all.

# ALEXEI'S GODMOTHER

The man stood in the pouring rain; his threadbare cloak gathered in folds over the bundle in his arms. It did not help; both he and his newborn son were soaked.

In their tiny hovel, his wife lay dead in their bed, worn bedclothes red with blood. These were the only bedclothes the man and his wife possessed but he did not care; he believed that soon both he and his son would be dead too, and so the practical issues of laundry, disposal of the body, and finding a wet-nurse would be irrelevant. There was only one thing that weighed heavily on his mind. Before his son died, he must be baptized.

The man knew his family would be reunited in heaven, where hunger and cold would no longer trouble them, and instead of a tumbledown hovel, they would reside in a golden palace with jeweled floors and windows of purest crystal. But if the baby died unbaptized, he would not be joining his parents. He would be stuck in the grey limbo, presided over by stern foster parents of the angelic host. The man could not bear the thought. His wife had given her life to create another soul, and the thought that her sacrifice might be in vain tarnished his hopeful anticipation of a heavenly reunion. The child must be baptized before he died. But the man and his wife lived alone; the nearest village was a couple of miles away, and their horse had died in the last famine and was eaten long ago. There was an abandoned church within walking distance, but the man knew he had to have a godparent for his child. And there was nobody around to ask.

That was why he was waiting on the highway in the pouring rain with his newborn in his arms—waiting for a passer-by whom he might implore, for the love of God, to help him baptize his son.

For a long time nothing happened, and the man was fearful the baby's fragile soul would fly away before it could be given a pass to Paradise. But then he saw a dim light approaching. The man ran to the center of the road, trying futilely to shield the baby from the cold arrows of rain.

A carriage slowed down and then stopped. It was inlaid in gold; its large wheels had bejeweled spokes; and the window curtains were of wine-colored damask. The horses were roan, and their harness was studded with rubies. The coachman wore opulent red livery. The woman who drew away the curtain and peered out of the carriage's window carried a king's ransom on her person. Her raven hair was twined with golden filigree; her lips and eyes were painted with gold dust; and her low-cut velvet gown showed off a chest so covered with precious necklaces that not an inch of skin was to be seen.

"What do you want?" the woman asked in a husky voice. "Money? I have to spare."

And she threw down a golden coin.

The man explained that money would be of no use to his family in Paradise. All he needed was a godmother for his newborn son.

"I have no use for peasant superstitions!" the woman responded indignantly. She slammed down the window, and the carriage rolled away, almost knocking the man down. The golden coin that was slowly sinking into the mud bore the inscription *Caveat emptor*.

Some time passed, and another carriage rolled by. This one was even more beautiful than the first one. Its sides gleamed with painted flowers; its roof was blue; and the horses drawing it were white and had pink plumes on their heads. The coachman was a young boy in a silk waistcoat and ruffled shirt. The carriage shone like the sky at dawn in the middle of the black night. Even the cutting wind and the icy rain seemed to die down when it stopped. A white hand drew away the curtain, and the most beautiful girl the man had ever seen poked her head through the window. Her hair fell to her white shoulders in elaborate ringlets the color of ripe corn; her eyes were like sapphires; and her lips were like roses filled with snow. But her beauty meant nothing to the man whose wife had just bled out in giving birth to their baby. The only thing that mattered was that here was a potential godmother for her child.

"What do you want?" the girl asked in a voice as sweet as candy. "You are a beggar, aren't you? Here!"

And she tried to put a golden coin into his hand.

The man shook his head and explained that he wanted the girl to go with him to the abandoned church, so his son might be baptized.

The girl drew away, scandalized.

"You don't need baptism!" she exclaimed. "All you need is love!"

She withdrew, and the carriage disappeared down the road, the sleek horses snorting contemptuously at the man and his son. The golden coin lay in the mud; and the man saw that it bore the inscription *Amor vincit omnia*.

The man opened up his threadbare jacket and cradled the baby next to his heart. The newborn was wet and cold; the man could feel his breath flutter like a guttering candle.

Nothing happened for a while, and then yet another carriage slowly creaked down the road. This one was pulled by a pair of black horses, so emaciated that their bones poked through their skin. The carriage itself was black and unadorned. Its coachman was muffled from head to toe in a heavy black cloak. Its single window was shuttered.

The man dropped down to his knees in the mud before the carriage. It did not slow down, and the man saw that the horses had no eyes in their sockets, and that the coachman's face was covered by a mask in the shape of a rat's muzzle. But the man was desperate and refused to move. If he were to be run down with his son, so be it!

The carriage stopped, so close that the man could feel the sulfurous exhalation of the horses on his cheeks.

"What do you want?" a voice asked. The voice was female, but so deep and sonorous that it seemed to reverberate in the man's bones.

He explained. There was a long moment of silence, and then the door of the carriage creaked open, and a woman stepped out. She was tall and straight, taller than the father, and wore a simple gown of black wool girdled with a chain of silver. Her hands were encased in black gloves, and on her head she wore a thick veil called a mantilla that could hide the face entirely. But it was pinned away, so the man could see her, and his heart skipped a beat. She looked like his dead wife Maria; or rather, she looked like the woman Maria could have been had she not been stunted by hunger, pockmarked by disease, and drained by miscarriages and then the delivery that killed her.

"Let me see the boy," she asked. The father wordlessly offered her the baby, whose lips were turning blue, and whose breath would not be strong enough to mist a mirror.

"Your son is dying," she said.

"I know," the man said. "But if we die together as Christians, we will be reunited in Paradise."

The woman's pale lips twitched in an ambiguous smile.

"If he were to live," she asked, "what name would you want your son to bear?"

"Alexei," the man said. "It was my father's name, and it means 'defender of the people.' I would want my son to defend Justice, and to help those in need. But if he is not to grow up, I want him to bear this name with him to Heaven, so he would know it when he is called to sit in judgment on those who do evil, as all innocent souls are called."

The woman who looked like the man's dead wife smiled even wider.

"I will be your son's godmother," she said.

Alexei hated his father.

The old man was craggy and bent but he still had strength in his muscle-bound arms, and by working as a farmhand he made a living for himself and his son. Their hovel looked as if it were about to fall apart but it never did, and the old man caulked the roof every year to keep the rain and snow out. There was food on the table and fresh flowers were placed every Sunday on the grave of Alexei's mother.

But poverty was not the reason for Alexei's contempt. His father's acceptance of it was.

The old man never complained. He never shook his fist at the fancy carriages that rolled on the highway by their hovel, splattering with mud their tiny front yard. He never talked of the injustice whereby the rich grew richer, and the poor poorer every year. He never mentioned the King, who was supposed to be the Father of the People but instead favored his fancy courtiers, whose elaborate wigs and bejeweled snuffboxes could feed a rural family for a year. Alexei's father was compliant and content.

Alexei, on the other hand, was keenly aware of the humiliation of their poverty. Their hovel stood in the shadow of a large mansion perched on top of the hill that towered above the exhausted fields and starving villages. The aristocratic family who lived in the mansion were called the Bogolyub, which meant "God-loving." They were considered tolerably good landlords, though they were absent most of the time, as they were heavily involved in the Court's endless intrigues. The family was composed of the father, named Theodor, the mother, Zenaida, and the little girl, Nina, who was the same age as Alexei. When they did come to visit their country estate, they would have a celebration for their tenants in the gardens where long tables overflowing with roast and beer would be set out among the formal flower beds and many-colored lanterns. Theodor and Zenaida would distribute coins to farmers and their wives, while the little girl offered sweets to the small crowd of dirty, rickety urchins.

These celebrations maddened Alexei because they made their abjection so much worse by comparison. Every chink in their hovel's walls gaped wider by contrast with the smooth plaster and carved stone of the mansion. Every piece of rough bread his father put on the table was seasoned with the memory of the cream-cakes he got from Nina. Every time he had to wash his tunic until the homespun fabric became as thin as a fishnet, he thought of Theodor's fur-trimmed coats and Zenaida's many-layered mantua dresses. He would forgive his father their poverty if the old man were as resentful as he was. But after each celebration, the old man would go back placidly to their hovel, put away the coins, and after a prayer, sleep soundly, while Alexei tossed and turned, consumed by unfocused anger.

One day when Alexei was ten and the Bogolyub family came back to the mansion again, the customary tenant party was postponed, and the rumor went that it would not take place. Eventually summons were issued, and the tenants and their families gathered at dusk in the gardens. But Alexei noted that Theodor looked shrunken in his embroidered waistcoat; his wife was pale and biting her lips; and Nina, her brown braids lavishly decorated with ribbons and her short frock even fancier than usual, seemed bewildered.

Theodor made a speech, using long words Alexei did not know but the gist of it was that his family would now reside in the mansion permanently. Zenaida shed a tear, and an uncertain murmur went over the crowd. Less money than before was distributed, and Nina walked around with her eyes downcast, silently offering honey cakes to the children. But when she got to Alexei, she had run out of sweets. She pulled a blue ribbon out of her hair and handed it to Alexei.

"Give it to your sister," she said and ran away before he could tell her he had no sister.

The customary feast followed, but even wine, beer, and roast piglets could not calm down the apprehension that settled over the farmers. They had learned the hard way that any change was usually for the worse.

As they were walking back home, Alexei's father told his son that the reason must have been that the Bogolyubs fell out of favor with the King.

"Does it mean the King will now exile or kill all the courtiers and rule as the Father of the People?" Alexei asked. The old man shook his head.

"No," he said sharply and refused to continue the conversation. But when they came back home, the old man lit a homemade candle and took out something from the secret hideaway where he kept his cache of coins. It was a book wrapped up in linen.

Alexei looked at it curiously. He knew his letters because his father had managed to scrape together enough money to pay a defrocked cleric who acted as an itinerant schoolteacher for the children of the countryside. But the only book he had seen so far had been the Bible in the church, and it was in a language he did not understand.

"This was a gift from your godmother," the father said. "She requested I give it to you when you reach the age of reason, and I think you have."

Alexei, who did not know he had a godmother, took the book gingerly and unwrapped the linen cover elaborately embroidered with golden thread in the pattern of stars and bones. The book was bound in soft calfskin that was stained deep scarlet, almost black. There were no inscriptions on the front board or the spine. But when he opened it, the stiff pages rustling, he saw that the title read "The Book of Justice." Below was a picture of a woman with a sword in one hand, scales in the other, skulls rolling under her dainty feet. She faced away from the viewer, so only her long hair could be seen.

Alexei nestled in the corner by the guttering candle and started reading.

When Alexei was twelve, his father told him they would celebrate his coming of age with a feast for their neighbors. He said there was enough money in his secret cache to have a big party. He would go to the mansion and ask Theodor whether they could hold it in the gardens, and he wanted Alexei to come with him.

Alexei knew that there would be no party. He had read the Book of Justice from front to back several times, and he had plans of his own. He also knew where his father kept his money. But out of some residual sense of obligation, he agreed to accompany the old man.

First, they went to Maria's grave, and the old man talked to his wife, as he did every Sunday.

"Look at our son," he said. "He has become a man."

Alexei stood by the tombstone awkwardly, averting his gaze. He had no concept of his mother's face, as there were no portraits of her, and his father's attempts to describe Maria to the boy were too vague to conjure up any image. And so, he associated his mother with a severe tombstone made of rough unpolished granite with a spidery cross hewn into it. When he was younger, he used to have nightmares of the tombstone creeping toward their house at night like a faceless stone turtle.

Next, they went to the mansion, and Alexei's blood boiled when he saw his father doff his cap and bow deeply to the landlord. In the years since coming to reside in his country estate permanently, Theodor had aged, his back became curved and his eyes rheumy. But he still strutted around his tenants, wringing every drop of submission out of their dependency on him. He hemmed and hawed, while Alexei's father stood with his eyes lowered deferentially, and thanked Theodor with humility when the permission was finally granted. Alexei could not wait to leave.

On their way back home, he saw a glint of blue in the shrubbery and lagged behind his father, until Nina stepped out from her hiding place. She had become very pretty, with her long brown hair worn in loose ringlets, and her large amber eyes shadowed by butterfly-wing lashes. Her blue gown was now hooped and gored and long enough to cover her ankles because she had already had her coming-of-age.

"I can't give you another ribbon," Nina said. "I'm now allowed to stop braiding my hair. My father wants me to get married, so we can regain our position at the Court."

"I see," Alexei rasped. He imagined Nina in the arms of some fat arrogant courtier, as old as her own father. He turned away and ran toward his hovel, fingering the worn blue ribbon in his pocket.

Alexei walked down the road in the dark. The new moon, a spiky scimitar in the star-sown sky, barely provided enough light for him to see the boundary between the grey ribbon of the highway and the black masses of the woods on both sides of it, but he pressed on. The capital was far away, and he wanted to reach it as quickly as possible.

Though Alexei had never seen it, he knew what he would find. The stately homes of the rich and the slums of the poor. The marble pavement of the Royal Square and the stinking mud of the Dustmen's Quarter. The bejeweled walls of the Summer Palace where the King lived in luxury, forgetting his duty to the people.

Never mind. Alexei was about to change all of this.

In his satchel, he carried all the money his father had put aside in his secret cache. It was more than he had expected, and at first Alexei had hesitated as to whether to leave some for the old man. But he had decided against it. His father was content with his degraded, meaningless existence, while he, Alexei, needed funds for what he was about to do. He was surprised to find two coins with inscriptions in a language he could not read, but after some consideration, he took them as well.

He also carried the Book of Justice, carefully wrapped up in the gold-embroidered linen. He had spent uncounted hours reading it over and over again, until he knew it almost by heart. But the woman who had left it for him remained a mystery. He puzzled over the frontispiece picture trying to visualize the face of Justice. He tried to ask his father, but the old man adamantly refused to talk about Alexei's godmother, which only made his son resent him more.

Suddenly he heard the rattle of wheels and the neighing of a horse. But as he looked back, the darkness seemed to grow thicker, veiling whoever was coming behind him. Alexei stepped to the side and almost tumbled into the ditch.

Emerging from the murk like a snake from the undergrowth was a large carriage drawn by two horses. The horses were pure black, and so was the carriage. Large and imposing as it was, it was also plain and unadorned. The coachman was muffled up in a heavy cloak and Alexei could not see his face.

The carriage drew to a stop next to him, and the door opened. A woman stepped out.

She was so tall that Alexei gasped. She towered above him like the biggest spruce in the forest. He was sure his eyes were deceiving him as he looked up and saw her wavering silhouette dissolve into the night sky. Her gown fell around her slender hips in folds of black velvet. She wore black gloves. And her face was veiled, so that not an inch of bare skin showed.

Alexei's knees went weak, and he felt like bowing deeply to the lady, but he reminded himself that all people were equal, and stood his ground.

"Well met, Alexei," the woman said, and her voice was unexpectedly pleasant and reassuring. It reverberated inside Alexei's head like the echo of a familiar but half-forgotten melody.

"How do you know my name?" he asked. "Who are you?"

"I am your godmother," the woman said. "And I am here to give you my gift on your coming-of-age birthday."

And with that, she took off one of her gloves. Her hand was a collection of bony sticks, the joints rattling as if loose, the nails long and painted scarlet. With the tips of her fleshless fingers, she brushed Alexei's eyes.

"Now you have the gift of seeing me when I go about my business," the woman said. "And when you call me, I will come."

She turned around and folded back into the carriage, and as Alexei blinked away tears, his eyes were burning. The carriage rolled away, the coachman staring back over his shoulder, the cloak slipping off and disclosing a mottled greenish skin and putrefying mouth.

Shaking off his awe, Alexei ran after the carriage.

"Godmother Justice!" she cried. "Let me see your face!"

But the carriage disappeared sown the road.

The Revolution was in its fifth year, and the King's Summer Palace, now renamed the Palace of the People, was resplendent, decorated with red banners and fresh flowers. The scaffold in the Royal Square (now called the People's Square) was draped with scarlet silk that hid the stains of fresh blood. The heads on the spikes surrounding the Square had, unfortunately, decayed, though attempts had been made to preserve them, so future generations could gaze with righteous anger at the swinish features of the last King, his harlot Queen, and their bastard children. But these attempts were unsuccessful, and as the heads were now hardly more than anonymous skulls, scrolls were affixed to them, describing the former owner of each head and their crimes against the nation.

People were now trickling into the Square to celebrate the anniversary of the Revolution: bakers, carriage-makers, tailors, seamstresses, ironsmiths, cooks. In the past, they would have been dressed according to their occupation and rank, with more prosperous merchants and their families sporting jewelry, furs and silks. But now sumptuary laws prohibited such displays, so all men wore simple grey jackets and undyed breeches, and all women unadorned sack-like gowns in brown and black. All golden jewelry had been confiscated to buy arms for the Republic, so nobody wore as much as a wedding ring, while the custom of allowing more adornment for unmarried maidens had been abolished. This created some confusion among young people, though most had no time or inclination for courting.

Alexei stood on the balcony of the Palace, slightly to the side of the Triumvirs, who greeted the crowd with plastered smiles. He tried to remember their names but concluded it did not matter. These particular men had been in office for two months, and their execution was imminent, as the fever of the power struggle in the Secret Council had reached the boiling point. In Alexei's time of service to the Revolution, he had seen one Assembly, two Supreme Councilors, one Leader, and two sets of Triumvirs come and go. But he was a fixture in the People's Palace and especially in its cellars, where speedy trials took place. He was the youngest of the Revolutionary Judges and the longest-serving. He was untouchable.

The First Triumvir started on his long-winded speech to the people, exhorting them to more sacrifices and calling upon the faithful to unmask slackers and traitors, but Alexei's attention was wandering. His eyes were burning.

He blinked and focused on the three men in their red linen waistcoats (they represented the Revolution, so it was only proper that they wore distinctive clothing, though Alexei himself disdained such displays, invariably dressed in a simple leather coat). The First Triumvir still went on, ratcheting up the heat of denunciation, as saliva blew from his mouth. The Second and Third Triumvirs nodded in unison, trying to demonstrate the unshakeable unity of the governing body of the Republic, which was necessary for their survival. But Alexei saw what he expected to see.

Standing by the side of the First Triumvir was a slender black figure, her face veiled. She took off her glove put her hand on the First Triumvir's shoulder. He blanched and stammered, but got hold of himself and went on as the people listened in silence, their heads bowed.

Alexei kept his eyes on his godmother as she faded out of sight, still hoping, after all these years, that she would linger to talk to him. But she did not.

When the speech was over, the Triumvirs filed out of the balcony, while below in the Square, musicians were playing, and the first condemned men and women were being led to the scaffold, their eyes blindfolded as the executioner checked his ax.

Alexei slipped out and caught up with the First Triumvir, placing his hand on his shoulder, in the same place as his godmother had done, feeling the fading chill in his fingertips.

"You are under arrest for treason," he said.

The Triumvirate was dissolved, and a new squabble for power ensued. Alexei did not care. His loyalty was to the Revolution, and the pitiless Justice it meted out. Whoever ended up on top in politics did not matter to him. He would continue his service. He knew people shied away when they saw his leather-clad figure, and whispered behind his back, calling him names like "Devil's son" and "Hell's judge." He considered them a compliment.

But he was beginning to feel that his service could be endangered if the political situation did not stabilize. There was unrest in the Republic. Common people grumbled that there was even less to eat now than there had been under the monarchy. The shops stood empty, and the few remaining clerics preached treason. Moreover, several neighboring kingdoms had declared a holy war on the Republic, and though they had been beaten back, the military threat remained. Alexei realized that in order to safeguard revolutionary Justice, he would have to declare himself the Leader.

He was extremely unwilling to do so. He cared nothing for the accoutrements of power; he despised wealth; he ate coarse bread and drank only water. He had no wife or mistress and wanted none. All he wanted was to serve the Revolution, hoping that eventually he would gather enough merit to be vouchsafed his heart's desire. When the land was pure, and the people had been avenged, he believed that he would finally see his godmother's face. But to achieve this, he would have to take over the reins of power himself.

So he cleaned out the Secret Council. That was easy: all he had to do was to stride in during one of their raucous sessions and whisper the summons. His eyes would burn. And then he would see his godmother standing by each of the condemned men, her hand on their shoulder. They would go pale; their knees would buckle; they would collapse, and cover their faces, and weep, knowing their time had come. Sending them over to the executioner felt like a waste of effort; and indeed, many of them never got up, dying on the floor of the Council Hall as the hand of Alexei's godmother touched them.

As the Leader, Alexei's first decree was that each town, village, farmstead, or former landlord's holding was to have a census, and each man, woman, and child above the age of eight was to be interviewed by an itinerant Judge. If any stench of treason was detected, the person would be sent to the capital, there to be questioned by the Leader himself. Only thus purified could the land be strong enough to withstand the imminent military attack by the corrupt kingdoms on its borders. And also, Alexei promised, the harvests that had been mediocre in the last five years, due to sabotage and conspiracies, would improve. The people would be well fed now that no fruit of their labor was stolen by the rich. Only Justice could ensure prosperity. And because Alexei believed this with all his heart, people listened and obeyed, set on fire by the sincerity of his words. Even those who had been tired and grumbling, worn out by arrests and executions, succumbed again to the allure of pure faith.

Every day Alexei would see hundreds of people brought into his Hall of Justice. Some cried; some pleaded; women begged for their children's lives; men were cowardly or defiant. Alexei pretended to look in the accused's face, listen to their words, consult the accompanying reports. But it was all for show. He would nod his head as the accused spoke and wait for the burning in his eyes, and for the black-veiled figure of his godmother to appear by their side. If she did and placed her gloved hand on their shoulder, the scarlet silk on the scaffold in the People's Square would acquire one more stain before it was washed for the next batch of executions. And while Justice was being served and heads rolled, Alexei told himself that his godmother was happy with him. But she still refused to show her face.

One morning; Alexei, unusually weary and out of sorts, sat in his high-backed chair, leafing through the bundle of new reports on his desk. He started when he saw the name of the village. That was his birthplace.

The first accused was ushered in the Leader's presence, and fell to his knees, striking his head on the cold flagstones. Thin and bedraggled, his face crisscrossed by deep wrinkles and his clothes torn, the man was unmistakably his former landlord, Theodor. He mewled something incomprehensible, trying to plead for his life, but Alexei was not listening. Instead he was staring in surprise at what was happening before him.

His godmother stood by Theodor's left side without touching him, as if hesitant to do so. But she was not alone. By the man's right side stood another woman. She was beautiful and regal, her hair wreathed with diamonds, her eyes and lips gilded. Her gaudy attire stood out in the plainness of the Hall like an insulting challenge to the Revolution.

"Who are you?" exclaimed Alexei. "What do you want?"

Theodor blubbered but Alexei shut him up with a flick of his wrist, focusing on the strange woman. He had never seen her in his life, yet she looked familiar.

"I will buy this man's life," the woman said in a voice as mellow as dark honey. "Remember the coin I gave your father? You will have thousands of those if you spare him. You will be the richest man in the world, and you will be able to buy whatever your heart desires."

Alexei involuntarily glanced at the small pine box on his desk. Locked inside were the two strange coins he had taken from his father's secret cache. He had spent the rest on his arrival to the capital, acquiring education and forging ties with the secret societies that eventually fomented the Revolution. But he could not bring himself to spend the two coins with the strange inscriptions which, he eventually learned, meant "Buyer, beware" and "Love conquers all."

He looked full in the woman's face and saw in her bold eyes and provocative smile all the insults and humiliations he had suffered in his childhood.

"No!" he cried. "Take your coin! I won't be bought. This man is condemned to death for his treason."

And he tossed the coin with *Caveat emptor* at the feet of the richly dressed woman. She paled and faded away. And Alexei's godmother who had been observing the interaction from behind her impenetrable veil placed her ungloved hand on Theodor's shoulder.

Alexei sat for a long time staring at the plain surface of his desk. The Book of Justice, still in its original cover, lay in the center. He had ordered copies to be made and distributed to all parishes, so the clerics could read it to the people instead of the Bible.

A knock on his door and a guard asked if the second accused from the same holding could be brought in. Alexei nodded.

He was not even surprised when he saw the woman. She looked older than him: years of hardship had put lines in her forehead and around her mouth. But her brown hair was still thick and rich, with red highlights, and her amber eyes still clear. Unlike her father, Nina stood straight and looked Alexei full in the face. He noticed that while she wore the same plain gown as every other woman in the Republic, her hair was braided but not covered. That meant she was a widow.

"Well met, Alexei," she said.

"You know me?"

255

She smiled. "How would I not know my most famous countryman? But I would recognize you anywhere. You don't forget your childhood playmates. Those were happy times."

Alexei's hand went to the pocket of his coat. Nested among drafts of execution orders lay pieces of a blue ribbon, so worn it had fallen apart.

"Wasn't so happy for your father's tenants," he said sternly.

She shrugged.

"My father tried to do the best he could, as bound by the rules of the system as his tenants. But even if he had done something wrong, we have paid for it in full. My mother was killed by the mob; my husband was executed, and my baby starved to death because we, as the family of the former landlord, were not allowed to receive grain from the communal storehouse."

Alexei pretended looking at the report on his desk, but he could not read them even if he tried. His eyes burned, and the letters swam before him.

When he looked up, he saw two women flanking Nina. His veiled godmother stood on the left side, as immobile as a funereal statue. On the right side stood a girl Alexei had never seen before: as lovely as dawn, as radiant as noon, as enchanting as twilight. She wore no jewelry, but her flaxen curls were encircled with a wreath of fresh roses.

"Love conquers all," the girl said. "You loved Nina as a child. You still love her. Spare her life, and you will be blessed with the greatest happiness a man can ever know. No money can buy it but the coin I gave your father will be my pledge."

Alexei looked at her for a long time, and then laughed.

"I sent countless men and women to the scaffold and watched them die," he said. "I slept on stone and ate moldy bread. I have no home, no children, no possessions. I gave up everything so future generations can know Justice. And you think you can buy me off with the pleasure that whores provide for a penny?"

He tossed the coin he had stolen from his father with the inscription *Amor vincit omnia* at the girl's feet. She faded away like morning dew. And Alexei's godmother placed her bare hand on Nina's shoulder.

Alexei called for the guards to lead Nina to the scaffold. Before she went out, she looked back at him.

"I wanted to be your friend," she said.

Alexei sat for a long time, staring blankly out the window of the Hall. The window opened out onto the Square, and he could hear people's cheers and the meaty whack of the executioner's ax, as each new traitor paid their debt to Justice. He went over to the window and drew the curtain.

The next accused was ushered into the presence of Alexei. It was his father.

Father and son had not seen each other for over ten years. Since the night Alexei had stolen out of their hovel, he had neither written to the old man nor tried to find out what had happened to him. Subconsciously, he believed that his father's silence meant he was dead.

But now he stood before his son. Alexei's first thought was how little the old man had changed. He did not seem to have aged. His weather-beaten face was the same ruddy color as before; his still-thick hair and eyebrows were steely-grey, just as they had been as long as Alexei remembered; and his clothes were neither better nor worse than what he had usually worn when Alexei was a child. Only when he shook off the guard's restraining hand and stepped closer did Alexei noticed that his father now walked with a limp.

The old man was the first one to break the silence.

"Well met, son," he said. "I suspected it was you when I heard about the Hell's Judge, but I was not sure. And as you see, after they broke my leg when I tried to help the Bogolyubs escape the mob, walking is tough, so I could not come to the capital to look for you."

"And if you did find me," Alexei asked, "what would you do?"

"I would kill you," the old man said without hesitation.

"So you confess to aiding enemies of the Republic, plotting against the life of the Leader, and being a sympathizer of the Old Regime?"

His father shrugged. "I confess to being a good Christian, which means all of the above."

"How could you?" Alexei cried out. "We lived in abject poverty, while the King and his courtiers hoarded wealth. You worked your fingers to the bone providing for me while the Bogolyubs were waited upon hand and foot! Where is Justice in it?"

"And where is Justice in spilling innocent blood?" the old man retorted. "Your mother died giving birth to you, and you kill other mothers' sons and daughters. Even your godmother is afraid of you now. She was an angel of God; you made her the executioner's whore."

"My godmother? What do you know of her? My godmother is Justice, and once I have purified the land, I will finally be given the privilege of seeing her face!"

The old man laughed.

"You godmother is Death," he said, "and she was the only one to pity a desperate man and help him baptize his child. And you need not work hard to see her face. It was the first face you saw when you opened your eyes, and it will be the last one you see before you close them forever."

And as if on a signal, Alexei's godmother appeared on his father's left side: slender and implacable, veiled in black. She took off her glove and raised her hand.

"No!" Alexei cried.

She paused uncertainly, and then for the first time after the roadside meeting, he heard her familiar voice. The veil fluttered as she spoke.

"Once I come at your call, you cannot dismiss me. A life has to be taken before I go away."

"Then take mine," Alexei said.

His father gasped, but Alexei went over to the black-clad woman and lifted her veil.

She smiled and put a hand on his shoulder. She beckoned the old man, and he came over and embraced his family.

The bodies of the treasonous farmer and the Leader were found lying side by side. No marks of violence were on either, but it was clear that was the result of a counter-Revolutionary plot. The new Leader ordered a great purge, and the executioner had to be given double pay as he worked overtime in pursuit of Justice.

# LITTLE MOTHER

The first child disappeared in June. It was on a bright, sunny Californian day—all the adjectives being superfluous except the last one. In June in the Santa Cruz mountains, all the days were sunny and bright; the feathered plumes of redwoods swaying high in the cloudless azure sky. The child was a boy, and he was eight years old. He stepped onto the deck of his parents' house, watching giant dragonflies swoop and dance in the light-saturated air. The tangle of manzanitas, tanoaks and madrones that fell away from the deck glowed like a pile of emeralds, but the boy knew better than to step down. There was poison oak mixed in with other vegetation, and there were coyotes and even mountain lions lurking in the woods. He was a good boy and did as he was told. He just wanted to see the dragonflies.

When, after calling several times, his mother went looking for him, he was not there.

They lived in the forest and considered it home, but the forest had other opinions, which were never consulted because the people who owned expensive houses surrounded by pristine redwoods felt they were friends of the trees. They drove their SUVs down into the valley, where they all had high-paying jobs, and came back in the fragrant

261

dusk, watched Netflix, and went to sleep lulled by the gentle soughing of the wind in the dense foliage. Their wives—those who did not have high-paying jobs of their own—stayed home, drove the children to school and back, cooked organic vegetables and low-carb pasta and thought of themselves as ecologically sound. But the forest kept to itself, as it had done throughout the centuries before the white man—or any man at all—penetrated the green darkness lying on the mountains of Northern California. The forest kept to itself, mocking and aloof, and brooded, and bided its time.

The man who owned a house built into the side of a hill and overlooking a steep ravine overgrown with redwoods, Chisos oaks and red firs had some inkling of the true nature of the forest, because occasionally the trees would speak to him. This happened at night. The slim black silhouettes like exquisite skeletons against the velvet blue of the sky would nod and wave their many-fingered hands, and in their haphazard gestures he would sense malice and mockery and obscure hints of something buried but not dead. Still, he loved his house with its glass walls and double garage and would not consider leaving. He lived alone because his wife had divorced him and moved away. His name was Mark.

One day, while vacationing in Italy, Mark met a woman and fell in love with her. Her name was Lucia, and though she lived in Milan, she was Croatian and had grown up in London. She had dark eyes, white skin, and hair the color of ash-covered embers. She spoke English with an accent that sounded like Slavic Cockney.

After a brief interlude of intense lovemaking and marathon conversations, Mark returned to California. But he could not get Lucia out of his head. They started WhatsApping in odd hours of the night because of the time difference between the Old and New World. She described a lifestyle that seemed to him hectic and unreal: crowded piazzales, the smell of overheated asphalt, clubbing, tiny apartments, and a strange assortment of friends who moved across the map of Europe like a flock of multilingual birds. After a month of red-eyed fatigue in the morning and vivid memories in all hours of the day, he bought her a ticket to California.

Lucia came fresh and excited, ready to marvel at the glass house, the woods, the deer, and the banana slugs. At first, she did not mind the nodding silhouettes of the trees at night, primarily because she hardly saw them, as they were busy making up for their separation. But Lucia did not drive. And after a couple of days when Mark had to go to work and leave her alone, surrounded by miles upon miles of redwoods, live oaks, manzanitas and hophornbeams, she grew restive. She complained of silence and of strange noises; she started when a crested jay landed on the sundeck and became unreasonably angry when a squirrel watched her from outside the bathroom window. And on the eighth day of her stay, she disappeared.

When Mark came back to the empty house, his first bitter thought was that Lucia had had enough. But in the bedroom her bras and panties still poked from the drawer and her Italian dresses, eminently unsuitable for country living, still hung in the closet. Her wallet and phone were there.

Mark called the police.

Two deputies came, poked through Lucia's belonging, eyed Mark with prurient interest, and disappeared, promising to pursue all available venues of inquiry. He did not expect to hear from them again.

Next day he paced his spacious living room and stared into the golden-green chiaroscuro of the woods outside. The myriad leaves watched him like Argus's eyes. How many of them were there? He thought of miles and miles of trees, each bearing an uncountable number of green protrusions, toothed, lobed, smooth, hairy, oval, oblong, arrow-shaped.... He waited for the night to blind those green eyes, but instead there came a long pale dusk, in which he could almost imagine additional eyes opening, unfurling like spring buds, all focusing on him. He regretted his glass walls and thought longingly of the tiny windows of Lucia's flat in Milan.

The police had been useless after the children's disappearances. First, the boy on Skyline, then a girl down at Felton ... and wasn't there another one? Mark had tried to not to think of the abductions, reasoning that he, a grown man, was in no danger. Now he cursed himself for an idiot. Lucia was not a child, but who knew how a serial killer's mind worked?

He was nervously scrolling through apps on his phone when a ping informed him that he had a new text. The number was withheld.

He opened it. The message said: "If you want to see your girlfriend again, click this link."

Now he felt in his element again. The digital jungles had many predators, but they were of a familiar kind. The link could infect his phone, of course, but so what? He had another one.

When he touched the link, the tiny screen went pitch-black. Mark cursed; a virus, after all.

But then a green dot appeared in the center, grew into an irregular amoeba-like cloud of radiance, out of which a face assembled itself.

Mark stared at it open-mouthed. It was obviously a CGI with a smooth glabrous skin and unnatural regularity of features. But it was one of the most unpleasant images he had ever seen.

Its face was hard and ashen. Its head was wrapped around with a sort of greenish turban, so that not a single hair showed. But the most shocking part of it was the color of its eyes and lips: both were bright coral-red, wetly gleaming like fresh wounds.

The creature opened its mouth to reveal small, seed-like, black teeth. The mouth gaped wider and wider, the turbaned head tilting backward, so he could see the greenish fibers that packed the creature's nostrils. The mouth filled the screen: a funnel of sultry red shading into the blackness of some vertiginous whirlpool. The blackness sucked him in, causing him to sway and pitch headlong onto the desk. But instead of hitting its edge, he felt himself being drawn into a cool and wet nothingness, filled with a smell of leaf mold and monotonous susurrus of the wind.

Mark came to lying on his back, staring into the tracery of boughs against the star-studded sky. A millipede crawled upon his bare neck. He sat up with a yelp and hit his head upon a crooked tree trunk that snaked close to the ground.

"Watch out," said a female voice.

A tiny flame sprang up. A woman was holding a fat moss-smelling candle that dimly illuminated her grey dress and threw enough light upon the turbaned head to reveal that the image on his phone had been no CGI. The smooth skin, the doll-like features and the glistening redness of the irises and lips flaunted their impossible reality, as the shadows played across the living face made of blood-stained wood.

"Who are you?" whispered Mark.

"Rowan," responded the woman. "We don't have much time, so listen. Little Mother has your girlfriend on her farm. We put up with this bitch for too long. She is an interloper, an intruder. She does not belong here. She crawled in dragging her domain with her, and we thought: as long as she keeps you people in check, who cares? But now it's getting too much. She is too strong. We can't get rid of her, or her farm. You have to help."

Mark bit the inside of his cheek and tasted blood. Not that he needed it. He knew he was not dreaming. The shivery air, the rustle of invisible bugs, and the reek of rotting vegetation were not generated by his sleeping self.

"Did you say 'bitch' or 'witch'?" he asked inanely.

"Both."

"And what are you?"

The creature shrugged, took his hand, and guided it toward her chest. Her breasts were as smooth and hard as wooden bowls; her skin had the texture of smooth bark.

"We don't play your animal games," she said, turned around and went downslope, gliding through the contorted trunks of manzanitas. Mark gulped and followed. The puny flame of her moss-candle was the only light, and he did not want to be left alone in the dark.

Mark thought he knew the woods, but he realized now he only knew the sunny face they presented to their human tenants. After five minutes of following Rowan down the overgrown slope, stumbling through the springy layers of dead needles, snagging his clothes upon clutching boughs, and brushing aside tough spider webs, he was totally lost. What unnerved him most was the absence of sound: no passing cars, flapping night birds or howling coyotes. Nothing but the underhanded whisper of trees.

Rowan stopped so suddenly that he ran into her unyielding back. "There," she said, pointing ahead.

There was a scarlet glow, bleeding through the black strokes of tree-trunks.

"It's her farm," she said. "Go through the rock gate. Your girlfriend is there."

And before Mark could open his mouth, she blew out the candle and dissolved into the shadows.

Lucia pulled the bucket out of the well. The rope was slippery and rough, leaving burns on her palms. The bucket was full, and droplets of reeking viscous liquid splashed into the inky surface below.

She looked around fearfully. The Red Moon was just clearing the tops of the trees surrounding the farm, its rocky face, mottled with dark markings, frozen in an eternal scream. The Red Moon was bad. The Black Moon was worse.

She hitched the bucket to the yoke and lifted it to her shoulders. There were calluses under the worn fabric of her smock. Lucia dimly remembered the time when her body was sculpted by daily gym sessions; when her hair was expertly cut; when her face was protected with creams and enhanced by makeup. Now the knotted muscles of her arms and legs ached with the deeply ingrained fatigue of hard labor; her unkempt hair snaked down her back in an untidy braid; and her face ... well, Little Mother's demesne had no mirrors and that was a mercy.

She carried the bucket to the farmhouse that squatted against the tangled, spiky fringe of the trees, black on black. There was a quivering blue light in one of the windows that, Lucia knew, was Little Mother's bedroom. She had to prepare her bath before the *striga's* bedtime, but how was she supposed to know when? No clocks, no sunrise or sunset, time moving as sluggishly as an algae-choked stream and then suddenly rushing forward like foaming rapids ...

It did not matter. There was no place for excuses on Little Mother's farm. She had to do what she had to do. Otherwise, what had happened to the children would happen to her. Lucia's skin crawled just thinking of it.

She passed the pigpen and averted her gaze from the reeking enclosure. The Red Moon had risen high into the sky, and while normally Lucia would appreciate the additional illumination that helped her navigate the trees in the yard, now she would be happy for the Black Moon to appear instead. She had gotten used to the diet of dry bread and water; to blows and curses; to the hard pallet for sleeping and heavy labor when awake. She had even gotten used to Little Mother's loom. But she could not get used to what was in the pen.

Trying to look away, she stumbled and the liquid in the bucket splashed onto her smock. The sickening metallic stench assaulted her nostrils.

Lucia started to cry.

Mark pushed through the vegetation toward the red glow, assaulted by thorny bushes, scratched by branches, whipped by leaves. He felt betrayed by the woods. He fervently wished for his cell phone, but tech had betrayed him too, sucked him into the black hole of this nightmare.

The only thing that kept him going was the thought of Lucia. The Rowan monster had said she was there, and he was going to find her, no matter what.

Rowan ... Something about her name niggled at Mark. Then he remembered. Rowan tree was another name for mountain ash. The tree was of European origin, brought to America by colonists in the eighteenth century. *She is an interloper, an intruder,* the creature had said about Lucia's captor. But so was she: an invasive species. Or maybe not. How long until an immigrant became a native?

The glow was getting brighter, flooding the forest floor with the feverish scarlet light. Mark slowed down: what if he was blundering toward a forest fire? These were common in Northern California. But no, there was no heat or smoke, and the light was even, not flickering. It allowed Mark to look around and get his bearings. He almost wished he had not.

The forest had shifted, changed, like a familiar face disfigured by a hateful scowl. Layers of dead leaves crunched underfoot, releasing the pungent smell of mold, and some of them twitched and scurried away on slimy pseudopodia. Thorny, twisted stems the color of old bones nosed up from the mulch. Among their exposed roots, pale fungoid bodies pulsated rhythmically like asthmatic toads. And the trees were the worst. They were familiar trees: redwoods, oaks, madrones, Douglas firs. But the bare lower branches on the redwoods clawed the air when he squeezed by; the squat boles of the oaks had grown into baroque swollen shapes fissured by tender-looking scars; the straight reddish trunks of the madrones were hung with peeling bark that looked like skin and oozed dark drops that looked like blood; and the Douglas firs' needles were steely and sharp. Moss rotted in big squishy cushions, and the only sound was the harsh incessant cawing of some invisible bird.

Mark took a deep breath and went on. The slope was getting steeper, the ground falling into a wide ravine whose bottom was choked with the dense huddle of vegetation. The light was emanating from somewhere behind it but he could not figure out what the source was. The Rowan creature had said something about a "farm," but this was the unlikeliest location for a farm he could imagine.

The closer he got, the stranger the forest became. Mixed among the familiar flora were European broadleaf trees—larch, chestnut, ash—that did not belong here.

Mark realized that the direction of the red light had shifted: instead of coming from below, it was now streaming from above, painting his hands lurid scarlet as if they were dripping blood. Mark looked up and froze.

Swimming in the dark sky was an inflamed red orb. He had seen blood moons—but that was something else, a monstrous swollen planet, twice as big as the full moon and luridly red. The markings on its surface looked like a screaming face.

Mark stared at the thing while his mind tried to come up with—not an explanation, it would be too much to ask for—but rather a story that would make sense of what was happening. He was a sci-fi fan and would not be averse to imagining himself in some sort of parallel universe, but he could not think of a parallel universe that would encompass Rowan, the red satellite, and the strange trees.

In front of him was a large boulder shaped like a rough-hewn arch, draped with moss and lichen. A curtain of damp tendrils hung from the top, obscuring the hole of the arch.

Rowan had spoken of "the rock gate." Mark prepared to dive in.

"I wouldn't do it if I were you," said a male voice.

Mark spun around. A man was leaning against a tanoak. He wore what appeared to be a samurai outfit with a lacquered breastplate and russet-colored skirt. He was a thin and stooped fellow with a decidedly un-Japanese cast of features under his close-fitting lacquered helmet. Huge swathes of purple rash covered his face, arms, and legs.

"Why not?"

"Because Little Mother will unravel your life and spin it anew on her loom and then put whatever you become in her pen. And trust me, you don't want to be there."

Mark took a deep breath.

"Rowan told me my girlfriend is there."

The man nodded.

"True. But it is a trap. Rowan is working for her. They all are. Interlopers. Intruders, invasive species."

Rowan, mountain ash ...

"And you are not?"

"I am native. California born and bred."

"Wait!" Somehow it all clicked. "You are Poison Oak, aren't you?"

They used to make Japanese lacquer out of it.

269

The man smiled, showing uneven broken teeth.

"Indeed. You uprooted quite a lot of me, didn't you? But I don't bear grudges. So I tell you, man, go back home. Little Mother is not to be trifled with."

"But I need to find Lucia!"

"She is the one to blame for this whole thing! You should have never brought her here, man. An invasive species, this one is!"

"What?" Mark blinked. "What are you, a Republican? We are the country of immigrants!"

"There are immigrants and immigrants. Do you know what forests are, man? They are history. We feed on your stories; we root in your memories; we are fertilized by your dreams and pollinated by your nightmares. There are bad forests where she comes from. Very bad juju. And she brought them with her. Seeds in her mind; saplings in her memory. Little Mother would never reach our redwoods if it were not for your girlfriend!"

"But she's only been here for a week!" Mark cried.

Poison Oak smirked. "You think trees care for your Apple watches and digital calendars? We have our own time, man, and it flows as we need it to flow."

Mark took a deep breath.

"All right," he said. "Whatever you say, man. But it doesn't change anything. I want my girlfriend back. And if this Little Mother is as bad as you say, shouldn't we get her out of here? I once spent a whole week cleaning out invasive species in Point Reyes. I know how to deal with them."

Poison Oak looked at him dubiously and then shrugged.

"You have a point. We can't let her stay. And she brought her goons with her—ash, and larch, and alder, and spruce, and European oak. The whole mountain is infected. All right go ahead! But sorry, man, can't help you. You're on your own."

"Aren't you supposed to give me some magic gifts?" Mark asked. "Or at least valuable advice?"

"That's not how it works. All I can say is that you better get your ass in gear before the Red Moon sets and the Black Moon comes up.

Sure, the White Moon would be better, but I wouldn't count on it happening any time soon."

"How about waiting till the sunrise?" Mark asked.

Poison Oak smirked.

"You would be waiting for a very long time."

Lucia walked into Little Mother's empty bathroom and with a sigh of relief lowered the bucket onto the scrubbed floorboards. The light shifted from ghostly blue to warm sunny gold, and for a second, she let herself forget where she was and luxuriated in the cozy ambiance of a traditional bathhouse, with pine-aromatic wooden walls, a portly china pitcher and a claw-footed freestanding tub in the middle.

From behind the door leading into Little Mother's quarters came the clacking of her loom, bringing Lucia out of her reverie. She hefted the bucket and poured its contents into the tub, instantly shattering the illusion.

The thick liquid left scarlet splatters on the tub's rim. Lucia knew she would have to scrub them off after they coagulated to black. The butcher smell made her empty stomach heave and filled her mouth with bile.

"Lucia, dear?" the dulcet tones of Little Mother came through the half-opened door.

"Yes, Mother," Lucia responded. She hated herself every time she spoke that word, even though she knew she had no choice. The fact that she was estranged from her real *majka* did not help.

"Is the bath ready?"

"Yes, Mother."

"Thank you. Be a good girl and check on our last addition to the pen. The poor thing took a lot of work to adjust. She must be still getting used to her true form. Go talk to her."

Lucia stood still. Her nausea intensified to the point when even the emptiness of hunger would not prevent her from being sick.

The witch had stolen another child!

"It is my fault!" she whispered, savagely pinching her wasted forearm that sagged like an old woman's. "My fault! My fault!"

"Lucia?" This sugary-sweet voice again, leaving a residue in your mind like the scum of a cheap candy on your teeth.

"Going, Mother!" she responded grimly and headed for the yard.

Mark stepped through the vine-choked archway and was not even surprised when he found himself in a cavernous tunnel. Compared to everything else that had happened, a hole in the rock extending into a tunnel seemed almost normal.

He groped in the thick darkness for what seemed like hours. Finally, he reached the end of the tunnel and, swiping aside another curtain of creepers, went out. Nothing jumped at him, so he crouched by the side of an identical boulder that marked the exit on this side of the tunnel and looked around.

Apart from the Red Moon hanging over his head like an overripe pomegranate, the place looked quite ordinary. He was in a big unkempt yard. The yard was overgrown with tough clumpy grass and cut through with a web of unpaved paths. There were some small trees scattered here and there, getting thicker close to the piling of tall stakes driven into the ground that encircled the yard. Beyond the piling, redwoods loomed. Across the yard, a structure of some sort—a barn or an outhouse—nested in the shadows. When Mark looked over his shoulder, he saw a modestly sized farmhouse on the other side of the property. There was light in one of the windows.

Mark hesitated. Lucia must be in the house; perhaps the light was coming from the room where she was held. But common sense reminded him that he had nothing that could be used as a weapon. The barn would have farming implements and hefting a pickax or a hammer would make him feel better.

Keeping low to the ground, Mark scurried toward the barn. He brushed by a thin tree that rustled even though there was no wind, but otherwise the place was deserted.

As he came closer, he realized that "barn" was a wrong designation. Mark knew little about farming, having grown up in the suburbia of San Carlos, but the structure seemed to him more like something he had seen in a zoo: an open enclosure with a shed attached. There were huddled forms dotting the enclosure, too small to be cows. Sheep?

One of the forms stirred and rose up, tottering toward the wire fence. Mark recoiled.

There is a moment when the brain becomes so saturated by atrocity that it shuts down, refusing to let in any more unbearable sights, smells, and sounds. Mark's brain was reaching this point, but he fought against it. He had to see. He had to understand.

The creature was a child. There was no question about it: an eight- or ten-year old child, still wearing a *Go Giants!* T-shirt and ratty shorts. But his face lengthened into a blunt snout, as if somebody had grasped a handful of his flesh and twisted it like putty. His eyes migrated to the sides of his misshapen head and blinked desultorily, trying to focus; his stick-thin arms ended in totters; and his legs were bowed and curved.

The Pig-Boy made a squealing sound, and others sleeping on the ground woke and rose, joining him at the fence, looking pleadingly at Mark, their medley of animal noises still bearing some remnant of articulated speech. There was a girl whose arms were plucked wings and whose legs had lost their flesh and were reduced to bone sticks. There was another girl whose face drooped in the soft curly-haired folds of a sheep. And there was a small boy, hardly older than a toddler, whose nose and mouth had been fused into a duckbill. This seemed to have been done so recently that the bill was still raw, dripping blood and lymph.

Mark backed off. The desire to turn around, dive back into the tunnel and run away from this hellish place was irresistible. He resisted it.

He came back to the fence, slipped his hand through it, making soft calming sounds. The Sheep-Girl grasped his hand—she was the only one capable of doing so, even though her palms were slippery with wool. She bleated something that almost resolved into words but not quite.

"I don't understand, I'm sorry," Mark whispered.

The Pig-Boy turned his malformed head, balding in uneven patches. Mark followed his line of sight.

Weaving among the thin trees and approaching the enclosure was a woman.

As Lucia made her way toward the pen, she also made a resolution.

She was not going to bear it anymore. She would try to kill Little Mother. She finally remembered how it could be done. The knowledge had been buried in her memory all along, and she cursed herself for not thinking of it earlier. Of course, doing so would require facing the past she had not wanted to face. But the time for running away was over.

And if she failed, and the *striga* managed to unweave her on her loom and weave her into some monstrous degrading form, so be it! Nothing could be more degrading than collaborating with a witch, drawing blood out of the well for her daily bath, soothing the poor kids turning into livestock for her table.

Probably the most nightmarish thing about this nightmare was its familiarity. Lucia had grown up with dark Slavic fairy tales told by her mother. When she got older, the fairy tales got increasingly mixed up with her mother's equally dark memories. Her mother Lena had been a teenager during the bloody Balkan Wars, but her stories of the siege of Sarajevo and the massacre at Banovina blended with tales of *strigas* and *moras* into a heavy burden of history that her daughter did not want to bear. Eventually she changed her name, Lucija, to the bland international Lucia, moved to Milan, and reduced the communication with her mother to the bare decency of Christmas and birthday phone calls. She had never known her father, and from Lena's evasiveness on the subject, she suspected he had been a one-night stand.

Her meeting with Mark was another opportunity to leave it all behind: the stench of blood and smoke, the pulse of ancient hatred that seemed to be encoded in her genes. In the sunny woods of California, she could reinvent herself, become somebody else, somebody new, with no history and no memory of the atrocities she was not responsible for. After a week in his gold-and-green retreat, so different from the dark woods of her heritage, she had resolved she would stay there.

Only it turned out that the dark woods had followed her to the Golden State.

Very well, then. Her mother's stories also contained moments of high courage and doomed resistance, from the partisans of World War II to the peacemakers of the Balkan Wars. If you can't run away from your history, you had better embrace it.

She would set the children free and kill Little Mother.

And when her decision hardened into grim certainty, she saw a man standing by the side of the pen.

Mark rushed toward the stopped, thin figure in a ragged smock and they clung together. But when they separated, and he saw her clearly in the light of the Red Moon, he was shocked.

Lucia had been missing for only a couple of days. But the woman standing before him was emaciated, her hair long and matted, her face gaunt.

*Time flows as we need it to flow.*

"You shouldn't have come here, Mark," she said. "It's not your place."

"Wherever you are is my place," Mark said, and meant it.

She smiled and took his hand.

"Let's go," Mark said pointing to the holed boulder. "It leads back to ... well, to California."

She shook her head.

"We can't. The children."

"We will take them with us," but even as he said it, he realized it would be cruel to do so unless they could be returned to their natural state.

"No. The spell must be lifted. We must kill the *striga*."

And as she said it, the red orb in the sky blinked out.

For a moment, they were submerged in the claustrophobic black, filled with the susurrus of the rustling foliage and the panicky cries of the children. But then Mark's eyes adjusted, and he realized the darkness was not absolute. It was diluted by writhing shadows and patches of grey as the light from the farmhouse's illuminated window fanned out. It actually seemed that the darkness was not falling from the sky but advancing in a dense front like a fog bank from behind the trees.

"The Black Moon!" Lucia whispered.

The edge of a tenebrous circle rose in the sky, obliterating the stars, as impenetrable as a black hole.

And at the same time, a cold wind blew, and the pervasive rustling of foliage increased so much it sounded like cries in an unknown language. Boughs whipped through the murk, slender trunks bent and dipped....

No, not just the wind. Trees in the yard were moving on their own, straining against the soil, pulling their roots out, and waving them in the air like tentacles.

"Her trees," Lucia said. "She brought them with her. Larch, pine, oak, chestnut. When the Black Moon is up, they walk."

Mark's hand tightened in Lucia's. The horror of walking trees was like something out of his worst nightmare—the nightmare of the owner of a house in the woods, waking up in the middle of the night to listen to the creak of a redwood threatening to fall upon the roof, or sniffing the air for the smoke of an approaching wildfire.

Lucia touched his cheek reassuringly.

"Don't worry," she said. "They won't touch me. Their sap is in my veins. My cradle was made of their wood. They are my brothers and sisters."

Mark stared at her. That was a different Lucia from the cosmopolitan urbanite he knew.

She started walking toward the farmhouse and he followed. The trees reached out with their clawed twigs toward him but calmed down when Lucia passed them, whispering their names in an unfamiliar tongue: *kesten, ariš, hrast.…* The half-formed faces jutting out of their trunks melded back into the bark.

Lucia seemed to be looking for something and not finding it. The light in the farmhouse suddenly flared up and then dimmed.

"We need to do it quickly!" she exclaimed. "She is taking her bath and we can catch her unawares. But once she is done, she will come out looking for me!"

"So let's go!"

"I need one tree! I know it must be here, but I can't find it. It's our only chance! A *striga* can only be killed by a twig of mountain ash."

Mark started. Dropping Lucia's hand, he stepped into a clearing where the darkness of the moon poured over him like a stream of ice.

"Rowan!" he yelled. "You brought me here; come and help us!"

Nothing but the increasing wind. The Black Moon was clearing the treetops.

"When it rises, she'll be out of the bath!" Lucia cried.

"Rowan! You grow in our mountains; come and help us!"

Nothing. Only the lower edge of the black orb was hidden behind the trees.

"Rowan! We are all guests in this land that is our home; come and help us!"

A slender tree with long pinnate leaves and clusters of berries shook and unfolded, the branches flowing together, the smooth bark metamorphosing into a grey dress, and Rowan stood before them. Her blood-red eyes looked like dark pits.

"So you've come into the trap," she addressed Mark. "You men! So easily led!"

"You don't want to side with the witch," Mark countered. "Why grow in the blood-watered forest when you can grow in the sunny woods of California?"

Rowan snorted. "As if there was no blood spilled in your backyard!"

"Little Mother will enslave you as she enslaves everything she touches," Lucia said. "Give us a twig, let us pass, and I promise that when my daughter is born, I'll call her Rowan in your honor."

277

Mark's mouth fell open at this declaration; but Rowan seemed impressed. And still, she hesitated. The black orb rose into the sky, floating above the treetops.

"Please!" Lucia begged.

Rowan cracked her long fingers and broke off one of them. There was no blood as she handed it to Lucia.

"You had better hurry!" she said, disappearing into the shadows. "Little Mother is coming!"

The light in the farmhouse window blinked out and the door swung open.

The darkness was complete now, the Black Moon greedily drinking up the remnants of ambient light, and Mark wondered whether they would even see their adversary approach. But he needn't have been concerned. Little Mother brought her own illumination with her.

He did not know what to expect. A giantess? A Halloween witch on a broomstick? An ogre? But he did not expect *that*.

The slight figure wreathed in the misty glowing halo that glided toward them was smaller than Lucia, hardly the size of a teen. Her filmy garments fluttered in the breeze; her white hair fell down her narrow shoulders in a luminescent waterfall; her narrow hands gracefully wove spirals of light. Her face was as pretty as a doll's, with the pouting rosebud mouth and a pert nose. Only her eyes, shadowed by long lashes, were impenetrably black, with no whites.

"Lucia!" Her voice was like chimes: sweet and tinkling. "Come here, silly girl! It's dangerous to be outside when the Black Moon is up! Spoils your complexion, brings wrinkles to your skin! And you want to be beautiful for your suitor, don't you?"

Mark, confused, glanced at Lucia, and was shocked by the look of pure hatred on her face.

"*Striga!*" she hissed. "Go back to where you belong! Hide among the bones and the ashes! There is no place for you here!"

"Really? But there is a place for you? An interloper, an intruder, a liar! Daughter of a war criminal! Why don't you ask your mother who your father really was? Do you think your beau would have anything to do with you if he knew your history?"

Lucia reeled but now Mark found his voice.

"Doesn't matter to me who Lucia's parents were. Just shut up and go away. And make those poor kids whole again!"

Little Mother threw her head back and laughed. Her rosebud mouth opened wide. And then wider and wider, splitting her head into two. The upper half fell back like the lid of an open box and another smaller head rose up from within the skull on an undulating neck: a flat snakehead with a sloping scaly forehead and yellow eyes. It hissed; a forked tongue spitting gobs of poison emerging out of its mouth.

"Now!" Mark screamed and rushed at the creature, but Lucia was ahead of him. Wielding Rowan's finger like a spear, she charged the witch that was visibly growing, the petite body swelling into the coils of a serpent, a sinuous tail emerging from under the white gown. And before Mark reached her, she stuck the wooden finger into the monster's chest.

The scream was so piercing that Mark fell to his knees, clapping his hands to his ears, hiding his face on his chest to escape the intolerable high-pitched noise that seemed to burrow into his brain. And so he missed the final transformation of Little Mother. But whatever it was, it was over quickly. When Mark rose to his feet, shaking and all but deaf, there was only a pile of ash mixed with charred bones and broken sticks.

Lucia was lying on the ground. Mark rushed to her, but she stirred and sat up. Her face was pale and smudged by soot and ash. He suddenly realized that he could see her clearly, even though Little Mother's luminescence had winked out with her death. He looked up. The Moon swam in the sky, its white orb too large but bearing the familiar markings.

"The White Moon," Lucia sighed. Mark put her arms around her.

"We need to break her loom," Lucia whispered. "Then the kids will be restored."

"No need," said the voice behind them. "I'll take care of that."

They turned around in unison. The man who stood behind them was almost as wide as he was tall, with ropes of muscles winding around his bulging arms, and his sturdy legs emerging from beneath his tattered tunic. His skin was smooth and brown, like an acorn.

"She used my wood to make her loom," he continued in a rumbling bass, "and didn't pay what was owed. Now I am taking it back. Whatever she spun will be restored to its true form."

Lucia bowed.

"Thank you, Father Oak," she said.

Mark felt that he had had enough conversations with trees to last him a lifetime. One more, though, was forthcoming. As they approached the boulder tunnel, he carrying the exhausted boy who had shed his pig features and Lucia with the toddler in her arms, while the two girls trailed behind them, he saw a scrawny fellow in the lacquered suit waiting for him.

"Well," Poison Oak rasped, "so you got rid of the witch and got your girlfriend back. Congratulations, man! But you know the *striga* will be back. These invasive species are like weeds. The more you whack them, the more they keep coming."

"That's fine," Mark responded. "We are all invasive species here."

# SUN, MOON, AND TALIA

he *rio* was choked with dead bodies.

The canals smelled worse than they did in the height of summer, when dead fish and household slops combined into a gooey mess under the steamy sun of La Serenissima. But it was early spring now, the water cold and grey, the dome of San Marco tracing a fading outline against the cloudy sky. And yet the Most Serene One, the Queen of the Adriatic, the Republic of Venice, stank like a charnel house.

Talia staggered out onto the embankment. There was a swollen bulk bobbing by one of the wooden posts that gondoliers used for navigation. A large gull was lethargically pecking at its head. It did not move when Talia clapped her hands and she let it go. It was easier to see corpses when they were balloons of anonymous flesh, half-eaten bird meals. Then it meant you did not have to think of them as people. The fresh bodies were unbearable, because they looked as if they would wake up and smile or talk to you. The bloated buds of buboes that the Black Death scattered over the flesh of its victims were mercy, really, because they marked the final separation between the living and the dead. Once they bloomed on you, you were carrion. Meat.

Talia sat on the wet coping, oblivious of the fact that her skirt was soaked through. She was constantly cold anyway; even when there was still wood to burn, the small fire could not counteract the chill of starvation. And she needed the respite from the constant feeble crying that she seemed to hear even now, emanating from the house, though the blinds were tightly closed as were the blinds of every house along the canal.

A rat skittered on the rubbish-covered pavement, dragging a rag of flesh. Talia followed it with dull eyes. There had been many more rats after the council ordered cats and dogs killed on the suspicion that they were spreading the pestilence. The Black Death only picked up after that: the dancing skeleton whose footsteps Talia heard in the depth of night when the wailing finally stopped but she still could not fall asleep, as if the unusual silence screamed in her ears. She was skeptical of the idea that domestic animals were to blame, anyway. The rumor that the Jews living in the ghetto had cast some malevolent spell over the city seemed more reasonable to her.

The rat, though ... it was sleek and well-fed, as were all the scavengers of La Serenissima: rodents and birds alike. Thinking of it, Talia felt saliva flood her dry mouth.

The babies were finally silent, and Talia let herself hope ... and recoiled from the hope with a flash of shame. They were her charge now. She had sworn on an image of Santa Maria Della Salute to take care of them.

But was it fair?

A splash of water in the dead silence of the dying city. Talia lifted her head wearily and stared at the canal. Her mouth fell open in surprise.

Rounding the bend in the *rio* was a fancy gondola, its six-pronged bow-piece smoothly cutting the steel-grey water. And standing in the bow was a tall figure swathed in a voluminous black cloak. Under its wide hat, its face was beaked and bone-white like the skull of an enormous raptor.

*Il Medico della Peste!* The plague doctor! At the beginning of the pestilence, there had been many such on the streets of La Serenissima, walking around in full costume, confident that the aromatic herbs in the curving beak of their mask protected them from the foul vapors. There had been fewer and fewer as the Black Death strode over the

Laguna of Venice; and once Talia saw a flock of pigeons pecking at a black-cloaked body, she had lost faith in their curative power. Still, her ingrained deference to the authorities reasserted itself as she curtseyed deeply before the imposing figure. The gondola slowed down, the plague doctor moored it at the post and stepped out. Talia shivered under the glassy stare of his blank, round eyes and had to remind herself these were spectacles. A plague doctor covered up every orifice through which the Black Death could enter a body. Except that the dancing skeleton apparently had its own secret entryways.

"Who are you, maid?" the plague doctor asked in a high, squeaky voice that reminded her of squalling birds.

"My name is Talia Barbarigo, Signore."

"And is your house marked, Talia?"

Talia licked her chapped lips.

"I lived with my elder sister, Signore," she whispered. "She died a fortnight ago and her body was removed. Our parents are long dead."

"And are you healthy?"

"I am untouched by the pestilence," Talia exclaimed eagerly. "Look!"

She uncovered her neck and shoulders. Her wasted flesh was as dull as parchment and as wrinkled as if she had been thrice her age of thirteen summers. But it was clean of buboes and lesions.

"Very well," the doctor said. "Our glorious Council of Ten that prays daily for La Serenissima has sent me to deliver provisions to those whom the divine mercy has spared. It has also authorized me to remove those showing signs of sickness to the plague island of Lazaretto Vecchio where they can die in peace. Are you alone in your household, maid?"

He hefted a sack from the bottom of the gondola, balancing it in one gloved hand, and Talia saw the rounded shape of a loaf underneath the burlap. She licked her lips again.

"Yes," she said. "I am alone."

And a baby's shrill cry came from the house, echoed by a second one. The doctor lowered the sack back into the boat and cocked his head, his curving beak pointing at Talia.

"These are my sister's bastards!" she cried. "She left them in my charge, but I have no more food to give them. Mercy, Signore!"

"Bring them out," the doctor said.

Talia rushed back into the house and brought out two swaddled bundles, which she put on the pavement.

The boy's face was red with crying, but the girl's big black eyes opened wide as she stared at the *Medico* in fascination, reaching out with a twig-like hand.

"What ages are they?" the doctor asked.

"They are twins, one year old. My sister, God forgive her, conceived them in sin, though she always denied it. She called them Sun and Moon instead of giving them Christian names because she claimed they were born of light."

"Remove their swaddling," the doctor said, and Talia complied.

The blank eyes studied the small bodies, so thin that each frail bone stood out in sharp relief under the transparent skin.

"I see signs of sickness upon them," the doctor said. "They are inconclusive, but the council charged me with power of judgment. They have to go to Lazaretto Vecchio."

"Those are but flea bites!" Talia cried. "The children are healthy. When their mother died, they stayed by the corpse and yet showed no contagion!"

"The judgment is mine," the doctor repeated. "They have to go to Lazaretto. However, since they are babes incapable of reason, their caretaker has to accompany them. Gather your belongings, maid, you are going to the plague island."

Talia prostrated herself at the doctor's feet, sobbing and kissing his embroidered shoes. Under the rich brocade, a sharp bony hardness seemed to repel her entreaties.

"It is sad, indeed," the doctor said meditatively. "You are healthy and when the pestilence leaves La Serenissima, as it has always done, you would have been spared. The babes, on the other hand, will die—whether from disease or hunger. Too bad you have to accompany them to the Lazaretto since no one comes back from the island of the dead."

Talia's sobs petered out and she stood up. The plague doctor towered above her, his bird-face looming against the dusky sky.

She glanced at Sun and Moon. They did not cry. The boy's blue eyes stared blankly at nothing; his sister's black lashes were lowered, as if she were asleep—or faint.

*The babes will die anyway....*

"Signore," Talia asked, "if these unhallowed children were dead, as are so many of our upstanding citizens of La Serenissima, would you give me food and let me stay in my parents' house?"

"Yes, indeed," the plague doctor said. "It would be better for all if they were dead."

With one swift movement, Talia swept the children off the slippery embankment, pushing them into the thick water of the canal. They sank like stones.

The plague doctor's beak dipped toward Talia and his cloak swooshed, spreading out, as an enormous bird silhouette blanked out the dregs of daylight. A clacking, chittering sound came from behind the mask—except Talia suddenly realized that the mask was not attached by ties to the head. It *was* the head.

The beak opened up, disclosing not a cavity filled with aromatic herbs but a wet, scarlet gullet. A stink of rot washed over her.

She woke up in darkness that closed in around her, squeezing air out of her chest. Talia realized where she was. The oubliette under the Doge's Palace; the place where heretics, traitors, and murderers were locked up to experience in life the tortures of hell reserved for the damned. She tried to scream but could not because with consciousness came the memory of what she had done. She deserved it. She had killed Sun and Moon!

Talia sank into a huddle on the ground, sobbing and trying to utter the holy name of Santa Maria della Salute, but she could not. The guilt sat on her chest like an incubus, squeezing out everything but a dull despair. Her hand scrabbled in the dirt, closing around a dry clump of grass....

Grass? Talia sat up. There surely could not be any grass in the oubliette! And as she finally drew in a full breath of air, the dampness of night vapors, the briny smell of rotting seaweed, and the touch of breeze told her she was outdoors. She heard the rhythmic splash of water as it beat against the embankment and the remote cry of a night bird. She was not imprisoned!

But why was it so dark? There should be a gibbous moon tonight; and though many people had stopped putting candles out in their windows to provide street illumination after the Black Death came, some still did, as per the order of the Council of Ten. But there was no glimmer of light in the thick, humid murk.

Talia got up and let her eyes adjust, confident that eventually she would be able to see *something*. And indeed, as her pupils dilated, she could discern the shaggy outline of a cypress against the inky sky. To her relief, she also saw a star winking at her from a tear in the scudding clouds. It was night; she was outside; and she was alive.

But where was she?

The familiar salt of the Laguna spiced up the air, telling her she was home, in La Serenissima. But the splashing of waves on the shore was louder than what she would expect from a *rio*, and the breeze was coming from an open space. If she was not on the Rialto anymore, how had she gotten here?

Talia's mind kept bringing up glimpses of verminous feathers and an inflamed beak, but she squelched them. There would be time later to think about what she had done. First things first.

Behind her, a bulky structure loomed indistinctly, black on black. Talia groped her way toward it, stumbling on loose paving stones and unkempt bushes. The building was long and low; she could not see how far it stretched in both directions. Her fingers caressed the eroded bricks and the plaster decorations around the door. She touched the ornate handle that seemed to have been cast in the shape of a screaming face and pushed it. The door swung inward.

Talia's nose was assaulted by the stench of human waste and dying breath. She backed off. She knew that stench only too well.

When her parents had died, and then her sister, it had lingered in the house for days and weeks like a reproachful ghost.

But now her light-starved eyes focused on a dim flickering flame somewhere in the vast expanse of the night. Inside the vague space before her a candle was burning.

Talia gingerly stepped across the threshold. Now with candlelight seeming to grow stronger, she saw pallets lined up along the vast hall. Shrouded bodies were laid out on the pallets.

Lazaretto Vecchio! The place she had been so frightened of that she murdered her baby niece and nephew to escape! And here she was. Well, that was what she deserved, didn't she?

And suddenly, a weight was lifted off Talia's soul. She realized she was dead already. And thus, she had nothing to be afraid of. The dead are fearless.

And the dead are curious. She went on through the enormous hall lined with corpses toward the guttering candle.

An old woman was sitting at the table, her head in her hands. She looked up when Talia approached. Her face was tired and lined but she was beautifully dressed in a patrician gown of purple velvet with a fanlike collar and gold-embroidered linen peeking out from under her low-cut bodice. Her grey hair was piled up in two plaits above her forehead like horns and woven with pearls. Talia was simultaneously cowed and reassured by the woman: cowed because she had seldom met ladies of nobility; reassured because the expanse of the woman's sagging flesh exposed by her gown was free of buboes.

"Who are you?" the woman asked.

Talia curtseyed.

"Talia Barbarigo, Signora."

"How did you get here to the Isle of the Dead, Talia? You have not been touched by the Black Death."

Talia dropped her eyes.

"Il Medico della Peste brought me, Signora," she whispered.

The woman's wrinkled lids flew up.

"He only brings those who have sinned so much that they deserve life in death," she said. "What have you done, Talia Barbarigo?"

*The dead are fearless,* Talia repeated to herself. But shame locked her lips.

"Tell me!" The old woman insisted. "There is nothing you can say that will shock me, maid. Look at me. Do you know why I am here? I poisoned my husband because he consorted with courtesans and left me alone in our big house on the Grand Canal. I was tired of watching boats going on below my window, so I put Aqua Tofana into his food. But after he died, I was even more alone, and so I went willingly with Il Medico della Peste. Now I keep watch on the boats bringing in the sick and the dead. But something strange has happened. I count hours by the burning of the candle because there is nothing else to do. By my count, it should be close to midday, and a new load of the dead should be brought in. But the Sun has not risen, nor have I seen the Moon in the sky."

Talia's hand clapped to her mouth in horror.

"Do you know something about it?" the old woman pounced.

"I killed my niece and nephew, Signora," Talia stammered. "I thought I could not survive if burdened by two babes. Their names ... their names were Sun and Moon."

"So you are to blame for this season of darkness!" The old woman shouted. Her trembling hand pointed at Talia accusingly. "Do you know what you have done? You have doomed La Serenissima herself! She has survived pirates, and raids, and wars, and floods! She has survived more visits from the Black Death than you can count! But now, because of a stupid, selfish girl, our city, the Queen of the Adriatic, will be shrouded in eternal darkness and will pass from memory of mankind! I am a poisoner, but you are worse than the Devil!"

Talia fell to her knees.

"Forgive me, Signora!" she cried. "Is there any way to atone for my sin? I may be the murderer of my kin, but how can I live knowing I am the murderer of my city? Tell me what to do to save La Serenissima!"

The old woman's wasted lips moved soundlessly as if she was praying or chanting to herself. Finally, she looked into Talia's face.

"You have to go down into Hell and bring back Sun and Moon," she said.

"Is this not Hell?" Talia asked, sweeping her arm around to point at the innumerable shrouded bodies.

"This? This is just a plague. It comes and goes, and we live or we die. Hell is something else. Hell is where all hope is lost, all anger is spent, and time itself is dragging its feet like a palsied beggar. Hell is where there is no past and no future. Are you willing to go there, Talia? If you bring back Sun and Moon, the Black Death will be over, and your sin will be forgiven. But if you don't ..."

"What if I don't?" Talia asked.

The old woman chuckled. "Then this Lazaretto will be what you will yearn for and can never go back to."

Talia dropped her eyes.

"I will go," she said.

"Come with me," the old woman said and, rising to her feet, hobbled over to a small door in the wall. Talia followed and caught a glimpse of the old woman's feet. She was wearing chopines, very tall platform shoes made of wood. Talia expected that from a noble lady. What she did not expect was the way the wood seamlessly flowed into the wasted flesh of the bony legs.

Talia stood by the entrance to Hell. It was a small inconspicuous white door, rather scuffed and splintered. The brass handle was in the shape of a coiled serpent. Above the door, a torch burned noiselessly, sulfur smoke dissolving in the black air.

Talia laid her hand on the brass snake, and it uncoiled and hissed at her, baring metallic fangs. Talia cried out and the snake subsided into a cunningly wrought handle again. Twice more Talia tried to open the door, and twice more the snake woke up.

*Am I to be stopped even before I started?* Talia thought in frustration. *No!*

She threw her body against the door without touching it with her hand. The door flew open, the snake remained dormant, and Talia tumbled into a murky place filled with an incessant susurrus like the plashing of a distant creek. The door banged shut behind her back.

She looked around and recognized the row of brightly painted houses with pointed arched windows and ornate doorways. She was back on the Rialto, close to her own home. Ahead of her, a bridge arched above the *rio*. The houses, the brick pavement, and the low embankment were familiar, but everything else was strange. There were no lights in any of the windows; even the candle that always burned in front of the icon of the Virgin set into the wall and protected by glass was not there. The sky was black and starless, and an even blacker orb hung above the roofs, surrounded by the halo of corpselike luminescence. Its strange, pale glow was the only illumination. The water in the canal was agitated, beating against the coping, but there was no wind at all: the air was stagnant and close as if she were indoors. Talia approached the lip of the canal, looked down and recoiled. The pitch-black surface was covered with a thick layer of refuse, and among excrement, food scraps and rat carcasses, she saw a swollen human head, its mouth filled with writhing worms.

She decided to walk home, but as she walked, she realized that while Hell might look like Venice, the resemblance was only superficial. The familiar alleyways she followed twisted and turned, leading her into dead ends. Canals that should not be there barred her way, while bridges she had crossed every day were gone. Palaces she had passed by often, dreaming of the luxurious and sheltered life of their noble inhabitants, were now reduced to damp-swollen ruins, the broken sidelights of their windows gaping like screaming mouths. And every pointed door decorated with the emblem of the house was marked by a cross. The Black Death had passed here and claimed the city as its own.

Talia stopped in front of a blank wall that suddenly appeared across her way. Affixed to the wall were partial human bodies: pelvises with legs attached; arms with open-palmed hands; chests with lowered heads. There was no blood, as if the bodies had been bled dry before being cut up and scattered around the wall like bizarre decorations. Above the toothed crenellations, mop-like treetops loomed against the dim sky. Gardens were rare in Venice, and often belonged to monasteries. Remembering what the old woman had told her, Talia decided to try to get in. She followed the wall as it curved away, leaving a narrow crack between two blank-faced brick structures. Talia wriggled through and found herself in front of a tall ironwork gate. The gate was ajar.

Beyond was a *fondamenta* Talia did not recognize. The light was better here; the waters of the Laguna shone with a pale greenish radiance. To her right was a church whose walls were clad with flower-painted, blue-glazed tiles. The door was open and inside she could see richly decorated pews and twisted blue columns. Talia walked toward the church but then she saw that instead of a cross, its dome was topped with an open hand. Talia hesitated, peering into the nave. There was a gathering of robed monks at the altar, their backs turned to her. Talia remembered the old woman's words.

*Follow the sign of the open hand. Blue monks may be treacherous, but red nuns are your enemy.*

What was she to make of it? A blue church with an open hand on top: friend or foe? Talia backed off and walked to the edge of the *fondamenta*. She looked down and gasped. Floating in the water were children.

She could not count them; there were so many. All were naked, their arms folded on their chests, their eyes closed. None appeared older than five. And they were all tethered to long flexible cords like waterlily stems that disappeared down into the luminescent cloud at the bottom spreading its radiance through the water.

They looked peaceful and serene. As opposed to the hacked-up bodies on the wall, these infants were whole and unharmed.

Talia's gaze traveled along the rows of angelic faces with their rosebud mouths and closed eyes. And then it snagged on a familiar sight.

Moon!

Her baby niece floated in the water at the end of an umbilical cord as she must have done in Talia's sister Lucia's womb. She was at the far edge of this vortex of drowned children, so Talia could not

293

reach her from where she stood. And Talia did not know how to swim. Many people in La Serenissima did not. Plunging into a polluted *rio* was folly; and the Laguna was for boats and ships, not people. Staring helplessly at Moon, Talia made up her mind to ask for help. She went back to the church.

The figures at the altar turned around. They were dressed in cowled robes belted with rope like Franciscan monks, but their robes were blue rather than brown. Their white faces had a black hole in the middle, like the blank mask called the *Moretta* that women wore to cover their faces, but not their hair and jewelry at the Carnivale. But these monks were not masked: the hole was just that, a hole, leading into the darkness inside their heads.

Talia curtseyed.

"Dear Signori, please help me," she said. "My niece, little Moon, is in the Laguna, and I need help bringing her out."

"Isn't it true that she is in the Laguna because you put her there?" asked one of the monks. His voice issued from the hole in the middle of his blank face and sounded hollow.

Talia hung her head.

"It is true," she whispered.

"You need to pay a restitution," the statue monk declared. "Give us the sight of your eyes, and we will help you."

"But how will I look for my nephew Sun without my eyesight?" Talia objected. The monk hesitated.

"True," he said. "But we can take your pretty blue eyes and give you other eyes. They won't be so pretty, but they will do."

His marble hand snaked from under the folds of his cloak holding a pair of round dark spectacles. Talia gasped. But what was she to do?

"I agree," she whispered.

A moment of blinding pain, as her eyes wriggled in their sockets and flew out. Talia was plunged into darkness. But then a cold hand placed the glasses on the bridge of her nose, and her sight returned. It was even sharper as it used to be, but everything seemed surrounded by swirls of murky smoke. Talia now could see into the farthest corners of the church where voluted blue columns twisted and untwisted leisurely like upright snakes.

"Now come with me," the monk said. In the depth of his black face-hole, a pair of blue eyes floated freely like shiny fishes.

Talia followed to the *fondamenta*. The monk crossed the paved embankment and, without breaking his stride, went on walking on water. The drowned infants bobbed and swirled under his feet, their cords whipping through the greenish cloud of luminescence. He stopped by Moon and pulled her out, snapping her cord. Her eyes opened and she wailed, sputtering, and coughing out water. The monk handed her to Talia.

"She is yours," he said and disappeared back into the church.

Talia wiped the baby with the hem of her cloak, and wrapped her up, fashioning a sling out of her clothes. Moon, used to the feel and smell of her aunt, calmed down and fell asleep, her heart beating rapidly against Talia's chest. Talia went on.

Following the *fondamenta,* she came to another wall. There was a gateway in the wall shaped like a giant opened hand. Thick fingers curled around the doorway. At first Talia thought they were made of plaster, but then she realized they moved slightly, and there were deeply etched lines on the fingertips.

The idea of stepping through this living doorway made her queasy. But the old woman had told her to follow the open hand. Short of retracing her steps or walking on water as the monk had done, that was the only way to proceed.

Talia ducked through the gateway, passing through the hole in the palm. The fingers twitched but did not try to hinder her.

Beyond the wall there was just more darkness but diluted and threaded with fires that burned on the campo surrounded by abandoned buildings. In the center of the campo was an ornate covered well, its sides carved in indistinct intertwined figures. Wells provided La Serenissima with drinking water by collecting rain into the clay-lined cisterns. To protect them from pollution, they were always covered with stone gratings. This well, however, yawned open.

Talia approached and looked inside. The small fires around her provided enough light to see. The well was half-filled with inky water that seemed unclean to her. Instead of the brackish smell of the Laguna or the calming scent of rain, the well stank of decaying vegetation. Whitish shapes bobbed on the surface. She leaned over the curb, straining her eyes, and saw pale babyish bodies half-submerged in the water.

Sun must be there! But how was she to reach down and pull him out? Talia looked around for the basin or the bucket that would be provided for the convenience of the public and saw one by a building's wall. But as she tried to back away from the well, she could not. Something was holding her fast.

The carved figures on the curb leaned forward, detaching themselves from the marble matrix, and one of them grabbed her cloak with long stony fingers. The fires flared up, and Talia saw that the carving was that of a nun in a wimple and habit. Her face was splashed with red paint that some vandal had thrown at the well: an ugly scarlet splotch against the white of the marble.

The fingers dug into her flesh, and no matter how Talia tried to wriggle free, she was held fast. Moon, dozing against her breast, woke up and started crying.

"Please, Signora," Talia implored, "my nephew Sun is in the well. Help me bring him up!"

"Talia Barbarigo," the marble nun squealed in a voice liquid and choked by phlegm like the rotting rainwater in the well. "The murderer of your kin! How dare you appeal to us for help?"

"I am trying to atone for my sin," Talia whispered. "It is true I tried to kill my niece and nephew. It is true I chose my own survival over the promise I made to my dead sister. The Black Death has made cowards of all of us. But I am still a daughter of La Serenissima, the Queen of the Adriatic, the most beautiful city in the world. I was ready to kill my kin; I cannot kill my city. To bring back the light into her darkness, I have to rescue Sun and Moon. Please, dear Signora, help me lift up my nephew!"

The frieze of marble nuns leaned even further forward; their faces, disfigured by erosion and spotted with red pain, turned to each other as a chain of whispers went around the curb of the well. Finally, the nun that had first spoken to Talia, spoke again.

"We will help you, Talia Barbarigo," she said. "But we require a payment for our services."

"I have little," Talia sighed, "but I will share with you whatever I have."

"As you can see, we are immured in the marble of the well, with no ability to leave. Give us the living flesh of your young arms and legs, and we will bring up your nephew."

"But how will I carry the babies if I have no arms or legs?"

"We will give you a magic cloak that will wrap up your nakedness and serve you as sinews and muscles."

Talia hesitated. Surely, that was too much to ask! She was young and healthy; everybody around here had died but she survived. Should it not count for something?

But then she remembered the old woman's words. She was as good as dead already; all she had to choose was between the life in death in Lazaretto and a chance at redemption by bringing back light to the benighted streets of Venice where the Black Death roamed free. It was no choice, really.

"I will do it," she said.

In the next moment, a piercing pain like nothing she had ever experienced went through Talia's body. She dropped to her knees, Moon in her arms crying. She felt herself unraveling, strips of flesh and skeins of arteries unwinding from her bones. In the fervid light, she glimpsed the raw musculature loosening from her like the wrappings of an Egyptian mummy. But then a black cloak flapped down, its voluminous wings covering her from head to toe. The pain lessened, though it did not disappear completely, settling into a dull throbbing ache.

Talia lifted her spectacles and saw that the frieze of nuns had stepped out from the curb and stood around her. They had grown to an ordinary human height, but the flesh from Talia's limbs had not improved their appearance. They were ugly oozing scarecrows, their white habits spotted and stained with blood. The red paint that marked their marble faces had transformed into slicks of raw weeping flesh.

"Help me," Talia whispered.

One of the red nuns turned to the well and tried to reach down but the surface of the water was too far away. Another nun grasped the first one's ankles, as she vaulted over the edge of the curb, and then another one joined this chain. The first nun disappeared into the black hole of the well, held by the two others.

There was a splash, and then a baby's cry. The nuns pulled on the living chain and the first nun flopped onto the stone paving, clutching a wailing infant.

Talia rushed toward them. She was afraid that she would not be able to walk, but the voluminous cloak that covered every inch of her depleted body carried her easily, moving the joints and bones in her legs. She almost felt as if she were flying.

She grasped her nephew. Sun looked up at her and smiled his milky smile; his blue eyes big and shining.

Clutching the two babies, Talia glided to the exit from the camp. Beyond the gates, she saw the familiar black glimmer of a *rio*. She stopped, uncertain. Now she had to find her way out of Hell. But how?

A glimpse of movement on the canal. A gondola was approaching, its six-pronged bow-piece cutting the oily darkness. She tensed, remembering how she had ended up in Hell.

But as the gondola approached, Talia saw that the gondolier was even stranger than the Plague Doctor. A giant hand stood in the prow, two of its fingers planted in the bottom of the vessel, the rest wrapped around the oar.

The gondola approached, smoothly cutting through the tarry water. Talia hailed the gondolieri.

"Please, Signor, take me out of Hell! I need to return Sun and Moon to Venice."

The gondola paused. The hand had no mouth to speak with, but its fingers moved in a complex dance which Talia, familiar with the secret language of thieves and pickpockets, understood well.

*What will you pay me?*

"I have no money," Talia whispered. "I have no more pretty eyes, or strong and unblemished flesh. I have nothing to give you."

*But you still have your mouth and your tongue. Give them to me, and I will carry you out of Hell.*

And Talia agreed.

With only a blank expanse of flesh where her mouth used to be, she sat in the gondola, cradling the two babies, as the hand rowed her out of Hell. She did not notice the transition, but gradually, the darkness became less solid; the houses more familiar, and she found herself on the Grand Canal. The gondolier rowed to the stairs that led up to the embankment, and Talia went up. Standing on the slick stones on La Serenissima, she released the toddlers.

They could barely walk but they made a couple of uncertain steps toward the Rialto Bridge. And as they walked, they grew.

Moon blossomed into a lithe young woman with long white hair streaming down her back and a coronet of opals on her head. She lifted her arms, and a new moon rose into the air, shedding its silvery light onto the gilded dome of San Marco and the statuary of the Doge Palace.

Sun became a strong young man, his cheeks ruddy and his eyes summer-blue, a golden crown on his head. He lifted his arms, and a flood of fresh sunlight poured over the dank alleys and the deserted *campi,* banishing the vermin breeding in the dark.

Talia would have called out to them in her joy. but she had no mouth to cry with. She sank onto the pavement, when the flapping of wings made her lift her head.

A raven stood in front of her, its strong beak clacking as it minced toward her on its clawed legs. Its cawing formed itself into words.

"You saved our city. I gift you with my beak for the service you have done to La Serenissima and her children, human and nonhuman alike."

And Talia felt the bony protuberance of the raven's beak fuse itself with her features. She lifted her skeletal hand, feeling the contours of her new face: the round dark spectacles, the curving beak, and the folds of the velvety cloak covering up her despoiled body.

Sun and Moon had disappeared into the maze of awakening streets, but Talia knew that the Black Death was still out there. Even if she had retreated, she would be back, as she always was.

Venice still needed her doctor, and always would.

She turned back to the *rio* where the gondola still waited for her. The hand-gondolier bowed; his stolen mouth spoke.

"I am at your service, Signora."

The new *Dotoressa della Peste* stepped into the gondola, and it glided away into the watery heart of La Serenissima.

# ACKNOWLEDGMENTS

"My Lady of Plagues" first appeared as "Lady of the Plagues" in *The Dogstar and Other Science Fiction Stories* (Leaf Books, 2007).

"Death in Jerusalem" first appeared in *Zion's Fiction: A Treasury of Israeli Speculative Literature,* eds. Sheldon Tetelbaum & Emanuel Lottern (Mandel Vilar Press, 2018).

"Turnadot" first appeared in *Midnight Circus: In the Age of Miracles* (EAB Publishing, 2016).

"Rattlesnake" first appeared in *The Fabulist,* December 19, 2020.

"Dancer from the Dance" first appeared in *New Realm Magazine,* 2016.

"The Two Courts" first appeared in *Fantasia Divinity Magazine* 13.

"Angelo" first appeared in *Fae Wings and Hidden Things,* Anthology (Wolf Pack Publishing, 2017).

"The Bone Forest" first appeared in *Another World : Stories of Portal Fantasy,* ed. Abigail Linhardt, 2021.

"Wings" first appeared in *Retellings of the Inland Seas,* ed. Athena Andreadis (Candlemark and Gleam, 2020).

"Melissa and the Stone Troll" first appeared in *The Future Is Short: Science Fiction In a Flash* vol. 3, eds. Sharon Kraftchack, Paula Friedman, J. J. Alleson & Emily Johnson (Lillicat Publishers, 2017)

"Little Mother" first appeared in *Silver Blade* 48.

"Alexei's Godmother," "Green Bird," "In the Lava Fields," "Jack the Giant-Killer" and "Sun, Moon, and Talia" are original to this collection.

# About the Author

ELANA GOMEL is an academic and an award-winning writer. Born in Ukraine, she has lived and taught in many countries, including the U.S., Israel, Italy, and Hong Kong. She is the author of six academic books and numerous articles on subjects such as narrative theory, posthumanism, science fiction, and serial killers. As a fiction writer, she has published more than a hundred fantasy and science fiction stories, several novellas, and four novels. She is a member of HWA and can be found at **citiesoflightanddarkness.com** and on social media.

# ABOUT THE ARTIST

**NICK GREENWOOD** graduated from East Carolina University with a BFA in illustration. He has worked as an illustrator/concept artist/designer in the advertising, gaming, and publishing industries for over twenty years.

A brief list of clients include AT&T, Modiphius, Rubbermaid, Dias Ex Machina, Hardee's, IBM, Goodman Games, Green Ronin Publishing, Wyvern Gaming, and Poisoned Pen Press.

Nick lives in Jamestown, NC, with his wife of 30 years and is the father of four daughters, two dogs and a cat.